The People Trafficker

The People Trafficker

Keith Hoare © Copyright 2009

All rights reserved

No parts of this publication may be reproduced, stored in a retrieval system, or transmitted in any form or by any means, electronic, mechanical, photocopying, recording or otherwise without the prior permission of the copyright owner.

British Library Cataloguing In Publication Data. A Record of this Publication is available from the British Library

First Published 2009 by:

Ragged Cover Publishing

II

The People Trafficker
© Copyright 2009 Keith Hoare

ISBN 978-0-9560191-6-5

http://www.raggedcover.com

1

Karen Marshall sat quietly in the rear of a small dinghy as it approached the submarine. The weak light of a waning moon spreading across the still water, made the submarine look dark, ominous and forbidding. This starkness was broken only by a few small handheld lights moving about on the narrow deck. She looked back towards the fast diminishing coastline of the Lebanon, collected only minutes ago from a remote cove - finally the nightmare was over and she was going home.

Soon the dinghy was alongside and hands were grasping hers, helping her onto the deck. She was directed to an open hatch, a ladder leading down inside, lit only by dim bulkhead lights. A man wearing the uniform of an officer was waiting for her at the bottom of the steps, as she climbed down into the submarine. He asked if she'd eaten, and when she said no, he took her directly to the galley. She was to see the Captain as soon as possible, but he wasn't available for another hour.

In the galley, Karen settled down to eat a huge helping of stew followed by apple crumble and custard. A few of the crew had given her a cursory look but said nothing. She felt quite put out over this, expecting at least some civility, but none had been forthcoming. What Karen didn't know was that they were under orders not to talk to her, go near her, or make any comments to each other about her being there, until she'd had her meeting with the Captain.

The officer she'd met earlier entered the galley a short time later and came over. "Have you finished your dinner?" he asked, looking at the three quarters demolished tray, her utensils now laid at the side of the plates.

"Yes thank you, it was a little too much for me. I hope I won't upset your cook, thinking I didn't enjoy it. I did, but I don't usually have such large portions and couldn't take another mouthful."

The officer smiled. "No, he'll be fine, besides you did well. Food on a war ship is a very important part of the day, but you're right, sailors do tend to have rather large portions. Anyway, now you've finished, the Captain is waiting to talk to you."

Karen made to stand, but an injury to her side sent pain down her leg and she fell forward a little with the shock.

The officer looked at her with alarm. "Are you alright he asked?"

She shrugged, giving a weak smile. "I'm fine, it's just I got injured on my side and it gives me a little pain at times. Shall we go and see your Captain?"

She followed him down long, narrow corridors - it was very different to the ship that had taken her to the Lebanon - finding she had to climb through stepped doors to get from one section to another. Eventually they stopped outside a door and the officer knocked. Rewarded with an acknowledgment, they went inside.

A man, smart but casually dressed, was sitting at a small desk. He stood as they entered and offered his hand.

"Karen Marshall, it's good to meet you at last. I hope my officers are looking after you?"

She looked at the man, deciding he must be in his fifties. "Yes thank you, Sir, the food was very welcome and English for a change."

He nodded. "That's good; anyway may I offer you a drink, tea, coffee, or something a little stronger perhaps?"

"Coffee's fine, but no sugar please," she replied.

They both sat down while the officer left to collect the coffee.

"I know you must be tired, Karen, but we're still in a holding pattern, waiting to collect the soldiers who came for you. Perhaps you can tell me why you were at the pickup point alone, and more importantly who brought you there?"

"The SAS soldiers brought me to within fifteen miles of the cove, Sir, and then while I hid they created a diversion for the search teams, so I could get through. But they didn't hold out much hope of being able to rejoin me at the pickup point. There were thousands of soldiers searching."

"I see, Karen, but was this split up necessary? Surely it was a big risk, on your part, to go on alone? Would it not have been safer if you'd stayed with them? After all, if you had been picked up, it would have been by the authorities and not the traffickers. They would almost certainly have sent you home. I would think the decision to send you on alone strongly risked you coming across marauding groups, with no allegiance to the legal government, or maybe the traffickers themselves?"

Karen shrugged. "Depends how you look at it. If I'd remained with the SAS soldiers, and we'd been captured, I'd have wanted them to put a gun to my head. So to go on alone gave me a chance to get home, but still with the option of taking my own life, if I'd been caught."

The Captain's reply to her contained disbelief at the way she was talking. "Perhaps a little exaggerated, after all, what were you so scared of that you'd want to commit suicide?"

"You mean was I prepared to return to a life where I'd have been raped every day? Where I'd even be sold again and again to different abusers, as they tired of me, or until I was too old or ill to carry on, and then have my throat cut, like I saw them do to a girl? I think not, Sir, I'd have taken the suicide option rather than that future, wouldn't you think?"

He didn't reply, as the officer returned with coffee. The Captain thanked him, and then called him back as he was just about to leave the cabin. "Karen tells me it is highly unlikely that any of the SAS will get to the cove. We're already two hours past our deadline so stand the rescue crews down and resume the patrol."

"Yes, Captain. We've made a cabin available to Karen when you've finished your meeting." Then he glanced at Karen before looking back to the Captain. "The Medical Officer would like to take a look at Karen, Captain, before she settles for the night? He was concerned when I mentioned to him she was injured and would like to check for himself, if that's agreeable with you, Karen? We do have six female crew members on board and you may have one with you during his examination."

She smiled at him. "Thank you, I'd like to have another woman present please."

"Well give us ten more minutes, Number Two, and Karen is all yours," the Captain said bringing the conversation to an end.

When the officer left, the Captain looked back at Karen, who was, by now, sipping her coffee. "Returning to our discussion I can now understand your concerns about being captured, Karen, you must have been very scared? In your own view do you believe that we can get the soldiers back?"

She shrugged. "I don't really know. What I do know is that the reward for their capture was very high. Then according to the SAS officer in charge there was very heavy fighting at the warehouses. I would think the gunrunner they targeted was annoyed at his own home being destroyed, as well as the warehouses, besides losing me, which he'd just paid around forty thousand dollars for. By what I've seen of the men there, they were not the sort to stick to any Geneva Convention if any of the soldiers had been caught."

"Yes, you could be right there. I think you did very well to get yourself to the cove. Of course I've also read the report put together about you. It shows a very level-headed girl, who wouldn't fall apart under pressure. This assessment was reinforced by your parents, particularly your father, who spoke very highly of your abilities. You should be very proud of yourself."

"Thank you, Sir, I only wish things had turned out a little better. It would have been nice to see everyone get out."

He stood as she finished her coffee. "Well don't worry yourself; it's not your problem. We'll have your injury looked at, and then perhaps you'd like to get your head down? We're not due to arrive in Cyprus for ten days. The submarine is still following a planned exercise, and the diversion to the pickup point was added later to the orders. I understand, because of this, I'm to transfer you to a supply ship the day after tomorrow. This ship is en route to our base in Cyprus. It'll be an experience for you, as we transfer by cable winching between the two vessels. It's actually a good live exercise for my crew. I hope you're not afraid of heights suspended across water?" he asked with a hint of amusement in his voice.

Karen shuddered inwardly at the thought, but never displayed any reluctance to him. "I don't think so Sir, but I'm happy with whatever you do to get me home. Would I be able to wander round your submarine while I'm waiting, or am I expected to stay in my cabin?"

He smiled. "This isn't a prison, Karen, you're free to go into the mess areas, and talk to the crew. Providing they are not on watch. You cannot of course go to operational areas, alone that is, but I'll arrange for you to be shown around if you're interested in seeing how a submarine works? You will join me and the other officers for dinner tomorrow night. Breakfast and lunch will be in the galley where you've just eaten. I'll also have you provided with basic ship's clothes but you'll leave the submarine with your own clothes, after they've been laundered."

"Thank you, Sir, I'll try to keep out of everyone's way, but I would love to look around the submarine, after all it's not something ordinary people, like me, ever get the chance to do."

Later Karen was lying alone in a surprisingly comfortable bed, inside a cabin usually used by the Engineering Officer who'd doubled up with the First Officer. She could hear the deep and constant thud, thud, of the engines, with the odd vibration of something on the shelves of the cabin, but little else. She'd been surprised no one had looked in her backpack when she'd come aboard, or if they had without her knowledge, nothing was said about the large amount of cash inside. The knife from Chapman was not in the bag but attached to her ankle, and wearing jeans, it wouldn't have been found anyway. So after they had left her alone, and with the cabin door locked, she'd removed her jeans and tried, without much luck, to find how she could attach the knife and its holder to her thigh or knickers. After all, she still wanted to carry protection and often wore short skirts. Deciding to check out the internet when she got home for a strap that would suit, Karen placed the knife and its sheath in the very bottom of the backpack, removed her t-shirt and then climbed into bed. Her confidence was growing now she was going home.

Over the next day, apart from feeling better in herself,

Karen was no longer the girl who'd left England. She'd become more alive to the fact of how attractive and sexually desirable she really was to men, and began experimenting with this belief. She'd flirt with the ratings; besides making each officer believe they were special to her as well. When she wasn't around, there was friendly rivalry among the crew, who'd been able to talk to her, as to who she fancied. This went for the officers as well; eyeing each other with suspicion, believing Karen really liked them that little bit more than their fellows. She was taken everywhere, by the officers of course, but Karen didn't ignore the ratings and chatted to them all. The few who'd plucked up enough courage and asked her for a date, didn't get a direct rejection, more 'I'll see what happens when we arrive in Cyprus', so none had gone away with the idea she'd actually said no, but of course she'd not actually said yes.

On her part, Karen had only just reached eighteen, living a relatively sheltered life, where boyfriends were concerned, and she was using this opportunity to practise how to be relaxed among men. In particular, how to make them want to be with her, and how to make them do what she wanted. For Karen though, with the submarine crew it was just a game, but with the background reality of a serious agenda. She'd no intention of letting any man get as close as her so-called boyfriend again, but she needed to understand how far she could go with a man and still keep his interest. This need had suggested itself during her forced captivity when promises of help often came with sexual demands, making for particularly difficult situations, in that she risked giving them everything, but in return would have received very little or even nothing, if she had done what they initially wanted of her.

Why was this so important for her? It was because Karen had every intention of going after the crew who'd raped her during her time on a ship called the Towkey, which had taken her to the Lebanon. Then there was Grant and Susan who'd pretended to be her friends, when in reality they were helping in the setting up of her abduction for money. However, to pursue these people, Karen was convinced she'd need assistance, and to ask for that required confidence in her ability to control a situation.

The Captain had also begun to realise Karen was playing up to his crew. He'd never been an advocate of using females on a submarine, although to be fair, the ones he had aboard were hard working, professional and no trouble. But this girl was very different. He'd expected a real problem with a girl who'd been through such an ordeal, but she showed no such after-effects. However, Karen was the sort of girl who could turn men against men, cause arguments and increase tension to the point that discipline may become a serious problem. He was very glad she was leaving the ship; because to have her for the entire exercise, might have caused discipline problems resulting in her being confined to her cabin.

"So have you found today interesting, Karen?" the Captain asked, avoiding any reference to her actions over the day, when they had all sat down for dinner in the early evening.

"Yes, Sir, it's been fantastic and everyone's been really kind and helpful. Would you thank them all for me, after I leave?"

"I will of course, but we'd all be very interested in how you managed to get to the cove alone. Not all the details Karen, just the general story."

Karen had no intention of telling the complete truth - or even the complete story - after all most of the problems encountered by the SAS were caused by her. "It's a bit of a long story but I'll try," she began. "First you need to understand that it wasn't me that the SAS had come for initially, they had come to destroy warehouses belonging to a gunrunner called Sirec. But this Sirec was also my new owner, so in reality my rescue was an afterthought. Two SAS soldiers from the main group were sent to rescue me from Sirec's house, where I'd been taken. The two SAS soldiers destroyed Sirec's house when they came to get me, but they had to pinch a car because the one they had ran out of fuel. I suppose the car they pinched must have been reported stolen because we were chased. We turned off the road and tried to make a run for it across some fields, but there were gunmen in the car chasing us and one of the SAS soldiers was shot. He died and we were forced to leave him and move on. Then later during another gunfight the other SAS soldier was injured very badly. He told me to go on alone, rather than be captured; after all it was only a few miles to go before joining up with the leader of the SAS troop, Commander Farrow. I was with them a couple of days, but they'd had a hard time trying to destroy Sirec's warehouses, and had lost their transport. That's when they pinched a helicopter.

She hesitated for a moment, collecting her thoughts, everyone listening intently. "You have to understand I cost my buyer around forty thousand dollars and the SAS had destroyed hundreds of thousands of dollars in property and weapons. Sirec, had put up half a million dollars for my capture, along with the SAS soldiers as well. The whole of the country was looking for us, so it was hard going. The captured helicopter was shot down. There were so many injured and some dead that the only two uninjured SAS soldiers decided to move on, with me of course. In fact it was hopeless; the searchers had spread out for miles and were approaching us in three directions. We'd no chance of escape but they as soldiers in uniform would only be arrested, perhaps made to stand in front of cameras and admit what they had done, before being sent home or exchanged. I had no such option. I'd have been returned to my owner if I was lucky, otherwise I'd have been given to the searching soldiers for the night. Either way I would never have gone home so they decided we should split up. They would head them off while I hid - until the searchers past my hiding place - then I'd move on. I was buried and breathed through a straw while the SAS soldiers diverted the searchers. They stuck a radio in my ear and told me over the radio when the searchers had passed. I lay there ages, my hand around a hand grenade in case I was found. If that had happened I'd have pulled the pin. With twenty or so miles to go, a map and compass, I'd not much of a problem navigating, but I could only travel at night and hid during the day."

She again hesitated for a moment. Now was the time to change her story of how she finally ended up at the cove, in order to protect Martha, a local lady who'd helped and looked after her while on the run in the Lebanon. "I was caught by two conscripts, we had a fight and I was injured when one threw his knife at me. I'd no real problem as my self-defence training meant I could down them quite easily, but it was a stupid mistake to get myself injured. After that it became more difficult with the loss of blood. I fell into a ravine hiding from a searchers helicopter and banged my head. But further on I found an abandoned farm and managed to get water out of a well and clean myself up. There were still searchers everywhere so I hid, but I realised that if I waited too long, you'd be gone and I'd have close on a hundred mile walk to get to a border. Anyway all of a sudden the search was off, why I don't know, but it was. The last six miles were simple, I was in pain yes, but it was easier without having to hide all the time."

The room was silent as they all tried to take in what she'd been through to get out, then the Medical Officer spoke. "What about the injuries, Karen? When I checked them over for you last night, I was very impressed in the way they had been stitched. Who was it who stitched them up for you?"

She looked at him indignantly. "I did," she lied, as in reality it was Martha who had stitched the wounds.

He shook his head in wonder. "I'm impressed, but I don't know how you had the nerve, Karen; it must have been very painful?"

"Tell me about it, in fact it took me the best part of a day, with a few swigs of whisky from a bottle I'd found in the farmhouse, besides pouring some on the wound, and even then I nearly passed out," she replied, hoping her explanation sounded feasible to the medical officer.

However, it was not the medical officer who spoke but the captain.

"It's a fascinating story, Karen," the Captain said as he leaned across and refilled her empty glass of brandy. "You're certainly a very resourceful young lady."

"She is, Captain, we should get her to sign up," the First Officer added.

Karen raised her hands. "Oh no, this is it for me. I just want to go home, find a boyfriend and do what normal girls of my age do. From now on I'll leave the soldiering to the professionals."

"That's a pity. You've displayed some remarkable skills. But you could be right. The services are more a vocation these days and require commitment and working as a team. You sound a loner rather than a team player," the Captain replied.

"Tell me, Karen, what sort of lad are you looking for in a boyfriend?" one of the junior officers asked.

Karen liked the fishing question; after all she'd really laid it on today, so she began to think about what sort of lad she was looking for as she sipped her coffee.

"I don't know really. He'd have to be quite tall; after all I'm close to six feet in heels. Not so bothered about him being really good looking, it'd be a bonus for any girl, but I'd rather have someone with a sense of humour, great personality and who's able to control me. I prefer a man to take the lead. I'm not some background control freak."

Karen had lied in her last sentence; she would always be in control of her destiny and never the man.

"There you are then, Karen, the forces are for you. There are strappingly fit and tall commandos, well educated officers trained to lead and most have great personalities, besides being up for a laugh," the Medical Officer added.

Karen looked at him with mischief in her eyes. "You know you could be right there, I never looked at it that way before. I'll have to seriously think about it. What do you think, Captain, should I become a soldier?"

He smiled. "I'd keep to the civilian bit, Karen. You'd be a disturbing influence with the troops. They'd all want to go partying with you every night, you'd wreck discipline."

Karen grinned at the thought. At that moment brandy was brought round.

The Captain stood. "Gentlemen, I propose a toast."

They all stood holding their glasses.

"To Karen. A remarkable and very brave young lady."

experienced sexually, so she couldn't claim she was just a child. He had some idea she might convince someone to help her, but if she was already a whore, so to speak, no one would want to help. So for this to happen he hired a man to seduce her before she was abducted. Of course it was naivety on the part of Whittle. Any girl soon learns to open her legs, learns she's got two orifices and men want to use both, when she's dumped in a brothel. Usually after a week she will know how to please a man or she ends up with a good beating until she does. But I'm deviating. Karen knows all about how her so-called boyfriend duped her. She also knows about her school mate who tricked her for money and of course she knows Assam and his ship called the Towkey that transported her to the Lebanon. The best part of it is, she thinks I'm dead and no longer pose a threat to her. How wrong that girl is. So what will she do with all this information? She'll either squeal like a pig to the authorities or she'll go after her abductors herself. Don't for one moment think she wouldn't be considering the latter course of action, that girl would relish seeing them squirm before she put a bullet in their heads, and believe me she's quite capable of doing that."

Again he stopped, his injuries were still serious and he constantly needed to take breaks. "Because of either possibility, this is where you come in. Before Karen had even been collected from the ship, to be prepared for sale, I'd already carefully selected five more children to be taken in the UK, all just as attractive and intelligent as Karen. It would seem I'd hit on a market that was silent previously and they wanted me to still fulfil their requirement after Sirec had outbid them for Karen. These new girls' photos have been circulated and the buyers are very excited. I've just less than a month before they are taken. A lot can happen in that time now Karen's free, so I don't want to take a chance that any of the people originally involved in Karen's abduction, may have picked up some knowledge of even the tiniest part of my UK operation. If they talk, whether that's to Karen, or to the British police to save their necks, my planned collection of the five girls could be in jeopardy. So everyone who was involved in Karen's abduction must be silenced."

Saeed handed the document over to Janssen, who hadn't commented.

He looked at the pages then back at Saeed. "The child as well? Surely she wouldn't know anything?"

Saeed shrugged. "If she's there, and could be a witness, get rid of her, otherwise don't bother. She knew nothing, only the father's the risk."

"Five thousand a hit, plus expenses, the kid's free, if she's in the house," Janssen said.

"It's a deal, twenty per cent up front and the rest when I've proof they are eliminated."

"What's your timescale on this?"

"It's got to be sorted within a couple of weeks. I can't take the chance of Karen talking and of anyone being taken in for questioning."

"I'll leave at once. Are you the contact?"

Saeed removed a sealed envelope from the folder he had in front of him, handing it to Janssen. "No don't contact me direct. Inside the envelope are known addresses, photos and other details, plus a contact name and number in the UK. The contact will supply you with untraceable weapons and updated information. He'll also give you the first payment."

When Janssen left Saeed dialled a number in the UK. "Pat, Saeed here, can you talk?"

"Yes."

"Janssen's on his way. You know what to do?"

"I've got it all in hand," Pat replied.

"What of the competition results?"

"Went like a dream, we sent entry forms to each of the schools the girls attend, saying because of the desert trip and staying with a nomadic tribe, only ones over sixteen could enter. With free entry and the chance to win the trip of a lifetime, we received plenty of entries including the girls we wanted. Anyway of course they were the winners. All have been notified and have returned the parent consent forms."

"What has it cost us?"

"The hotel is two star and for only one night, the flights out are booked and paid for, so too is the agency. Altogether we've paid out two grand. The agency and parents have a return date and flight number but it doesn't exist, well the flight does, but their kids are not booked on it. Anyway the desert trip leaves first thing on the second day. We'll make sure the girls have no mobiles, so none will be able to contact the outside world. That will give you ten days at least before any parent would expect to talk to their daughter."

"How about the organisers you employed, do they know you?"

"No, the agency doing all the work believe they are dealing with a charity based in Morocco that are something to do with the tourist board, promoting a better understanding between the cultures there. The agency sent the entry forms to a P.O. Box number and we returned the winning names and schools they attended. Two representatives are going with the group, but they return to the UK after the girls leave on the desert trip. The drivers of the Land Rovers are hired locals and know their destination. They of course won't return, along with the vehicles."

"Good work, Pat; I'll move things along on my side now. What about the press in the UK, is Karen top news?"

"Yes, many have managed to get copies of the professional photos we originally had taken at a local studio for her sale. So she's splashed across every morning paper, I would think after the live interview today, the frenzy is going to increase and not die down."

"I have to agree with you there. It's a mess and means the Towkey will have no use to us in the future. I've not heard from Assam, its captain, but if he's heard the news he must now be a very worried man."

"He was a fool, Saeed, letting her talk to the crew. He even gave her his own name. Armed with all that information it's only a matter of time before the ship's found and the crew's arrested."

"Yes… well let Assam's errors be a warning not to make similar mistakes."

"I will, I'll speak to you soon and confirm when the girls leave the hotel."

Saeed switched his phone off and leaned back. He felt it was ironical that if it hadn't been for Karen and offering her for sale, he'd have never met the other private buyers who were after a top class girl. Even before she'd been finally sold he'd secured forward orders for similar girls. Four weeks of finding the right girls and planning had come to fruition at the right time. The deals he'd secured would not only cover his costs in the hospital, but return a very nice profit. He opened the folder once more and looked at the photos of the new girls, then read through the details carefully. Of course none had Karen's self-defence and survival skills, but each was seventeen, five foot nine, intelligent, very attractive, good education, hadn't touched drugs and came from stable homes. His only change since Karen's preparation for sale was to secure accommodation far away from towns or villages, have the rooms set up with proper chain restraints and add a television and chair. This would mean the girls never needed to leave the room, meet and talk to any of the others and so add to the belief each was there alone and importantly had no possibility of help. His mother, along with two other women had already left for the house. He'd no intention of having men around with the chance that a girl might convince any to help her. With only a week to prepare the girls once they arrived, it was going to be tight. However, he had obtained two cattle sticks that used electric shocks to control animals. He'd had them altered to produce a higher voltage with a larger soft pad placed on the tip that would not only give the girls an instant and painful electric shock, but leave no lasting mark. This method, he believed, would avoid the use of physical and violent punishments that would render the girls unsalable to his clients if they were injured or even worse sustained broken limbs. As a final method of control he'd been able to obtain far more effective sedatives than he had used in the past. He'd had his mother make up small packs with just the right amount to subdue the girls, but not enough for them to become completely lethargic, as had happened with Karen. Satisfied everything was covered this time he leaned back closing his eyes. Soon he would have a great deal of money and already planning to take more of these very desirable and valuable girls.

3

Grant Martin nearly choked on his sandwich when watching lunchtime television. They had suddenly broken into a report on traffic wardens, to say they were going live to Cyprus because Karen Marshall had just arrived at the military headquarters and was about to give a live interview. As Karen's former boyfriend he was now desperately worried. He'd never been comfortable with the arrangement Frank Whittle made with him, but it had paid well and they needed the money. After all he was happily married and although his wife understood his part-time job as an escort, it was one thing escorting a single or married middle aged lady, but it was another thing to have been paid for seducing a seventeen-year-old schoolgirl. He was also very alive to the fact that Karen herself could make a complaint against him, particularly if she'd been told by any of her abductors of his involvement in her abduction, or that he never loved her anyway.

"You look worried, Grant, is it anything I've done?" his wife, Lucy, asked as she took the seat opposite him at the table.

He sighed. "No it's nothing to do with you, but it's best you know my problem, Lucy, after all it's already on the lunchtime news and its more than likely that the police will soon be paying me a visit."

She gasped. "The police! What've you been doing?"

Grant looked sheepish but didn't reply.

"Come on, Grant, out with it," she demanded.

"Okay," he eventually replied, "about three months ago, when I lost my full time job and we were really on our uppers, a Frank Whittle contacted the agency. I was to take a woman, in her forties, to a wedding. It wasn't a job any different to what I'd done in the past, just a quick hundred quid and maybe a bonus if she was generous. Anyway when I was at the wedding Whittle came over and introduced himself. Told me to forget the woman, she'd gone home. I wasn't bothered, after all I'd been paid. Then he asked me to join him for a drink as he'd a different job I might be interested in. This wasn't through the agency, but if I took the job no one, no one, was to know of the arrangements."

"I hope you said no, Grant?" Lucy cut in, then kicked herself as she realised he must have taken it to have a problem.

However, Grant ignored her comment and carried on. "At first I said I wasn't interested in anything not through the agency. I remember that he just smiled and pushed a small piece of notepaper towards me. It had the figure of three thousand pounds written on it. I just stared at the paper. You know we've never had a thousand pounds in cash and this man was offering, what to me, was a fortune. It seemed easy enough, at first. He just wanted me to spill a drink on a girl at that same wedding, offer to get her clothes cleaned, by collecting them from the girl's house and returning them. When I took them back I was to get a date with her and that was it. Once I'd done that and I'd got the date, he met me again. This time he raised the payment to ten thousand pounds. I was gobsmacked to say the least. But I'd had a good date with her, the girl was young yes, but she was really attractive and fun to be with, however to earn the ten thousand had strings. I was to stay with her, but I was to escalate the relationship and teach her how to please a man. I was supposed to be with her for three months, and then she was going away for good. But never once did he say she was going to be abducted."

Her eyes narrowed. "You're telling me this girl Karen, that's on every news channel and across every paper, you pretended to be her boyfriend, went as far as fucking her and Whittle paid you?"

He nodded in agreement.

"Well you've done it this time. It's been hard enough accepting you going out with other women all the time, but to do that to a seventeen year old, still at school, you'd better get down to the police station yourself and tell them what you've told me, before they come for you. Because Grant, you can be sure they will come, this girl's news and if the papers catch onto what you've done, they'll have a field day. You have to think of our children in all this."

He stood and paced the room, before stopping and glaring at her. "That's you all through isn't it? You weren't complaining when I paid the arrears off the mortgage last month. How do you think I earned ten thousand pounds? It wasn't escorting some old biddy to a stupid tea dance."

She lowered her head, looking at the floor, avoiding his stare. "That may be so, Grant, but never in my wildest dreams did I think you were raping a child to pay our mortgage."

He smiled to himself as he thought back to the wild times with Karen. "I never raped her, she wanted it, in actual fact loved it. That girl was a quick learner, believe me! Besides she was seventeen and no child."

She shook her head. "And you think that makes it okay then? Just because the kid was so besotted with you, that she'd even allow you to make love to her? No Grant, you're nearly thirty, married and took money off someone to seduce a naive and vulnerable schoolgirl. That will be the reality in the court, and if you think 'Miss Goody Two Shoes' is going to say anything different, think again? Somehow she'll have to explain this to her parents and she'll be looking after her own arse, believe me. Her brief will claim you were a professional escort, with no intention of being a real boyfriend, and couldn't even marry her, all you wanted was to get inside her pants. Besides all that, the real killer to your defence is that they will claim you were, along with a man who's now dead, grooming a naive schoolgirl, destined to be abducted and used in a brothel. You'll go down for this; the papers and public opinion will see to that, have no doubt about it. We'll be lucky if she doesn't sue you for damages."

"Ha...she'll not get anywhere that way, we're broke."

"Not exactly, Grant, what about the house, it's worth close on two hundred thousand, since the house prices went wild and over a hundred of that is ours?"

He downed his drink and ran upstairs. Moments later he was back, his shoes on and fastening his coat.

"Do you want me to come with you?" she asked meekly.

He sniggered. "I'm not going to the police, there's no way

I'm going down for this. I'll get twenty years so I'm off, you and the kids can keep the bloody house. If she'll let you that is."

Her mouth dropped. "You can't be serious? You can't leave me alone with two kids, I couldn't cope."

"Oh, I'm deadly serious. Besides, Lucy, we've not exactly been getting on, and your mother will love me gone. She's done everything to get you to leave me for months now."

She stood and moved over to him, putting her arms round his neck. "I still love you, and we've had a great time this morning, I really believed we'd turned the corner," she whispered kissing him gently on the lips. "And you're imagining it with mum. She really likes you. It's just that she doesn't understand your job, that's all. Anyway it's between you and me and mum's got no say. I don't want you to leave and I'll stick by you, Grant. We'll fight it in the courts, say you were duped as well."

He kissed her back. "I know you would Lucy, but it isn't fair on you or the kids. Both you and I know I'll have no chance; I can't even get them to call Whittle as some sort of defence for me, so I'll take the complete rap and go down. It's ironical, only a few weeks back I thought we were home and dry when they said Whittle had killed the girl. With ten grand we were made, but now that's all changed with her not being dead."

"But where will you go? Will you come and see the children? I need to know these things, Grant? Besides, I don't even know if you want me to wait for you."

He shrugged. "I've no idea, Lucy, and that's the truth. This wasn't planned, you know? But I'll probably look in on my sister, she'll bung me a few hundred for my car, then with the money I'll go abroad. There's bound to be a warrant out for my arrest, when they find I'm not here. If anyone asks, particularly the police, stall them, say we had an argument or something and you're expecting me back. They will wait a day hopefully, and that'll give me time to get out of the country."

She held him tight, she knew he was right but she couldn't imagine him just walking out and leaving her and the children to fend for themselves. "Keep in touch, Grant, for the children's sake?" she whispered, still holding him tight.

He kissed her gently on the lips. "I'll try, Lucy, look after yourself and say goodbye to the kids for me."

With that he left the room, the front door slammed, then silence. Lucy returned to her chair, sitting there in a daze – only an hour before they'd been fooling about in the bedroom, the kids already at school. She'd run back home, after dropping them off, because he'd a rare day off and she wanted time alone with him.

4

Susan rushed into her house, through to the back kitchen. Her father was just pouring hot water into a cup for coffee.

"Careful, Susan, this is boiling water."

She flopped on a chair and looked at him. "Have you heard?"

"Heard what?"

"Karen's back."

He spun round. "When you say back, what are you talking about?"

She sighed. "Well if we'd a telly that worked, or you'd brought a paper from the pub you'd know. Apparently she was picked up two days ago and she's just been on telly offering to sell her story to the papers. We, Dad, are in the shit. It was one thing lying when we thought she was dead, it's another thing now she isn't. Once it gets round we took money to get her to come to our house, for Whittle to abduct her, we'll go down for sure. The papers will see to that."

"Then, Susan, you must see Karen. Convince her we knew nothing. No one knows of the money, only Whittle and he's dead."

She rolled her eyes back. "Oh yes, it's down to me again, like the first time I lied about having a CD she wanted and offering to copy it for her. The girl will beat the shit out of me. She was raped Dad, probably put in some brothel and forced to go with loads of men day after day, who knows?"

"You talk as if she's some tomboy. You're a big girl, Susan, she'll avoid you that's for sure," he urged.

Susan laughed. "Pushover is she? Karen is no pushover, she was head girl, feminine yes, but I never saw any girl even try to go up against her. She went to judo and kick-boxing and some other place for self-defence. You saw the state of this house after the fight she had with Whittle? Karen can be very violent if she wants."

He stood looking at her, as he sipped his coffee. "So what do we do? Go to the police and admit we were part of the abduction and took money for it?"

"I don't know, Dad, I really don't know."

They sat for some time, not saying anything, both in their own thoughts. Susan, on her part, had been devastated that luring Karen to their house, after school, on the pretext of copying a CD Karen had wanted, which in reality was to get her there for a meeting with a family-shunned uncle, turned out to be for neither reason. In fact she'd brought Karen unknowingly to the house to meet her abductor, resulting in a vicious fight between Karen and Frank Whittle, when Karen refused to go with him. Susan had spent the next week in hospital. She had broken her jaw when Frank Whittle pushed her accidentally into the door jamb after she'd come out of her bedroom to see what all the noise was about. Added to that, he'd kicked her a number of times in the ribs, broken two and badly bruised the others. Even today her jaw was still wired, and she was in constant pain.

"I vote we go to the police, tell them everything and let's see what they do?" Susan said suddenly. "After all I was injured so it was hardly a set up on our side. We genuinely believed he was a friend of her family and this was just a meeting to attempt to heal a rift."

Her father nodded. "You're right, let's go now before Karen can get in first."

Forty minutes later they walked into the local police station and asked to talk to the officer who had dealt with Karen's abduction. It was a further twenty minutes before they were sat in an interview room.

A plain clothes man entered the room. "I'm Detective Inspector Morris. I believe you want to talk to us about Karen Marshall?"

"I do, but I'm not sure where to start?" Susan's father suddenly blurted out.

"Perhaps Sir, if you give me your personal details and that

of the young lady, who I'm presuming is your daughter, we can go from there," Morris advised.

He made notes as they gave him their details, then looked up. "Did you know Karen Marshall to talk to?"

"Yes we did know her, well rather my daughter knew her from school."

"I see, so what do you want to say about Karen?"

"She was abducted from our house. We told the officer then we didn't know anything, but we did and we suspect Karen knows we did as well," Susan's father answered.

"So you've come here, after finding out that Karen wasn't dead, to give the truth about your involvement, before Karen returns to the UK and we come round to talk to you?"

"Yes, we'd like to make a new statement," he answered.

"Are you sure you don't first want to tell me about it, before you make a formal statement?"

Susan nudged her father. "Just tell him dad."

Her father went on to tell the officer about the chance meeting in a pub. How the man, Frank Whittle, had told him that he was a friend of Karen's family and wanted to meet her again, at a meeting to be set up by Susan. How Whittle believed that Karen was the key for a reconciliation of his and Karen's family. Susan's father waited while the officer made more notes then continued.

"He offered me money to arrange it. Susan duped Karen into believing she was copying a CD for her, when in fact Frank Whittle was waiting in the house when Karen came. Susan hid in the bedroom so that he could talk to Karen privately. Then she heard the fight, the screams of both Karen and Frank Whittle as he battled to tie her up and get her to his car. When Susan came out to see what was happening, she got caught up in the fight and ended up in hospital."

Detective Inspector Morris looked for some time at his notes. Susan and her father sat silently.

Then the Inspector sighed. "Okay, I'll take new statements from both of you. It will be under caution but I will release you on bail pending further enquiries. Truthfully this is a problem for the DPP. I'm not sure if you have actually committed an offence, apart from withholding information that could have been useful in the original investigation. So you will have to wait for a letter from the DPP, or from us after decisions have been made. I'd advise you to keep well away from Karen, when she comes home. You must not talk to her about what really happened in any way. We may do nothing, I don't know. But Karen might make a complaint against you, particularly if she knew about money changing hands, then it would be a completely different ball game. Do you understand?"

"We do, Inspector, we'll not go near Karen," he replied.

5

Karen, following her statement and offer to the press, had been ushered into the main building of the army barracks by a woman in her late forties, dressed smartly in a skirt with matching blazer, accompanied by a security man. They went down the main hall and into a room at the end. Inside the room there was a large table with ten chairs surrounding it and nothing else. The security man left them inside alone.

"Can you take a seat, Karen? Would you like a drink, coffee, soft drink, tea?"

"Coke please," Karen replied selecting a chair at the very bottom of the table.

The lady returned with a glass of Coke. Karen was rummaging through her backpack, but replaced it under her chair when she realised the woman was not going to leave her alone.

Time went on, Karen was getting fed up. "Why am I here? It's been close on an hour now," she asked.

"I'm sorry, Karen, we were to begin as soon as you arrived. However, they are all still in another meeting."

"Yes well, they'd better hurry otherwise I'm out of here. Anyway where's mum and dad, why haven't they come to see me?"

Karen's statement of wanting to leave disturbed the woman. "I'm afraid I can't answer any of your questions. Let me go and see what's holding everything up. I'll be five minutes."

"Okay... but any longer and I'll go for a walk and come back when the people I'm supposed to be meeting, have the courtesy to actually turn up themselves."

The woman left the room and walked quickly down the hall, up the stairs to the next floor and knocked on a door, before entering.

"Yes Miss Frogmort?" a man sitting at the head of the table

asked.

"It's Karen, Sir Nigel, she's getting fed up and is very annoyed just sitting there. She threatening to go for a walk and only come back when someone is ready to talk to her."

"Who the hell does she think she is?" Sir Nigel asked. "If the stupid girl hadn't made such a naive and explosive statement to the press we'd have been able to begin. As it is I've had not only the Home Secretary on the phone but the Prime Minister as well. They're livid, wanting to know who allowed her to make such a statement without us being aware, and armed with a prepared statement for the press. Already questions are being asked around Parliament as to why the government is relying on a young girl to lead the way in the fight to stop the human trafficking trade, besides using her own money? The ministers of course had not listened to the interview and were taken completely by surprise, unable to give any rational explanation, from questions made in the House, causing severe embarrassment all-round. I did ask you to bring her directly into the building Miss Frogmort and ignore the press."

"There was little I could do or say, Sir Nigel. I could hardly drag her away bodily, with not only the world's press assembled, but live on television. I'd asked Karen to keep it low key, just to say she felt a little tired but happy to be out. Karen said she understood so I knew nothing about what she really intended to announce."

At that moment the telephone rang. Sir Nigel answered and listened. He looked annoyed. "No you don't let her go out. What are you running down there?"

He listened to the answer. "She's already gone… and you call yourself security. Go and bring her back now," he said, then slammed the phone down.

"I suppose, by my conversation, you can gather that Karen has walked out of the building, Miss Frogmort? Would you please go and collect her from security, then keep her in the meeting room."

"Yes, Sir Nigel, immediately, but please come and see her soon, otherwise she'll go again. Youngsters these days have no discipline or respect for their elders."

"We will be along shortly Miss Frogmort."

Miss Frogmort ran down the stairs to the main entrance, stopping at the security desk. "So where is she?"

The security man shrugged. "Outside the main gate with the press again I presume. I'm on my own here, my mate's gone for our brews, so I could hardly leave the desk and go and get her, as lord high and mighty upstairs demanded."

She went outside to find Karen, as he'd suggested, sitting on the wall with at least twenty members of the press surrounding her.

Karen stopped talking and looked at Miss Frogmort approaching. "Hi, are they ready yet?"

"Please, Karen, come back inside with me. Sir Nigel's very annoyed."

She grinned. "Oh it's one of those posh people is it; think they own the world because they're a Sir? What about me? I'd been sat in there for over an hour. Anyway I'll be in later; I've been invited by some of the press to have lunch with them."

Miss Frogmort stared at her open-mouthed. "You can't do that! You'll get me sacked."

Karen laughed. "I'm only joking you know, lead the way," she replied jumping down from the wall. "Sorry lads, seems like I've upset a Sir," she said with a cheeky grin. "So I'll have to take a rain check on lunch. But I am open for offers to be taken out for dinner, and I'm really cheap to feed, if anyone wants to take me that is? Mind you, that's if they don't lock me up and throw away the key for escaping."

Many of the reporters began to laugh, this really was the sort of girl they wanted for their paper and already they were handing her their cards, or ripping a sheet out of their notebook with their name and number on, urging her to ring so they might arrange a night out and dinner.

Once inside and again in the room, Miss Frogmort shut the door. "You'll get me shot, Karen. Then to ask reporters to take you out for dinner, Sir Nigel will go absolutely berserk."

Karen shrugged. "I can't see why, after all, who I go out

with is my own business. Besides, no one has ever taken me out for dinner before, apart from the odd family do, which doesn't really count. Now I've got loads of offers, I could live for nothing at this rate."

"You really are a very strange girl. I'm used to dealing with girls who are traumatised, introvert and as such very difficult to get through to, while you're exactly the opposite."

"Yes well, this is the public side of me, trying to sell my story to help others," she replied soberly. "The other part of my life is private."

She looked at Karen with concern. "When you say private, you mean you're having trouble coming to terms with what's happened to you?"

"I never said that. I'm fine; I just don't want my private feelings discussed among a load of strangers."

"We're only here to help you know."

"So go and help someone, like I said I'm fine," she retorted.

In Miss Frogmort's opinion, Karen had responded too quickly. She had a great deal of experience with victims of rape and abuse. Karen, even if she didn't want to admit it, was already showing signs of delayed shock and trauma. But this girl was not approachable just yet; she would be as she started to go downhill, but at the moment she was holding herself together.

"You need to think very hard, Karen. Try to suppress your anxieties, your thoughts, and both will only give you pain. No matter what you think now, we can help, believe me it isn't a sign of weakness to ask for help. Ignore the signs and you risk your own sanity."

Karen shrugged with indifference. "Thank you for the advice, but I won't be taking it up."

At that moment the door opened and four people came into the room. Miss Frogmort left.

"Karen, Sir Nigel Henderson, I'm sorry about the delay but you caused quite a fracas with your announcement. We've been trying to explain to the British Government that your offer wasn't that serious, after all we're talking very low sums of money these papers often pay."

Karen grinned. "So the current bid of a quarter of a million is low is it? Whatever you say, Nigel, if it makes you happy? Or should I call you by your title?"

He raised an eyebrow and looked at her over his glasses. "You are joking?"

"No, why should I joke? But don't worry; it's from a foreign paper so our government won't have to stump up anything."

"I have to tell you, Karen, the military and the government are not happy with what you propose. We have men still missing, the operation was in a country we should not have been in and you intend to make it public. I'm of the mind to have a D notice placed on it."

She frowned. "What's that mean?"

"It means, young lady, your story couldn't be published."

Karen grinned. "Yes, I remember the word now; you did a D notice on some spy didn't you? But he just had it printed in Australia and you couldn't do a thing about it? So I wouldn't take that tack with me. I intend to help the kids sold by Saeed and other scum like him into brothels, no matter what you say, or try to do to stop me."

"Even if I told you you're causing severe embarrassment to your government. Questions are already being asked as to why we as a country are expecting a young girl to pay for what is primarily a governmental problem."

"You mean I should be a patriot, keep my mouth shut so politicians, who have swept this problem under the table for years, because it doesn't get them votes, can sleep at night? I don't think so, Nigel, but you or the government could contribute if you want? I'd be happy with that."

He sighed. "We'll leave that part of the discussion for the moment, Karen. Perhaps you can tell us your story from the beginning? We will be recording it and also some of the people here will be making their own notes."

Karen began at the beginning, however at every point she arrived at where she accidently injured or killed someone, she twisted or just left things out. In fact her story had become so farcical it sounded like she'd been on a walk in the park.

When she finished Sir Nigel decided to break for lunch. They called Miss Frogmort back, told Karen she was under no circumstances to leave the building again, and she reluctantly agreed, while Miss Frogmort was given the task to make sure she did as she promised.

Sir Nigel joined the others who'd listened to her story for lunch. "She's lying, it's obvious. Does anyone else agree?" he asked as he opened the conversation about Karen's story, after coffee was served.

James Gulliver, a psychologist nodded. "I agree, she is lying, Sir Nigel, and being very convincing in the way she's doing it."

"Can you explain?"

"In my view, Karen's withholding a great deal of information. Why? I'm not sure; however, she's either traumatised and is genuinely confused, pushing the horrific times she's experienced to the back of her mind as if it never existed. But I don't think so. She's too articulate and that leaves one other explanation. I believe she was involved in the loss of life of our soldiers and perhaps others, more than she's saying. If I'm right, and she's decided to leave her involvement out of her story, it would account for the fragmented explanation of what happened to her out there."

"I can't believe that," a lady from the local Social Services within the camp cut in. "It's very clear, Karen has been under a great deal of strain. She's a little jittery about her escape, that's obvious. But the girl is just eighteen, still a child and very feminine. Girls like her don't go round killing or fighting for that matter. They go with the flow, attach themselves to people to survive. I see a lot of children who experience violence. A child will try to put it to the back of their mind, even come to believe it never happened, as a means of protecting their own sanity. Karen has seen a great deal of violence both against her and others, she's also seen people killed or beaten. The girl is traumatised, acting exactly as I describe and how I'd expect a child to react."

James smiled. "Miss Sharp, she's hoodwinked you. That girl is cold, calculating and manipulative. She's been very clever in convincing you to believe what she wants you to believe, which is not the truth. As a man I can see her clearly leaning towards the males of the room. Effectively flirting with them, wanting them to see her as you have, vulnerable, needs to be looked after, butter wouldn't melt in her mouth syndrome."

"Rubbish, James, I'll tell you this though, the young girl's traumatised and trying to protect herself," Miss Sharp cut in, with obvious annoyance that this man would question her assessment.

"If you are right in your thinking James," Sir Nigel said, "the point is why? Why is this girl doing what she's doing? Is she hiding something she's done, but afraid to admit it?"

"I think, Sir Nigel, as I've suggested, Karen was very much more involved out there than she is admitting, maybe she's even killed herself and the killing has been a form of closure for her," James replied.

Sir Nigel frowned. "Would you like to expand that line of thinking?"

James leaned forward. "Take the scenario of a loved one passing away. Everyone is very upset; they feel loss and often walk around in a daze, not knowing how to handle it. Then the day of the funeral, the loss is still there but reality begins to return. Why? I'm suggesting that the actual event of the funeral is a sort of closure, an acceptance that the loved one has passed on, maybe to a better life, who knows? Except the mourners realise the deceased is at peace and it's time to pick their own lives up again. Now take a girl who's been raped, abused, whatever. She will be scared of the person, hate them with a vengeance besides be traumatised very much like with the loss of a loved one. However, if the abuser is punished, shown up for what he or she is, or even killed, that for the abused is closure of a sort. Karen has closure, Karen has either killed the abusers herself or others have done it for her, so this is why she can move on and why she is acting like she is."

"It is possible that what you're suggesting is true. Karen is using everything she's got to try to control the situation I agree, but either way, Karen will still need help," Miss Sharp suggested.

"Precisely, Miss Sharp, she will need help. However, as you pointed out Karen is still a child and we all know children can quickly become introvert. She's learning in her interview how to control a situation. Unless we can break this build-up of resilience we will never get at the truth. It will be lost in lies and counter-lies as she builds this impenetrable wall around herself."

"Have you experience of this sort of behaviour?" Sir Nigel asked.

"Unfortunately no, and I don't think many psychologists have, they are extremely rare. If you look at Karen's situation she has lots going for her. She's attractive; some would see her as decidedly sexy and because of her experience maybe available. However, she is young, and quite naive in her dealings with men. I have no doubt we will see over the next few days a steady rise in her confidence. She will use every trick in the book to convince us that what she is saying is true. So with your permission, Sir Nigel, after lunch I'd like us to ignore what she's already told us but go direct into really in-depth questioning of her. Study her reaction, her mannerisms and most importantly her answers. I believe I can get inside this girl's head, draw out the real story before she closes the door forever. Then I'm certain you will see a very different Karen Marshall, laid bare she won't be the nice feminine little girl she's very cleverly portraying, and what she hopes you believe she is. But a dangerous killer, whose words about helping others are a smokescreen to hide her real intentions."

"And those are?" Sir Nigel asked.

"To find and kill everyone who took part in her abduction."

Miss Sharp burst into laughter. "You really believe that James? If you do, you shouldn't be here, your suggestions are ludicrous. Because go down that route and you risk awakening painful memories for the girl. Do that and Karen will end up on drugs for the rest of her life, trying to stop the nightmares of a particularly violent and abusive experience for any child."

He shrugged. "Possibly, Miss Sharp, but soldiers are missing, only Karen knows the real story and she must be made to tell it."

"You are right, James, do it and see where we get," Sir Nigel said. He disliked this girl intensely, and had no qualms if, as Miss Sharp claimed, she'd have to live with her actions.

6

Lucy returned home after taking the children to school. It had been two days since Grant had left her and each night she'd cried herself to sleep. The police hadn't come, however she didn't expect them yet, as Karen was still in Cyprus.

After washing the breakfast pots she went upstairs to her room and into the shower. Five minutes later after drying herself she put on her Lycra one-piece and trainers. In twenty minutes her best friend Janet would call and they'd both go down to the gym for their weekly workout.

While she waited she collected clothes from the children's bedrooms and ran down to the garage to put them into the washer. It was then the front doorbell rang.

Lucy looked at her watch and sighed. *"God she's early, I've not even got my tracksuit on,"* she commented to herself as she went to open the front door.

A man, around six feet three, was standing there when she pulled open the front door, it was Janssen.

"You Grant's wife?" he asked.

"Yes…," she replied slowly with some hesitation.

"Where is he?"

She frowned. "Excuse me, who are you and why do you want to know?"

Janssen suddenly moved forward, pushing the door with a great deal of force, she stumbled back in surprise. But by then he was inside and had slammed the door closed. She screamed, but was silenced quickly by a blow to the head.

"Don't piss me about, just tell me where he is, or I'll beat the shit out of you," Janssen drawled with little or no compassion in his voice.

"I don't know where he is, but if you don't leave my house I'll call the police," she answered bravely.

Janssen sighed then grabbed her long hair dragging her into the lounge and forcing her face down on the couch. Then he ripped open her one-piece exposing her back and bottom. Suddenly his face was inches from hers. She felt his other hand touch her bottom with something cold. "Listen, lady, we can do it the easy way or the hard way. The easy way is you tell me everything I want to know. The hard way, I turn you over and run this knife you can feel on your bottom from your throat to your fanny, and gut you like a pig. They'll struggle to sew you up, if you survive, with all your guts hanging out, believe me. Or maybe I'll just dig your eyes out with the tip of my knife, rest them on your cheeks, and pop them?"

Lucy was terrified, tears streaming down her face. "Please, I beg you, I've two children. I'll tell you anything you want, even do what you want with me, but don't use your knife."

"Then tell me where that husband of yours is, before I start cutting," he said quietly, at the same time sliding the flat of his knife up her body, letting it rest on the back of her neck.

"I didn't lie. He read the paper two days ago about a girl called Karen, who was abducted. He thought she'd died in an accident. Then he just panicked believing she'd tell the police about him and he'd be sent to prison. He told me not to bother waiting for him, as he was going abroad and never coming back."

Janssen remained still, looking down at Lucy. He knew when the truth was being told to him. This woman was terrified but she still might tell him less than the complete truth, if she wanted to protect her husband.

"Had he any money?"

She shook her head.

"Then where would he go for some? Has he a family, mother, father, sisters, brothers?" he asked.

"I've his parents' address, his sister is married and lives in London but I only have her phone number, I don't know her address," she answered without delay, hoping he'd believe her about Grant's sister which at least would give him time to leave the country.

He grinned, the oldest answer in the book. He was at his

sister's and she was trying to protect him. "You married women don't learn do you? Still have some misplaced loyalty to your husband. Well lady, he's not here, you're alone naked and vulnerable. When I ask for the truth, I mean all the truth. What is his sister's address?"

She said nothing.

At that moment she felt the tip of the knife start to prick her right buttock, as if a needle was injecting into the skin. Then as the skin would first resist a needle so it did with the knife, before finally giving, allowing the knife to enter her buttock. The sudden pain was intense. She wanted to scream, try to push him away, but face down she couldn't get any strength in her arms to do it. Then he forced her face into the couch, so she couldn't scream or breathe. Lucy felt faint, as the knife sank in deeper, but fought it for all she was worth. He pulled her head up and she started begging him to stop, she didn't want to die, and she'd find his sister's address for him if he'd just let her be.

Suddenly Janssen pulled out the knife, stood back, looking down at her. Blood was pouring from the wound to her buttock; the woman was close to passing out. "Get the address," he demanded.

She tried to stand, but the pain was too much, so she crawled, leaving a trail of blood following her. Pulling a drawer open on the sideboard, but unable to stop it at her level, the drawer fell off its runners, missing hitting her head by inches, spilling the contents over the floor. Lucy rifled through the contents, found no address book and pulled open the other drawer Again it came crashing down off the runners. However, she saw what she wanted and grabbed the address book, flipping through the pages until she found the address.

"This is where she lives," Lucy said offering him the open book.

"I suppose that's where he's heading, and why you claimed you didn't have the address, is it?"

She nodded. "I'm sorry I deceived you, he's my husband and I still love him. He's leaving the country and going there first to pick some money up. I just wanted him to have the chance of escape that's all."

"It wasn't worth it was it? Now what should I do with you?"

Her mouth dropped, he was stood over her playing with his knife. "Please, I beg you don't kill me, don't leave my children without a mother and father."

He grinned. "But if you live you'll tell the police where I'm going."

She shook her head. "I won't, I won't say a word. I'll just tell them someone came looking for him and I couldn't tell the person as I didn't know where he was."

Her breathing was coming fast and short, close to falling completely apart. "My children come first, Grant's made his bed. Please, Sir, don't let them be left alone, they're only five and six." Then the emotion and fear of perhaps never seeing her children again was too much, Lucy broke down and began sobbing uncontrollably.

The next moment Janssen was down at her side. The knife inches from her face. She stopped crying, her eyes as big as saucers, staring up at him.

"I'll let you live, for your children's sake. Say one word to the police, telephone his sister or anyone else and I'll find out. But it won't be you I'll come back for, it'll be your kids. Then after stringing them up naked I'll gut them in front of you so you can watch them die slowly. Believe me lady you'll remember their screams of terror, with their guts hanging out, the life blood running from their tiny bodies for the rest of your life. Do you understand?"

"Yes I understand..." she stuttered. "I'll say nothing; I'll not risk my children's lives for anything or anyone."

He stood and took one last look at her lying there then turned and left the house. Lucy closed her eyes thanking God. Her body was shaking, both with cold and fear. Dragging herself along the floor once again she pulled the telephone off the side table and began to dial the emergency services, but she didn't complete it as moments later she blacked out. However, her friend came, as arranged, to go to the gym, found the door wide open and came in calling her name.

When Lucy woke she was in hospital. She lay there for a moment trying to remember what had happened and why she was here. Alongside her a machine was bleeping constantly, a bag with some red stuff inside hanging at her other side. Then she remembered, all at once everything came back. Grant, the stranger, her children... Her children, what had happened to them, where were they? Were they safe? She began screaming and shouting, a nurse followed by a doctor then a policewoman ran in.

"My children, where are my children?" she kept shouting.

The policewoman moved closer to her while the doctor, with the help of the nurse gave Lucy an injection.

"Don't worry about your children, Lucy," the policewoman said quietly. "We have already collected them from school and your mother is looking after them. They are perfectly safe, believe me. Now you need to calm down and tell me what happened."

Lucy stared open-mouthed at the policewoman, shaking her head. "I can't. I can't help you; he'll come back and kill my children. Please don't ask me any more questions."

She was shaking uncontrollably in obvious terror, but at the same time slowly calming as the sedative they gave her took control. Within minutes she just lay there staring up at the ceiling. The policewoman knew they'd get nothing out of her at this time. Whoever had done this to her had instilled absolute terror in her mind for the continued safety of her children, this mother would tell them nothing.

Janssen hadn't gone directly to London to find Grant. He'd climbed into his hired car and drove round to Susan's home. The street was deserted, the children had gone to school, people were at work, leaving the odd housewife or pensioner at home. However, Janssen knew that Susan's father was at home. He knew this because the old car he drove was still in the drive. He was made redundant an while ago and not due to go down to the post office until later to cash his giro and collect his unemployment money, then he'd go directly to the pub. Janssen didn't go to the front door, he walked round the side, elbowed the window of the back door in and put his hand inside, turning the lock.

Once inside he stopped and listened. The house was quiet.

Making his way upstairs he pushed open the main bedroom door. A man was still sleeping; the room stank of stale beer. Taking out a gun from his pocket he carefully screwed on the silencer. He walked over to the man, placed a pillow over his head and fired twice. The body shook and contorted for a minute or so then fell still. Carefully unscrewing the silencer, it was then when he heard a noise. Someone else was in the house. Janssen moved swiftly to the door and looked down the short landing. A woman was shuffling along carrying a night potty to the bathroom, at the end of the landing. Janssen knew from the document Saeed had given him that this was the grandma, completely gone in her mind, with very few lucid moments. He took the silencer out once more, screwed it back on and walked towards the bathroom. As he pushed open the door she was bent over the toilet emptying the night potty. Janssen raised the gun and fired twice. The old woman just fell forward onto the toilet. She'd not uttered a word. He walked over and shot her once more in the head then left the bathroom.

Leaving the house, he climbed into his car, took one last look round the deserted road, started the engine and headed off towards London.

7

It was two days after Karen arrived in Cyprus that she walked out of the debriefing sessions. Karen's parents and her sister were already staying in a hotel on the island, but on the first day she was in Cyprus they were not allowed to see her until the evening. This was because Karen had been scheduled to attend preliminary interviews, counselling and medical checks. The following day, for Karen, was much the same as the previous day and again the family returned to spend the evening with her. Tonight though, unlike the night before when they just visited they joined her for dinner in the camp Social Club.

"So when can you go home?" her mother asked. "We're getting a little fed up of being fobbed off all the time."

"God knows. I'm stuck in a small room with a guy called James. Some sort of psychology nerd. All he does is ask stupid questions, going over and over the same thing. I'm not sure if he really believes I've been abducted, he's more interested in making me agree to his thoughts, rather than what happened to me."

"Can't you object and tell him to get lost?" her sister, Fay asked.

Karen grinned. "Funny you suggested it; tomorrow if he starts I'm going to do just that."

"Are you sure you can?" her father cut in.

"I can't see why not, after all I was told I was here voluntarily, to help sort out what happened to me. If he doesn't believe me, so what, he's not getting me to admit things I've never done."

"She's right Dad," Fay said. "If it's voluntary they can hardly object if Karen complains this man's being obnoxious and only interested in discrediting her all the time."

"Well don't get their backs up Karen, you know what you're like, with that short temper of yours?" her mother added.

"I don't have a short temper," she retorted indignantly. "I just can't stand someone who wants to pull me down all the time, I agree. But this man really winds me up."

"You mean you can't wrap him round your little finger like all the lads you meet?" Fay ribbed.

Karen laughed. "You might be right there. Mind you, Fay, if you see him you wouldn't want to."

"Well at least you can get off the island, whether you leave or they chuck you out. Mum never sent your passport back, when they told us you'd died in Wales, so she's got it with her," Fay said.

"Yes well, don't volunteer that information to them, otherwise they'll pinch it and leave me stranded here."

The conversation went onto what had been happening at home and they left Karen around midnight. After waving them goodbye, until the following night, Karen made her way slowly back to the single room in the women's barracks they'd put her in. She didn't like going there; it was stark, uninviting and above all lonely. She'd been alone enough and just wanted to go home, sleep in her own bed, and cuddle her teddy which she'd had ever since she could remember.

Karen entered her room and shut the door. She sat on the side of the bed looking down at the floor. After all that had happened to her, never did she feel as low and scared as she did now. Since boarding the submarine Karen had been trying to put everything behind her, block it from her mind. It had begun to work, the constant strain she'd been under on the run had gone. Even the people she'd met were at last becoming a blur, in reality as if it never happened.

However, James and his constant questions, making her go over and over everything again and again, forcing her to relive her experiences had awakened the terror of her ordeal once again. Last night she woke a number of times, her body was shaking, and she was absolutely soaked in perspiration. However, she didn't mention it to anyone, afraid they'd put her through more tests.

Tonight she was terrified of even lying down and closing her eyes as she clasped her hands together trying to stop them shaking. Karen knew what was happening to her. But it was as if she was in some slow-motion film watching herself as she began to fall apart, not knowing how to stop it.

"Pull yourself together," she demanded of herself. *"Saeed's dead, they're all dead. You've won."*

She sat there considering the statement.

"I have, I've won, haven't I? I can go home and forget it. Yes that's what I'll do, I'll tell them I'm going home," she decided.

Satisfied with this decision and desperately tired, Karen closed her eyes, her head was spinning. Again the screams, people shouting, and guns firing returned. Then the visions, the faces, though when she opened her eyes, everything was quiet. Karen fell back onto the bed, staring up at the ceiling. But she just couldn't keep her eyes open. Soon her nightmares began again, she was in Saeed's big room, and her gun was firing, people screaming. But when she tried to stop the nightmare by opening her eyes once more the screaming inside her head, mixed up with gunfire, persisted. She put her hands to her ears, trying to block the sounds out, everything was so real. She wanted to scream out loud herself. Tell everyone how she desperately needed help. But her pride, her determination to show the world she was Karen, bullet-proof, calm and composed, made her discount the urge.

How long she lay there, she'd no idea. The room was cold; she was cold, her body soaking the same as the night before. Looking out of the window it was still dark outside. Why can't the night finish?

Eventually Karen stood and left the room. Outside she felt better, the sounds inside her head now gone leaving her only with a splitting headache. She could see the beginning of dawn appearing on the far horizon, the sun just beginning to peep over the edge as it bathed a reddish light across the parade ground, highlighting the flagpole in silhouette. Lights were coming on in different buildings; even in her own block she could now hear the sounds of stirring. Karen felt relieved, the night was over, and somehow she'd managed to sleep, but not much, although she couldn't remember doing it.

"Are you just coming in?" a voice came from behind her.

Karen turned to see who was talking. A girl was stood in

pyjamas, lighting a cigarette.

"Excuse me?"

"I was just asking if you'd just got back."

"No I've just got up, what time is it?"

"Five forty-five. Would you like a cigarette?"

Karen shook her head. "No thank you."

"Do you always go to bed in your clothes then?" the girl asked.

"No never, I just couldn't sleep, so I got dressed."

"Oh…"

"What's that supposed to mean?"

The girl sighed. "Listen it's no odds to me if you've sneaked out for the night. We all do it you know, but you should go in before someone sees you."

"I told you I've just got up. What's this going out for the night thing all the time?" Karen snapped back at her.

The girl held her hands up. "Okay, you've just got up, so don't get heavy on me. Anyway I'm going in. You need to as well and clean yourself up, you look shit."

Karen never replied. *"Look it,"* she thought, she also felt it.

Back in the bedroom Karen stared at herself in the mirror. Now she understood. Her face was streaked in make-up and mascara, her eyes red, her hair looked dirty and unkempt. It was no wonder the girl didn't believe her, she wouldn't have either now.

Throwing her clothes off, and pulling a large bath towel round her body, she wandered down to the shower room spending a good twenty minutes tidying herself up, trying to look more her usual self. By the time Karen dried her hair, put a little light make-up on and a set of clean clothes her mother had brought, she looked and felt tons better.

After breakfast she was back with James. He went on and on, she still had a splitting headache, so she just sat there completely ignoring him, her mind drifting. Thinking about anything and nothing so long as it wasn't what he was going on about.

James, as usual, was pursuing his absolute belief that she

was telling a complete pack of lies and subjected her to intense interviews and questioning. After lunch they returned to the interview room and James began again.

"You know, Karen we're getting nowhere. You sit and tell me that all around you people were dying and yet you talk as if it's some comic book adventure, and you're just the token dizzy girl among all this carnage. This is not what's coming out from the Lebanon. They are demanding your return, claiming you killed a number of civilians. Of course this is just talk, as they know full well you couldn't be extradited because there are no arrangements for this between our countries. The Lebanese are talking that way because they want strength in negotiating the release of two SAS officers still held captive. They also have another officer who's in hospital and paralysed. His name's Garry Stafford, who you say in your statement, is one of the officers that collected you from Sirec's house?" He fell silent for a minute deciding to try to frighten her. "We want to be convinced you have not committed murder, because if you have the government may decide to hold you for an indefinite time, for your own safety, under the mental health act."

Karen had gone cold at Garry's name being mentioned. Out of all the SAS officers only Garry knew she'd shot and killed Saeed. But would he talk, after all he fancied her and wanted to see more of her when they let him go? She'd said yes at the time, after all she thought he was dying and would never return, but the mutual arrangement of meeting each other again could be very important to her now.

Because she didn't reply James pushed on. "Come on it's very simple. Is what you've told me the truth or fabrication?"

She gave a soft smile, deciding to call his bluff. "So you believe you can frighten me by talking about mental health acts and holding me? Tell you what James. I've had enough shit from you. You've had my story, believe it or believe it not I couldn't care less, but it's all you're getting. So I'm going to walk out of this building. I'm going to sell the real story of my captivity and escape to the highest bidder. Try and stop me and I'll have dad call the papers, I'll tell them how you're treating me as some criminal. I'm not, I've done nothing but the minimum to stay alive and get myself out of that hellhole. So arrest me or shut up."

He knew then he'd failed to get through the barrier she'd set up. Every time he tried to breach it she gained strength in her story, which was now unshakable.

He shrugged. "Okay if that's what you want, I'll call Sir Nigel. He will give you permission to leave, if it's possible, I cannot. You and I are finished, Karen, I hope to god you can live with what you've done out there? I know I couldn't, if I were in your shoes."

She glared at him. "Who the hell do you think you are; pontificating as to what you think went on? You don't know and neither do you want to understand, apart from your own belief that I'm some sort of murderer. No man can really know what it's like to be a girl alone and on the run. If a man's caught he can expect a beating. If a young girl's caught what can she expect? I'll tell you. She can only expect rape, rape and more rape. Stretched out on some bloody table, more than likely tied down like I was, until everyone has had their turn. Maybe she'd get lucky and they'd kill her, but probably not. After all there's always the brothel, or more soldiers to satisfy the next day and the next day and the next? Faced with that, my option was to fight for my freedom or die. Well I decided to fight and believe me, I can live with myself. I was brought up as a Catholic, taught to turn the other cheek. I didn't, and I really, really hope one day you're faced with decisions like I had, and see just what you'd do. Although looking at you, you'd shit yourself if you had just one day of what I had to endure for weeks. So just get lost. From now on I no longer want to see you, talk to you, or listen to your patronising bloody twaddle anymore."

James left the room and five minutes later Sir Nigel entered. "I hear you want to leave," he said.

"I don't want to talk to that idiot or another like him, that's what I want," she retorted.

"I see Karen and you really have nothing more to add to your story of the events in the Lebanon?"

"No, nothing although I'd like to meet Garry again. We got

on well and I thought he'd died of his injuries."

"That may be possible, although I'm not certain he will be released before you return to the UK, Karen. But you are free to go; shall I call a cab for you?"

"No I don't want a cab. Besides, they cost a fortune and I'm not made of money. I'll walk; maybe thumb a lift, it's not your problem. Anything's better than being beholden to you lot."

He looked down at the open file in front of him and signed the release paper, then looked up at her.

"You know all we wanted was the truth Karen, it seems you don't want to tell us, so you can hardly expect us to be all nice and pally can you?"

She shook her head. "No you didn't want the truth. You wanted me to admit what James decided in his mind was the truth, not what really happened. So you're just pissed off he couldn't break me and force me to tell a load of lies to make him and you look good. All he's done is make me relive times I wanted to forget. I had nightmares last night, stayed up half the night afraid to close my eyes. You have no right to do that to me. But I'll tell you this. Every bit of what he's done to me I'll tell the papers. Its harassment and he'll bloody pay."

"I think that is a bit of an exaggeration, Karen," he replied, not really believing what she was saying.

She laughed. "You do, do you? Well we'll see won't we, when I get dad to take me to a solicitor."

She stood and looked at him watching her as she picked up her backpack; she'd kept it close to her since coming to the building. "Anyway I'm off, is it left to the town or right when I get out of the gates?" she asked.

"I did say we'll drop you off, Karen, you don't have to walk."

"You won't. I don't want to see any of you again. So I'll find my own way thank you."

She left the room and walked down to the main entrance door of the building. The security men made to stop her by one of them putting his hand on her shoulder telling her to wait there. This time her composure dropped, she snapped inside, her mind began to play tricks, making her believe he was something to do with Sirec and this man was trying to send her back.

"Take your hand off me," she demanded.

"You're going nowhere young lady, until I'm told different," the man replied, with authority in his voice, confident he could hold this young girl with ease.

"I said take your hand off me, this is the last time I will ask," she replied very softly but with aggression in her voice.

Still he ignored her.

However, before she took the next step of taking this man on, Sir Nigel caught up with her and intervened. "Leave Karen alone, just let her go. Ring the gate, tell them she can leave," he demanded.

Karen turned to look at Sir Nigel; he could see the change in her, the wildness in her eyes.

"Tell that James of yours if he comes near me again, I'll kill him." Then she walked out of the door.

The security guards and Sir Nigel watched her walking down the path towards the main gate.

"These kids, they say some stupid things. Thinking she could do something like that. I blame the television and the video games. She'd run a mile if someone even said boo to her," one security guard commented.

Sir Nigel never replied. Suddenly he'd seen another side of this girl. For nearly three days James had tried to pull this out of her and failed. Yet it only took one person to try to restrain Karen and in that second, her mask of naivety and femininity slipped, ever so slightly, but it slipped. Then he saw it in her eyes; heard it in her tone of voice. Her comment was no comment from a video game, or TV show as the security man believed. That was a direct threat from a very capable killer. Although he now knew there was nothing he could do about it. Her recorded answers gave nothing away; the others that were with her in the Lebanon were missing. Their only chance of perhaps getting at the truth would be if she was traumatised, and James's questions had disturbed her to the point she needed counselling. But not by James, he must be warned to keep well way from her; he'd not a shadow of a doubt that Karen would almost certainly follow through with her threat, given a chance.

Karen arrived at the gate. No one said a word as she walked out. However, just outside were a few newspaper reporters hanging around, stopping and asking people going in and out if they had heard what was happening to Karen.

To say they were astonished, seeing her walk through the gate, was perhaps an underestimation. But unlike her attitude with security Karen had slipped back into her naïve young girl role.

"Hi, I don't suppose anyone would like to give me a lift into town?" she asked.

8

Inspector Morris watched the ambulance take Susan away. An hour before she'd called the emergency service. The girl was hysterical, screaming down the telephone that her dad and grandma were dead, there was blood everywhere and she wanted help.

The emergency call centre couldn't get out of Susan, at the time, who she was, or where she lived as the girl was so distressed. They could only trace the call and re-direct a police patrol car, in the area, to find out just what was going on. The police patrol that responded found her sat on the front step sobbing her heart out, and it was they who'd called for medical assistance.

Going inside, he watched as the forensic team finished their photographs and the pathologist completing his initial inspection of the bodies.

"Well Henry, what are your first thoughts?" he asked the pathologist.

"The man in the bed, two shots to the head, through the pillow to stop the blood from splattering, it's professional, probably a contract killer. The old lady in the bathroom, two shots from across the bathroom to stun her, then one in the head to ensure she was dead. The first two killed her anyway, the last shot again the work of a contract killer ensuring the victim was dead. This was no opportunist looking to rob; nothing in the house has been obviously touched, like you'd see in a robbery. It was an ordered killing, you can be sure of that."

"Thanks Henry," he said, and then wandered back to the front door.

A sergeant came up to him. "I'm not sure if it's related Inspector, but I was called to another house this morning. A woman had been assaulted. Not strange in itself, I grant you, but it wasn't rape or robbery. Someone had forced their way in and by the look of it interrogated her. Whoever it was used a knife and she has a very nasty wound to one of her buttocks. The point is, Inspector, she is terrified of talking. Whoever it was knew what they were doing, just how far to go to terrify their victim and again took nothing from the house."

"Very strange; what of the neighbours around here, did anyone see anything unusual?"

The sergeant shook his head. "Most were at work, the few who weren't tend to live in the back rather than the front. No one saw or heard a thing."

"Okay, I think I'll visit this woman, is she in hospital or at home?"

"St Wilfred's, ward twenty-two. There's a policewoman outside the door.

Forty minutes later Inspector Morris entered Lucy's room in the hospital. She was awake, but just staring ahead. He could sense the tension in the room, the fear this woman had.

"I'm Inspector Morris, Lucy. Now I know you don't want to talk about your ordeal. Whoever it was who assaulted you threatened your children didn't he?"

She nodded, tears beginning to trickle down her face.

"I understand. I also understand you don't believe we can protect you and your children from him, do you?"

Again she nodded.

"Well we can, but I have to admit to do that we would need to put you and the children into a safe house until he's caught. Whether you tell us what happened or you decide to remain silent, I recommend you don't return to your house. The man could still come back, even if you tell us nothing he wouldn't know that, believe me."

She looked up at him. "I can't help you Inspector, I won't help you. My children are all I've got. You can't expect me to risk their lives? They are so young and innocent."

"That's all right Lucy, but I'd like you to answer me one question, it's nothing about what happened to you. It's just a stab in the dark that you may be able to help me with another incident."

"What is it you want to know?"

"Do you know, or have you heard of a girl called Karen Marshall?"

Lucy suddenly went cold, her mouth dropped open and she began to shiver. "I know of her," she whispered.

"Was this before she was splashed across the national press?"

"No, I'd not heard of her before then. But it turns out my husband was her boyfriend. He told me this two days ago. We split up over it."

"Thank you, Lucy. Now one more tiny question. Did your husband ever mention a Frank Whittle?"

She nodded. "He did, at the same time he told me about this Karen Marshall. It was this Whittle that introduced him to Karen."

After thanking her once more he left the room, wandering slowly down the corridors deep in thought. Whatever was going on, someone was eradicating anybody associated with Karen's abduction. But why, what was there to gain? After all he'd a statement from Susan and her father; there was nothing in it that would warrant him being killed? The only connection between these two incidents was Whittle, but he was dead and Karen was coming home.

Back outside he climbed into his car. Then called control for Lucy's address. Once there he went into the room where the assault took place. Staring for a time at the drawers on the floor with their contents scattered. The line of blood told him that it was Lucy who'd gone to those drawers. She'd taken something out to give the man, but what was it?

At that moment he heard someone coming down the stairs. Going out to the hall an elderly woman was just at the bottom holding a suitcase.

"I hope you don't mind, it's clothes for the children? I'm Lucy's mother."

"No that's fine, I'm Inspector Morris. Tell me, would you know if anything is missing from the drawers in the lounge?"

She followed him in and went carefully through the items,

then looked up. "The address book isn't here. Lucy normally leaves it in one of these drawers."

"I see. Do you have other children?"

"No Inspector, Lucy is our only child. Grant, her husband has a sister in London. I'm not sure where she lives, as his part of the family never communicates with us. His mother would know, she lives in Marple, on some farm. I can give you her address, if you'd care to come back to my house?"

"Yes I'd like that address. I'll follow you. Before we go, the photographs on the sideboard, which one is Lucy's husband?"

The woman handed him one. "This is the most recent. Taken at Joshua's birthday last month."

It was the next day after picking up the address of Grant's parents, that he was able to contact them by phone. They'd been away and only arrived back in the early hours. After talking to them on the phone, Inspector Morris had called Scotland Yard and asked if they would go round to see Grant's sister, to find out if she'd seen Grant. Already he'd put a general all points notice at airports, ports and other places of exit for Grant.

The Inspector was sitting in the police canteen having breakfast, when the telephone call came through.

"Chief Inspector Grays here, Morris. The lady you sent us to call on is dead. Shot in the head twice, we believe it was professional. Can you give me the background of your request?"

He listened to all Inspector Morris had found out the day before, then told him to wait for a call. Twenty minutes later the call came. He was to go down to London urgently, bring everything he had on both the killings, the statement by the victim and details about the woman being attacked in her home, to meet a Sir Peter Parker of Special Branch.

Arriving in London four hours later, Inspector Morris was collected at the railway station and taken direct to New Scotland Yard.

After meeting Sir Peter, he spent the best part of an hour carefully going through details of both incidents with him.

"This seems to have escalated Sir Peter, for Special Branch to be involved?" Inspector Morris commented.

Sir Peter, a tall ex-commando officer, with greying hair, leaned back on his chair. "We are worried Inspector. In themselves they seem innocuous. However, if you take the return of Karen Marshall into account and the involvement of both families before she was abducted, it seems to indicate that whoever is behind the contract killings, wants every link between them and Karen broken. It could be because, with Karen back and talking of her ordeal, just maybe someone involved was worried in case these families panicked. We don't know but the families may even have been part of the ring itself, and to save their own skins, might have decided to tell us more about the traffickers' operation in this country."

"I can go with that scenario. But it would mean this Grant is also very much on their hit list."

"Of course, and I would think his sister was subjected to threats and intimidation to tell whoever it was, where her brother had gone. But more serious than that, all this wiping out of tracks seems to indicate there is to be another abduction by the same gang. But whoever they are abducting must be very high profile. Someone like Karen, even at forty thousand dollars, wouldn't warrant a contract killer to be engaged."

"Say it isn't one, but a number?" the Inspector suggested.

Sir Peter shook his head. "They'd never pull it off. Girls commanding high values are selected, they are not random ones taken from the streets. To coordinate that sort of operation would involve a number of teams to snatch at the same time. Very difficult for criminals to do. Very high risk of someone talking. So although we discount nothing, it is nigh on impossible for the trafficker to achieve, I would think."

"Would you like me to stay on the case, as far as the Manchester link is concerned?"

"Yes I would. I've already talked to the Chief Constable and he's agreed for you to work directly with my department. Another important part for you is Karen herself. She lives in your patch and is due home in a few days. I talked to Sir Nigel Henderson, who's attached to the Embassy in Cyprus only an hour ago. They have had a great deal of trouble with the girl. In fact she walked out on them, refused to talk to them anymore, but still intends to sell her story. Doing this sort of thing, for her, risks the traffickers wanting to shut her up, the same as happened to these two families, so they can get on with what they do without reporters and such snooping around."

"I see. So this Karen's a very foolish girl talking out like she has?"

Sir Peter took a sip of his coffee in thought. "I think the answer to your question is yes and no. Although they would like to shut her up, Karen might have considered that saying nothing made her a bigger target. I've seen pictures of her on the television, the same as everyone, but apparently when you meet her, even the photos don't do her justice. She is, by all accounts an extremely attractive, well educated, intelligent girl. The papers love her, she will sell papers for them, believe me. So taking out a girl with such a high profile, her death would burst the traffickers' bubble good and proper. Every paper in the world would be up in arms. Governments and politicians alike would be looking to clean their act up, so no blame was directed at their country. On that basis she could be bulletproof."

"Very well, Sir Peter, I now understand things better, and your concerns. You can be assured I will keep my ear to the ground and also pursue these incidents. Just maybe the girl Susan can shed some light. Who knows, we can only try."

"We can only hope, Inspector, in the meantime I'll work this side looking for Grant. I'll also keep you informed of any intelligence we receive as to the real reason these families have been targeted."

9

Angela, better known as Angie to all her friends and family, took one last look at herself in her bedroom mirror, before picking her teddy up, kissing him goodbye and then sitting him on an already made bed leaning against her pillows. Then she left the room pulling the door closed gently behind her. Only a week or so from eighteen, five foot nine, slim with long blonde hair and deep green eyes, she was popular with all the lads, fun to be with and full of vitality. Now with all her exams finished, and a long summer break spread out in front of her before university, that also included a holiday of a lifetime she'd won in a competition, Angela couldn't have been happier. Although her boyfriend Simon wasn't at all happy with her going away without him. He'd wanted her to go along with him and his mates, clubbing in Benidorm for a week, in fact it was being seriously talked about until the letter informing her that she'd won one of the places in the competition dropped through the letterbox.

"Come on, Angie, you'll miss the plane if you don't get a move on," her father shouted up.

Angela appeared at the top of the stairs grinning and began making her way down. "There's no chance I'm missing it. Besides, I'm ready now."

He watched his daughter coming down. Dressed in jeans and a short cropped jumper she looked so grown-up, a far cry from the little girl who used to grasp his hand tightly not so many years ago. "Have you got everything?" he asked as she came up alongside him.

"Yes, Dad, I'm ready so don't panic me into thinking I've missed something, because I haven't. Where's Mum?"

"She's just slipped next door to tell them you are off."

They went outside and climbed into the car. Angela's mother ran out from the front door of the next house, followed by her neighbour and best friend Carol.

"Have a great time Angie," Carol said looking in the car. "Bill and I would like you to have a little something extra," she added at the same time handing her an envelope.

"Thank you, what's inside? Can I open it?" Angela asked.

Carol shook her head. "No later, besides it's only a few Euros we had left from our holiday. Just enough to buy yourself and your new-found friends a Coke or two."

After the last farewells they were off. Angela, sitting in the back, opened the envelope. It wasn't just a few Euros; it was close to a hundred. Not sure if she should mention it to her parents Angela slipped the currency into her purse, already deciding to buy Carol and her husband brilliant presents for their generosity.

They arrived at Manchester Airport an hour before the short flight to Gatwick. Angela hugged her parents at the entrance to security.

"Look after yourself, love," her mother said as she held her daughter tight, "and call us as soon as you arrive at Gatwick just to let us know you've met up with all the others."

"I will, and don't worry I'll be fine, meet loads of new friends and have lots and lots of photos so you can see everything I've done."

She let go of her daughter and they watched her go through the security of the domestic gate, before a final wave from her as she disappeared inside the departure lounge. They both walked back slowly to the main hall and found a coffee bar to wait until the aircraft left.

Her mother sat fiddling with her cup half watching the television. "That poor girl, her parents must have been over the moon to find she was still alive."

Angela's dad looked at his wife. "What are you talking about?"

"On the television, that girl who was abducted. Apparently she's just finished a two-week holiday, courtesy of a newspaper and finally arrived back in the UK. Now the poor girl is giving yet another press conference. I bet she'd just like to get home and shut the door on the world for a short time."

He swung round to look up at the screen. "Oh... that girl. They're making a lot of fuss over it. She's on the news quite a lot. They were saying the other night close to 20,000 people go missing a month, most are back in a couple of weeks, some never."

The mother sighed. "I don't think they are making too much fuss. Can you imagine if it had been Angie, you'd have been shouting from the highest mountain for someone to bring her back? Besides, I feel for that poor woman, knowing what her daughter must have had to go through. They should do something about it; the police are bound to know where they all are and what's going on."

"I suppose they do, but it seems the way of the world these days. We're lucky Angie wouldn't get mixed up in that sort of thing. She's level headed and would never walk off with strangers.

"Yes we are, but I'm not sure if that girl intended to get involved, it just happened. Anyway shall we go up to the viewing platform and see if we can catch a glimpse of Angie getting aboard?"

Angela sat quietly alone in the departure lounge. Because the winners of the competition were from all over the country they were all to make their own way to Gatwick. Her father had decided not to drive to Gatwick, as it would have needed them to set off in the middle of the night, so he'd booked the shuttle for her. She would have preferred that they were with her when she met the group, mainly because although she'd a lot of confidence among people she knew, she was still very shy and nervous with strangers. Angela was brought from her thoughts when the announcement came to board the aeroplane.

Within the hour Angela was making her way from the domestic arrivals at Gatwick airport and along the seemingly endless passages towards the International Terminal, when a huge crowd of photographers, newsmen with security were coming down the other way. Angela stopped, a little nervously, unsure where to stand as a few photographers, ahead of the main group, pushed past her, not even apologising when one knocked her handbag onto the ground spilling the contents. Cursing them, she knelt down to collect everything together, then another girl was at her side helping. When they finished Angela and the girl stood. They looked at each other for a moment. The girl in front of Angela was the same height as her and particularly attractive.

"Thank you for helping me," Angela said.

The girl shrugged. "It was half my fault, since I arrived in the country this bloody lot won't leave me alone and talk about rude. Anyway forget them; I'm Karen, what's your name?"

"Angela, I won a holiday in North Africa and it includes a sort of desert safari. There's a few of us who won a place so I'm just on the way to meet them."

Karen smiled. "You must be really excited?"

"I am, it's the first time I've been away; on my own that is." Then Angela suddenly recognised Karen. "Aren't you the girl who's in all the papers, besides being on the news?"

"Yes unfortunately, I've not had a moment alone since I first arrived in Cyprus a couple of weeks back."

"You were really, really brave, I couldn't have coped like you did."

Karen laughed. "Don't you believe it Angela, when the choice is to live or die, you cope – it's self-preservation? Anyway I must go, have a brilliant holiday."

"Yes thank you, I will, and it was really nice to meet you, besides good of you to help me."

"Think nothing of it, maybe we'll meet again one day?" she remarked, and then walked away down the corridor Angela had just come up.

Angela watched her for a while as Karen made her way down towards the shuttle lounge, then she herself turned and began pushing her luggage trolley to the main terminal. It seemed strange bumping into someone so famous. She'd not expected Karen to be her height. She'd always considered herself too gawky when she was growing up and only now was she finally beginning to fill out and look, what she considered, a little more balanced. However, Angela did have a touch of jealousy over Karen. She was really attractive, with a fantastic sheen to her skin and she'd love to look like her. Now she couldn't wait to find the others then she could ring her mother and tell her who she'd just met.

In the main terminal stood a man holding a placard up in the air with 'Conort Holidays' plastered across it in bold print. Angela saw this and made her way over.

"Are you Angela Bandom?" the man holding the placard asked, at the same time looking at a photo he was holding in his hand when she approached.

She nodded.

"Well you're late; we have to get you all through security and customs yet."

"I'm sorry, but the plane was delayed in landing and I got held up waiting for my luggage," she retorted to his offhand tone.

He urged her to join the others and they made their way through to the departure lounge. Angela was looking at the other winners as they passed through security. She knew it was a holiday competition but they all were tall, slim girls, like her, all particularly attractive and well spoken. How did a competition end up with similar looking girls and no lads? However, another point that disturbed her was the man had a photo of her. She wondered how they'd got it and he seemed to be checking she was who she said she was, by comparing the photo. However, once in the departure lounge Angela put her concerns behind and telephoned her mother to say she was safe with the group, and also tell her that she'd met Karen.

10

"You need to transfer what you want immediately into your rucksack. The rest goes on ahead in your suitcase."

Angela looked at the driver confused. "But I have to take my suitcase; it has all my personal things in besides underclothes."

The driver came closer to her. "Listen little lady, you're going out into the desert for the first few days, not a hotel. Just keep jeans, shorts, tops and knickers besides something warm for the nights. The case will be at the lodge when we arrive back."

She sighed, took out a few things from the suitcase, pushed them into her rucksack then let him put her suitcase into a small van. It was just before five in the morning, she was still a little tired from travelling the day before. The hotel was really dirty and the food pretty awful so she just wanted to get out and on the real trip. Then last night they had collected all the girls' valuables and money then placed them in large jiffy bags which the girls had signed over the sealed top flap. They'd been told there were no shops until they got to the village where the lodge was and money and jewellery had gone missing on last month's trip, or been lost by the person themselves, so they weren't taking any chances. Even their mobiles were placed in the valuables bags, but Angela insisted in keeping her watch and her grandmother's ring that she had received for her sixteenth birthday. She climbed into the back of the second vehicle; sitting alongside the girl she'd shared a room with last night. Her name was Dawn and she came from Essex. They'd got on well but she'd taken simply ages to get ready for bed, then kept Angela awake for at least an hour telling her all about her cool boyfriend.

"I feel a bit naked without my mobile, don't you, Angie?" Dawn asked, as Angela settled down.

"Not so much naked, more disturbed. Dad always insists I have it with me at all times and fully charged. He wouldn't like me leaving it behind."

"Yeh, mum would be the same. Mind you, they say they won't work where we're going so I suppose they're a bit pointless and I'd probably lose it anyway. I've already lost two this year; dad's gone mad having to keep getting me new ones."

When everyone was in the vehicles they were off. The girls hung on for dear life as the vehicles sped through the still deserted streets and out on the open road. For three hours they never stopped, finally slowing and turning off the highway, pulling to a halt in a clearing.

"There's Cokes in the hampers girls, if you want the toilet it's behind the bushes I'm afraid," their driver called back into the vehicle.

Dawn stood at the side of the vehicle and lit a cigarette, after offering one to Angela who declined. "It'd better improve this trip; otherwise I'm out of here and taking the next flight home. I'm not into squatting behind a bush," Dawn said, drawing on her cigarette.

"I think I'm with you on that. I ache all over with the banging about in the back of that vehicle and the noise of the engine's giving me a headache. Besides, it's a bit embarrassing to have to go behind a bush to wee; we're not lads who couldn't care less," Angela replied.

"Right girls, time's up, back inside," the driver shouted.

This time when they set off they never returned to the main highway but travelled slowly down a long, narrow track towards the coast.

Dawn grasped Angela's arm. "Look it's the sea, which means a beach and sunbathing."

"How, Dawn, I've got no clothes for the beach with me. We're supposed to be going into the desert; this is a bloody funny way," Angela replied.

Dawn frowned. "Oh! I never thought of that. Hey driver, why are we going down to the beach?"

"You'll see," he called back.

Now they could see in front of them not so much a beach, more a very stony and deserted cove where only a small boat was moored up. The vehicles stopped short of the cove and the driver in Angela's vehicle turned to the girls.

"Okay girls lunch is served, and then the adventure begins," he said with a huge grin on his face.

"Are we going in a boat? I hope not, I get seasick," one girl sitting opposite Angela asked.

"No you're going into the desert, Sammy, but this is a small surprise beach party the agency arranged before we turn inland," he replied.

No one objected, or rather didn't have time as the girl sitting alongside the driver, had wound down her window then hurriedly begun to unfasten her seat belt. "Come on you lot, can't you hear the music, there must be a beach party going on," she called back.

As the girls piled out of the vehicles they too could hear the music and they ran down to the cove to find a barbecue smoking away with three African chefs dressed in whites calling everyone over for food. Alongside the barbecue an oversize ghetto-blaster was thumping out the music they'd heard. Soon the girls and their drivers were sitting around with huge platefuls of sausages, burgers and salad including cans of cold beer and Coke. For the girls, it was at last beginning to be the start of a fantastic adventure. Besides which all the concerns many had of it being a pretty naff experience, had gone out of their heads.

However, rather than what was the intention of many of the girls, to dance after the food, everyone who'd eaten was beginning to feel very sleepy, so much so, already some had lain down and closed their eyes with the final ones following quite quickly. Within fifteen minutes none were awake. Boats began to arrive at the beach, more men climbed out. Among them was one carrying a briefcase. He set the case down on the now empty barbecue table and opened it. Inside were a row of glass capsules, a syringe and rubber gloves. Quickly putting the gloves on he drew all the liquid from a capsule into the syringe. Then he walked over to the first girl, injecting her in the arm before filling it again from the next capsule. Finally he came to the last girl, stopped and looked back at the ones he'd already injected.

"We seem to have six girls, I thought there were only five?"

he asked a chef who'd just finished packing the barbecue items into a large box.

He shrugged. "Five, six what's it matter we get paid per person."

The man never replied but drew some more liquid from the last capsule, injecting the sixth girl.

After each girl was injected they were carried to the waiting boats and laid down on hastily fitted flat boards across the bench seating. Once they were aboard, the man who'd injected them walked over to the sleeping drivers, who'd brought the girls. Pulling a gun from his jacket he fired twice into the head of each then went back to one of the boats, climbing aboard quickly. Within a few minutes they set off at speed.

The small boats came alongside a ship. This was old, the hull rusting, desperately needing a coat of paint. The crew looking over at the boats were of African descent, many from Nigeria. Their usual pastime was modern piracy, boarding cargo boats in the dead of the night, sometimes holding out for ransom, other times stripping them of any valuable cargo. And of course if payment was offered they have no qualms about collecting human cargo for delivery anywhere in the world.

The small boats had ropes attached fore and aft then were winched up into their normal position. Each girl, now heavily drugged was carried into the hold and taken to individual containers set out in a line. Inside the container was a bed, a table and chair, with a chemical toilet set in a corner. A single bulb was set in the ceiling and was the only source of light. Angela, like all the others, was laid on a bed. Then she was stripped of her clothes and jewellery including the clips holding her hair back. Once the two crew members, who'd carried her in, had completed this task they left the container slamming the big door.

It was nearly four hours later when Angela awoke. She lay there shivering, staring up at the single bulb, rocking slightly. In the background there was the constant thump of an engine running. Getting off the bed and standing gingerly she looked around, not understanding where she was, why she was naked or how she'd got here. Automatically she looked at her watch. What watch! It was missing, so too was her grandmother's ring which she'd worn since the age of sixteen.

"Hello…" she said softly, "is anyone there," in some way afraid of a reply.

Of course there was no reply, and then she became bolder and shouted louder and louder, still no response. Grasping the single sheet on the bed, she wrapped it round her naked body and sat on one side of it. Slowly awareness dawned as all the warning signs she'd been concerned about came together. Everything that had happened, the competition, the man looking at the girls' photos, then the girls themselves, all the same age and particularly attractive, then the leaving very early with no one around to see them go. Their money, passports and other valuables including phones left behind. Now even her clothes, ring and watch had gone as if none of it mattered any more. She was sure they'd been abducted. Tears began to form in her eyes; she couldn't forget the images on television of Karen, then meeting the girl in the airport. But in Karen she had seen a strong girl, very capable, athletic and fit, where she had always relied heavily on her parents and now she was alone.

How long she sat there she'd no idea, then the door of the container opened and two men came in. One carried a stick, the other a tray with a carrier bag in the other hand. He placed the tray on the small table and opened the bag. Pulling out two tatty looking books he put them on her bed. Then he pulled out a pair of knickers and a t-shirt which he handed to her.

"These are what you wear from now on. The books are to help pass the time. You will be taken to the bathroom once a day, where you can clean your teeth and shower before being returned to this room. Shouting, screaming or kicking the door will mean nothing. No one will come and no one will hear you. You eat, we will return in fifteen minutes. The food will be taken away finished or not," one man said.

They turned to leave.

"Please… where am I, why am I here?" she asked hesitantly.

However they ignored her questions and left, slamming the door behind them.

Sitting on the small chair, she finished the food quickly, the stew was spicy, the bread dry and the hot drink a very weak coffee. After a short time, which she could only imagine was fifteen minutes, they returned and took the tray away. Again she tried to talk to them but they ignored her and left her alone. With nothing to do she lay back down on the bed and soon fell asleep.

11

Beryl was woken by a knocking at her door. She'd finished the ironing and had settled down with a coffee and biscuit, closing her eyes for a short time. Going to the door she opened it to find Carol stood there.

"Hi, Carol, sorry I must have dozed off, come in," Beryl said opening the door wider.

"Have you heard from Angela?" Carol asked.

"No, but we don't expect a call from her until Friday when she returns to the hotel. She's out in the desert or somewhere and there are no telephones."

"Didn't she go with Conort Travel?"

"Yes, why do you ask?"

"Well according to the lunchtime news there's a parent of one of the winners complaining she can't get in touch with her daughter. Her father has been involved in a road accident and is in hospital but this Conort Travel Agency has closed its doors and gone away."

Beryl frowned. "That must be worrying for her, but I can't see what she can do about it, after all I don't think you'd find a telephone box in the desert."

"I agree, but you'd think they'd have some emergency communication equipment with them, say one of the group had an accident, they'd need to get help?"

"You've a point there, it would seem sensible? Anyway I'll put some tea on, why don't you change the channel to the twenty-four-hour news and see if there's anything on about it?" Beryl said, walking into the kitchen and filling the kettle.

They'd sat for some time through all different types of news and were about to switch the television off when the newsreader was handed a note.

"We have some breaking news over the Conort Travel

Agency closure reported earlier. Moroccan police are appealing for the parents or relatives of the winners of a competition held by Conort Travel to get in touch with them urgently. They understand there were at least five winners from the UK. The contact telephone number is shown at the bottom of our screen."

Carol looked at her friend. "Why would they want the parents to contact them, surely they have all the details of the winners?"

"I've no idea, but I'm going to give them a ring and find out," Beryl replied.

For the next ten minutes, they couldn't even get through, the line was constantly engaged. Then all of a sudden Beryl could hear the ringing tone and at last it was answered by a man.

"Hello, this is Angela's mother; I'm ringing about Conort Travel Agency."

"Yes Madam," the man replied in perfect English. "Is Angela on holiday with Conort Travel?"

"Yes she left at the beginning of last week, is there a problem?"

"I cannot tell you Madam, I do not know. This is a request from the local police for contact information. Can you give me your full name and address, also the name and age of your daughter?"

Beryl gave him all the details.

"Have you spoken to Angela at all?" he asked.

"No, not since she arrived at the hotel in Morocco, she's due back at the hotel tomorrow and she promised to call me as soon as she got back. Do you want me to ask her to ring you?"

"No, that won't be necessary; we will be at the hotel. Anyway thank you for the information, we'll be in touch."

Beryl replaced the telephone on its cradle. "Well that was a strange conversation. He just took details and virtually cut me off. I hope it was a genuine Moroccan policeman, you never know you hear all sorts of things these days."

Carol shook her head. "It must be genuine, Beryl, the BBC is hardly likely to put out a prankster's number."

"Yes I suppose so. But I'll be glad to hear from her

tomorrow, it's been really quiet and lonely around the house with her gone. God knows what it'll be like when she goes to university and only comes home on holidays."

At Scotland Yard, Senior Detective Russell Joyce of the Child Investigation Division settled down in the video conferencing lounge with three other detectives. On the other end of the video link were two Moroccan policemen.

"Gentlemen," one of the Moroccan police began in perfect English. "We have a problem. An hour ago it was confirmed that the two men found shot in a remote cove, were the drivers who collected the five English girls from the Hotel Crispin. Estimated time of shooting is nine days ago. The daughter of one of the victims is also missing. We believe the girls may have been abducted and we are at this moment trying to ascertain just who these girls are, and what they look like. We've already had nearly a hundred calls from concerned parents whose children are alone in Morocco and haven't heard from them. This was to be expected, as lots of kids don't keep in touch. However, we are only concerned about the competition winners who were taken to Hotel Crispin. We've been informed, by the proprietor of the Hotel Crispin, that there were five girls of around sixteen to eighteen who left in the two vehicles. Unfortunately the hotel did not take details of the girls, as they are required to do for guests staying in the hotel. We are not sure if it was deliberate, or an oversight. Either way this will be investigated. In the meantime we'll pass all the names and addresses on to you, of the people who have called our contact number, for your local police to investigate. We'd appreciate if you would confirm back to us, as soon as possible, the names and photos of the actual girls we're looking for."

"Holy cow," Russell muttered. "We've just got one back and now we might have lost five more. The shit will really hit the fan now."

The Moroccan policeman nodded. "I can understand that, we also are in the firing line as they were taken while in this country. There is no way out of the cove except by the single track dirt road and there are no extra wheel tracks, so they must have been taken by boat. So at this stage we are assuming they were taken to a waiting ship and we're currently studying the movements of ships in our territorial waters at the time the girls left the hotel. Like you say the shit will hit the fan. We, like you will have people in government demanding action, so we've already placed over thirty detectives on the case and will leave no stone unturned. However, using the cover story of the girls being taken on an outward-bound type holiday, the traffickers have had a considerable time to get the girls to another country without any alarm bells ringing. The only reason the drivers of the vehicles were found, was some local kids go snorkelling sometimes from that cove, they had time off from school and decided to spend the day there."

By ten that night Angela's parents were distraught. With the strange telephone call and the failure of Conort Travel and no contact from Angela, already they feared that there had been an accident and they weren't being told. The television was still on the news channel and coming up to the hour.

After the usual welcome the newsreader carried on.

"Tonight the country is reeling with the news that yet again British children have been taken by people traffickers. Scotland Yard tonight have confirmed that it is almost certain five girls aged between seventeen and eighteen have been snatched. A travel company called Conort Travel, which was found earlier today not to exist, took these girls on a so-called desert trip ten days ago. Alarm bells began to sound when in Morocco, the two vehicles hired to take the girls, were found abandoned and their drivers dead. We understand names are being withheld until all the families have been contacted. These abductions follow close on the heels of that of Karen Marshall who was snatched some weeks ago. She of course escaped and vowed to use the money raised by her story to help children taken by these people. Already reporters are assembling outside Karen's house trying to get her reaction to these latest abductions. In the meantime it is understood that the Prime Minister has asked Sir Peter Parker of Special Branch to head a high powered investigation team to find these girls."

He fell silent a moment. "We are going over live to our

reporter outside Karen Marshall's house."

The picture changed to show Karen stood outside her house surrounded by reporters.

"I feel very sad to hear the reports." Karen had just answered a reporter's question.

"Will you be assisting the police in finding the girls?" another asked.

"I don't think so, after all they could have been taken by anyone and they could be anywhere in the world by now. How parents could allow their daughters to be away with strangers with no means of communication is unbelievable."

"But you wouldn't refuse to help if you were asked?"

"No of course not. But like I said, I can't see what I could do."

"What in your opinion will these girls be going through?" the BBC reporter asked.

Karen looked at him. "What sort of question is that? You're talking about girls just out of school. Kidnapped for the sole intention of being used for some man's sexual gratification and you wonder what they will be going through?"

"Did you know there was a girl of only fourteen taken?"

"No I didn't, but if it is true her mum and dad must be devastated. The little girl terrified."

Beryl was just staring at the television, her mouth open, tears beginning to run down her face. She couldn't believe what the reporters were saying. It was a mistake, it must be, nobody would take their Angela? She was such a kind and thoughtful girl, never did anyone any harm. She looked away from the screen towards the telephone willing it to ring and hear their daughter's voice, but it was keeping steadfastly silent.

"What are we going to do, Donald?" she whispered.

He shook his head. "I don't know, Beryl, and that's the truth. I pray to God that there is some simple explanation and the girls are safe."

She looked at him with tears running down her face. "She will be all right won't she? Promise me, Donald, our little girl will be all right?"

He didn't reply, just held her hand tighter. How could he promise her that Angela would be all right?

It was six o'clock the following morning when the doorbell rang. Donald opened it, the police were standing there. He asked them in.

Beryl was still sitting on the settee staring at the telephone, she looked up, her heart was racing.

"Angela, you've found Angela?" she whispered.

The policeman shook his head. "I'm sorry, but it has been confirmed by Special Branch, who are in contact with the Moroccan police, your daughter is one of five abducted. The two locals who'd driven them away from the hotel have been found. They are both dead and also a daughter of one of them is missing. The vehicles were abandoned on a narrow lane leading to a cove. Interpol is now involved, so too is Special Branch."

Beryl put her hand to her face, her eyes wide with fear. Suddenly everything she'd listened to about Karen's ordeal was flooding into her mind. Then seeing her on the television only hours before, she realised what sort of girl Karen must be. But her Angela was not like this Karen, a girl obviously relaxed with herself, tough, well used to survival, where Angela was very feminine, with no capability of dealing with what was possibly going to happen to her.

However, it was Donald who brought up a problem, a very serious problem. "What about her medication, Beryl?"

Beryl gasped. "God yes, her medication," and then she looked up at the policemen. "Angela needs regular injections; she has a serious blood problem. We go every six weeks; she was due her next one three weeks after she would have come home from holiday."

"And if this medication is not available to your daughter, what would be the result?" he asked.

"Our daughter will fall very ill, we are waiting for the results of tests she took a week ago to determine what the underlying problem is," Donald replied.

Beryl grabbed her husband's hand, her voice faltering as she spoke. "Please, Sir, you have to get our daughter back from these people no matter what it costs. She wouldn't be able to cope, with their demands and her illness, it would destroy her."

"We understand, Madam. I can assure you very experienced police officers are involved. This is not only a serious abduction of six young girls, but murder as well. You can be assured we will be working with many police forces to find them."

As they left the officer turned. "There will be a policeman outside your door for the next day or so. He will be in constant contact with control and inform you of any progress. I'm afraid you can expect the press to be here in force. These girls came from all over the country so it is a national story."

12

How long she'd been on the ship Angela had no idea. The food came regularly. She was taken blindfolded to a shower room, given a toothbrush and soap then locked in for ten minutes before being returned to her container. She saw and heard no one else besides her guards. They never struck up a conversation with her, only gave orders. Then the engines suddenly fell into silence. After a short time she was awakened and they sat her up. Pulling her t-shirt sleeve up slightly one gripped her so she couldn't struggle, while the other injected her. Seconds later she began to feel light-headed. Try as she might she couldn't keep her eyes open then she slumped unconscious onto the bed. A stretcher was brought in and she was placed on it before being taken out onto the deck and put back into the small boat she'd arrived on. The other girls were done the same way and the boat set off for the shore. Within twenty minutes they had been transferred yet again into the back of a lorry which set off without delay. Two hours later they were again laid in separate bedrooms, on single beds. None had been sufficiently awake to see where they were going, who'd taken them or put them in the rooms. It was, for them, as if they'd fallen asleep and woken up in another place.

Angela was beginning to come round. She could remember the African injecting her and very little else. Her mouth was dry; she felt sick and very cold. Opening her eyes, she knew immediately she was somewhere else. The room was large and bright; two other people were in the room. One, a woman in her thirties, stood some way back from the bed holding a stick in her hand. The other person was also a woman, but she was old, dressed in heavy black clothes and rubbing her hands with a towel.

"Where am I?" Angela asked.

Saeed's mother looked down at her and grinned. "You're

awake then? That is good; we were just about to wake you. You need to shower with plenty of soap."

Angela sat up, and for the first time she looked down at her naked body. He mouth dropped open; all her body hair had been removed.

"What the hell have you done?" she demanded.

"You are being prepared for sale, body hair removal is necessary before the oils to your skin are applied. Now you will come for a shower."

"Sale, what sale?"

"First you shower, then I will explain. The creams on your body need to be washed off before they begin to burn your skin."

"I couldn't care less. Besides I'm going nowhere," Angela retorted bravely.

Saeed's mother looked across to the other woman stood behind Angela and nodded. She touched Angela with the stick she'd been holding. The shock to Angela was immediate. Her body arched throwing her back onto the bed. But the woman hadn't finished. Grinning as she kept touching Angela on the most sensitive and intimate parts of her body, laughing as her body moved in severe spasms, only stopping when she was crying uncontrollably, her body still shaking with the bolts of electricity sent through her.

"Now will you shower, or should we give you more punishment?" Saeed's mother screamed at her.

Angela had had enough and she followed Saeed's mother, with the other one behind her holding the stick, into a shower room. They stood watching her as she rubbed the soap all over her body before rinsing it off. Then she dried herself with a towel hanging on the door.

Back on the bed Saeed's mother began with the oils, rubbing them in vigorously, until every part of her body had been covered. She stood back looking down at the girl, before taking some clothes laid out on the chair, throwing them at her.

"Put these on."

Angela was glad to finally dress, although they were only knickers and blouse.

"Sit on the side of the bed."

She did as instructed and Saeed's mother knelt down on the floor and taking an ankle iron from under the bed, which was attached by a chain to one of the metal bars of the bed, clipped and locked it around one of Angela's ankles.

After checking the lock she looked up. "You will be showered in the mornings and oiled three times a day. You will not be allowed to leave the room. I've provided books for you to read. When you have finished them, tell me, and I'll give you more. Object to anything I ask you to do, try to escape and you'll feel the electric stick on your body. In three days' time you are to be offered for sale by auction. You're a very pretty girl, if you keep it that way, rather than be subject to beatings every day then you will be purchased by a very nice man, who will look after you. The alternative to no one buying you is the local brothel. They will take anything; you'd be good for six months of twelve hours a day on your back."

Angela said nothing, what was there to say. Already she felt dirty, abused and angry with herself that she'd been duped so easily, when all the signs were there to tell her something was not right.

The two women left the room, slamming and locking the door after them.

She sat there in the silence and began to think back to meeting Karen. She had managed to escape, was it possible that she could do the same? But if she did, how would she survive? Karen was already used to survival skills; she'd never even slept in a tent, let alone stayed out all night hiding in some field. The more Angela mulled it over in her mind, the more she realised, for her, there would be no escape. Her only hope would be that the local police would find her, or somehow she could contact home. Walking over to the chair, she sat down and picked a book up, already she was scared and fed up. The oils on her body stank making her feel decidedly sick.

13

Donald entered a small room at the rear of an adult interest shop. He felt a little embarrassed going through the black painted front door, past all the hard-core pornography DVDs and racks of books. However, in other ways he couldn't care less provided the end justified the means and this was a risk he needed to take.

There were two men inside the room; one stood, the other sat behind a desk. The desk was covered with papers obviously just thrown down without much thought of what was on them. The man behind the desk nodded towards a chair. "It's been a long time, Donald, take a seat," he said. "I hear you are no longer in the force, so I presume this is a private matter?"

"It is, Chad, and I desperately need information and maybe your help."

"If I can help in any way, Donald, I will, after all you did me a favour once, and I said then, if you ever need something just come and see me. You laughed saying you'd not got to the age when you needed one of my girls, still happily married. So what is it you need from me?"

Donald sat down and removed a photo from his inside pocket. It was a photo of Angela, his daughter. He placed it on the desk in front of the man. "I'm still not in the market for one of your girls, Chad. I want my daughter back and the people who did this to her punished. There's a hundred thousand in the pot, it's all I can raise, but time is not on my side. Angela is very ill. She has a rare blood disease that if left unchecked will poison her. She needs an injection every few weeks to counteract this build-up and there's only three weeks left."

Chad looked at the photo. "A pretty girl Donald, I presume Angela was one of the girls abducted?"

"Yes she is."

"If she can be found, do we have to get her back here for

the injection, or can it be done where we find her?"

"She can be injected anywhere, Chad. Then she'll need around twelve hours before coming back to normal. Of course that would depend on how far she'd gone, so the twelve hours is only a guess. You see it's only happened once before when she first showed symptoms of the disease, so that's why we don't really know timescales."

Chad said nothing for a short time. He rubbed his chin with one hand as he leaned over the desk gazing down at the photo. "This was an abduction to order, no girl from the five who went missing has, to my knowledge, been offered out to the brothels. We didn't like this snatch. To take five British girls in one hit like that has caused our business real problems. The press are hounding our girls. They're snooping where they shouldn't be, believing the girls are back in this country, and splashing our outlets across the papers. The man who took these girls is known to the industry as Saeed. We don't think it's his real name; in fact it's probably certain it isn't. He has a smallish organisation in this country but specialises in supplying the market around the Mediterranean. If you remember, a girl called Karen Marshall was taken. She somehow escaped, that has never happened before, but she was one of Saeed's girls. Now we come to your daughter. Saeed was very badly injured by this Karen, in fact there's an open contract out on her, but unknown to her she's protected. Not by the government, but her original purchaser, a man called Sirec. Even in this country you don't go up against that man. He's a gunrunner of the worst kind and has many contacts throughout the world."

Donald frowned. "You seem to know a great deal of what's gone on. Why is that?"

Chad shrugged. "It's a very small business, as traffickers themselves go that is. In fact there's only a handful throughout the world. We as outlets, so to speak, know the majority of them, as each trafficker specialises in who and what they supply. Although since the break-up of the Soviet Union, more traffickers have begun to appear, offering anything you want at cheap prices. But Saeed caused so much trouble by this snatch, there was a meeting some days ago, and it's been agreed to freeze him out completely. Now we come to the problem of finding your daughter. We believe and it's only a belief that these girls were ordered for private buyers. No brothel would take the chance of using them after all the publicity. Even in the Mediterranean countries the brothels are frequented by many Europeans. It would take just one of their clients to recognise one of the girls and the brothel would be in the shit. You have to remember most brothels use registered girls; among these girls are the so-called specials. These girls and boys as well are usually underage and kept in the background for special requests. They are under very strict control and have no chance of escape. But if one of these snatched girls was recognised the client would probably say nothing to the girl, except minutes after leaving the brothel he'd be in the police station trying to claim the reward for information."

"I see, so you're suggesting that because my daughter has gone to a private buyer it will be more difficult for her to be found?"

"Impossible, it's as simple as that. The only way to find your daughter is to find Saeed. The problem is no one knows where he lives, or what he looks like. His dealings in other countries apart from the Lebanon are through strings of agents, he never gets his hands dirty. I say never, but that's not strictly true, he doesn't use agents in his own country, there he deals direct. Mind you, even to get into the Lebanon, for a white guy like you that is, and then start asking around for this Saeed would get you nowhere, maybe even killed."

"So what does this Saeed usually deal in, after all this is the first big snatch of English girls?" Donald asked.

Chad nodded. "You're right, he rarely gets white girls. His usual stock in trade is children from Asia, sold by their own parents to raise much needed cash. At one time these girls would often be drowned at birth, now this is a way to still get rid of the girls but bring money in for the family. They go through auctions he runs once a month."

"What if I made it known, through you, I was in the market for a girl? Would Saeed deal?" Donald asked.

Chad shrugged his shoulders. "Of course he'd deal, get anything you wanted, boy, girl, baby, even an adult. But you would only deal with an agent not Saeed. No, the route to find your daughter is through someone who knows him. The only person I've heard of, who's actually met him is that Karen Marshall."

"How do you know that?" Donald asked.

"She lived at Saeed's for a time, in fact saw him every day, and if you read her story of the abduction in the paper, she talks of the house and her captivity, besides the bizarre gambling night that led to her being taken to some other house where she had been clever enough to trick them into letting her call home. Get her to agree to go back and I'll supply the muscle. They will force Saeed to give the names of the buyers, then armed with that, we can find your daughter."

"I hear what you're saying, but would she go back and more importantly how will she get there?"

"That, my friend, unfortunately, will be your problem. After all she had a hell of a time getting out. Then even if she agrees, just to get her back in the country would be difficult. She'd have to be flown to Cyprus, after which she'd need to go by sea to a port in the Lebanon. It would be a long and difficult journey and she'd be in great danger, both from Saeed and her purchaser who also lives there."

"Thank you for the information Chad, I will see this Karen Marshall and get back to you."

Chad stood and offered his hand. "Good luck with this, Donald, if I hear anything I'll be in touch."

Donald left the shop and took a taxi into the city centre. Then he walked briskly down a shortcut between two main roads and took another taxi. This one travelled some distance before stopping outside a large office block. On the sixth floor he entered an office with the words 'Farman Transport Service' on the door. Once inside he was shown into a large meeting room. There were six people already sitting at the large centre table. All of them were studying documents from a folder in front of them.

The man at the head of the table stood and offered his hand. "Donald, it's been a long time."

Donald shook the man's hand. "It has, Peter. I believe you're now knighted so should I be calling you, Sir Peter?"

Sir Peter laughed. "I suppose you should, but we go back a long way so let's forget the formalities. Anyway how did our underworld friends treat you?"

"Very well, in fact they are just as peed off as the government is, and prepared to supply people to sort it out. They are incensed that this mass abduction has happened in their neck of the woods."

"Yes I can believe that, besides which, we've really been keeping the pressure on them and also around the Mediterranean. So what did they say?"

Donald told the meeting what had been talked about then fell silent while others in the room finished making their notes.

Sir Peter looked up. "Their information tallies with ours, even as far as the man called Saeed, is concerned. We also agree the girls were destined to private buyers as none have appeared in any brothel. As for Saeed, we like them believe this is not his real name and he's based in the Lebanon but we have no information beyond that. However, you mentioned they said Karen Marshall would know? Why is that?"

"They're convinced about it, Peter. You see apparently it's in her story that was sold to the papers. How she'd lived in Saeed's house for a week. Then been taken to another local house and even a church, before returning later with the SAS So she'll certainly know him and I suspect the area around his house. But I was quite shocked to hear that a contract was out on her, set up by this Saeed, and the involvement of this other man Sirec."

"I agree that is disturbing. She must really have opened a hornet's nest with this Saeed. I never read the full story, I suppose I should have done really, but until now I hadn't appreciated the content would have such significance. I think I'll go and see Karen Marshall, and attempt to get a better picture of this Saeed from her experiences. In the meantime Donald, you need to go home and give your wife comfort. Let me handle this for a while and I'll let you know just what is going to happen."

"I'll do that Peter; as you can imagine my wife is devastated?

But I don't want a backburner job here. We will have to move fast, whatever is decided, time is not on Angela's side."

"We all understand the urgency, however, I've a feeling any sort of rescue attempt will hinge very much around Karen. By what you've managed to find out from the cartel, she is the only person who could actually identify Saeed, the location and the house," Sir Peter answered.

When Donald had left a General Ross from army headquarters asked who he actually was.

"It's not who he is now, General, but what he was," Sir Peter answered. "Donald for eighteen years was in MI5, the same as me. He was marked for taking over when he had a stroke leaving him very ill for nearly a year. He requested and was granted early retirement from the force, and for the last three years has been advisor to the government on security, among other things. It was he who had the contacts into the cartels that now run most of the organised crime in the UK. That is why I value his input and professional approach to help find his daughter."

Sir Peter looked at his diary. "I suggest, after I talk to this Karen Marshall, we reconvene in two days time, say around two just after lunch?"

With this agreed they all went their separate ways.

14

Karen was sitting in the conservatory reading when Sir Peter arrived at the front door. He had telephoned a little earlier and asked if she would meet him. Karen agreed although she'd no idea why he wanted to talk to her.

Her mother had answered the door and brought him through. Now Karen and Sir Peter were sitting alone, both with freshly brewed coffee.

"Before I say anything," Karen began. "I've had my fill of you lot. I was treated badly in Cyprus, looked down on as if I was shit. God I had more respect from the traffickers than they gave me. So if it's your intention to go through it all again forget it, read my story in the paper if you want. I've had enough."

"I can understand your aggression, Karen. I was sent some transcripts and I was appalled at their attitude. In the police force if we'd done that, we would have been subject to disciplinary action. I can only apologise. However, I'm from Special Branch, attached to Scotland Yard, and assure you I've come for information which only you can give. And please call me Peter; I'm not one for formality."

She sighed. "I'm sorry, but that man left me having to relive my time out there, it wasn't fair. But I suppose I'll have to take your word you're nothing to do with him, so what is it you want to know?"

He leaned back. "Thank you Karen; I believe you know a man called Saeed?"

Karen looked down at the floor, the very mention of that man's name sent shivers down her spine. "I did, but he's dead. Why do you ask?"

"All in good time, Karen, but why do you say he's dead?"

"Is this official and off the record? Or more importantly are you carrying a recording device?"

"Like I said, Karen, I'm here only for information. No judgement, no long interviews, but your answers are very important. And yes, this is absolutely off the record and I assure you I have no recording equipment. But I do really need to know why you think he's dead?"

She shrugged. "That's simple, I saw him shot. In fact more than shot, he had a fair few bullets put into his fat carcass."

"That maybe so, Karen, but Saeed's not dead, he's very much alive and probably put out a little, over your escape?"

She lifted her cup from the coffee table and took a long sip, at the same time watching him carefully. "Yes when I saw him last, he was a bit peeved even then that I'd escaped my owner. But it's not good, if he still lives. I'm beginning to suspect the reason why you're here; you believe Saeed had a hand in the abduction of the five girls?"

"You're correct in that thinking. But we don't suspect, we know he did, Karen, except we have a problem."

"And I suppose your problem includes me in some way?"

"Very much so; you see Saeed took those girls to order. They have not appeared in any brothel; we're checking them regularly so that could only mean one thing. They were bound for private buyers."

She frowned. "I'd agree with you there, after all a private purchase, like I was to be, is at least four times more money than what he'd get from a brothel and there's a great many out there who would buy from Saeed. But why should I be interested, after all I got out?"

"You did, but you're also the only one, we know, who has actually met Saeed, who knows where he lives and who else he employs there."

"I suppose I must be one of the few who escaped that would know him. But I can assure you a great many children he's trafficked will know his name and would like me have met him. Of course his friend Assam, the Captain of the Towkey, also knows him besides his sidekick Garrett. Mind you I don't think they would be much help, if you found them that is. But whatever information about Saeed I can give, I'm very happy to do so."

"Thank you, Karen, it is appreciated believe me, but would that help expand to you returning to the Lebanon in order to identify him for us?"

Karen stared at him, her body had gone cold at the very thought. She stood and walked to the window putting her hands on the glass. He watched her carefully, knowing what must be going through her mind.

She turned. "Have you any idea what it's like out there?"

"Possibly, Karen, but I'd be very interested in your experience."

She said nothing for a short time then turned to look at him. "I was treated like shit, chased across the bloody country because some man had bought me for something to shag. I had to stand and watch people being killed because of me besides kill myself, to survive. Even my so-called rescuers eventually abandoned me to save their own necks. I'd hide in ditches afraid of every noise, without food and drinking dirty water. All the time I was hiding, I was trying to build up enough courage to be able to put a gun to my head, rather than be taken alive. I'm only just eighteen for god's sake. All I wanted was a boyfriend, someone to love me who I could love back. Now I'm home, I still look round corners, still jump when I hear only a click. I fear closing my eyes to sleep, just in case this is a dream and I'm still in the hands of that scum out there. If you want the truth it was me who killed Saeed, or thought I had, he raped me, and then four of his friends followed. Outwardly I suppose I look the same, judging by the number of times I get photographed, but I'm a wreck inside. My life is shattered and you want me to go back. How can you even ask me to do such a thing, knowing what I've had to endure?"

She looked down at the floor, tears trickling down her face. "I feel for those girls. I know what they're going through. The loneliness and despair when you're alone, not knowing what will happen next. Then there are the constant threats of violence towards you if you step out of line. Do you not think I'd help them if I could? I would, believe me, but if it means I have to return to that hellhole, I can't. My confidence is shattered; I'm still on pills from the doctor to get me through the day, after what that

James subjected me to. I have nightmares about the people who died; I wake up shaking in fear. What good would I be to you?"

She turned away and looked out of the window once more.

Sir Peter stood and walked over to her, stranding at her side, he was also looking out through the window.

"One of the girls is dying, Karen," he said softly, still looking outside. "Suffering from a rare blood disease and desperately needs medical attention. You met her at the airport, helped her pick up the items knocked out of her bag by a reporter. She's got only three weeks left then she will die in agony. They also took a little girl, who'd just gone with her daddy for the ride. Put a bullet into her daddy's head then took her. She's just fourteen, a child. Do you know what they do with girls and boys that age? The child rings buy them. They're subjected to perverted sexual actions every day of their short lives. I say short because many don't last a year. When you were taken everyone thought you were dead, but when they found you were still alive, people came for you. The world is a hard place, life a hard taskmaster. Often we have to do things we don't want to do. Do you really think I'd let you go into the same sort of danger without protection?"

Karen was thinking back to the airport and the girl she met on the way to the domestic departure lounge. "I remember that girl; she was pleasant and really attractive. I also remember Saeed saying he'd more than one offer for me. I wouldn't put it past him to have brought those girls in, to sell to the ones that were outbid for me. If you'd seen her she was a similar height, just as slim and probably my age. But trying to play on my conscience won't make me change my mind, Peter, whatever you say. No matter how much they are down on their luck, it won't work. I know what protection is. I was supposed to have it. But when your protectors begin to die one by one around you, soon there's no protection and you're alone."

"Then at the very least will you come to London with me and go through everything you can remember that will help the ones who are going in?"

She nodded. "I'll do that for you, if you think it will help the girls?"

He turned and faced her. "Thank you, Karen; I really can now understand just what you are going through. However, your input will be very valuable and I appreciate you agreeing to help us. Here's my card, the mobile is direct if you just want to talk or anything else for that matter. Now I must be going. I've a number of meetings in this area. I'll come for you at nine in the morning, if that's alright and we'll travel down together?"

More relaxed, now he didn't want her to go to the Lebanon, she smiled. "I'll be ready; I'll see you out shall I?"

15

Later that day after Sir Peter had left, Karen was dropped off in town by her mother, who'd an appointment at the hairdressers. They'd arranged to meet in two hours, leaving Karen to browse around the main shops to find something to wear in London.

She'd decided on a black trouser suit with a white thin jumper to wear underneath the jacket, and she was busily looking through the racks. Finding some suitable contenders she took them off to the changing rooms. These rooms were solid cubicles, with a curtain at the entrance, set in a row either side of a corridor at the back of the shop. She'd tried a sweater, discarded it and was just going to pull another over her head when a man entered the cubicle. On the verge of demanding why he was there, he'd pulled a gun, the tip of the barrel inches from her eyes.

"One word, one sound and you're dead, understand?"

She remained very still, one arm already in a sleeve of the jumper and her other arm she was just about to push through. "I understand, what do you want?"

"Put your own clothes back on then we're going to walk out together. Try to escape and I'll shoot you in the back to stop you running, then one in the head to make sure you're dead. Call for help and I'll kill the ones that try. So get your clothes on and let's go."

Karen did as she was told. Her time in the Lebanon had taught her not to panic, but assess the situation, all the time watching carefully for even the slightest error on his part. But with this man there was none as yet. Once she was ready he turned her round to face the wall. Checked her pockets and pulled her mobile telephone out, putting it in her bag, then ran his hands over her body as a final check. Satisfied she carried nothing that she could use as a weapon he took hold of her hand and urged her out of the cubicle along the passage and through the main entrance. A car was waiting outside and he pushed her into the back, slipping in beside her. The car roared off.

"Where are we going, and who are you?" she demanded.

He grinned now, satisfied she wasn't a threat. "You and I have an acquaintance, who would dearly like to have come himself, but someone put a bullet into his knee and he lost a leg. So he sent me to get you."

Her features hardened. "Not Saeed? You're not from him are you?"

"Got it in one, kid, now shut up and just enjoy your last ride."

Karen was happy not to continue with the conversation, she was already deciding on her exit. With her jeans on and trying tops, he'd only checked the pockets, more interested in running his hand over her breasts and bottom. She didn't bother about him doing that, so long as he didn't move down to her ankles. Because in a holder, strapped round her right ankle, was Chapman's knife. A knife he'd given her in the Lebanon and she'd worn ever since, he had told her that one day it might save her life. Never was he so close to the truth as now, that's if she could get at it. He'd also spent time showing her how to use it, how to hold a knife and how to stop any person from taking it from her. She looked at the driver, he was concentrating on the heavy traffic, the man at her side still held the gun, but it was on his lap facing away from her. Karen decided she should try for the knife.

"Can I tighten my shoe laces?" she asked.

"If you want, then no more talk and keep still," he replied.

She leaned forward and tightened her left shoe lace, retying the bow. The man watched with little interest. Then she moved to her right foot, again she refastened her lace, but as she pulled up she grasped the handle of her knife. Fitted in an upside-down sheath, drawing it out was easy. Sitting up again with the knife in her right hand Karen was gaining in confidence. Casually looking at him she decided if she followed Chapman's instructions on how to disable someone quickly she'd have to go in with the knife under the rib cage, in an upwards penetration to puncture the heart. But the man was wearing a heavy coat and she doubted if she was in the correct position to thrust the knife hard enough to penetrate the coat and do the damage she wanted. The next option was to go for the throat. That would be messy, his hands would be free and he held a gun that could easily be turned and injure her. Still considering both options, and now out on the motorway, an opportunity came her way. The driver had called back to the man at her side for help. He had a map on the passenger seat and was asking if it was exit nineteen or twenty? The man slipped the gun in his pocket furthest away from Karen and leaned forward to take the map.

This was her opportunity.

As he went forward she grabbed his hair with her left hand, yanked his head back and tried to draw the ultra sharp knife across his throat. However, the man was a great deal stronger than she imagined and soon they were wrestling in the back, she still trying to use the knife, he realising what she had in her hand and forcing her arm away from him. During the struggle the knife caught the driver in the back of his head. He screamed in pain as he pushed his head down away from the knife. But with the car travelling close to eighty miles an hour, the second's loss in concentration sent it out of control. The driver panicked making the problem even worse. They hit the outside barrier, bouncing back into the centre lane, the rear end clipped by an overtaking lorry sending them into a spin, the tyres screaming. The next moment the car crashed through a wooden fence then down an embankment. The driver was suddenly engulfed in air bags. The man Karen was struggling with, was thrown sideways and hit his head on the door pillar, passing out instantly. Karen followed the same direction, but she was cushioned in doing the same by the bulk of the inert body of the man, as the car careered down, coming to a jarring halt at the bottom of the banking. The engine raced on for a moment before the fuel cut-out operated. A device designed to stop fuel pumping out in the event of a crash, and shut the engine down. Karen lay still for a moment, not sure if she was injured. Everything had happened so fast she was completely disorientated. She sat up, looked at the man by her side. His head seemed to be in an odd position and he wasn't moving, the driver was beginning to moan. Cars were stopping at the side of the motorway, people running down to help. Karen slipped the knife back into its holder and tried to open the door, but it was jammed. In the meantime drivers and passengers who'd stopped to help managed to wrench the door open before pulling Karen out. They attempted to open the driver's door but that too was so badly damaged it wouldn't move. Now there were flashing blue lights up on the top, police were running down moving the helpers away worried that fuel spilled around might ignite. One was calling into his radio for an emergency service team who'd arrived by then, to bring cutting equipment.

"Are you all right, love?" a policeman asked.

"Just a little shaken, I'll be okay. May I have my handbag from the car please?"

The policeman went over to the car, talked to a fireman who handed him her bag and he brought it back. "Would you like to sit in our car until the ambulance arrives? They will take you to the hospital with the other occupants just to check you over?"

She smiled. "I'd like that, thank you."

Once inside the car she pulled out the card Sir Peter had given her. Then using the mobile from her bag she dialled his number.

"Hi it's Karen," she began when he answered. "I need your help."

Sir Peter listened to what had happened. "Are you injured?" he asked with concern.

"No, just a little shaken, otherwise I'm fine. But I'm going to have trouble explaining why I was in the car with a man carrying a gun and I've a knife if they search me. That's illegal as you know. You have to get me out of here."

"No problem, Karen. I'll call control and have a car sent for you. In the meantime say you feel unwell, you're confused and have a headache or something. But don't let them interview you."

"Okay; and thank you."

A police car arrived in less than ten minutes and after they spoke to the officer in charge Karen climbed in the back and she was whisked away. Twenty minutes later Sir Peter joined her in an interview room at the police station. She was sitting quietly holding a paper cup containing coffee.

"You certainly get yourself into some scrapes, Karen," he said taking a seat opposite her. "But everything's sorted. In actual fact you were never there and will not show up in any police report."

"That's what my life's all about these days, Peter. I'm never going to get any peace am I?"

"If you want the truth, Karen, we'd heard that this Saeed has offered a reward for you, dead or alive. But ten times the payment if you're delivered alive. He's a bitter man and determined to make you pay for what you did. However, it's made more complicated by a man called Sirec who has made it known you are under his protection, which has deterred a great many from trying for Saeed's reward. Although there will always be some who will try, like you've just experienced. We of course know of this Sirec and his dealings in the illegal armaments trade but again no one we know has met him or knows what he looks like. On a good note we've found your mother, she's going home after we assured her you were fine and we'd bring you home later."

She said nothing for a time. How she'd hoped it was all over but it would seem these people, once they got their hands on you, were determined not to let go. Changing the subject she looked up at him. "What about the men who took me in the car, what will you do with them?"

"One is dead; his neck broken when he hit the door pillar. The other has crushed legs besides internal damage. You can't attempt a kidnap in this country without going down for a long time so he will remain in custody. It will be expected that you give evidence. It will be in a closed court where, you will be known as Miss X and give evidence on camera. If the press got wind of just what has happened to you they would have a field day, and the other girls would be at even greater risk."

She shrugged. "You know Saeed's mother said I brought death to their land. It seems death is not confined to over there; it's following me. So to try and sort out my life, I've made a decision. I'll go back to the Lebanon with your team. But for me to do this, I need to feel safe in myself. I've been there and know what to expect so there are conditions."

"And what are those, Karen?"

"I want to be armed with weapons of my choice, a map and GPS with a planned emergency route out of the country if I get split up from the group. I also want to be allowed to sort Saeed once and for all, if I can that is. I don't intend to go through life with him chasing me all over the world."

"You're saying in a roundabout way you want to kill him?"

Karen looked him in the eyes. "Peter, it's either him or me. I prefer it to be him, after all the man's not stopped taking girls. He's learnt nothing; even in his hospital bed he's directing his operation. I wouldn't be surprised it's his mother sorting the girls out for him, because I don't think he's the type to rely on strangers looking after his payments for the girls he sells."

"You're playing a very dangerous game, Karen."

She gave a weak smile. "Not that dangerous, I've been in worse scrapes."

"Okay, Karen, we go to London. I'll put your request to the team and get their opinions. If it's agreed you go in armed, with your own mandate - providing we have secured the location and collected the other girls, you can do as you like. I agree with you, this man will not give up on you. It is I'm afraid you or him."

16

For three days, Angela went through the same routine. She was bored, scared and lonely. But above all she was constantly sleepy, hardly able to keep her eyes open. In the afternoon of the third day when the continued preparation to her body had finished and Angela had dressed in the usual knickers and shirt, Saeed's mother didn't leave the room but sat down on the easy chair.

"You are now ready to be sold. You have experience in pleasing a man?"

"What sort of experience?"

"You know how to make love, keep a man happy?"

"Of course I don't."

The woman smirked. "Then you are a virgin yes?"

Angela nodded.

"That is good, very good. You will fetch very nice price. My son will be pleased. Within the hour you will, along with the other girls who came with you, be paraded in front of men wishing to buy themselves a young girl. However, we have only four buyers so you will be competing against the other four girls."

"If there's only four what happens to the girl no one wants?" Angela asked, with apprehension.

"The girl who's not bought by a private buyer we sell cheaply to a brothel. It is something you don't want to contemplate. You see our selected brothels for shall we say unwanted girls, or girls who still believe they are above all the others and scowl or reject the man offered to her, are not very nice places to be sent. There, both boys and girls are worked for twelve hours a day, with one or two clients an hour, it takes its toll, they usually only last a year. Then they either fall ill, catch diseases you wouldn't believe, or just die."

Angela was becoming scared. She had little self-confidence in playing up to a man as it was. In her mind the other girls were far more attractive than her, probably with more life experience as well. Apart from this she wasn't feeling well, her reactions were slow, she'd a blinding headache and had begun to have pains in her stomach.

"You're very quiet, child, why is that?"

"I don't feel well, I've a headache and a pain in my stomach and you're telling me I've to compete with far more attractive girls, play up to a man who's only interested in fucking me every day when I can hardly stand up? What do you want me to say? Thank you for giving me the opportunity to avoid the brothel, when you know full well that's where I'll end up, none of the men will want me?"

She shrugged indifferently. "That's your problem, not mine. Now there are nice clothes in the bag I've left on the table. Dress, comb your hair and be ready when I return."

After she and the other lady left Angela took out the clothes. The knickers were tiny and see-through. The top just long enough to reach her waist and the hipster skirt very short. Finally the shoes were heeled, adding nearly two inches to her height. In some way they could be what she'd wear for a party, perhaps not the knickers though, and certainly not see-through ones. Sitting at the side of the bed now dressed and ready she suddenly felt sick and ran over to the chemical toilet, retching for a good time before she tidied herself up and went back to sitting on the edge of the bed.

An hour later she was being taken past the shower room and down the stairs into what looked like an old barn. Already the other girls were stood spaced out across the barn with one of their wrists attached to old metal rings in the walls, by handcuffs. All of them looked under strain, not daring to talk to each other after being warned to keep quiet by a woman who constantly walked round carrying the electric stick. Angela was taken to the far side of the barn and like the others one of her hands was attached with handcuffs to an iron ring set in the wall.

One was taken out of the room, returning in about ten minutes and followed by another. As the second girl returned Saeed's mother pointed to Angela. "That one's next," she said to the woman who was watching the girls.

The woman went over to Angela and unfastened her hand from the ring and then re-fastened Angela's hands together behind her back with the hand-cuffs. Saeed's mother had followed the woman and she grasped one of Angela's arms tightly. They left the barn and walked across a small courtyard into what looked like the main farmhouse. She stopped Angela before they entered the room where the buyers were waiting. "Smile, be pleasant and do what I tell you without objection. Remember there are only four buyers so one of you won't receive an offer. Believe me you don't want to be the one who doesn't sell."

Angela just nodded, she still didn't feel well, her headache had increased and the stomach pains made walking difficult. Looking at the other girls waiting, she suspected they had been told the same as her, and not wanting to be sent to a brothel would go all out to attract a buyer.

The room was quite large, the buyers sat well spaced from each other around the walls leaving a clear and open area in the centre.

"Walk round the room till I tell you to stop," she said, at the same time removing the handcuffs. "My buyers want to see you nicely dressed first and how you present yourself. Then go to the centre and remove all your clothes and don't move. Delay or refuse to remove your clothes and I'll get my assistants to strip you and you'll be punished in front of all the buyers with the electric stick. That wouldn't look good for you; they'd lose interest and probably not make a bid. You know what that would mean?" Saeed's mother said as she urged her to start walking round.

"Gentlemen this is our third girl of the day," Saeed's mother began in a language Angela couldn't understand. *"Her name's Angela, she's seventeen, five feet nine with a nice developing figure. She speaks French and English originating from the UK. This girl is also a virgin so there is a premium of ten per cent on top of the bid. Bids are opening at thirty thousand and she's available like the others to take now."*

Angela did as she was asked, walking round then going to the centre after being told and removed her clothes. She stood still, shivering slightly, unsure what to do now.

Saeed's mother looked round at the men. "Put your arms up above your head," she demanded.

Angela did as she was told. Saeed's mother pushed her head back a little so her breasts were more pronounced.

"Now gentlemen you can see what a nice body this girl has. The firm pert breasts, the flat stomach, the hips perfect, her bottom beautifully shaped and her skin radiant," she began at the same time turning her round. *"This is a very special girl, looks after herself. You only have to inspect her nails, her hands, her teeth to realise that, and as I said a virgin. Take your time; check her body over yourself and then the bidding begins."*

She looked at Angela. "Put your arms down and go to each of the buyers. Smile; allow them to check you out. Remember one must buy you otherwise you know the alternative."

Now Angela felt really embarrassed and scared as she went to each of the buyers, who stood and started looking into her mouth, her ears and hands before rubbing their hands over her body. She pulled back as one pushed his hand between her legs, but she was rewarded with an instant sharp stinging slap across the bottom from Saeed's mother stood behind her. The last buyer spent longer with her, he pulled her eyelids up and looked into her eyes. Then he opened her mouth and smelt her breath. He seemed concerned and putting one hand in the small of her back he pressed her stomach with the other. Angela wanted to scream, the pain intense. She tried to stifle it the best she could, but gasped anyway.

The man frowned, confused. *"What are you trying to sell us old woman?"* he demanded. *"Pushing a girl into the sale who's obviously ill. I can see it in her eyes, the pain in her stomach, the difficulty she's having breathing, she's also very cold to the touch. I didn't come here to be conned, neither am I a hospital."* Then he looked at Angela. "Go and get dressed, girl, you need to keep warm."

Angela hesitated, looking at Saeed's mother, scared that she'd use the stick on her if she moved. But the mother was clearly shaken, prices might tumble if they thought she was conning them. "Do as he says," she demanded. Then she looked back at the man. *"It is just a stomach upset, a change of food that's all. But she will soon be better and she is a very beautiful girl. The other girls are all very fit. It is a shame you don't want her, but no matter I will send her to the brothel, they will look after her until she's ready to work. But by way of compensation with this girl not being at her peak and no longer available, I do have another. The girl I'm going to show you is just fourteen, her name is Natasha, born in Morocco but her parents are English. She's lovely long legs, nicely developing body and has bids of thirty thousand from the children's rings. They are very excited at the prospect of getting hold of such a child, but of course she'd only last six months and be badly abused. I think she will be such an attractive and loving girl in a year or so, that is why I'm prepared to offer her to the highest bidder of the day for half the bid price of the girl they buy. That means if you pay forty thousand, you get the young girl for twenty, take her for what she will offer you now and in the future, or get yourself an instant profit from the children's rings by reselling her."*

"Bring the girl in," one called.

Saeed's mother seemed to have forgotten Angela as she rushed out and grabbed one of her assistants.

"Give the buyers refreshments. I need to prepare the young girl, that one in there is ill and they are not happy," she said with more than a hint of annoyance in her voice.

Running up the stairs she burst into a room. Natasha was sitting on a mattress on the floor, in an otherwise empty room, her legs pulled up to her chest, staring down at a tin mug and cracked plate. She was starving, the only food given to her were leftovers, if there were any, from someone else's meal. The tin cup usually filled with water had been empty since the night before. The girl had been forgotten, already sold so no-one bothered with her, the time being taken up on the other girls, who required preparation, before the sale. She'd been crying, her face streaked in tears, not understanding why she was locked up and why her parents hadn't come to collect her. Saeed's mother pulled her up and dragged her into a bathroom. There she ripped her t-shirt off and began to pull her jeans down her legs. Natasha started struggling, trying to prevent her but Saeed's mother stood back, removed her stick from under her shawl and poked the girl on her bare shoulders. The severe shock threw Natasha across the small bathroom, but Saeed's mother followed and touched her chest this time, rewarded by seeing the girl's body arch back in spasm. She grinned, enjoying the girl's distress and kept poking the stick inches from the girl's face demanding she remove her jeans. However, Natasha didn't react quickly enough for Saeed's mother, so again she touched the girl's shoulder. Thrown back like some rag doll with the shock, Natasha was begging her to stop, unfastening her jeans and pushing them down her legs as fast as she could. Ironically Natasha shouldn't have been here. Her father was a driver who'd collected the girls from the hotel and was to take them to the so-called desert camp. She'd badgered him the day before to take her, even her mother thought it a good idea and an opportunity for her daughter to be with English girls, so finally to keep the peace he'd agreed. But of course she'd also eaten the food and the crew from the ship didn't know this girl wasn't included. Besides which her father was dead, so they could hardly leave her there anyway. Saeed's mother was ecstatic when they turned up with her. She was a bonus, whose sale, for no preparation at all would pay the transport cost of all the others.

"Get the pants off as well and into the shower."

Again Natasha didn't object and was soon washing herself in the cold water.

"That's enough," Saeed's mother shouted dragging her out. "Dry yourself and replace your knickers."

When she'd finished Saeed's mother took the towel and rubbed the little girl's hair vigorously, until it was nearly dry then brushed it before pinning it up in a ponytail. She stood back; the girl looked nice now and clean.

"Come with me," she demanded of the girl.

Natasha grabbed her clothes but Saeed's mother snatched them from her. "You won't need those; we'll come back for them later."

"Am I going home?" she asked somewhat naively.

"If you're a good girl, I will ask your daddy to come and collect you? But first you're to meet some friends of mine."

"But I've got practically nothing on," Natasha protested. "Can't I wear my t-shirt please?"

"It's dirty, you'd look a sight. I have clothes downstairs you can wear. So no more delays or I'll use my stick."

Frightened of the stick on her nearly naked body the girl went down the stairs, stopping in front of the lounge door. Moments later Saeed's mother opened the door, grabbed the girl's hand and dragged her into the centre of the room, all the men looked at her.

"Now gentlemen, was it worth the wait? This is Natasha, nearly fourteen and of course a virgin."

Saeed's mother told Natasha to raise her arms above her head arching her body back, the same as she'd done with Angela, to push out the girl's small breasts. *"You can see she is developing well, her skin is beautifully tanned with living in Morocco, her body just right and is of course just coming into puberty."*

One of the buyers liked the look of the girl, telling her to come over to him. Saeed's mother told her to put her arms down and go to him, giving her a push from behind. As the buyer had done with Angela, he looked into her mouth, her ears, checked her hands, her nails then ran his hands over her body, at the same time roughly grasping her thin cotton knickers, trying to pull them down, but being only flimsy he ripped them clean off her. Natasha was in a panic now, standing completely naked, she didn't like this man and even more so when he grasped her buttock with one hand, while he worked his other hand in between the top of her legs, trying to push his fingers inside her. The girl began screaming hysterically, not knowing why she was here, what these men were going to do to her, so she pulled away from him and tried to escape. But Saeed's mother had come up behind, quickly touching her bottom with the stick. The girl froze, as a severe shock, once again, went through her body. Then she touched her back, the man stood back laughing as she arched back, before collapsing on the floor. Her body was still jerking in spasms but Saeed's mother kept on touching different parts of her body. The other men had come closer enjoying seeing the young girl squirm on the floor.

Angela felt for the young girl. Her mouth was dribbling with saliva, a pool of water spreading around her as she urinated uncontrollably. The look of terror in her eyes said it all. However, the men seemed mesmerised with the young girl's punishment, now all stood round her urging Saeed's mother to touch her again with the stick.

"Leave her alone, for god's sake. Her body won't take much more, you'll give her a heart attack," Angela shouted.

They all looked round at her, Saeed's mother was grinning. "You want to take her place and give the men some sport?" she shouted at her.

Although Angela felt decidedly ill, her head pounding, she didn't back down. "What sort of men are you allowing a woman do that to a little girl? She's just a child, even wetting herself with the shocks to her body. Then after this so-called sport she can only expect to be sold into a life of rape and abuse. Not have a chance to just be a little girl, to grow and develop. So if you want your kicks, then yes, do it with me, if it saves her from more pain?"

One of the buyers shrugged. "You have spunk girl, but are very stupid wanting to take this child's place," he said in English, then changed to his own language. *"Get her better old woman and I'll take her at thirty-five thousand. But she's right, this girl has had enough, I didn't come here to waste time. But I will also take her so get her cleaned up,"* he said.

"No I will take the little girl," another demanded.

Saeed's mother was pleased, they both wanted her. *"Whoever bids the highest for their choice of girl will get her. As you can see she is a beauty, her slim body will develop and she will be a very beautiful girl. In the meantime she will keep you warm, when your own girl can't amuse you at the end of the month. Maybe perhaps take them both together after you teach her how to perform? This is a very rare find and if my son was here he'd want top money for her."*

"Then get rid of that one who's ill and bring in healthy girls, so I might add to my bid for the child," another buyer replied.

Taken back in to the room with the other girls, Angela's hand was once again handcuffed to the iron ring. Another girl was released and taken in. The girls were left alone for a short time while the one guarding them took Natasha back to her room.

Dawn turned to Angela. "I bet you got a bid, you're the most attractive in here, so I'll have no chance."

Angela shook her head. "I got no bid; they threw me out so

I'm the one who's going to the brothel."

Dawn's eyes went big. "You're joking, if they don't want you how about me? I'm next."

Angela shrugged. "Don't worry there's four of them, so with me out you've definitely got somewhere to go. We can only pray that someone comes to find us. I'll not survive being raped every day."

Dawn touched Angela's hand with her free one. "I really feel sorry for you; but I don't think any of us will have an easy time. You were gone ages and the woman watching us went outside for a fag. Anyway we've been talking and made a pact while you were in there. If any of us gets out, that one will do her best to get help for everyone else. Sam was saying that she'd mentioned Karen Marshall in passing while the old hag oiled her. The woman went berserk over her name. She said she'd never seen a woman so frightened. So she is the girl, if anyone gets out, to talk to. That Karen could beat the shit out of the old hag and find out where we've all been taken."

"I'll do the same if I get out, but I don't think I'll get much chance of escape from a brothel. Anyway I met Karen Marshall at the airport? She was really, really attractive and very nice. But she had something about her. Stood at her side, although she seemed really feminine, she gave you the feeling that inside she was a real tough, hard girl. God I wish I was like her, you have to admire someone who has gone up against this lot."

"Yes," Dawn answered. "I read some of the things that are supposed to have happened to her. You're right she must have been really strong to get out like she did. I hope we get the chance, that's all?"

At that moment they stopped talking, when Sammy was brought back and Dawn was taken.

17

Sir Peter was on time when he knocked on the door. Karen's mother opened it and smiled.

"Karen's nearly ready, she's spent ages in the bathroom this morning, you've made a great impression on our daughter, Sir Peter."

"Mother, do you mind, besides I've only spent the usual time in the bathroom," Karen said coming up behind her carrying a small overnight case.

"Yes, dear, call us when you arrive and we'll see you tomorrow."

Then she looked at Sir Peter. "Look after our daughter, I was very concerned yesterday when the police called and said you needed to see her urgently."

"You can be assured Karen will be very well looked after Mrs. Marshall."

Once in the car Karen turned to him. "Don't mind mum, she gets in a flap if I'm five minutes later than I'd told her, panicking that I might have been taken again."

"It's understandable; Karen, abduction can be harder on the family back home, not knowing what is happening. Besides she might have had a real reason to be scared yesterday, if you'd not managed to escape."

Karen laughed. "Some escape, I nearly bloody killed myself, as well you know."

"Yes, I saw the car later, it was a mess. You were very lucky."

She shook her head. "That, Peter, was not luck. That is what happens to me all the time. People around me die, I seem to always survive. I'm really beginning to believe God is looking after me for some reason known only to himself."

"Perhaps so Karen, who are we to understand the grand

design? Anyway I must tell you a few things before we arrive. When we go into the meeting I will ask you questions and perhaps even put objections to you in what you ask. Don't take it personally, I need the rest of the committee, which has been formed, to understand just what you are asking for and why. At this point it has not been agreed, as no one knows you have the intention of going back to the Lebanon. So I will lead with that. Whatever, I don't want you to compromise your position or your very real fear of being left or taken by these man again."

"I think I understand, I won't take offence," she replied after some thought.

"Good girl, there is one other thing, Angela's mother is there. She won't be in the meeting, but I think she would like to talk to you. She of course like everyone else has no idea that you want to go back in. I think she just wants some reassurance that a girl can survive this sort of ordeal. Again keep your responses low key, give her a little confidence that even though her daughter is under severe pressures, if she plays ball like you did, she will get through it."

The car drove directly onto a private airstrip and they transferred to a waiting helicopter.

An hour later, after again being met by a car, they entered a military camp, stopping at the main building before being shown into a large room. Already around a meeting table there were ten other people. Sir Peter acknowledged them all and walked round to the head of the table, Karen taking a seat at his side.

"Ladies and gentlemen. Thank you for being so prompt, I'd like you all to meet Karen Marshall, many will know her by sight as she's been hounded by the press, with pictures of her not being out of the papers for well over a week. I'd also like to thank Karen, for agreeing to come and speak to us so quickly. So to business; I believe, Jim, you have some very important news?"

Jim Squires from Interpol stood. "I do, Sir Peter. We now know the girls were picked up and transported by a ship run by people who claim to be modern day pirates; I'd rather call them gangsters. They were taken to the Lebanon and onto a remote farm, prepared for sale and after the sale three went directly with their purchaser, one was an overseas buyer and that girl would be shipped to the purchaser's home. We know this because, more by luck than good management, a container originating from a port in the Lebanon arriving in Italy was routinely checked, following a tip-off that it contained arms. In actual fact they had the wrong container, but inside the one they searched was a girl. She was on a stretcher, strapped down and heavily drugged. We understand she was placed inside before the container was lifted from the ship and left on the quay awaiting collection. It was a close thing as a lorry had already arrived at the port entrance with documents to take the container. Anyway we had just enough time, while the port authorities messed about with paperwork for collection of the container, to change the girl for an Italian policewoman of similar size and looks before we let it go. It was delivered to a warehouse last night. Two men were waiting for the container's delivery and they took the girl. Fortunately they had never seen her before and the policewoman was driven to a large private estate outside Milan. Five minutes after they arrived the estate was raided. Apparently there were thirty police cars, special SWAT teams, the lot. The Italian police were taking no chances apart from being irate that one of their countryman could have done this, particularly as he was also a prominent and very wealthy businessman. This man was arrested and is now in custody. It now all rests on the girl's evidence. If she identifies him as one at the sale the Italian government intends to send him down for life. It is a very clear statement to others who decide to purchase a girl by this means."

"Is this girl you rescued one of the five?" a man asked.

"She is, but we are not telling the public that. In fact she is being kept under wraps, even her family doesn't know she's been found. The Italian's are in on it and only saying the man they have arrested is suspected of having sex with underage children. It gives us a breathing space of about a month to find the others. The girl is unharmed, but she's been able to give us plenty of information and understands her rescue must be kept quiet for the sake of the others."

He fell silent when coffee was brought in, then continued

when they were alone once more. "The girl's name is Dawn Perrick. She told us that four girls were sold to private buyers and the fifth girl was unsold. Her name was Angela and she was originally to go to a brothel. However, she was very ill and Dawn overheard the old woman, probably in her seventies and running the operation, saying she was going to take her to her home and bring a doctor. She heard that they thought it was pneumonia but she still had a private sale for her if they could get her better."

"Wasn't there a sixth girl?" Karen asked.

"There was, one of the driver's daughters. She's fourteen and has been sold to a buyer who also took one of the five original girls."

Karen frowned. "The old woman, was she small, constantly bent forward and spoke broken French when she tried to talk to them in English?"

"Yes she did."

"Can you tell me if they used oils on this girl and shaved her body hair?"

"Yes, is that important?"

"It is, apparently Saeed's well known for doing this to his special girls. He has this thing about how the girl should look tanned and smell nice. So if that's happened to the girl then the old woman is more than likely Saeed's mother. She's probably running the operation until her son is better."

"You seem to know a great deal about this family, Karen," one of the men in the room said.

"I should, after all I spent a very unpleasant week in both her and her son's company."

The room fell silent for a moment, many taking the opportunity to sip their coffee.

"Right gentlemen, Karen was originally going to just give us help by briefing the team who will be going in. However, Karen's circumstances have changed and she wants to go with them. There are conditions from her, so I propose we listen to them and then Karen will leave us while we discuss her proposals."

Karen looked around the faces looking at her. "My proposal is simple. I carry weapons, for protection, of my choice. I must be allowed to talk to and interrogate Saeed, and his mother myself, and in my own way. Those two are the scum of the earth and there is no such thing as the Geneva Convention when it comes to dealing with them. If any of the girls have been sold to buyers living in the same country, we move on and bring them out."

Sir Peter looked round the room, no one had commented, it seemed it was down to him. "If you were to go, Karen, it would be with the full protection of the soldiers selected to go in with you. So some of your conditions may be agreed, but you let the professionals carry weapons and they interrogate. You acting as observer, would you still be happy to go in?"

Karen looked him directly in the eyes. "If you think I'm going in there relying on others to protect me, you're one off. I've had to shoot myself out of that country once so I'll do it again if necessary. Then you seem to be suggesting I couldn't get information from Saeed, or his hag of a mother? Believe me if she's there and she sees me, she'll be terrified, not only for her own life but that of her son. The woman reads palms and stupid as it sounds she told me my future. She believes I only bring death and destruction. She wasn't wrong in that. Since the prediction nearly twenty people have died as a direct result of me being there and that was without counting how many British soldiers died. So you can be sure she will be more scared of me, than any of your people."

"I see, but what about going for the other girls in the same country? Once we have addresses our teams can move on to them without your help."

"I suppose they can. But this is a big decision for me to go back. If I do, I want to be fully involved. I don't go in for one girl. For me it's all of them or none at all. I couldn't live with myself just bringing Angela, or some other girl out and leaving the rest to endure what I had to. So I'll not be coming back from that country till I find them all. If I have to go on alone, I will."

"Has anyone at this stage any more questions for Karen?"

He waited. "No, then perhaps, Karen, you can leave us to discuss just what we are going to do from here and if we are agreeing for you to go in on your terms?"

Karen was sitting in the dining room on her own. She was really glad they had found one girl at least. She could also understand that if it got out the other buyers may panic and kill the girls rather than be found with any of them.

A woman approached her. "Excuse me, are you Karen Marshall?"

Karen sighed. "Yes I am, but I need some time alone."

"I'm really sorry, Karen, but I desperately want to talk to you, it's about my daughter Angela, may I sit down. I'll only take a few minutes of your time?"

Karen looked at this woman, the desperation in her face, her eyes. "Of course, if you think talking to me will help," she answered, resigned to having to listen to this woman.

She sat down opposite. "My daughter met you; she was so excited on the phone and couldn't stop talking about you. Saying how kind you were to her, taking the time to help pick her things up."

Karen shrugged indifferently. "I did what any other person would have done. Besides, I'm nothing to look up to, no hero or role model. I went through hell, but I was only a seven-day wonder and people couldn't really care less, most men probably only interested in hearing about the sex bits while the women were more interested in the human cost? The only good thing in it all, was being able to sell my story, it gave much needed money to the charities trying to help the ones caught up in trafficking."

The woman looked away; tears were running down her cheeks. "I know what you've done, Karen, and you're wrong, you are someone to look up to. It was a very courageous thing to offer your story, which must have hurt you deeply inside to talk about and admit to the world what had been done to you. But unlike you, who's strong willed, with the skills to take them on, our Angela won't be able to cope, it will kill her. She's our only daughter and that man has taken her away from us."

Karen sipped her coffee looking at the woman. "You're wrong, you do cope. It helps in some way that you never stop believing that somehow you'll be rescued and go home. You even become detached from the abuse, try to think of other things, because the men don't treat you as a lover, just something to use, so the abuse is over in minutes," she looked down, "but it always leaves you feeling dirty and cheap, perhaps a little more despondent as the day's turn to weeks and still you're at their mercy."

"But you survived and Sir Peter has told me you're prepared to go back to help find Angela and the others?"

Karen sighed. "I am going back, but I'm afraid my reason is to kill Saeed, and probably his mother. But you must keep in mind no one is even certain Saeed is involved; it's just what everyone's presuming. Then even if it was him, the odds of finding Angela are miniscule. The girl might already have been spirited away into some private house anywhere in the world, not local to Saeed's; anywhere."

She looked back at Karen. "I understand that, Karen. We can only pray that she can be found. But you and the others going in are her last hope; if we can't get to Angela quickly she's dead. Angela suffers from a rare blood disease where something in the blood is produced which is alien to the body. If it's not stopped it becomes a poison to the body over time, so Angela needs regular injections to prevent this happening. Her captors will not know this; even Angela doesn't know the whole truth as to why she gets progressively ill over a few weeks, the test results only arrived yesterday. My daughter will first feel unwell; it'll seem like she has pneumonia symptoms, like headaches, vomiting and severe stomach pains. But it won't be pneumonia; her body will have begun to break down as the poison enters every organ. Angela will die in excruciating pain."

She'd fallen silent; tears were running down her face as she grasped Karen's hands. "All I'm asking is you do your best to save my little girl's life. Only you know what she will be going through. You'll know her fears and the nightmares she'll endure when she's alone at night. The abuse will break her spirit. As her mother, I can only imagine what's happening, not really understand what's going through her mind, where you can. I'm begging, as only a mother can, find our daughter before it's too late."

Karen leaned forward. "I'll do my best; it's all I can say. But as her mother are you prepared for the alternative."

"I don't understand," she whispered.

"It's a hellhole, with those people, for any child, believe me. There could be a time when for Angela there's so much against her she has nowhere to run, nowhere to hide. Then her only way out is for someone to put a gun to her head." She fell silent reliving the moment it happened to her. "I was in that position. The searchers had blocked every exit, and I had nowhere to run and decided to end my life rather than be taken. But even up against those odds I was convinced by others I could get through. I was buried and lay for nearly an hour underground, breathing through a straw, my little finger in the hoop of a grenade so I could blow myself apart if I was discovered."

Karen looked at Angela's mother, who was watching her and listening intently. "Wherever she is now, she's being looked after, a captive yes, but alive. Once you are out and on the run that's different. She'll be hunted like a dog, lucky if she can find food, or a way out. She'll be aware, if she's caught, she'll be punished maybe even killed. Don't believe for one moment that the troops will get her out. They may not and she could find herself alone. Would you want Angela to be in such a position?"

Angela's mother sat for a moment, and then looked back at Karen watching her. "If my little girl can only be saved from what to her would not be a life, but an agonising death without her medication, then, Karen, if she can't be brought home, I pray that you would end her torment. Has that answered your question?"

Karen sat for a short time, neither of them spoke, then she stood and looked down at Angela's mother. "Then I advise you go home and pray for her, God turned his back on me, but he might just take pity and help your daughter. Even if that means by me going back, I may even be going as her executioner."

Angela's mother stood and shook her head looking Karen directly in the eyes. "God never turned his back on you, Karen. I'll not believe that for one moment. When I go home I'll pray not only for my daughter, but for a very brave and courageous girl who has every reason in the world to walk away, and everyone would understand, but hasn't."

18

On the day the auction of the five girls was held, Natasha the fourteen-year-old, and another girl of seventeen called Sammy had been sold to the same buyer. Sammy was every lad's dream girl. With her natural shoulder-length blonde hair, hazel green eyes, hourglass figure and at five feet eight she could easily have been a model. However, her time with Saeed's mother had been hard. She was not from a wealthy family, but brought up in the East End of London; Sammy was a tough streetwise girl. In order to suppress the anger in this girl. Saeed's mother had used more drugs than she had with the other girls. Even then Sammy had lashed out twice and injured one of the helpers. Before the sale she'd been stripped in advance and handcuffed, with a sedative added to her food, just to get her in front of the buyers without trouble. However, when the buyers saw her, the bids were high; in fact she fetched the best price of all the girls, with the winner also taking Natasha for half price. Salem, a drug trafficker from the north of the country, was ecstatic, collecting one very attractive girl and the younger one who he'd already decided to keep and not sell on. However, he had been warned of Sammy's violent outbursts and Salem had decided to curb this girl's aggression from the outset.

The two girls had been locked inside the back of a small delivery van, among boxes of various items and began the long journey to Salem's home. They were prevented from moving around the van by a leg iron welded to the van floor, giving the girls less than two feet of movement. The back of the van was lit up by a single light inside. Sammy was looking at the young girl. She'd seen her in the other Land Rover, but hadn't talked to her and didn't know her name.

"What's your name?" Sammy asked.
"Natasha, what's yours?" the little girl asked.

"Sammy, but you can call me Sam if you want."

Natasha was dressed in a t-shirt and jeans. She had no shoes or socks. Sammy was in a shirt that ended just below the knickers she was wearing, she too had no shoes.

"What's going to happen to us Sam?"

"We've been sold to some man. I suppose they're taking us to his house. It's no use me not telling you the truth, Natasha, but we are in deep shit. More than likely he's bought us for sex; it seems to be the norm around here. We can only hope someone will be able to find us and get us out."

"Do you think he'll have one of those electric sticks to use on us? It really hurt and I still feel shaky."

Sam shook her head. "I've no idea, but you can be sure he'll have some means of making us do what he wants."

"I hope he'll feed us better than where we've been. I've not eaten for two days, apart from leftovers, which were just the chicken bones and some uncooked potato."

"I can't see why he shouldn't; after all he's paid a lot of money. It'd be a bit pointless starving us, we'd be worthless," Sammy replied after a little thought.

"I've never had sex, will it hurt a lot?" Natasha suddenly asked.

Sammy had been with her boyfriend for over six months and lost her virginity nearly two years before. She'd never been promiscuous and her sex life had always been restricted to her current boyfriend. "It's not supposed to hurt, Natasha, it's supposed to be enjoyable, part of life really. My first time was a bit painful as my boyfriend knew even less than me. I can't see the man who has bought us being like that, but you can never tell."

"Sam, do you think they will find us before Christmas? Dad said he was going to take me to the ice show that was coming to our town?"

Sam grasped her hand. "Listen, Natasha, don't keep your hopes up too high. It could be weeks, even months, before they find out where we are. Let's just live one day at a time shall we? At least for the moment we're together, can you imagine the other girls? They have no one to talk to and must be really scared."

They both fell silent; Natasha lay down and was soon asleep. Sam just sat staring at the single light bulb thinking back to the story in the paper about a girl who'd managed to escape. She decided because a girl had done just that, this man and the others who bought the rest of the girls would be very careful and not give them the chance.

It was four hours or so later when the van stopped. They were taken out, allowed to go into the bushes for the toilet then sit on the verge where they were given food. The two men who were driving never said a word to them and after an hour's stop they were on the road once again.

They travelled on through the night, by the time the van arrived, just after dawn, the girls were asleep. They were shaken roughly, while the leg irons were released. Climbing out of the back, they saw the man who had been in the auction room standing watching. At five feet one, with a large pot belly and balding head, he spoke quickly, in a language neither girl could understand, to the two men. Each man grasped a girl's arm and they were taken into a large virtually empty barn. The girls were made to stand alongside two ropes hanging over one of the huge wooden cross members holding the barn roof up, and told to hold their hands out. Both did as they were asked and handcuffs were fitted to their wrists. They passed ropes between the chains of the handcuffs and began pulling the other end of the ropes. Soon both girls' arms were stretched high above their heads; their heels raised just enough for the girls to stop themselves from swinging around by pushing the balls of their feet onto the floor.

Already Sammy's arms were aching, the sockets really being pulled. Salem stood and watched; the men left the barn and closed the doors. The light inside was now very dull; to the girls he looked intimidating.

"My name is Salem and you are both inside your punishment room. I own this land for thirty miles around us. That means all the people who live on this land work for me. The guards who protect this house work for me. Every person who works inside my house works for me. I'm telling you this, so you have no illusions about getting ideas of believing you can run away. You will not get far and you will be caught and brought back to this room for punishment. I also have paid good money for both of you. That means in my book I own you. I decide if you live or die. I decide when you speak or don't. I decide what you wear, what you eat and more importantly what your role is in my house."

He walked up to Natasha. "Do you understand?"

"Yes, I think so."

"Why is it you only think so? What don't you understand?"

"I can't understand why you should own me; I have a mum and dad, why should I want you to own me?"

He walked over to Sammy. "Do you understand?"

"Of course. We've been abducted and sold into slavery by the sound of it?" Sammy replied.

"That is correct, perhaps later you can explain in great detail to Miss Stupid there?"

He grasped hold of Sammy's shirt and began to roll it up, exposing her hips, then he pulled her knickers down to her feet. She felt frightened and embarrassed but said nothing. Going over to Natasha he rolled up her t-shirt then pulled her jeans and knickers to her feet, her hips and legs were exposed the same as Sammy's. Saying nothing he then walked across to a large wooden box, opened it, and took out a two-inch-wide leather belt before walking back and standing in front of them both.

"Now as I was saying before our Natasha got confused, this room is called the punishment room. It's where you're brought if you disobey my orders. You will be strung up naked for major punishment, or as you are now, your pants pulled to your feet exposing your bottom and legs for a minor offence. This strap will be used to punish you. The number of strokes will never be less than three and maybe ten. Three will just make your bottom and legs sore, but you will feel considerable pain. Ten will be across your back, bottom and legs, hard enough to cut your skin. Believe me with ten strokes you'll want to die, the pain is so bad. Do you both understand?"

The two girls nodded and answered yes.

"That is good, so now we're nearly finished with your

education. But you Sammy have been very stupid, caused a great deal of trouble for an old lady, injured someone, and have this belief you shouldn't be here. I can see your point but the truth is you're here and this is where you'll stay. The rebellious actions and violence must stop right now. You see I came from a working class family. My father would beat me often for no reason apart from he'd drunk too much, or just wanted to hear a child scream. One of his beliefs was that the actual punishment is something that is far better learnt by the experience of feeling it, rather than just being threatened with it. That way you know what to expect if you step out of line. You Sammy are to learn just what to expect. You Natasha will also receive the same experience as Sammy. Sammy, there is an even worse dilemma for you. You see, after today, every time you step out of line and we come to this room, Natasha will also come. She too will receive what you get. That means Sammy; any repeat of the actions with the old lady will meet not only with your own punishment, but this young girl's."

Then without another word he walked up to Natasha and turned her round so the back of her faced him. The girl hadn't understood just what he had been saying and Sammy stared wide-eyed as he raised the belt, bringing it hard down across Natasha's bare bottom. Not expecting it Natasha screamed, then suddenly began to choke and vomit.

Sammy panicked, shouting at him to cut Natasha down before the vomit stuck in her throat and choked her to death. But Salem ignored the warning and turned Sammy round. She knew what was coming, gritting her teeth as the strap hit squarely across her bottom, but it was far harder than he had done to Natasha.

Sammy, although expecting it, screamed with the stinging pain. She tried to struggle free but only succeeded in taking her feet off the ground, nearly pulling her arms out their sockets.

Salem had moved up behind her, his mouth close to her ear. "Now you know what a punishment will feel like don't you?"

"Yes…" she stuttered, tears running down her face.

"I'm glad you know that, Sammy, because for your outburst, without my permission to speak, you've earned a visit to the punishment room. But you're already in here, aren't you? Already strung up, your knickers at your feet, your bottom and legs exposed awaiting the strap. What are you going to say to stop me carrying out your punishment?"

Suddenly she was very scared, realising that the strap across her bottom was just a taster. He was threatening to punish her just for shouting out. "I'm sorry Salem. I really believed Natasha was going to choke to death. You have to believe me, I was worried for Natasha but I promise I'll never shout at you again."

"Oh, I didn't realise you had Natasha's health on your mind, perhaps I'd better check," he replied walking over to Natasha. She'd stopped vomiting and only tears were running down her face. "No, Sammy, your outburst was unnecessary, Natasha is perfectly all right."

Then he returned to Sammy, turning her round to face him with a hint of a smile on his face. She'd relaxed a little believing she'd escaped further punishment.

"You know my father would never accept verbal apologies the same as me, Sammy," he began, at the same time re-rolling her shirt up which had slipped back down covering her bottom, stopping it again just above her hips. "They don't have any value you see, and the one who apologised then believes you're soft, laughing behind your back."

"Please, Salem, I'll not be laughing or think you're soft."

"I know you won't, Sammy, do you know why that is?" he asked grasping her hips.

"Because I've apologised and promised never to speak out again?" she answered hoping that's what he wanted to hear.

"No? It's very simple why you won't be thinking it, Sammy, because your punishment goes ahead."

Her eyes went big, her mouth dropped open as he turned her round once again. She began begging him not to hit her. But her begging was turned into screams of pain as the strap first hit her across the top of the legs. This was quickly followed by a second a little lower, then finally a third one across her already sore bottom.

Salem put the strap back into the box and walked out of the barn. Both girls were left tied up, Sammy sobbing uncontrollably, the pain intense and already a pool of urine spreading around her feet. She'd begun urinating with the shock to her body, during the punishment. Natasha could only look on at her distress, unable to go and comfort her.

A man and the woman entered the barn after a few minutes and let them both down. After the handcuffs were removed; they were stripped of the soiled clothes and taken naked into the house through the back door and up to a bedroom. Off the bedroom was a small bathroom where they were left to shower. When they came out of the bathroom, the bedroom door had been locked. There were two bowls of stew and two glasses of water left on a side table with a t-shirt for each of them laid on the bed.

For the rest of the day they were left alone, neither spoke much, both still very shocked over their ordeal in the barn.

A woman came early evening and brought more food taking the empty soup bowls away. She never spoke even when Sammy thanked her for the food.

The next morning the girls were woken and sent into the bathroom. A woman brought clothes for them to wear. Very short flared skirts, knickers and crop tops. After they'd dressed they were both taken in to see Salem. He looked at each one of them stood in front of him. He lifted Natasha's skirt looking at the red mark on her bottom from the strap.

"Does it still hurt, Natasha?" he asked.

"Yes a lot."

"So have you learned from the experience in what to expect if you step out of line?"

"Yes, I promise I will do anything you ask of me."

He then went to Sammy and lifted her skirt, rubbing his hands over the red marks on her legs and bottom, noticing her flinch.

"So, Sammy, are we going to see a repeat of what happened with the old lady?"

"No never, Salem."

"That is good, what else have you learned?"

"Your word is law, speak only when spoken to."

"Then you have learned a very important lesson haven't you?"

"Yes, Salem. You will have no problems with me I promise."

"As my father said, promises mean nothing, only actions have meaning. Remember that."

He moved away and stood in front of them. "Now we have an understanding you are free to roam inside the house. Go outside without my permission and you will return to the punishment room. Natasha, go with cook and give her some help. Sammy you stay."

When Natasha left, Salem took a seat and looked up at Sammy stood there. "I would think for the moment you'd prefer to stand?"

"Yes please, I'm still very sore," she replied.

"Find the cook after and ask her for some soothing cream."

"Thank you I will."

He said nothing for a short time, reading an article in the paper. Sammy just stood there afraid to move until he said she could leave.

"It seems all you girls have caused quite a stir," Salem suddenly said. "The British government is stumped, not knowing what's happened to you. But you see, Sammy, no matter how much they look, or who they talk to, they will never find you. This country is effectively closed to foreigners and in the area we live, full of marauding gunmen. So you must forget all about your past life, there is no chance of a rescue. You are, to all intents, already dead to the outside world. So we now come to what is expected of you. Your role besides light housework is to keep me company at night. When I retire around eleven to midnight you will join me, returning to your room a short time later. Sometimes I'll want you to stay all night. Do you understand what I'm saying?"

"Yes I understand."

"When you're not with me, you will look after Natasha as a sister, or if you prefer, her best friend. It will be harder for her coming to terms with never going home. For you also I think? But she's very young and will need help. I didn't expect two girls, so only one room was made ready. You will both keep this room spotless, you will put nothing in the drawers or wardrobe I haven't given you, or allowed you to wear. I will personally check the room regularly and if I find anything in the room I don't know about, you will be taken immediately to the punishment room. As you now know I never accept apologies or promises, it will always be punishment. For the time being you will share a bed with Natasha. Both of you will shower before bed and prepare yourselves for me. No nightclothes will be provided; Natasha must, like you, get used to no longer being a child from today, and always be available. Have no illusions for Natasha, because she's young, it has no bearing on her ability to please me. The girl's future and yours is for my personal pleasure alone, or together, in either dancing for me and my friends, or as I said joining me in my bed."

He fell silent for a moment, allowing her to understand her role. Then his voice changed, far sterner. "If either of you are found, or I hear that you have been with another man, be it in an effort to use the man to escape or just lust, expect no mercy. You will receive ten lashes and immediately be sent to a public brothel. There you will work as many hours as they can get out of you to pay me back. In Natasha's case she will be sold to a children's circle. Don't even try to think what would happen to her there, but she will be lucky to survive six months. Do you understand?"

"Yes, Salem, I understand."

He nodded. "That is good, because later you will explain all this to Natasha. You may despise me at the moment, because of your punishment or your new role in life? It is understandable but necessary that we start as we mean to go on. You will normally find I'm not a hard man, if you keep to the rules. We have television, books and the internet, which you may use under supervision. We will celebrate your birthdays, Christmas and other religious festivals. Natasha will still need education, so I will arrange that she is educated here in the house. Both of you will be taught my language. You will want for nothing and have nice clothes, which I will allow you to choose. We have a large swimming pool, I like to swim and I suspect both of you do too.

Shortly, if I'm satisfied with the progress of you both, as a reward, I will allow you to use the pool, besides sit out in the sun. I can understand you'd rather be at home, but the day you were abducted your future became a lottery. No matter what, you were never going home again. However, either or both of you could now be in a brothel pleasing a great number of men. You're not, and you should be thanking God you have only one man to please in your life. Think about that. Do you have any questions on what I've talked about?"

"Just one."

"And what is that?"

"If either of us become pregnant, what then?"

He looked at her carefully. "What would you want to do, Sammy?"

She stood there trying to think what she would want. It was such a simple and practical question to ask him, but he'd put the onus on her to answer and she didn't know how to. After all she couldn't even visualise having to sleep with a man old enough to be her father every night, let alone have a child by him. But if she told him what she really felt, would she be taken to the punishment room?

"You seem to be having difficulty in answering your own question. If I told you I'd like children, would that help?"

She gave a weak smile, deciding to answer the only way she could. "I've always wanted to be a mother. Perhaps not at this age, I wanted to live first. But if I became pregnant, I would want to keep my baby."

He seemed satisfied with her reply. "Because of the soreness from the punishment, I will not be calling you to my bed this week. Now you may go and have cream put on your bottom and legs."

"Thank you Salem. I know you don't think much of promises, but both of us will be no trouble for you, and I do realise how lucky we are to come to such a beautiful house to live. I'll work hard to please you."

"We shall see. Actions always speak the loudest."

19

"Comments gentlemen?" Sir Peter asked, after Karen had left the room.

The Captain of the proposed operation sniggered. "She's a naive school kid. Talks like some sort of female James Bond. We can secure the house, even bring out every resident and transfer them to the carrier for proper interrogation. Forget the kid; she's obviously unstable, possibly even still traumatised over her own captivity. I'd be very nervous taking her in if she's carrying live ammunition."

A man dressed in jeans and a jumper, who'd come into the room after Karen left, took a drink from a glass of water on the table, then looked round. "Many of you know me, my name's James Gulliver from division three, which deals with interrogation. I spent two and a half days with Karen, before she walked out on me. She's no naive schoolgirl and you'd be very foolish to believe that. She played down her role in much of the killing that went on out there, but her inexperience in being debriefed meant that I was able to gather information without her really being aware we had. Although she was doing her best to avoid saying anything that might have incriminated her, she probably still believes we got nothing from her, we did. With what I did get, I was able to begin to build a picture of just what went on out there. With the answers she gave, tied in with the reports coming out from the Lebanon, both officially and unofficially, we now have a very clear picture."

"That's an interesting approach, James. But I have looked at the transcripts and also talked to Karen. Your methods were, shall we say extreme and caused the girl a great deal of pain."

"Perhaps Sir Peter, but I now have no doubt that we are dealing with a girl who has killed on more than one occasion. Not might I add just for self-defence. I went hard in for the truth, in the hope we could find out what really happened to the SAS officers, but all we were getting was lies."

"I accept it was necessary, but were you able to come to any firm conclusions?" Sir Peter asked.

"I did, Sir Peter. My analysis of Karen, and it is only my opinion, is that you have a very dangerous and capable girl who is not averse to using extreme force to get her way. I say extreme in that I believe she has killed beyond her admission and like I've just said, I suspect not always when she's had to protect herself. On that basis it is reasonable to assume, that given the chance to interrogate Saeed or his mother, she will use excess violence because she still considers these people her abusers."

"Are you suggesting Saeed's in hospital because of her?" Sir Peter asked, although he already knew that she had injured him.

James sighed. "I'm suggesting more than that. I believe it was her who pulled the trigger. I agree with the Captain, she is still traumatised. So I'm warning you to keep her well away from Saeed and his mother, unless you want a war on your hands."

"I see, but what's your opinion of her saying she'd stay on? Is that talk or do you believe she'd do just that?"

James said nothing for a short time trying in his own mind to answer Sir Peter's question against his experience and not his opinion. "If you'd asked that question against a great deal of people I've interrogated, I'd have to say it was a bluff. But with Karen, I don't think it is. My reason in saying that is I think she wants to go back in to settle a score. She also perhaps has a belief that this abduction would not have happened if she'd succeeded in killing Saeed, rather than just cripple him. So yes, even though the danger of her getting caught this time is very high, she would take the chance and try to bring the girls out."

Sir Peter smiled to himself; he knew that was exactly why she wanted to go back, but he said nothing, as a few more in the room backed James's recommendation to keep her away. However, General Ross from military headquarters cut in.

"If what I'm hearing is right, this girl is ideal. We reject ninety per cent of soldier applicants to the Special Services groups for various reasons, but Karen would be perfect. You see, you have what's effectively a battle-hardened girl prepared to go back, after what she's been through. We have soldiers in Special Services that wouldn't do that. Snatch her hand off I say. Let her interrogate and see if she can break the wall of silence that our teams will almost certainly come up against. If the girl who has a serious medical problem isn't in Saeed's house, and Karen can find out where she is, so be it, we don't have time to pussyfoot around or the kid will be dead."

"I still advise extreme caution," James cut in. "You don't know what you're dealing with here, Sir Peter. The girl could be very unstable and I believe the risk to her has also got to be considered. The General is looking at Karen as some sort of trained soldier. She isn't, she's a girl just out of school, who has experience of survival yes, has managed to get herself out a very difficult and dangerous situation yes, but it's impossible to predict how much more she can take. I believe the continued pressure on her under battlefield conditions will break her."

"In that case," the General began, "it will take ten days or so to get everything in place for a team to go in. Why not use that time with Karen, and send her to an army training camp? Test her stamina, her ability to use weapons, her capability in protecting herself. But more importantly give her the opportunity to realise the professionalism of the people around her so that she has respect for their judgement. The trainers can also strengthen her weaknesses and assess her mental state."

Arguments came for and against until everyone had made their opinion heard, however, it was up to Sir Peter to actually make the final decision.

"Thank you all for your most valued opinions. I needed to understand this girl, that's why I visited her at her home. I also found James's assessment extremely enlightening and I tend to agree with his summing up of Karen. However, we're dealing with a civilian, who at present is still going through her own process of trying to come to terms with what happened to her. Besides which she is still in the media spotlight, so the slightest error of judgement on our side would end up in a blaze of publicity. Her need for excess personal protection is yet another indication of her perceived and very real vulnerability returning so soon to a hostile location."

Sir Peter took yet another look at his papers in front of him, then looked directly at the General. "Tell me, General Ross, is it possible to train someone in ten days?" he asked.

"Normally I'd say no Sir Peter, but we would be taking a girl who already has a background in survival, weapons and other disciplines including actual battlefield experience. I'm proposing that we hone those experiences and bring her more into a team, give her a real working knowledge of the weapons she will carry besides bring her fitness level up. That would be as far as we could go."

Sir Peter thanked him then fell silent while he sipped water from a glass which he'd taken from the table. He was purposely delaying the end of his summing up to be sure in his own mind what he wanted. "I'm going to join with the yes vote this time. Karen must go back, there is too much at stake not to have someone with the team who has in-depth knowledge of these people and the way they think. With the proviso that we insist she does what the General suggests and goes to a training camp, so we can assess first hand her strengths and weaknesses. I know it's high risk, I know Captain you disapprove, so I'm going to request another Captain take your place. Whoever goes in must be confident in the girl's abilities and limitations. We're very lucky Karen is prepared to help. It couldn't have been easy for her to make that decision, so every officer in the team must back her one hundred per cent and always remember the girl is just eighteen and could still be traumatised."

The room remained silent after his words.

"I presume from your silence, some of you agree and others still have doubts? Perhaps I should now call Karen back and put our conditions to her? However, before I do, I suggest you leave us, James, with our thanks. You're not flavour of the month with this girl, and I don't want to antagonise her."

James smiled. "I will leave, Sir Peter. You're right, Karen does not like me one bit. However, please take heed of my warnings. The girl, if she's allowed to carry weapons, will be very dangerous, believe me."

Karen took her seat in the large meeting room a short time after the meeting with Angela's mother.

"Did you enjoy your lunch, Karen?" Sir Peter asked.

"Yes thank you, it was also very enlightening," she replied with a little contempt in her voice.

Sir Peter didn't rise at her words, just gave her their decision. "It has been decided, Karen, to accept the terms by which you are prepared to return to the Lebanon. We do, however, have a condition of our own. This is, like yours, not negotiable and a condition of you going."

She smiled. "So what's that?"

"I've been told by the military that they need ten days to brief and train their personnel, besides get them to the point where they will enter the country, you will be flown directly to join them at the last moment. In the ten days before, you will go to a military training camp. You will learn how to handle weapons correctly and safely. You will be brought up to a high fitness level and more importantly you will learn discipline and teamwork. We don't intend to have a loose cannon in what is otherwise a well disciplined and trained combat troop. I know it's a very short training time, but with your experience on weekend mock military operations, plus your other skills in self-defence I've been assured this will alleviate you training starting from scratch. Finally while you are there we will be assessing your mental state and decide if it's actually possible that you could endure another operation so close to the last. You yourself have told me, besides independent reports have also confirmed, that you're still having difficulty coming to terms with your ordeal. It's perfectly understandable and I'll tell you now, if there was an alternative which meant you didn't need to go, we'd be taking it. As it is time's not on our side so you're in, providing we get a positive report from the camp. Whatever the risk to the other girls I don't intend to sanction an operation built around a girl who cannot cope mentally, as well as physically. Under those circumstances we would have to find an alternative, even if it was too late to save the life of Angela."

Karen sat quietly for a moment, everyone in the room was

waiting for her reaction. Then she looked at Sir Peter.

"When I was in the Lebanon, particularly when I was alone and surviving just on experiences from my limited training, both in self-defence and weekends doing mock exercises, I realised how little I really knew about what war was, besides trusting and working with men. You need to remember I was a schoolgirl, in fact head girl at a convent school. My abduction brought home the reality of just what the world was really all about and the vulnerability of a girl on her own. I was with people I couldn't confide in, couldn't trust and they always promised the world if I paid. The payment of course was to have sex with them. But if I'd agreed, I'd have got nothing in return, just empty promises. So you can understand once among the soldiers I'd lost all trust in men until something happened that left me completely confused and not knowing what to do."

"What was that, Karen?" Sir Peter asked with interest.

She looked away obviously ashamed. "An SAS soldier laid down his life for me, after our helicopter was shot and was coming down. He held me tightly, preventing me from being injured when the helicopter crashed, with no thought for himself. He could have just told me to keep my head down and saved his own life, stuff mine, after all I was not exactly flavour of the week, but he didn't, and like I said, it cost him his life. I tried to understand why, then when the going got tough, no one suggested I should be handed over to the Lebanese. After all I was the one the Lebanese were after, not them, they could have all gone home. But none did, they were soldiers, comrades and they looked after me," she hesitated. "Only I came home. So what I'm trying to say is I agree I should go to this camp. It's a good idea, and for me necessary, so that I can be sure I understand comradeship including discipline. But I don't want to receive any favours. I should be pushed to the limit and beyond. If anything goes wrong out there, my life and others' might depend on my ability to cope under difficult conditions and I need to know I still can."

"Thank you, Karen, for that very frank answer," Sir Peter began. "Perhaps, General Ross, you can take charge of Karen for us and make the arrangements with the camp you have in mind for her training?"

"I will, Sir Peter."

"What about your parents, Karen? Do you want to go home first and explain before you go?" Sir Peter asked.

She nodded. "I think I should."

"Then she's all yours General," Sir Peter said. "If you go through with Karen just how you intend to present her at the camp, then she can be taken home in the morning before moving on for her training, I'll be very grateful?"

"Consider it done, Sir Peter. Are we all right to leave now?"

"Of course."

Then Sir Peter looked at Karen. "Keep in mind, Karen, if it's not working out, call me or the General, and we will understand. But don't leave it too long, if you're experiencing any problems, as a new plan would have to be considered very quickly."

"I promise."

When Karen left the room, General Ross held back, asking Sir Peter for a private word. "I'd like you to back me, Sir Peter, in requesting Karen is made a Lieutenant, before she goes to camp. I'm not sending her to Sandhurst, but a camp that specialises in training troops for regions that require special training beyond the basics. However, I want her to stand away from the other troops, and them to have respect for her. My ideas for this girl are very specific, so I do need this."

Sir Peter rubbed his chin in thought. "All right, if you're sure, I'll make a few calls. Are you going directly to the MOD building?"

"Yes."

"In that case I'll have papers waiting there, ready for signing. Don't let me down on this, General, all our necks are on the line."

20

When Karen left Sir Peter with the General, they went directly to the Ministry of Defence building in Whitehall. Karen was left in the reception area with a cold drink, while General Ross, met by an officer, made his way upstairs and into a large office, with the name Lieutenant General H. Myers written on a plaque outside.

"Mike good to see you, how's Ethel."

General Ross shook his hand and smiled. "It's good to see you Harry, and Ethel's fine thank you."

General Myers walked over to a side table and poured two large whiskeys before coming back and sitting at his desk.

"So Mike, what's this all about? I've had a request from the Secretary of Defence office to sanction a commission for a civilian, who has not attended training or even holds a degree?"

"I know it is a very odd request, Harry, but it's absolutely essential, believe me."

"Odd isn't the word I was thinking of Mike. It's most unusual or should I say unknown, to make a civilian a Lieutenant without any formal training."

"These are unusual circumstances, Harry. You see we don't have time to push Karen through Sandhurst. So she must go to a special training camp and stand away from the regular troops in training. Then when she joins Special Operations, she must have the authority to take control of interrogation without her being looked on as a private or civilian by the other rankings with her. This commission will need to be, by all intents, above board and documented. But within a month she'll be discharged and returning home."

"Will you take personal responsibility for her, particularly if it begins to backfire on us?"

"Of course, that goes without saying, besides there will be daily reports, medicals and protection. We'd be alerted well before any problems get out of hand and pull her out, if there are any."

"She must be very valuable to the operation then?"

General Ross leaned back in his chair. "Without her, Harry, we may as well just abandon the missing girls. Because this Saeed, even his mother, or associates, could walk past our troops and they wouldn't know them. As for the government of the day, if we fail to find the girls, besides lose more troops trying, the political backlash could be serious enough to need an election."

"I see," Harry replied. "Very well, I'll sanction it. It's already been looked at by the legal bods and they have given the green light, so why don't you wheel her in?"

Karen entered the room, taking a seat opposite General Myers and alongside General Ross.

"My name is Lieutenant General Myers, Karen. Special Branch has requested you be trained at one of our camps. General Ross, who will be monitoring your progress, has asked that you be given the temporary rank of Lieutenant, during your time at the camp and on the mission. I have sanctioned this; however, you're not trained as an officer so you will hold the rank only for operational reasons. You will not take advantage of this commission. You will not under any circumstances give orders to any personnel you outrank. Sometimes though the training may require a team leader, and a ranking officer within the group would normally assume that position. It is in order then for you to lead the team, like any soldier given the task to act as the soldier in charge for the exercise. Do you understand?"

"Yes, I understand, but why give me any rank. I don't mind being at the bottom you know?"

"May I answer that?" General Ross asked.

General Myers nodded in agreement.

"It's essential that other trainees, and junior officers on the camp, don't treat you as a raw recruit, Karen. We don't have time for any tomfoolery. The rank will hold respect; you will be asked no questions. Even if you were, and you didn't answer the question nothing would be said. When you leave the camp and join the operation, it is intended your primary role is interrogations and looking after any girls who are found. They will possibly be traumatised and may not believe, or have confidence with male soldiers. So your job will also include giving them that confidence. Yet again the rank will mean you will not be questioned on tactics, but of course as General Myers said, you will not give operational orders to the soldiers. Except if it concerns the girls and their safety."

Karen gave an indifferent shrug. "I suppose what you say is right. After all I've never been to a military camp, so there's no chance of me giving orders; I wouldn't know how to do it."

"There are two other essential parts, Karen," General Ross added. "Your surname is to be your mother's maiden name, Harris. You must also dye your hair. It can be semi-permanent, as it only has to last no more than a month. I suggest blonde, it is a good colour to change features and looks to."

She nodded without comment. Considering blonde to be tacky and common looking, she didn't really want this. However, she also realised she needed to look very different, after all her photo had been all over the papers for weeks. General Myers opened a folder, took a pen, and signed at the bottom of the top document. He then passed the folder to General Ross.

"There you are, Mike, if you sign alongside my signature, then Karen you sign the other documents in the folder, you're in the army as a Lieutenant, and subject to military regulations."

General Ross took the folder and signed, followed by Karen.

"Thank you, Harry. Let's hope this is the beginning of the end for this particularly nasty trafficker."

When they left the office, Karen was first measured up for a uniform, then she was taken to the hairdressers. General Ross looked at her as she came out from the hairdressers. She was so different, in fact he thought, far more attractive with her intense blue eyes. However, when she arrived home, her mother went mad, said she looked a tart and what had possessed her to do such a thing. Then Karen told her parents what she'd agreed to do.

"You're going where? Are you out of your mind?" Karen's father demanded.

Karen looked at him. "I suppose I must be, but a young girl

is dying, she needs my help and I intend to do what I can for her. Anyway this time it's with the blessing of the government, I'll be with the armed forces and perfectly safe."

"And if things go wrong again, what then, Karen?" he asked.

She sat for a while then looked up at them both watching her. "I know what those girls are going through. People came to help me, without consideration of the risks they took. It's my turn to help a young girl not only abducted, but dying without medical help, besides the others. I couldn't live knowing I'd turned my back on them, no matter what the risk to me personally."

"Then you must go, Karen," her mother said softly.

"But surely there's another reason, Karen, why are you really going?" her father asked.

"You're right of course. After all if it's just people who can fire guns they wanted, I'd be useless. But it's not just that, Dad, I know the house, the people who do these things, without me they would be going in blind, not knowing if the people they talk to were innocents or the traffickers. That is why I'm going."

"That I can understand, so when is it you leave?" he asked.

"Tomorrow morning, the military will collect me, I'll be taken to a training camp first to assess my fitness and I suppose my mental attitude. If all goes well and I can cope, in ten days I leave for Cyprus and then to a ship standing off the Lebanese coast. Apparently we go in by helicopter, landing a mile outside the village. After that we walk."

"I presume that is why you've gone blonde and tried to change your looks?" her father said.

"Yes, after all I'm in the papers such a lot; I stand out like a sore thumb. This way I might get away with it."

"Well you certainly look different, Karen," he replied.

She grinned. "Well don't worry; I don't intend to stay like this when I come back. I prefer my own colour and, Mum, I'll be using your maiden name in the training camp."

Their conversation then reverted to minor points of the trip before going to bed. The following morning the doorbell rang. The car to take her to the camp had arrived dead on time.

General Ross was standing at the door, a soldier at his side carrying a small suitcase.

"Hi I'm ready," Karen said as she opened the door. "Would you like to come in and meet my parents before we go?"

"Good morning, and yes I'd like to meet your parents very much, Karen," he replied. The General took the small case from the soldier, who returned to the car.

He handed her the case. "I'd like you to change into the clothes I have in this case."

She left him with her parents and ran upstairs. While she was gone he assured them she'd be looked after and a medical team would assess her progress and any problems every day. Karen came back into the room. They all looked at her. Following measurements taken the day before she now wore a smart Lieutenant's uniform.

"So what do you think of your uniform then?" the General asked her.

"It's fantastic and really smart, but I feel a bit of a phoney."

"You could only be a phoney if you were not in the army, Karen. As it is the Secretary of Defence signed your temporary entrance papers and the Chief of Staff confirmed your position as a Lieutenant. From this morning you are, Karen, in the army and subject to army discipline. Besides, after training and becoming part of a well disciplined force you might consider army life, if it is your sort of thing."

Her mother smiled. "I can't help agreeing with you, General Ross, army life could be just what Karen needs."

He looked at his watch, then her parents. "Thank you for your hospitality, but we should be making a move. It's a six hour drive and I want Karen settled in for the night so she can begin training first thing in the morning."

Karen hugged them both and then left with the General. Her mother watched quietly as the car disappeared round the bend at the bottom of the street.

She sighed. "I hope Karen's done the right thing?" she said quietly.

Her husband put his arm round her. "Karen's grown up,

love. She has had a bad time and I think she needs this to try finally to put it all behind her."

They turned and went back inside.

As the General had said it was nearly six hours later, and early evening when Karen arrived at the military camp. The car stopped outside the main building and both she and General Ross went inside. Soldiers at the door came to immediate attention and an officer was waiting to meet them.

"General Ross, welcome, please would you follow me, the Colonel's expecting you?"

By the time they entered the Colonel's office the entire training camp knew a General from staff headquarters had arrived unexpectedly and everyone was on their toes, not knowing why he had come.

"Colonel Wright, General Ross. You have received communication from my office?"

"Yes General everything has been arranged. I presume this young lady is Lieutenant Harris?" he asked looking at Karen.

"She is."

"I've arranged for both yourself and the Lieutenant to join me and my fellow officers for dinner tonight, I hope that's acceptable, General?"

"Yes that's very acceptable, but first, if you could have the Lieutenant shown to her quarters, so that she may freshen up before dinner, it will give us time to talk. I won't be staying overnight, I must return to London immediately after I'm satisfied everything has been arranged here."

After Karen left the room, the General took a seat opposite the Colonel. "I'll not beat about the bush, Colonel, Karen is very important to a coming operation, and must be guarded at all times."

The Colonel frowned. "Guarded, General, for what reason?"

"Colonel, this is a direct order from the Chief of Staff. Karen has already had an attempt on her life, we certainly expect others. Whether or not they can find her here, I don't know, but we take no risks while she is in our care. The guard on her must be discrete, part of the group you are placing her with, and not obvious to her or other soldiers in the camp. She is to attend the medical facility daily, where a doctor has already been briefed. Have you received her training schedule?"

"I have General, and assigned Staff Sergeant Summers, ex SAS, along with six commandos to form her training group. The itinerary is specific in its objectives, so I hope the girl's very fit?"

"Yes, I hope so as well, but if she isn't, it will be up to your fitness instructors to pull her into shape. Now Colonel I come to information not in your memo. Karen has already been in a recent combat situation, we're not sure just what state she's in mentally, that is why she will be closely monitored by the medics. She is also very attractive; outwardly a very feminine girl and will be popular with the younger soldiers. She must have plenty of rest and no distractions. I accept she needs some relaxation, but in moderation. To this end, I don't want to hear officers, or ratings are keeping her up to the early hours in the bar. She must not under any circumstances leave the camp grounds. There are to be no inductions, or any silliness by other officers. Karen is due to join a clandestine combat group in ten days. It's a high risk and dangerous operation, already in the same region we have lost men. So have no illusions your camp and you yourself will be under the closest scrutiny. You follow our training instructions to the letter, knock her into shape yes, but at the same time you look after her. I hope we understand each other?"

"We do, General, and you can be assured your orders for Karen and that of Staff Headquarters, will be followed implicitly."

"There is one more thing before we go and eat, this is need to know and ends with you. Karen is not a serving officer, she is a civilian, and has been conscripted into the army under a temporary order signed by the Secretary of Defence. Chief of Staff has sanctioned a rank to ensure she commands respect from any soldier. In law Karen is in the army, but without basic training as she has not come through the ranks, she is though, subject to all army regulations."

The Colonel frowned. "Didn't you mention Karen has come from a combat situation recently, was she mixed up somehow in the operation as a civilian then?"

"That is correct, although Karen has had some basic military training, in an enthusiast's group, and she is also trained in self-defence, besides, I understand, holds a brown belt. But you should always remember, Colonel, we are in unknown territory. All the reports and analysis point to a girl who has been found to be very capable under pressure. But I've been warned by experts that under certain circumstances she could be extremely dangerous and has already killed. Now Karen's moving to the next level to receive training in close combat techniques. This will give her the knowledge not only to disarm, but have the ability to kill an opponent with little difficulty. So you can understand why we are monitoring her mental state?"

"I see, Karen must be very important to you to make such elaborate plans for her? But I'm glad that you have made me aware, General, the officers would have sussed her out very quickly, just by general questions of where she's been and what she's done. Now I will control that situation and ensure she does not have those sort of questions asked of her."

"You are correct Colonel, Karen is very important, but didn't you say dinner was ready to be served?"

The dinner, as far as Karen was concerned, was the best she'd ever eaten. She'd been placed alongside the General, at his request, to indicate to all the officers her importance. Although as far as anyone in the room was concerned, to arrive with a General from London, had already set her status. After the dinner the General had Karen walk him to the car.

"Remember, Karen," he said, out of earshot of anyone. "Any problems, doubts; call me. We appreciate all you've done so far and wouldn't think badly if you found you'd taken on more than you can cope with."

"I will, General, I won't let you down and I will see it through."

"I know you will, Karen."

He took her hand and shook it hard. "Good luck, remember, I'm always available to talk, we'll meet just before the operation."

Later, Karen lay quietly in her bed. She'd stopped, since yesterday, using the tablets the doctor had given her, deciding if she kept on with them, apart from her reflexes being slow, she'd not feel alert or in control of her own mind. She was very aware that to go through the rigorous training schedule the General had shown her, she would need to be very switched on and not suppressed with drugs. However, Karen hadn't really appreciated just why the doctor had given her the tablets and already she was wide awake, unable to sleep. Her mind was beginning to play tricks. She was back in the room at Saeed's. He was banging his baseball bat on the table, demanding she get up and follow him. But she was chained up and couldn't follow. Karen was in a panic, terrified of him using the bat and injuring her. Then she had to go to the brothel. She was sweating, struggling to bring herself back to reality. Then she was running, she could hear troops shouting. Faces of the dead kept coming and going in front of her, the sound of shots, their screams. She put her hands to her head, she wanted to scream at them herself, tell them to go away. But much as she tried to shout she couldn't. Karen screwed her eyes up, she felt sick, her head was still spinning. Then she began falling, falling, then suddenly she was back in her room; all the sounds left were the steady ticking of her bedside clock, the steady hum of an extractor fan out in the passageway. Her night clothes were soaking, tears running down her face. Karen got up, making her way down the passage to the bathroom, her legs felt heavy, every step an effort. Her body wouldn't stop shaking. She sat on the toilet for a time, before going to a sink to throw water on her face. Her mind was empty, engulfed with a feeling of loneliness, fear of the future. Leaning against the wall she slowly slipped down until she was sitting on the floor, her knees up against her chest, her head buried. She began to cry uncontrollably. How long she was there she'd no idea. It was so cold, her body still shivering, she went back to her bed. In minutes she fell asleep, finally the visions, the nightmares had gone and she could rest.

The next moment Karen was being shaken. "Come on sleepy, it's time you were up."

Karen opened her eyes, Shelly, a girl who had the bedroom

alongside her, who she'd met in the toilet area last night was standing there grinning.

"What time is it?" Karen mumbled, just wanting to close her eyes again.

"Five forty-five. The roll call is at six, breakfast after initial workout at seven then everyone joins their own group."

Dragging herself up she went into the bathroom and showered before coming out, with a towel wrapped round her body, and going back to her room. But the clothes she'd put out had disappeared. She looked round, then in the small wardrobe, but everything had gone.

"Who's pinched my clothes?" Karen shouted up the passage, but no one replied.

The six girls in the barracks were now coming out of their rooms, many grinning as Karen stood there still in her towel.

"Oh come on, it's my first day, I'll be late," Karen begged.

They all laughed and left the barracks as the bell sounded. Shelly hung behind and pointed to a door further down but never said anything.

"You're late, Lieutenant, take twenty," the Sergeant shouted at Karen, as she ran across to join the others.

"Excuse me I was sorting out my clothes," Karen answered, not wanting to tell tales that the other girls had hidden them.

Everyone looked at her, the Sergeant grinned. "Answering back gives another five."

Shelly sensed Karen was about to object. She pushed her gently, her voice low. "For fuck's sake, just do the twenty-five and don't say another word or you'll be doing fatigues on your first bloody day."

Karen did as Shelly asked and easily finished twenty-five push-ups. However, immediately after she had to join the others who were already in what was a hard and gruelling workout for a solid forty minutes. Then they were all dismissed for breakfast. Karen left them to collect a jacket from her room, promising to join Shelly in the mess.

As Karen left the group, a corporal caught up with Shelly putting his arm round her shoulder. "So, Shelly, who's the chick and where's she been hiding all my life?" he asked.

"Your so-called chick is a Lieutenant, Stubs, attached to Special Services so I'd keep away from her, they like to keep their 'chicks' to themselves."

"Oops, good job I didn't do my usual, in your face, chat up line on her then."

Shelly laughed. "You're right there, Stubs, but I'll try to introduce you later if you want me to?"

He shook his head. "Thanks, but no, there's no way I'm going up rank to find a chick."

Following breakfast the Staff Sergeant collected her and she was taken to a small office. Another man was standing there waiting, dressed all in white.

"This is your fitness instructor, Lieutenant, you will report to him after breakfast every morning for the first five days in the gym. You will wear your tracksuit over shorts and top. You will also need a towel. It's his job to bring your fitness up to scratch. I will be putting together your itinerary for specific afternoon training this morning and after lunch we will go over it and show you where you should be at any given time. Have you any questions?"

"I have an appointment with the medical team this morning, Sergeant."

"Yes we know that, your fitness instructor will collect you in two hours and he'll take you to the gym facility. Can you make sure you have your gym clothes with you so as not to waste time?"

"I will Sergeant."

Karen left them and after picking up her sports bag and dressed only in tracksuit she made her way to the medical centre. A girl on the desk showed her into a room, the doctor was sat behind a desk looking through a folder. He offered his hand then asked her to take a seat.

"A lot of our meetings will be informal, so do you object to me calling you Karen?" he asked.

"No that's fine with me, Doctor."

"Well, Karen, first on the agenda is a full medical. The nurse will be doing the majority of the tests and I will be monitoring at all times. I'd like to get it over as quickly as I can so that you and I can talk for a short time." He pressed a button on the desk and a nurse came in. "Can you take the Lieutenant to the medical room and begin the tests, Nurse."

For the next hour Karen was prodded and pulled, placed on a walker, with monitors attached to her, followed by taking blood and saliva tests. Finally with a paper cup full of sweet tea she was back with the doctor. She'd given him the bottle that contained the tablets she'd been taking.

"I stopped them just before I came here," she told him.

"So how do you feel now?" he asked.

"A little light-headed as if I'm here but not. I also shake at times for no reason. Last night was bad; I ended up in the toilets on the floor crying uncontrollably. But I didn't know why."

"That's understandable, Karen, these pills are anti-depressants and very strong. You're in detox, it's like a drug addict waiting for the next fix. Your body craving for the drug, making you feel inadequate, unable to cope without a fix. It was a very dangerous thing you did just stopping like that; you should have come for advice. Why were you taking them?"

She shrugged. "I kept getting nightmares. I'd wake at night in sweats. Basically I was unable to cope with just living."

"Would you like to tell me how you got into such a position that you needed drugs? After all you're a very fit girl, you're heart's strong, your lungs clear and you don't seem to be suffering any obvious illness."

Karen looked at him. "I'm not sure if I'm allowed to tell you anything. Is what I tell you confidential?"

"Anything you tell me is absolutely confidential, Karen, I can promise you that. To help you through whatever the problem is I need to understand what's going on inside your head. I'll make notes, but they won't go on your record, they're just for me to refer to. The instructions I have from General Ross are to monitor your physical and mental state on a daily basis. But I can't do that without knowing what's troubling you."

"I can understand that," Karen replied. "I was abducted and raped. While being rescued there was a great deal of killing, some

I'm afraid by me. I found myself alone and had to get out of the country without help. The whole experience took its toll. When I came out I was nervous, afraid of every shadow. It gave me nightmares as well as depression. I'm here to be trained in weapons, to understand the discipline the army runs under and to bring my fitness up."

"Why, Karen?"

"I'm going back in."

He shook his head in disbelief. "This is something you want to do is it?"

"No; it scares the hell out of me, but there is no one else and I've already had an attempt on my life since coming home. It has to be sorted one way or the other."

He made notes and then looked up at her. "To see this ten days through, Karen, you mustn't be on anti-depressant drugs, at the same time you need to sleep at night, we can't have you awake for half of it. I'll talk to the Sergeant and advise that you take the rest of the day off. You are to relax, read a book. Not alone but in public. The mind needs to be distracted so as not to allow the drug to take control of you which you've experienced when you were alone. Don't take any more of the tablets your doctor gave you, but tonight you will take sleeping tablets. The point is the drug will be weakening all the time, your body will crave it, but eventually that craving will stop. Then, Karen, whatever the drug was suppressing could be back with a vengeance. Only when the final effects leave your body will you know if you can cope without tablets."

"Okay, I'll do as you ask. What time do you want me back tomorrow?"

"You are booked to come here every day just before dinner at around six, Karen. We will then go through how you are coping. I will check your heart, your breathing for the records, and I think, until we are certain the drug has gone we'll take a blood test. But if you can't cope, don't wait until six, come and see me."

She stood. "Thank you for your time, doctor."

He nodded. "Thank you for being frank with me and take care, Karen. This is your health and your sanity you're messing about with."

The afternoon flew by; she'd taken a book and sat reading, as the doctor had told her to, in the regimental gardens behind the main building. A few times she'd fallen asleep, even once dropping her book, but by late afternoon she felt so much better. However, following dinner she returned to her room, lay down and fell asleep. Waking late in the evening she decided to clean her teeth, wash and go back to bed after taking two of the sleeping tablets she'd been given.

The next day, Karen didn't wake up until six thirty. She'd slept the entire night without waking and felt really good in herself. She didn't have to attend morning fitness, like all the other soldiers, so she went directly for breakfast and joined her own fitness instructor in the gym. It was always empty then and he took her through a very hard and rigorous routine, taking her to the very limit of her endurance.

After lunch she was in weapons training. They began at the beginning, taking her through all the safety in handling a gun containing live ammunition. How she was to keep the gun clean at all times, with a warning that a dirty gun can explode in your face, or fail when really needed. Her first introduction was followed by constantly assembly and disassembly until she believed she could do it blindfolded. And blindfolded she was, with the other soldiers urging her on as she struggled to actually assemble and disassemble the guns. Finally at the end of the session a vital part was taken from her, to add a little light relief. But Karen took it all in good spirit, after all this was the first real day of training. The last hour before her medical check-up she was back in the gym for close combat training. She did well at first, her previous judo and kick-boxing standing her in good stead. But it didn't last long. Close combat was nothing like self-defence training, judo or kick-boxing. Close combat was directed specifically to kill or disable. Because of this difference she was on the receiving end of mock attacks to her and she lost every time. However, by the end of the hour she had begun to fight back as the new and violent moves were explained and shown her.

She left the medical centre and wandered slowly to the mess

for dinner. Everyone else had gone and she sat alone eating. Karen wasn't bothered; today had been long and hard. But she hoped it would get easier, as her fitness level began to rise again after the three weeks on the anti-depressant tablets. She finished quickly then made her way to the barracks.

"Where've you been I was just about to give up on you?" Shelly asked, as she entered the woman's barracks.

"Medics, I have a check-up every day at this time, so it makes me late," she replied.

"Well now you're here, I'm out with two other girls for a drink tonight, and so are you. Have you got any jeans?"

Karen didn't really want to go anywhere, she was shattered, but decided, if she was to be accepted and fit in, she couldn't refuse to join in with the girls.

"I'll come, but for only an hour, maybe tomorrow I'll feel better and stay longer but tonight I'm really feeling like shit."

"That's okay, just so long as you show your face. There's lots of the girls who want to meet you, and probably the lads as well. It's not often we get a real live Lieutenant training with us. They all go to Sandhurst," Shelly replied, at the same time texting her boyfriend to tell him she'd be late.

Fifteen minutes later Karen was ready. Dressed in tight hipster jeans, a short t-shirt and heeled shoes, adding to her five eight, she'd left her hair loose and used a little eye make-up.

Shelly stood aghast. "God, is this how you always look when you go out?"

Karen felt a little worried wondering if this was not what they expected a Lieutenant to wear. "I've got a dress, but it's very short and figure hugging, if you think I should change?"

"God no, if you go out in that the other girls will have no chance; even now I think the lads are going to have one hell of a shock when they see you."

Karen just smiled; she was very used to this sort of attention.

As they made their way to the Social Club, they caught up with two other girls, one Maggie, the other Crystal.

"You've got competition tonight, Shelly; it looks like you'll be back to your boring old boyfriend. The Lieutenant here will stun the lads, you won't get a look in," Maggie mocked.

"Can't you just call me Karen when we're off duty?" she asked.

"Of course we will, if you want us to," Shelly replied.

The Social Club facilities in the camp were large, modern and very full. The girls struggled to get to the bar. However, two soldiers, who were in the same troop as Karen, made them a way through. Although unknown to any of the girls they were Karen's assigned guards for the night.

21

Annette sat quietly in the back of the car, staring out of the window. Just eighteen and from Leeds, she had always been a popular girl. As the others, she was five eight, slim with deep green emerald eyes and jet-black shoulder-length hair. Two had bid for her but an Englishman called Lomax was determined to have this girl and finally won at thirty-nine thousand dollars. Unlike Sammy, who she'd made friends with on the first night of the holiday, when they'd shared a room. Annette wasn't aggressive but very feminine and outwardly seemed to accept everything that had happened to her. However, Annette was not really like that, she was angry, frustrated and determined, after getting her bearings, of leaving to find her own way home.

The house she arrived at was in a compound with guards at the entrance. Although the house was nice it was small with only four rooms downstairs and five bedrooms. She'd been given one with an interconnecting door to Lomax's room. As she'd left the auction with only knickers and shirt, Lomax had stopped in a small town and taken her into a clothes shop. They fitted her out with two pairs of jeans, three dresses, t-shirts, underclothes and shoes. Finally he bought her a leather bomber jacket, telling her the nights could get quite cold.

Later, after showering and dressing in one of her new dresses, Annette joined Lomax for dinner.

"I suppose you wonder what you've got yourself into?" he asked.

She shrugged. "It's pretty obvious; I've been sold as some sort of sex slave. I suppose you're going to threaten me the same as that old hag with her electric stick?"

"I could if you want? But in my book Annette, this is your new home. It may not be what you'd choose but you can't return home, so why not buckle down and we'll get to know each other?"

She frowned. "But you're English; surely you wouldn't keep a girl against her will? Besides, you're not bad looking, it'd be easy to meet a girl who really liked you and wanted to stay anyway."

"That's your opinion, not mine. So from now on keep it to yourself. I'm not throwing away good money to send you home, because you and I are English. In my book, unless you can show me some real affection and learn to accept me, all I've paid for is a prostitute, and if that's the case I'll treat you like a prostitute. So based on the normal hundred dollars fee for a young girl, you've got 390 sessions to pay off before you can think of going home, plus interest and cost of food, accommodation, clothes etc., so probably you'll be here at least two to three years. During that time I could hand you around and get some money back that way. Alternatively you and I could look on it as an opportunity of two people being thrown together and finding out if there is common ground. You could learn to like me the same as me you and we'd become a couple. You'd want for nothing; in time we could even travel, eventually you could have contact with your family once more."

Annette, although young, was not that naive to think he'd ever go that far. But she would rather try and be a part of his life rather than be thought a prostitute working her so-called debt off.

"I've thought about it a lot, Lomax, and realise no one would ever come to find me, even if they could actually locate where I was. So I've decided to throw myself into this relationship and hope it works out."

"In that case, Annette, I'm happy to welcome you into my house. You will have your own room but at times I'll expect you to join me. You can even have time to settle in if you want. I'm looking for a girl for the long term not a quick romp and that's it."

She grinned. "Thank you, but I'm not a prude who needs time. I have had boyfriends in the past and perhaps gone too far, but I enjoy sex, the point will be, can you keep up?"

He smiled back, filling her glass. This was the sort of girl he'd hoped to get. "All I can do is try Annette," he replied, believing this girl would have her work cut out to keep up with him.

She on the other hand never replied, already she was planning her escape, her own future and it didn't include the likes of him.

22

Saeed shifted his position on the settee and lifted up the telephone handset. "Saeed here," he answered.

"It's Ashram here, Saeed, I'm currently in the UK."

"Asham, it's been a long time my friend. How are things with you?"

"They're good, but could be better. I spoke to your mother yesterday, but apparently you were in the hospital. She said you had some accident?"

"Of sorts, Asham, I have to go there every other day for the moment, but what can I do for you?"

"I heard on the grapevine there was this girl called Karen Marshall. Something about you were offering a large fee for someone to, shall we say, collect her for you?"

Her very name made him shudder, not with fear but hate. "You are right, I have made it known that I want this girl, but the price is alive, very much alive, there is nothing offered for her death even though I would have the satisfaction of knowing that the killer of my friends is at last meeting her maker. Why is it you're asking?"

"She's here."

His heart skipped a beat, but he was also confused, had Asham caught her?

"Here, Asham, what are you talking about, where?"

"Karen, she's in the same army camp that I'm stationed at. Walked into the Social Club large as life last night, no one ever said she was in the military."

"She isn't, you're mistaken, my friend, Karen Marshall was a schoolgirl up to three months ago."

"You're wrong, Saeed. The girl for two weeks was in the paper every day, really photogenic she was and the papers knew it. Okay she's gone blonde, which makes her look very different.

She's also changed her surname to Harris, but believe me this girl is Karen Marshall. She's a Lieutenant with Special Forces."

Saeed scratched his head confused. Why was she there? Had she joined the army, after all it was her sort of thing? But if she had surely she'd have started as some sort of beginner? "Tell me Asham, is a Lieutenant at the bottom, middle or where in the rankings?"

"It's a high rank and only one below a Captain, Saeed, apart from which she's something to do with army headquarters in London. She arrived with a four star General."

"And you say she's working with Special Forces there? How long's that been going on?"

"That's the strange thing, Saeed, she arrived three days ago. The camp was in panic I'll tell you. Usually when top brass arrive, it's with lots of notice and we even paint the side stones white, well not exactly every stone, but you can understand the place is given a good clean up at least. So you can imagine when a staff car arrived at the gate even the officers were shitting themselves."

"Yes, yes I'm not interested in that, more with Karen."

"Well like I said, she's now billeted in the woman's section, training each day, and no one seems to know, or will say, just how long she's here for."

"What's the chance of snatching her?"

"Inside the camp, virtually impossible. But I work in the supply depot and we had a request for full battle gear for the troop she's with to be available Thursday night. I checked the camp weekly training sheet and she's on field training this Friday. It's an overnight exercise so she'll be staying out with two of her group. There's weapons on the list, but no live ammunition, as it's an exercise. A few selected lads would have them all in minutes."

"Just who are these lads, can they be trusted?"

"They're all ex-marine, work on the doors of a couple of girly bars in the town. Bung them a few quid and they'd relish a skirmish with the army lads, there's no love lost between the army and navy you know."

"Do it, Asham. I'll have my man in the UK call you to make the handover arrangements."

There was a short silence.

"I don't like to ask, Saeed, but payment?"

"Five thousand, my agent will pay on delivery. If she's dead or badly wounded you get nothing. Except, that is, my gratitude, and hatred because I didn't get the pleasure of seeing her die."

"Consider it done, but cash Saeed, or you don't get the girl."

Saeed sat there in thought after he'd replaced the handset. He just couldn't imagine what she was up to, unless this girl wasn't Karen. Lifting the handset again he dialled a number and waited. Soon it was answered.

"Hello," came a man's voice.

"Pat, is that you?" Saeed asked.

"It is; who's this?"

"Saeed. I've just had a very interesting, but strange phone call," he began.

Pat, Saeed's agent in the UK, listened to what Saeed had to say.

"Do you think it's Karen? It sounds like this Asham's trying it on, or he's genuinely mistaken himself," Pat commented.

"I don't know, but if it is her, we have to take the chance. Anyway don't, whatever you do, hand over my money for just any old girl. Very few are worth that sort of money in the brothels, if they have it wrong."

"I understand that, should I go down myself and check out this girl?"

"You can, but I doubt you'd get very close to her. No, on second thoughts its better you keep well away, contact Asham, make an arrangement to meet him with the girl."

"Okay, Saeed, anything you say. Is there anything else?"

Saeed was thinking, and then he made a decision. "Slight change of plan, when you meet Asham," he began, "if the girl is or isn't Karen, the trail stops there as far as we are concerned. Do you understand?"

"I do, does that go the same for the girl if she isn't Karen?"

"It's up to you, if she's drugged just leave her, if she's awake and can identify you, I'd not take the risk."

"I understand; I'll keep in touch."

23

"You've done well, Lieutenant," the fitness instructor said after she'd just completed ten lengths of the swimming baths. "You're thirty per cent up on your length times, even the running earlier has shown a marked improvement."

She felt relief as he helped her out of the pool, handing her a towel. The last few days had been hard; often she just wanted to give up. "What have we on tomorrow?" she asked.

"You have a break, well not really a break. The Sergeant has arranged a team exercise on the moor. It's overnight, are you all right with that?"

Karen laughed. "I don't have a problem; I often did it with my dad and other enthusiasts. Although it looks like the rain has really set in, so it's going to be a pretty miserable exercise."

"They're always the best, Lieutenant; otherwise it's a pretty boring, mundane walk. Anyway if you go via the stores they'll fit you out with all the equipment you need. I've been told after lunch you've got weapons practise on the range, followed by an hour of close combat. The rest of the afternoon is briefings; apparently you're to be dropped off on the moor at seven tomorrow morning. Good luck and don't let the lads intimidate you."

The next morning, after an early breakfast, Karen along with two other soldiers was sat in the back of a lorry on the way to the moor. As she sat there quietly, she thought back to yesterday. The morning was as usual filled with fitness training, but the afternoon had been hard for her. Apart from collecting mountains of equipment for the exercise, she'd been on the shooting range. However, it had not just been aiming at a stationary targets; it involved lots of crawling about and taking shots at rising targets. With the relentless rain, she was filthy, cold and wet, just wanting to go to her room to clean up. But this was the army, so even after the exercise and before a warming shower, it was clean all the equipment until it shone like new. Besides all this, the close combat training had moved to another level. She had been hit on two sides at once, thrown about, kicked and very nearly trampled on as she struggled to hold her own, in an effort to score points as she touched certain parts of her opponent's body. Parts of the body that is, which would normally disable or kill them. Following that she had to attend the medical centre, again she was given a full medical check-up, including the treadmill. By dinner, she had been happy to finish and go back to her room, even declining joining the other girls for a drink in the Social Club. Although normally she loved going, never being off the small dance floor, and refusing so many requests for a date that it had become quite embarrassing being asked. It wasn't that she didn't want to have a boyfriend, it was in her mind pointless meeting and perhaps becoming attached to someone and then finding him living the other side of the country or stationed abroad. Then of course there was going back to the Lebanon. The last thing she wanted was someone giving her doubts, not wanting her to go. For her there was a score still to settle and she intended to settle it once and for all this time.

"Penny for them?" a soldier asked, nudging her arm and bringing her out of her thoughts.

Karen turned to him and smiled. "It'd cost you a lot more than that Terry, besides, you'd have so much dirt on me I'd be at your mercy for you not to divulge them."

He grinned. "Sounds intriguing, I've got ten quid, but it'll cost you a date as well for me to keep quiet."

"Shame on you," she ribbed. "Besides, you get to sleep with me tonight, what more can you ask of a girl?"

"Hey, what about me, can't I sleep with you as well?" the other soldier butted in.

"Yeah? What about your girlfriend, Gareth, how'd she feel if she found out?" Terry cut in.

At that moment the vehicle slowed and minutes after the Sergeant pulled open the back flap. "Right you scrawny lot, all out. I want to see you back at camp in time for dinner tomorrow. Miss it and you starve. That is if you can manage to avoid the enemy, who'll be attempting to stop you at all costs. Then it's a return to camp with your tails between your legs."

They climbed down and stood looking round. As far as the eye could see, it was open moor with little cover. Already it had begun to rain.

"On your way, you've got three hours start then all hell will break loose," the Sergeant urged.

They all began to fit the heavy packs on their backs as the vehicle started up, turned back the way it had come, and soon disappeared leaving them alone.

"Well, Lieutenant, this is your operation, which way?" Terry asked.

Karen looked at the map the Sergeant had just handed her, it was the first time she'd seen it, so she spent time before she answered.

"The direct way is due east, I would think that's the way they will be expecting us to go, so most of the opposition will just sit down, and wait for us to come to them. I propose we go south-west for ten miles, then swing south on a direct line, coming up ten or fifteen miles beyond the main groups wanting to stop us and to the east of the camp."

"You're adding on miles there. This is only an exercise?" Gareth commented.

Karen picked up her gun, then looked at them watching her. "Yes well, this may be an exercise, but I want to arrive back at camp with my head held high, rather than a bloody laughing stock, you lot can go east if you want, I'm going the other way."

No one objected again and soon they were struggling through boggy terrain, with the rain coming down relentlessly.

Two miles due east of them, a Land Rover with three men dressed in army gear stolen from the camp, were sitting in the back smoking. Alongside the driver sat Asham, with his mobile to his ear. "Stop here," he suddenly said to the driver. They slowed and came to a halt.

He turned round towards the men. "This is as far as we can go following them in a vehicle. They've gone south-west, Stewart, uld they do that?"

Stewart, who been made the designated leader of the men, looked at the map then back at Asham. "Are you sure?"

"Of course I'm sure; I placed a direction beacon in one of the soldier's backpacks. My partner has it coupled to the internet and he's giving me their position."

"Then they are trying to avoid the troops, sent out to stop them getting to the camp. My guess is they will have to swing south after they are beyond the main opposition. That's good for us as they will be out on a limb."

"If you're certain they will do that, then it's time you followed," Asham replied. "I'll call you if they turn. I'll expect you to catch up with them before nightfall. Remember the girl must not be injured or killed. I'm not bothered with the rest, in fact it would be better if they can't identify you, if you know what I mean? I'll bring transport when you confirm the snatch and you give me a pickup point."

The men jumped out from the vehicle and set off in single file in the same direction as Karen's group.

Meanwhile three hundred miles away in London, and two hours after Karen was left on the moor, Sir Peter entered General Ross's office. He took a seat opposite him. "I hear our girl's doing well?"

"She is, Sir Peter, in fact reports from all departments are confirming she is meeting their targets and will be ready to join the group as arranged."

"Yes, well that's why I'm here, General. The operation has been called forward. It's proposed to collect Karen, by helicopter, on Sunday afternoon. There are political problems with all this and we want them to be over there before the shit hits the fan."

"Yes, I had the feeling everyone was getting a bit twitchy. The papers haven't let off demanding some action from the government. I'll call the Colonel and make arrangements while you're here."

He dialled and waited. "Colonel Roberts please. This is General Ross…"

"General Ross, this is the Colonel, how can I help?"

"I must commend you, Colonel, on Lieutenant Harris's progress. We've been reading the reports and it would seem the girl has really taken to army life."

"She has, General, very much so. She has also, as you predicted, been particularly popular, both with the soldiers and her trainers."

"That is good, however Colonel, the operation has been brought forward and she goes on Sunday."

"You do know it's Remembrance Day; will she be leaving before or after the parade?"

"I do Colonel, she will be leaving after the parade, the time of departure is not fixed as yet. Is she available for a talk?"

"Not until tomorrow General, she's on an exercise with two of her group. It's a test in enemy avoidance, and the Lieutenant is leading."

The General fell silent for a moment.

"I hope you're not telling me she's left the safety of the camp, Colonel?" he asked quietly.

"Of course, they are on the moor. It's the usual training area for all units."

"But I specifically gave orders for her not to leave the camp."

"No, General Ross; you said she wasn't to leave camp socially, which she hasn't. This is training devised by her trainers to see how she copes, both with leadership and cunning. It's pointless training someone without giving them a real situation and it was sanctioned in our training schedule."

The phone had been on speaker and Sir Peter lit a cigarette. He reached forward and touched the mute button.

"I don't like it, General; we're too close to her leaving on the mission to risk even a simple accident like a sprained ankle. I think it would be prudent to bring Karen back into the safety of the camp."

He nodded, pressing the mute release, allowing the Colonel to enter the conversation. "We're not comfortable with this, Colonel, I suggest the exercise is cancelled immediately and she be brought back to the camp."

"I understand, General, but for our troops to find them, will depend on how well the Lieutenant can avoid detection. Normally with this sort of exercise, on their first command, we have them by dinner or even the worst case before dark."

Sir Peter shook his head slowly. "This is Sir Peter Parker from Special Branch, Colonel. You are talking about a girl who was able to avoid close on five hundred troops in a hostile environment. You're wildly optimistic if you believe that. Are you not in radio communication with them?"

"No Sir Peter, the whole point of such an exercise is to work on your wits, we don't mollycoddle our troops."

"Are the guards with her armed?" the General asked.

"No General, they all carry guns as part of their equipment, but they will have no live ammunition."

"In that case, Colonel, you'd better get every troop out there you've got, including helicopters, to find them. Without weapons she's very vulnerable."

"I'll do that right away, General."

The General replaced the handset. "Do you think they will struggle to find her, Sir Peter?"

"It'll be interesting. But if you want the truth, she'll use the same tactic she used in the Lebanon and travel at night, laying deliberately low in the day. You will need to use imaging detection to overcome that. But if she suspects that might be used, there are ways in which she can even avoid that equipment."

24

If Karen had been leading a larger group, according to the training sessions over the week, she'd have arranged the main body of the group's protection in the usual way. At least one man a hundred yards in front, then the same a hundred yards behind, with the main group in-between. However, because there were only three of them she closed the distance up so the centre soldier could see both the lead and rear soldier. The exercise gave points for the number captured from a group. This way they'd have advance warning and the ability to react positively with perhaps the loss of only one soldier rather than them all. However, when they settled down for a break, Terry, currently the one behind, moved up to join them.

"We're being followed, Lieutenant," Terry said as he sat down on the bank.

"How many and how close are they?" Karen asked.

"There's three, spread out with about fifty metres between each of them. They're staying around a quarter of a mile behind. What I can't understand is they stopped when we stopped and turned when we turned. It's as if they had observers watching us, but I couldn't see any and we're on higher ground than they are, at the moment."

Karen frowned, something was wrong, there was no way they could have caught onto them this easily. "Well we've a choice. We take them as prisoners and collect the points or we stay clandestine and avoid them by pushing further west. Has anyone any thoughts?"

"I vote we take them out of the equation, if we don't they will be constantly radioing back our position. Besides, I think they're waiting for dark and will come at us then," Terry said.

Everyone fell silent while each thought about the suggestion.

It was Karen who spoke first. "I agree, the longer we allow them to follow the better knowledge they will have of our intentions. I'll go ahead with Terry. Gareth you wait here and position yourself to take the one on the left flank. If our suspicions are correct and they do have an observer he'll report back that we're on the move, hopefully not realising only two have moved on. But if we have it wrong and it's just a coincidence you then leg it and join us…" she looked at the map, "at this point here," she said, her finger pointing to a location on the map. "It's showing high ground, which means we will also be able to see, just about, what's going on, if the rain stops that is and the weather clears a little."

With this agreed they finished the short break and moved on. Gareth positioned himself to lie and wait. It wasn't long to wait as sure enough, the men following began to move as well.

"This is really weird, it's as if they have some sort of homing beacon," Gareth thought to himself.

Karen and Terry settled down on a ridge nearly half a mile in front of Gareth. The bracken was thick and afforded very good cover at the same time as allowing them to watch what was going on with field glasses.

Further down the valley Gareth was relishing the annoyance for the group's leader, when in less than a hundred yards they would be caught. The fools were walking directly towards him.

Gareth jumped up from his hiding place, at the same time pointing his gun directly at one of the soldiers. "You are caught, and out of the search. I want your tag," he demanded.

The man grinned. "Are you for real? Is your gun actually loaded with live rounds?"

Gareth frowned. "No of course they're not, this is an exercise, but the rules say you're caught, so hand me your tags."

The man turned and called out to the leader. "Hey, Stewart, I've been rumbled, looks like we're caught."

Stewart and the other man joined him.

"Okay it's a fair cop, mate, we may as well come with you and the others," Stewart said as he approached.

"I don't think you're supposed to do that. You just go back

to the camp via the road," Gareth answered.

"Well that's not what the Sergeant said," Stewart replied looking confused. "He told us to stick with you lot. Anyway you've got the points for a capture so why worry?"

Gareth stood for a short time, and then shrugged. "Well it didn't happen last time I was on the moor, it's probably best if we go and see the Lieutenant, she'll decide what to do."

Fifteen minutes later Gareth, with the three men, was stood in front of Karen. Gareth had told her what they'd said.

I don't understand that idea," Karen said after some thought. "No one said we had to keep the prisoners we caught. God, if we keep on catching them I could be trying to hide a bloody army, and that would be impossible."

"Well are we coming or staying?" Stewart asked.

Karen shrugged. "I suppose you'd better come. But we avoid anymore we see, is that clear?"

The three men looked at each other, with a hint of a smile on Stewart's face. "Whatever you say, Lieutenant, you're in charge."

They all set off together, Sam looked at one of the weapons the men were carrying. "That looks like one of those CR-21 assault rifles used by the Afghans, why are we issuing those?"

Stewart cut in before the other two could say anything. "All the other weapons are out, so we were given these from the store. It just completes the pack, no one's got ammunition so they may as well have given us wooden ones. Anyway which way are we heading?"

"South-west, then we turn south before going directly east to come up at the far side of the camp," Gareth replied.

"That's stupid; you'll hit the wetlands way before that. I know a far better way and they'll never find us."

They all stopped and Karen looked at him with scepticism. "You mean you know a way direct to your mates, so we all get captured?"

He looked at her with a hurt expression. "No, it's just that I've done this a few times and found a brilliant way. You can please yourself but it'll get bloody boggy, so you'll be forced to turn earlier and walk directly into your searchers."

"Show me?" she demanded.

Stewart took her map and she watched as he moved his finger over the map indicating a line a good twenty miles further but bringing them in well north of the camp.

"So what do you think? It's too far over for them to expect you to actually be there, besides we hit a road six miles from camp, there's a pub and twice I've got a lift and didn't have to walk."

"It looks good, Lieutenant," Terry urged with Gareth also adding his enthusiasm.

While Karen couldn't help agreeing that it was a far better route than hers, she had really wanted to do the exercise without help from someone who'd already been on the moor. For her it was a learning curve to see if she could lead. Although the weather was becoming worse by the minute, so it was no longer a bit of an adventure but fast becoming a hard slog.

"Okay, why not, all we want to do is get back to some hot food," she said after a last look at the map.

"I'd prefer the bar to the food," Gareth added.

"You would," Terry replied.

"Either way, let's go shall we?" Karen cut in before it became a large conversation.

By the time darkness came the weather had worsened. Winds were gusting at around fifty miles an hour and the rain was virtually horizontal. The driving rain was stinging their faces, all of them thankful for the waterproofs they were wearing. Karen decided to call a halt and bunk down. It was pointless fighting the weather so they settled down among a few scrub bushes trying to keep warm.

Karen was sat between Terry and Gareth chewing a biscuit. The three men were some distance away, in another banked area, also trying to keep out of the worst of the wind. Every part of her body was beginning to shake uncontrollably. Karen knew by her symptoms she was close to hypothermia, but decided she should say nothing and try to add some light conversation to an otherwise appalling night.

"God I wasn't built for this; I should be in Spain sunning myself on the beach wearing nothing more than the tiniest and sexiest bikini you could imagine," Karen began. "As it is I'm freezing my butt off on some god awful moor in the middle of the night."

Terry laughed. "Well you should get some real food down yourself and put a bit of weight on. Fat keeps you warm so they say. Mind you thinking about it, then you'd not want to sit on the beach looking like a beached whale."

"Yeah, looking like stick insects is more for you men rather than choice. I'd rather have the stodgy puddings and be the whale," she retorted.

"But you look good as a stick insect and if you stop whingeing I might even join you on the beach," Gareth said joining in the conversation.

She turned her head and looked at him. "Oh yes, who invited you to my beach? I have to think of my street cred you know."

Gareth looked across at her. "What about my street cred, say your choice of bikini colour clashed with my really cool bathing costume?"

Karen grinned. "Then you'd have to get rid of it wouldn't you."

"Why me; why not you?"

"I'm a girl, my fashion sense is perfect," she replied indignantly.

"What fashion sense, have you looked at yourself today?" Terry asked laughing.

"Yes well, the less said about this getup the better. I'm bloody sure they dress you like this just to give the officers a laugh," she replied.

"You are an officer, besides before the night's out you'll be glad you have the trench coat and waterproof over trousers," Terry said.

"Oh… I forgot that little point. Anyway I don't feel very much like an officer. I'm so cold and tired," she answered despondently.

They all fell silent for a time.

Terry looked across at Gareth, and then slipped his arm round her shoulder. "If you're really that cold, Karen," he whispered in her ear. "Unfasten your water proof and you can snuggle up to me."

"I'd like that," she replied unfastening her heavy coat. Terry did the same and soon they were snuggled close to each other, Terry's waterproof wrapped round her.

"Feeling a little warmer now?" he asked.

"Yes, much, thank you."

"Then it's time you got some sleep. I'll take the first watch, Terry the second, then you see us through till dawn."

Karen did as he asked, drawing her waterproof coat and baseball cap down even lower on her head before closing her eyes. He pulled her closer to his body. He could feel the girl shaking, now realising just how close she really must have been to hypothermia, but there was nothing they could do. With no communication, and such bad weather they just had to sit it out.

Two hours before daybreak, Karen had taken over the watch and moved away from the other sleeping soldiers to sit on a mound looking out across the dark moor. She'd slept well and if she hadn't woken when she did, they would have left her, rather than let her take a watch. She'd also been a little put out when the captured soldiers had refused to do a watch.

"After all," Stewart had said, *"we're prisoners, so you could hardly ask a prisoner to keep watch?"*

Karen could see his point, but tonight in her mind was exceptional weather conditions and it was only an exercise after all. But it wasn't worth arguing the point and that was why she'd agreed and broken the night up into three-hour watches, just for the three of them.

For the last week she'd considered asking the General if she could actually join the army. The life seemed good - although the training since she'd arrived had been hard, it wouldn't always be like that, besides most of the lads were her sort, she felt at ease with them in the Social Club and on the camp. However, she realised if that was to happen she'd lose her mythical rank and she couldn't quite accept having to start at the bottom. She was brought out of her thoughts when Stewart came up to her.

"It's time we moved on," he said with some authority.

"I decide that, besides, the other lads, unlike you lot, have been on watch all night so they should have more rest."

He moved closer. "I don't think you understand, Karen. We're not soldiers playing your stupid war games - we're here to collect you. But before you even think about screaming out for help, unlike your guns, without ammunition, ours have. Now that leaves you with a dilemma. Decide to wake them, try to resist and we kill them where they sleep. So it's your choice, come quietly and they live, object they die, but you still come with us anyway? So what's it going to be?"

There was nothing to be said. Karen didn't want the lads to die on her account. "Okay I'll come with you, but you don't kill the lads. They're nothing to do with this."

"Then fasten your coat up and let's go before they waken."

She got up and fastened her coat. They moved out from the camp fast and quiet, not allowing her to take her backpack. After fifteen minutes of hard walking they stopped and Stewart came up to her.

"The coat, give it me."

She took her coat off and he checked her pockets. Then he checked her body, removing her belt and throwing it to the ground. "Just in case you have anything you can use as a weapon, Karen," he said before handing her coat back.

Karen said nothing; again a man hadn't checked her that carefully, preferring to rub his hands over her breasts and bottom. While all the time her ankle knife remained unnoticed but absolutely deadly in the right hands.

It was another four hours before they arrived at a road. Stewart had called on his mobile telephone around half an hour before and already a white van was parked waiting for them. A man climbed out when he saw them coming. He walked over, looked at Karen then grinned.

"This is good, very good," he said, at the same time removing two plastic tie wraps from his pocket. "Take her coat off and tie her hands behind her back with these," he continued, handing the ties to Stewart. "Then put her in the back of the van."

Soon Karen was sitting on the floor in the back of the van. "Can I have my coat back, I'm cold?" she asked before they shut the door. Stewart threw it in over her and then slammed the door.

"I'll be off then, a car's on its way for you three," Asham said.

"Where's our money?" Stewart asked.

"Oh! Yes, I nearly forgot, one minute," Asham replied, running to the driver's side of the van.

The men stood in a group; two were already lighting cigarettes when Asham suddenly came round the far side of the van, a huge grin on his face. He was holding a similar assault rifle as the men. Seconds later it came to life as he sprayed them with a full magazine of bullets. They had no chance and were dead before they hit the ground. He walked over to them, kicking each one, then satisfied they were dead he sauntered back to the van, threw the gun into the passenger well and climbed in, before starting the engine.

Karen sat quietly until the vehicle moved off; she'd already formed a plan and was hoping no one was going to join her in the back. When she'd heard the gunfire and although she couldn't see what had happened, she'd suspected the driver of the van had killed the men dressed as soldiers. Now, hoping she was right, and it was just her and the driver, she'd every intention of escaping long before he arrived at their destination.

The back of the van was only lit by a very small skylight just above the back doors, but once she'd got used to the gloom it was enough for her to see by. She shuffled around and ended up kneeling down with her boots hard against the van side. Leaning back she was able to pull one trouser leg up, exposing the knife in its sheaf. Gripping the knife in one hand she pulled it out of the sheaf before twisting the blade around in-between her wrists. Now it was a simple matter of applying pressure on the nylon tie wraps with the sharp blade to cut through. She rubbed her hands to regain circulation and replaced the knife in its sheaf. Then she put on the big coat and her gloves, still stuffed inside a pocket where she left them when she'd taken her coat off at the van. The back door of the van was of a modern design and had an inner handle. Hoping it wasn't locked from outside, Karen pulled the handle down. It wasn't and the door swung open. They were still on the moor road and she crouched holding the door, waiting for the van to slow sufficiently that she could jump out without injuring herself. The opportunity soon came at a particularly hard right bend. Karen jumped, rolling over and over on the road. Then she was up and ran onto the moor, slowing down only because of short bracken. After a good ten minutes of running she stopped, at the same time holding her stomach and bending nearly double with a stitch. She looked around and saw a small culvert with water running at the bottom. Not hesitating she jumped down, crouching low, with just her head looking over in the direction she'd come. There were no signs of life, it would seem either the driver didn't know she'd escaped, or hadn't any idea at what point she'd jumped out.

However, Karen was not complacent, she was all too aware that he had a gun, and if she returned to the road for a lift, or help, she risked other people's lives, if he came back and found them with her.

With no map, no communication or food she knew she must still move on. Deciding to now keep parallel with the road she climbed out from the ditch and began to walk. The terrain was up and down, sometimes she could see the road far in the distance, other times she'd not see it at all. The moor was particularly boggy, hard going and more than once she fell flat on her face trying to drag her boots from the soft slurpy bog that would grip her foot until the last moment and then suddenly release, sending her flying. She decided this must be the beginning of the wetlands everyone talked about as it was so hard going. The mud was a mixture of black sludge and rotting vegetation. Karen was filthy and unrecognisable. After forty minutes more walking and convinced now she had gone far enough that the driver could not follow with the way he was dressed, she found a relatively dry spot and settled down to rest. However, it worried her about where the soldiers, who'd taken her initially, had come from. Did the driver of the van, have access to others, if so would he send more soldiers to look for her? Then what of the two soldiers with her, would they realise something was wrong and call the camp? Whatever happened she'd have a dilemma, not knowing who to trust. With that in mind, she decided to do as she had done in the Lebanon. That was to treat everyone as the enemy and make her own way back to the camp, and hopefully safety.

However, Karen felt so cold; in fact she'd begun to shake uncontrollably. Even the clothes inside her big trench coat were wet, and she felt very down. In her mind she'd failed the test they'd set her, lost her soldiers, although perhaps saved their lives, and now her own life was in the balance, unless she could find her way back. She needed sleep, if only for an hour, but if they were out looking for her, they would almost certainly use imaging equipment. Imaging and portable cameras were now part of any search and in the right hands a camera was able to locate a person by the heat they gave off, similar to what police helicopters used when they were chasing criminals. If she didn't hide herself from such an instrument, and if the man from the van had brought others in, she'd have little chance of staying undetected. She pulled her wet coat up tight around her body, with the collar high and her baseball cap down hard on her head, so not even the tiniest bit of her skin was exposed. Happy she'd done her best to hide her heat signature, she began to close her eyes and was soon drifting into sleep.

In the distance a helicopter was following a grid search pattern. Inside Canadian Commandos, already on a training exercise, had been brought in to help with a search of the moor. They were sat on the floor of the helicopter with its open sides allowing their feet to rest on the skids. All had binoculars studying the terrain.

Sitting alongside the pilot a soldier was watching a monitor carefully. This monitor was specifically designed to display different temperatures fed from an infrared camera fitted at the front of the helicopter. The screen was very flat; nothing was showing up, apart from the odd heat spot of a rabbit stirring. He stretched, took his eyes off the screen for a second then looked back. Did he see a flash of a larger image then?

"Turn fifteen degrees north," he called to the pilot.

The helicopter turned.

Again he studied the image, and then he saw it again and grinned. This time he was going to see just what it was, and turned up the sensing equipment to maximum. Now the rabbits stood out like light bulbs, even down to a mouse. But of course he wasn't looking at those, more the larger image he'd seen a glimmer of earlier.

"Son of a bitch, I don't believe it," he shouted.

The Captain came closer to see what he was talking about.

"Look, Captain, I think it's someone who's blocking their heat pattern, or a dead animal, but I don't think it's an animal. Turn five degrees west," he again called to the pilot, "then slow down and I mean slow down."

The helicopter banked and slowed as the operator watched.

"Yes I'm certain it's no animal, it's human. This must be our missing soldier, trying to remain hidden, as most of the heat is purposely being blanked, probably by wet clothing, two hundred metres dead ahead."

The Captain didn't comment. It could also mean the soldier was already dead, and all he could see was what little body heat was left.

The helicopter began to descend, the Commandos piling out spreading wide, their guns primed and ready. Moving forward they found the source of the weak heat. Karen was still sat where she'd stopped, her big coat pulled round her, hat pulled down low over her face. She didn't really notice two soldiers at her side, or their medic joining them.

He glanced up at the Captain. "What's the soldier's Christian name?"

"Her name's Karen."

"Karen… Karen… Wake up love, it's time for you to go home now," he shouted into her ear, at the same time gently shaking her.

She opened her eyes, at first disorientated, not knowing

where she was. Then it all suddenly came back to her. She panicked thinking it was the people that had snatched her, then she saw the insignias on their combat clothes.

"Hi, I'm Lieutenant Harris," she said weakly. "I was just having a rest. I'm a little tired; I don't suppose you could give me a lift back to the camp?"

He smiled. It was obvious she was in a very bad condition and would not have been able to travel much further without help, but she was lucid and that was a good sign.

"That's why we are here, Lieutenant, to take you back to camp. Besides, you've got two very fit Commandos waiting to give you a lift?"

Seconds later they were either side of her and helping her to stand. She felt cold, light-headed; her legs didn't seem to want to work.

The medic looked at Karen; she could hardly keep her eyes open. There was no way she'd be able to walk over the bog to the helicopter. "The girl's at the end of her endurance, we carry her, link arms," he told them.

Within five minutes she was in the helicopter, a thermal blanket wrapped round her, the medic urging her to drink hot sweet tea from a plastic cup. Soon with all the Commandos aboard, the helicopter lifted off.

By now Karen had begun to come round, the hot drink making a big difference.

"Lieutenant, I'm Captain Starkey, Canadian SAR, how are you feeling?"

She looked at this very good-looking and well built Captain. "I'm fine thank you." Then she frowned. "What am I doing in Canada?"

He laughed, so did some of the others.

"You're not in Canada. We were on a NATO training exercise as part of their search and rescue teams. We were asked to help look for you. We carry heat-seeking cameras so we were ideal. That's always providing the person being searched for doesn't deliberately try to hide from such equipment."

She grinned. "Well I didn't do a very good job, after all you found me."

"Don't you believe it, Lieutenant, you hid very well and we wouldn't under normal combat conditions have taken a second glance. This search was exceptional, as we were looking for even the slightest heat source; it was suspected the signal might be very weak, if you'd met with an accident for instance."

"You mean if I was dead?" she added quietly.

"Yes, if you were dead as well I'm afraid."

"How did you know where to look for me?"

"We didn't. The two soldiers you were with joined up with others and said you'd gone missing along with three other soldiers you'd captured earlier. Everyone was totally confused as to who they were, as all soldiers had been accounted for on the moor. Then three men, dressed as soldiers, were found at the side of the moor road. They'd been shot. Roadblocks were set up for miles around by order of a General Ross. A man in a white van stopped short of one of the road blocks and tried to make a run for it. He was caught easily and his van searched. They found the gun that they think was used to kill the men and also two tie wraps cut and loose in the back of the van. It was then the search and rescue teams were called in. Everyone was convinced you'd managed to escape somehow, and were out on the moor hiding. What was confusing was why did you leave the two soldiers you were with originally?"

She shrugged. "The men had guns, with live ammunition, where we had empty ones. They threatened to kill the two soldiers if I refused to go with them. But they were not very professional. They searched me and missed my ankle knife, so after I was bundled in the van with my wrists tied, I just got it out and escaped. Mind you that part of the moor is pretty bad, it took a lot out of me to get far enough away."

One of the Commandos offered her a biscuit, which she took gratefully. Now with Karen much more alert, some of the Commandos were ribbing her, asking if it really was a real girl under all the mud and dirt.

"Of course I'm a girl," she replied indignantly. "Tell you what, are you staying at the camp tonight?"

"We are, because of the Remembrance Parade tomorrow, then we move on to NATO headquarters to begin a major exercise. Why do you want to know?" the Captain asked.

"I'll be in the Social Club later tonight and I would like to buy you all a drink, besides prove to you I'm really a girl."

Then she suddenly had a thought. "That's if General Ross will give me some money, otherwise I might have to sell my body."

One of the Commandos grinned. "Forget the body bit, Lieutenant, the way you look no one would buy you. Besides, we've never had a British Lieutenant offer to buy the drinks, or want to for that matter. You're more than welcome to join us tonight and we'll buy the drinks if you're out of cash. What do you say lads?"

They all wholeheartedly agreed, with the Captain adding a little caution as Karen would need to go to the medical centre and be cleared as fit to go to the club first.

25

General Ross had arrived at the camp minutes earlier and was walking up to the main building when the colonel came out through the main door.

"General, you're just in time. Would you like to join me in the Land Rover, apparently Karen's due to land in five minutes?" the Colonel asked.

"You've found her then, is she all right?"

"Yes, the Canadian search and rescue found her. They were extremely lucky to do so; she'd followed standard orders and cloaked herself from heat-seeking equipment. They said the signal was so weak they at first believed she was dead. Anyway the pilot reported she was very cold and close to hypothermia, but has pulled round while on the helicopter."

The General lit a cigarette as they drove across the parade ground just as a helicopter came down. This girl never ceased to amaze him with her resilience.

Karen climbed out and stood a little unsteadily in front of them. They both wanted to laugh, but refrained. The girl was looking at them from under her baseball cap with a face streaked in mud. Her clothes were absolutely filthy, even her boots caked in mud.

"Are you all right, Lieutenant?" the Colonel asked.

"A little tired, Sir, and I could do with some food, I've had nothing, besides a biscuit, since yesterday," she replied then grinned. "But the best part is I got myself an escort of real live Canadian Commandos to bring me back. I hope that it was in order to accept a lift, or should I have completed the exercise on foot?"

The Colonel was relieved she was in good spirits. "Under the circumstances I ordered the exercise aborted a good time ago. I also believe we could convince the mess to rustle up some food for you, Lieutenant, after all you deserve it. But you're in the army and normally, before anything, you should give your report. However, you are a little bedraggled and I wouldn't want you dirtying my carpet. How about I have you run over to your room, get yourself a shower, change into something more acceptable then come back and join the General and myself? Say thirty minutes?"

"Yes, Sir, that sounds fantastic."

"Lieutenant Harris?" a voice came from behind.

She turned to see who'd called her, and then there was a flash of light.

"Thank you, this is a brilliant shot for the camp paper," a young soldier commented looking at the result on his viewer.

"You're dead if you print that," she said. "My street cred will be on the floor, I'll never live it down."

The soldier grinned. "Maybe, Lieutenant, but it'll be the photo of the year. I'm not sure anyone's come off the moor in such a spectacular fashion before."

Karen just smiled and climbed into a waiting Land Rover. Going directly to the shower room she stood dumfounded looking at herself in the mirror. No wonder the Commandos all ribbed her and the soldier wanted a photo, she couldn't even recognise the person stood there. Never in all her life had she been so dirty. However, after ten minutes under the shower, her hair washed and dried; with clean clothes on she looked her normal self again.

"Take a seat, Karen, the General said as she entered the Colonel's office thirty minutes later. Only the General was in the office and he'd walked over to a side-table after asking her to sit down.

"Would you like your coffee topped up with a tot of brandy?" the General asked.

"Yes please, that would be great."

He poured a little in and took the chair by the side of her, bringing also a large plate of buffet items for her to eat. She thanked him and tucked into the sandwiches.

"Both Sir Peter and myself were concerned to find you'd

been sent out from the camp without protection. Our orders were specific in that you should be protected at all times. Then to find out another attempt to abduct you had happened, I was annoyed I can tell you."

Karen sighed. "It was my fault I suppose, allowing the other soldiers we thought we'd captured to come with us. After all it seemed a bit strange them saying the Sergeant had told them to join up with us if they got captured. But I couldn't understand how they found us so quickly, besides stopping when we did, so I was convinced they had a spotter and I'd end up with a whole army to hide."

"I can understand your dilemma, Karen, after all you'd never been on an exercise like that before, and my enquiries found out you'd not even been given the rules of engagement. In those rules it clearly states what to do with captured soldiers; normally they hand over their dog tags and leave the exercise. The fortunate thing was, if you had worked to those rules, then things could have been very different."

"Why do you say that?" she asked.

"Because, Karen, if they couldn't have split you from the other soldiers then they'd have killed them for certain."

"I suppose you're right there, so my naivety saved their lives. It doesn't bear well for me does it?"

He leaned forward. "Listen, Karen, stop knocking yourself it wasn't naivety not knowing what to do with prisoners in an exercise, you could hardly have shot them dead, and besides no one realised that there would be a possibility that you'd capture soldiers, after all you were the ones everyone was pursuing, you weren't the pursuer. Remember that you're only just eighteen; the pressures on you have been enormous. Sir Peter and I are really very proud of what you've achieved. The reports from your instructors couldn't be better. Unfortunately we're going to have to cut short the planned training. Believe me this is something I didn't want to happen."

Karen had suddenly gone cold inside, she knew it was going to happen sometime, but she'd hyped herself up to ignore it and concentrate on her fitness and training. "When do I go then?" she asked meekly.

"You're going in with Special Forces very early Monday morning. You'll be collected tomorrow at midday, flown to a military airport and then onto Cyprus. From there you'll be flown to a carrier currently steaming to a point five miles off the Lebanese coast. I know it's a rush and you'll be literally jumping from one means of transport to another, but there is no option. En route you'll be briefed in the operation and also meet the Captain in charge of the Special Forces."

She looked down. "It doesn't give me much time to say goodbye to the friends I've made here, or even talk to mum and dad."

"It's worse than that, Karen, you mustn't tell anyone you're going, particularly your parents. We cannot risk another attempt to snatch you. The first time anyone here will know you're leaving this camp will be when your helicopter is waiting on the tarmac. As no one has an inkling why you are here they will think nothing of it, after all you trained, did an exercise on the moor and left. The timing is perfect. But until the moment you climb on that helicopter, there are to be no more risks taken with your life, you will be guarded day and night with armed MPs."

"What if Gareth or Terry ask me what happened?"

"They won't, Karen. They are currently on an extended debrief. They will not be around the camp until you're gone."

"What about the MPs being with me all the time, won't it cause people to talk?"

"Maybe, but it can't be helped. This is the second time an attempt has been made to abduct you. Besides, we're only talking of today and tomorrow and most of that time you'll be in bed so don't worry too much as to what anyone says. Anyway, you must be tired, go and get some sleep and above all don't worry, this time next week you'll be home and hopefully the girls too."

She never said anything. In fact what was there to say? It was a place she really didn't want to go back to, but Saeed was making her life hell, not knowing when another of his people would try to take her, so she could see no option but to go and sort him out herself.

"You're very quiet, Karen."

"I'm, like you said, just tired General. It's been a hard week and the time on the moor, apart from the really miserable weather, made me realise just how easy it is for Saeed's people to find me, no matter where I am."

"Yes, that concerned me as well. But when you make it known in the underworld that a great deal of money is on offer, it brings out the opportunists who think it's easy money. Two groups have found it isn't when you're up against a girl who is streetwise and very capable of looking after herself."

Karen smiled. "It's nice of you to have confidence in me, but I live on a knife's edge, relying more on luck than real planning and one day my luck will run out. That, General, terrifies me."

He leaned back in his chair. "Tell me, Karen, have you considered joining the army? I agree you may have reservations, but you would be safe in the army and I believe it's a life that would suit you."

She sipped her coffee and looked towards him. "You know when I was on the moor, trying to work out how I was going to get off, I really thought about that. But I have a problem."

"What is that?"

"I'd enter at the bottom. Don't get me wrong, it's the right thing to do, but I feel a tiny bit more important as a Lieutenant. I get respect, apart from some Commandos ribbing me as to how I looked, but even then they had respect for the rank. I wouldn't want to lose that, besides with my luck I'd probably meet some of the troops from here, and that would take some explaining."

"I can understand your concerns, Karen. Let me think about it and perhaps when you return we'll talk further. But I'm keeping you, and you really do need to get some sleep."

As she stood to leave the Colonel entered the room, stopping her before she left. "I'd like you to join us for dinner tonight in the Officer's Club, Karen. I know you've been using the normal dining room over the week, but you are an officer and tonight it is a regimental dinner with Remembrance Day tomorrow and an important event in our calendar. It will be full-dress uniform."

"Thank you Colonel, I'd like that very much. Would it be all right if I left around half ten? The Commandos who found me on the moor, I promised to buy them a drink. With me going sooner than I thought I don't want to let them down. Besides," she added with a grin, "I'm determined to prove to them there actually was a very feminine girl under all the mud and not some tomboy."

He smiled. "That will be perfectly in order; dinner runs from seven until nine so you will have plenty of time."

"There is one other tiny problem," she said shyly.

"And that is?"

"I'm completely broke, the money dad gave me to come with is gone. I was going to ask if there was any way I could borrow some money, otherwise I couldn't actually afford to buy them the promised drink tonight."

He sighed. "Why didn't you say something? We don't expect you to use your pocket money. I'll have the Personnel Officer advance you fifty pounds, would that be enough?"

"Fifty, god, I don't want that much, I'm not working and would struggle to pay it back. I was thinking of twenty at the most, dad would help me out with that much, but he'd go berserk if I asked him for fifty."

They both laughed.

"Karen," the General began. "You're a Lieutenant, temporary I grant you, but you've signed up officially in the army all the same. This means you're earning twenty eight thousand pounds a year, that's at least five hundred pounds a week. I think personnel will be able to advance you fifty pounds without too much of a problem."

"Oh… I didn't know. But will that mean, because I'm leaving early I'll miss a week's pay?"

The General and Colonel looked at each other.

"She's quick, Colonel, I'll give her that."

"She is, so what do you think? Should we give her a month's employment?"

"I think so; otherwise we won't hear the end of this lost week's pay."

Karen thanked them and left. However, outside waiting for her were two MPs, both over six foot and well built.

"Hi, are you my protection?" she asked with a smile.

"We are, Lieutenant, but we need your cooperation. This is a military close protection order from the very top. You're also subject to the same order. You go nowhere unless we're with you, so no sneaking out of the back, otherwise when we find you, for your own protection, we'll lock you up. If anyone is walking with you, be it to the Officer's Club or the Social Club they will be searched by us. If any attempt is made on your life, you hit the ground and remain there until we tell you to move."

"God, that's a bit over the top. You don't come into the showers and my bedroom, do you?" she asked trying to lighten the conversation.

However the MP who was giving her the do's and don'ts, didn't seem amused. "We don't stay in the room once you're inside, but before we allow you in we will check the room, then MPs will be stationed outside the room, until you're ready to leave."

"Okay, I understand and I won't be doing anything foolish I can assure you. But I'd like to return to my room now for some sleep."

He nodded and they walked alongside her back to her room. She waited outside as instructed until told she could go in. Then once inside she threw her clothes off and climbed into bed. The MPs were professional, not wanting to be overfriendly, taking their job very seriously. Karen, for the first time since coming home, felt very safe.

26

Saeed was drumming his fingers on the side of a table listening to his agent Pat in London, trying to explain what had gone wrong.

"How in hell can the idiots over there have her twice and she escapes?"

"You tell me, Saeed, but that's what's happened."

"So where's Karen now?"

"She's back in the camp."

"What's the chances of snatching her again?"

"That's why I'm ringing; I think it can be done later next week. There's an end of training do in the Social Club. Basically everyone gets drunk and security is lax. If the girl just collapses everyone will think she's drunk too much and take her to her room to sleep it off."

"So what's the point?" Saeed asked, getting frustrated that Pat wasn't coming to it.

"The girl won't be drunk, she'll be drugged. A laundry van leaves at twelve every night, which an associate of mine drives. He and a friend will take her out the back way; the rest of the women will still be in the club so no one will know she's gone."

"I don't know, it's a bit close to the last abortive attempt, they are bound to be on their guard with her now."

"Maybe, maybe not. This is the army, and they'll be convinced she's absolutely safe on the camp itself."

"You have a point, they could have their guard down, and she'll certainly believe she's safe in the camp. What time will you collect her?"

"He's not told me that, just asked me to arrange for her to be collected ten miles south of the camp. What do you think?"

"Well we've nothing to lose, Pat. Make the arrangements, if he succeeds all well and good, if he doesn't, well it was a long shot and there'll be other opportunities."

check, the blood results after you came off the moor showed a few problems. The doctor thinks it was possibly a build-up of toxins in your body, with lack of food and exhaustion, so he's asked to see you. But you know what they're like, they worry about everything? After your tests, they will brief you on Angela's illness and the symptoms you need to look for. I've decided on you knowing this as well as the medic in the group, it's possible the girl might have been very badly abused and not trust men in any respect."

The car drew up at the military hospital and they went inside. Immediately Karen was shown to a small room, her blood was taken besides the normal tests of blood pressure, breathing and urine. Ten minutes later she was sat with another doctor who went through Angela's problems. Then Karen was back with her own doctor.

"You test out fine, Karen, in fact surprisingly good. Your body has put itself back to normal very quickly. I do however have a few concerns as to your ability to cope with going back so soon. I'm going to give you some tablets to take if you begin to feel tension and stress. Don't use them for nothing, they will slow your reactions down and put you at risk, but I think it's essential that you have them just in case."

She looked at him for a moment then smiled. "There was nothing wrong with my blood, taken at the training camp, was there, doctor?"

He smiled. "You're very astute, Karen, but you're right, although it was good to confirm you are in peak physical condition. I really wanted to talk to you about your possible mental state and give you the appropriate tablets without anyone else knowing. This is a high risk operation and the last thing we want is for any of the team not having confidence in your abilities. Use them only if you feel you can't cope. Remember though like any drug that suppresses, it can cloud your judgement and ability to operate rationally."

"Thank you for doing that for me, doctor, you could be right, but I hope not. Are they the same as I had from my own doctor?"

"No, these are very different. They are a new drug, with little or no side effects and the body won't begin to crave for more, so they can be used as required to calm you."

She sighed. "Well I hope I don't need them, I've been able to put it all to the back of my mind over the last week."

He stood and shook her hand. "Good luck, Karen, let's hope everything goes as planned and the girls including yourself are back safely very soon."

An hour's flight landed them on HMS Invincible. Karen was impressed with the size of the ship when they landed, and just how busy it was on the deck. Two MPs were waiting for her and she was accompanied to the galley for an early breakfast. Already the galley was half full, even at this time, as crew came off watch. Following breakfast she was taken to the stores and given her clothes. Her undergarments were army style t-shirt with knickers. Her uniform a close fitting jacket and pants in black, with a number of useful pockets. On top of this she fastened her bulletproof sleeveless jacket, then slipped on light boots. But the boots, although nothing like the normal army heavy issue, were steel capped and waterproof. Her leather waist belt was already fitted with a handgun holster and GPS unit in a pouch with an ammunition belt fitted diagonally across her chest attached front and back to the waist belt. This belt was able to accommodate three grenades and three spare clips for an AK47 gun. She finished off her combat clothes with a black baseball cap. On each arm and her cap was a small Union Jack with the word 'army' below. The word Lieutenant was in black on a grey background attached to one of her breast pockets. All the insignias were attached by Velcro allowing, if necessary, that they could be removed. Her backpack was already filled with a change of underclothes, jumper and a pack of personal items such as toothbrush, comb etc. Added to this were her emergency rations, spare ammunition and finally she was handed and signed for the guns and grenades.

The Armaments Officer who handed her the grenades laid them out in front of her. "You have two types Lieutenant. The first two are six second, stun and blast. They send hundreds of tiny shrapnel type bullets out. Nothing will survive, even you, if you don't get out of the way. This one is your last resort as you requested. As you can see, unlike the others it's coloured red. The delay time is less than a second, not long enough for anyone to take it from you. Its normal use is booby traps, with trip wire attached. So you can understand a delay would be pointless. It has approx. five metres by five kill area, going out to ten metres for stun. Use it and you're dead, so it's last resort as I said."

She thanked him and clipped the six second grenades in the top pouches with her final solution in the bottom. Once inside the changing room she stood and looked at herself, after finally winding her hair up and trapping it under her baseball cap. To her everything was as she'd requested, which gave her confidence the same as she had last time she was in the Lebanon. Her only problem, which she could never hide, was her slim figure and face, making her always think people believed she'd dressed up for a photo shoot, rather than being a formidable adversary.

Making her way through the maze of corridors, some of the sailors glanced at her, then took another look, before saluting her when they realised she was a Lieutenant. Eventually she came up on deck.

Sir Peter watched her approach, he felt sad to see such a young girl dressed the way she was with the gun slung over her shoulder and that deadly grenade in the pouch on her chest. He prayed she'd not have to use it, this was a very special girl and it would be a disaster to lose her.

"This is it, Karen, they're waiting for you. Good luck and please don't take too many risks. I want to see you come back with the girls. I don't want to lose any one of you," he said when she was close enough to hear.

"I'll do my best, Peter."

"I know you will, Karen. But before you go I have to ask you once more. Are you certain you want to do this? Even at this stage we would understand if you felt we were pushing you into something you didn't want to do. This is your life, your future you're risking; it should never be taken lightly."

She looked away, glancing at the three Apache helicopters,

their rotors turning slowly, and through an open door of one she could see troops already aboard.

Then she looked back at him and sighed. "It isn't a question of me not being scared of having to go back, I really am, Peter. But somehow this nightmare has to be finished one way or another. Saeed's mother believes I walk with the Angel of Death. After what I've seen, you begin to believe it. But if I don't make it back, it won't be because I didn't try. It'll be because my luck finally ran out, and the Angel came for me."

She then pulled a letter from her pocket. "I know you have my will, for what use it is, as I've nothing anyway. But if I don't come back, will you see mum and dad get this? I've just tried to explain why I had to go, told them I love them so very much and included some photos taken of me last night. I have nothing else to give."

He put his arms round her and pulled her close. "I'll keep your letter, Karen, and give it you back when you return," he whispered. Then he kissed her on either cheek. "Take care, whatever you think, God is with you in this, believe me?"

She gave him a weak smile, and then walked over to the helicopter. They helped her in and it rose quickly, turning towards the mainland.

Sir Peter didn't move until he could no longer see the helicopters. He had a feeling this might be the last time he'd see Karen, but he hoped not, after all she'd been through and what was waiting for her, she didn't deserve to die.

29

Fifteen minutes after her conversation with Sir Peter the three attack helicopters were sweeping low and fast over the water towards the coast. As they crossed onto land, and moved further inland, Karen became more apprehensive. To be back here so soon with the memories of last time still fresh in her mind frightened her. The men around her seemed so confident, but she knew different. They were in a country where rules of engagement went out of the window. It was every man for himself indifferent of the consequences. She gripped her gun even tighter as the air of expectation among the soldiers in the cabin rose.

The pilot turned round and shouted to the Captain to come forward.

"What is it?" he asked.

"We're being tracked by radar, Sir. Remember we're not transmitting our identity and we don't know if this radar is controlled by hostile forces. I might have to take urgent avoidance manoeuvres. Can you have your men braced for possible impact?"

The Captain went back to his seat. "Brace for impact men. Precautionary, we're being tracked by radar."

Karen went cold, this very thing happened last time and she knew what could happen.

However, the soldier at her side nudged her. "Don't worry, this often happens. These helicopters are well protected and can avoid missiles with ease."

"I've heard that before," she said without much belief in his words. "Last time we were hit and went down."

He looked at her. "You've been in one that's gone down?"

"Oh yes, we were hit and in the same bloody country."

The solder shouted to his mates. "Did you hear that, the Lieutenant's been here before."

"Quiet soldier," the Captain shouted. "Just follow orders

and brace for possible impact."

Suddenly a bleeper began. "We have hostile incoming," the pilot shouted.

"Fuck, they've detected us, now we'll have some fun," the soldier who'd been talking to Karen muttered.

She never said a word, inside her stomach was churning, the fear of being back, the repeat of what happened last time. Karen gripped her gun that much tighter, closing her eyes trying to block the constant bleeping of the missile detection from her mind. Deep down Karen knew she should never have come, now she was back and so too was the Angel of Death.

The helicopter was being thrown about like some puppet on a string, then all of a sudden there was silence.

"See, like I said, a piece of cake," the soldier commented at her side.

Then the alarm sounded again. Seconds later came the explosion, throwing the helicopter into a spin, plunging it down towards the ground. But again at the last moment the pilot pulled it out. This time the soldier at her side said nothing. Karen was terrified, her head spinning, the explosion still ringing in her ears. But there was little time to relax as yet again the bleeper began. The helicopter banked sharply then began sending out chaff to confuse the missile as they raced along less than fifty metres from the ground. Even above all the noise she could hear the scream of the missile, followed by an explosion, so close the helicopter veered sideways with the blast. The alarm was sounding once again, but this time the missile was wide of its mark. They carried on without further incident, everyone beginning to relax hoping they were past the defences. The pilot turned to the Captain and shouted into his ear.

"They've lost us on radar tracking; you can relax for the time being, ETA five minutes."

He moved to the back. "Right gentlemen and lady, we land in five minutes. This is hostile territory so don't hang about, the helicopter will be down for only one minute. Shaun, Carl and Eric protect the group. Jason and Paul protect the Lieutenant."

The helicopters were slowing; everyone was checking their

guns, pulling their backpacks on as the helicopters landed gently on open terrain. The troop spilled out, running to the protection of shrub-like trees to one side of the landing area. Three of the soldiers broke away from the main group and settled a short distance away scanning the area with powerful night vision glasses. Karen followed the main group, a soldier to either side of her, and within seconds they'd stopped on the edge of the scrub area, all down on one knee circling the Captain and Karen. In the distance further down the valley were the lights of the village where Saeed's house was. They waited for the helicopters to leave then the Captain gave the order to move.

Everyone did one final check of their weapons and they set off at a brisk pace. Already three men were well ahead of the main group with three well behind in a classic protection of the main group position. After forty minutes of nonstop marching they entered the outskirts of the village. It was dark, with the majority of the buildings shuttered up for the night, very few lights to be seen inside the houses. Karen took them past the church she'd prayed in, down two more streets and into the cul-de-sac of Saeed's house.

She grasped the Captain's arm. "I'll show you how to get in; there's a bit of a knack."

He nodded and pointed to two soldiers to go with her. Once in the courtyard many now followed, fanning out and settling in places that afforded hiding. Karen moved onto the front door and slipped the latch using the same method she had watched Saeed use, and done herself once - it opened silently. Then she, the Captain and two others entered the house.

The place was in darkness, even the kitchen was closed up for the night. Moving up the stairs Karen took them to an end room, then looked back as she stopped at the door. "This is where Saeed's mother sleeps."

They never replied but moved Karen from the door and in seconds were inside. Saeed's mother had no chance and before the light was on she was being held by two soldiers. They dragged her out from the bed and forced her to sit down on a chair in front of an old dressing table, demanding she place her hands flat on the table.

"The girls Saeed took, where are they?" the Captain demanded.

Saeed's mother grinned showing a row of bad and broken teeth. "Gone, all sold," she lied.

"Then we want names, addresses," he demanded.

She shrugged. "How do I know, I'm just his mother. What he does with girls, where they go you'll have to ask him."

Karen entered the room and walked up to her. The old women's face changed from one of confidence to a look of sheer terror. She raised a hand pointing at Karen. "Get that thing out of my house," she screamed, before placing her hand back on the table.

But Karen ignored the comment and came closer, talking in French. *"You're still frightened of me are you? That is good because you have reason to be. I'm not like these men, as you know? It's already believed by your people that I'm a killer, which I suppose is true. You will tell me where each of the six girls have gone, otherwise, I'll slit your throat."*

None of the soldiers understood what she'd said to the woman except they could all see the real fear this woman had with Karen standing there. The Captain began to wonder just what had really gone on in this house between this girl and the occupants to have the woman so frightened.

However, Saeed's mother had relaxed a little. "I know you Karen Marshall, you're just talk. You'll get nothing out of me. My Saeed is looking for you and believe me he will find you, then you'll wish you never lived," she said with confidence in English.

"You know the first time I entered this house your Saeed told me just how important you are to him. Threatened me with all sorts if I as much as touched you. The bastard should be dead, for some reason he's still alive. Next time he won't be that lucky, if I see him again," Karen replied in French so the others in the room didn't know what she'd said.

"Ha! You think he's afraid of you? My Saeed has dealt with your sort for a long time. Go home little girl before he returns, otherwise it will be you who's dead."

The Captain was beginning to get the gist of this one-sided conversation with Saeed's mother talking in English and Karen in

French. It was becoming obvious now why this girl was with them. She hadn't just been here before, she knew the trafficker very well by the sound of it. However, even he wasn't prepared for what was about to happen.

Karen sighed. "I don't have time for this shit," she said reaching down to her ankle and pulling the knife out of its holder. Suddenly without warning she lifted the knife and came down directly through the woman's right hand, the tip of the blade ending up in the top of the dressing table. The woman screamed in pain.

"That's just for starters. I want names and addresses for every girl," Karen shouted in her ear.

The Captain and both soldiers looked on in horror. Karen was so quick they had no chance to stop her.

"What the hell…" the Captain began.

Karen swung round and glared at the Captain. "Keep out of it; you heard her and her stupid threats. Well welcome to the world of trafficking, a world where violence is all they understand. But have no doubt I will find where the girls are, even if I have to cut her up into pieces," she shouted at him. Then she turned back to Saeed's mother and grabbed her hair yanking her head back. She'd already pulled the knife out of the woman's hand, and was now holding it millimetres from the woman's eyes.

"Talk or I'll use this knife to dig out one of your eyes."

The woman had no doubt in her mind Karen would do just that, only now understanding how she'd the nerve to gun down so many of Saeed's friends. But she was also frightened of her son, and what he'd do if he found out she'd told Karen anything. However, the girl who was ill was still upstairs and a search would easily find her. So she decided to give them her information and claim she knew nothing of the rest.

"There's a girl in your old room, she had an offer but he wouldn't take her till she was fit. She's ill and the doctor said he could do nothing, she's dying. We were going to take her to the desert and leave her. But you can have her, she's of no value," Saeed's mother answered as if throwing Karen a scrap.

Karen smiled. "So at last we're getting somewhere. Is she

secured with an ankle chain?"

Saeed's mother shook her head. "There's no need for one, she's too ill and going nowhere."

Karen turned to the Captain. "I know where Angela is, Captain, she's here. Leave a guard with the woman and we'll go and find her."

"The house has been searched, Lieutenant, while you've been in here. There's no one but the old woman," he replied.

She grinned. "Come on, I'll show you a room with no obvious door, I told you these people are very good, you have to know their secrets. But I suspect we will need the medic."

He called for the medic over the radio while he and Karen ran up the next flight of stairs and along a corridor she knew well.

She turned and looked at him. "Now watch this."

Grabbing what looked like an ordinary light switch's outer casing, she swung it open. Behind was another hidden switch. Pressing it, the blank wall in front of them slid open revealing a door behind.

"That's clever, how did you find that?" he asked.

"By chance, this was where they kept me. Saeed had taken me down for the afternoon to sit outside. When we came back up, his mother must have shut it, so he just opened the switch and pressed this button. Probably never thought I'd ever be a threat and so wasn't bothered that I saw it."

Karen turned the key still in the lock and pushed the door open, stopping for a moment before she entered; the memories of her time in here came back. But she didn't dwell on them when she saw someone lying on the bed. She knelt down recognising Angela immediately.

"Angela..." she whispered in her ear, "wake up, it's Karen, I've come to take you home."

The girl stirred, and opened her eyes staring at her for a moment. "Karen, is it really you? I'm not dreaming am I?"

Karen laughed. "No, you're not dreaming it really is me."

She sat up, pulling the blanket around her naked body. "Would you pass me my clothes?" she asked.

Karen swung her gun back over her shoulder and went over

to the chair grabbing the thin shirt and knickers for Angela, the same type she'd had to wear, returning to the bed and handing them to her.

Angela was already sitting on the side of the bed; she took them from Karen then sighed. "I don't feel very well, Karen, I don't think I've the energy to come with you. But thank you from the bottom of my heart for coming to find me, I always believed you would."

"Don't worry; we knew you'd not be well, so I'm here with your own personal medical team. They'll give you an injection, then take you to the waiting helicopter."

"How did you know I'd be ill?" she asked.

"Your mum came to see me, she told me of your condition and how urgent it was for you to have an injection, besides get you home. I'd hoped it was the work of Saeed and this would be where they would bring you, so that's why I'm here."

She gave her a smile. "I'm glad they did then. Anyway I love the getup, Karen, it's dead sexy, but that isn't a real gun you're carrying, is it?"

Karen laughed. "You bet it is, beside grenades, a handgun and an ankle knife. You don't go after these bastards without protection; believe me."

"No I suppose you don't, so is that how you got out last time, by shooting your way out?"

"Sort of, but there were lots of times, before I got a gun, that I was forced to agree to do anything they wanted of me."

"I wish I could be like you. I fell to pieces virtually the first day they took me. Just accepting there was no way I could escape alone."

Karen smiled. "Well don't worry about anything. Now you're with me they won't get near you. But before the medic arrives, what happened to the other girls?"

"They had a sale, it wasn't here though, it was somewhere else. I think they were taken immediately after the sale. An old woman was looking after me, probably them as well but I don't know as we were all kept separate until the sale. Then we weren't allowed to talk, but I did manage to speak to Dawn for a couple of minutes. She told me she'd had the same done to her. The old woman always had someone with her who carried a stick that gave you electric shocks if you didn't do as they said. It was awful, Karen, they removed my body hair and that woman kept pouring oils on me. I was so ill at the sale no one wanted me, so I was to go to some brothel, but I collapsed and they brought me here. I suppose thinking it was just flu or something and I'd get over it so they could sell me later."

"Well that's all in the past now, you'll soon be home. Maybe we'll meet back in the UK?"

"We'd better, Karen, you'll at least have to come for a weekend. Saturday night we'll go out and have a great time."

"Yes I'd like that."

Then Angela looked more serious. "There's another girl, she wasn't one of the competition winners. It was terrible Karen. The old women dragged her into the room naked. She was so young and scared and just went into hysterics when they started touching her. That old woman used the electric stick on the girl. All of them stood round enjoying her body being contorted every time the stick touched her. They only stopped when I made them feel ashamed of themselves, telling them to have their fun with me rather than her. You have to find the little girl, Karen, she's so young and frightened, her mother must be beside herself."

"I'll do my best, Angela, but it won't be easy."

"I understand, god I can't even believe you've found me. But I'm really glad you did."

By then the medic had arrived and Karen stood to one side as he opened his bag and pulled out a tiny bottle full of liquid, which he filled a syringe with. Seconds later he injected Angela. After assessing her he decided Angela wouldn't be able to walk herself to the helicopter, so they opened up a stretcher.

As she was being taken out of the room she looked at Karen stood there. "Are you coming as well?"

Karen shook her head. "Not just yet, I'm going to find out where the others are. If they are still in this country I'll go and get them."

"Good luck, I hope you find them and the people who have

done this to us."

"Oh you can believe that, Angela. But this time if our paths cross I really will make sure the bastard is dead."

Coming back down the stairs the Captain stopped her. "Good work, Karen, do you want to go with the medical team and we'll finish off here? The old lady is very shocked, we've had to use our medic to stop the bleeding and calm her down."

"It's okay; I'm staying for the moment. Besides, the old hag will be playing you up. She's as tough as old boots that one and bloody good at pretending to be a frail, little old lady. She won't do that with me, I'll cut her throat if she doesn't give me the locations of the other girls."

"Yes I suspected that what's she doing, but I don't think we'll get much out of her in the state she's in."

"We'll see," she replied.

Saeed's mother looked up as Karen came back in. *"You got the child then?"* she asked in French.

"Of course, now it's time you started to remember the other girls' locations, after all you've had plenty of time to think."

She shrugged, *"I don't know. But you've got one that's enough. Besides the others are settled with their new owners."*

Karen leaned on the side of the table and looked down at her. *"I'm glad you said that."*

She frowned. *"What are you saying child?"*

Karen didn't reply at first, but took the gun from its holster on her belt and clicked the safety off. *"Well it gives me the opportunity to try out my 'loosen your mouth' techniques. So for a starter how about I give you five seconds then blast your foot, then the kneecap before beginning on the next leg. It'll be a bit painful, as Saeed found out, but at least you can sit side by side with him in wheelchairs and compare each other's injuries."*

The woman's eyes went as large as saucers. *"You wouldn't dare, Saeed would kill you."*

Karen grinned. *"You don't get it do you? I couldn't give a stuff about him. I'm not even interested in your so-called threats as to what he'd do to me. Besides, he'd look a bit stupid chasing me down the street in his wheelchair. Anyway your five seconds are up, talk or lose your foot. I prefer the latter."*

She raised the gun aiming for the woman's foot.

"I'll give you them, for what good it'll do you," she suddenly shouted in panic when she saw the gun raised.

"Shit, why can't I have a little target practice, OK then tell me?" Karen muttered with obvious disappointment.

"You're sick you are, anyway give me some paper and I'll write them down."

"Right, now we have locations, Karen, I'll call control, give them the information and ask for new orders," the Captain said after Saeed's mother had written them all down. He turned and left the room, expecting her to follow, but she didn't.

Turning to Saeed's mother, she sighed. *"Saeed's just not doing well in his profession, since I came on the scene, is he? But unfortunately it's going to get worse. You see old woman I want all the money that you've brought back for him. But don't for one moment try to kid me you got paid by cheque, gave credit or any other shit. You wouldn't have, it'd all be cash because I know your son has a real distrust of banks."*

She glared at Karen. *"You won't get a penny out of me. That money is for my son's medical treatment, caused by you."*

Karen frowned. *"Yes I admit, old woman, it was caused by me, besides I was really upset when I heard he'd actually survived. After all I'd pumped a fair amount of bullets into that fat little body of his. So I'm thinking of going down to the hospital and blowing his brains out, just to make sure he's really dead this time."*

Saeed's mother's eyes went as large as saucers. *"You will leave my son alone. He's all I have."*

Karen laughed. *"I suppose so, if you insist, how about I just blow yours out instead,"* she replied indifferently. *"After all it's the money, you or your son's life. I'm not really bothered which. Well I am really, I'd rather just put a gun to your head."*

They both fell silent, then Karen shifted position, still messing about with the handgun and pulling back the stock to arm it. *"Right I'm off. I'll not say it was good seeing you again, it wasn't. Perhaps you can put a word in for me when you answer to God. Then I'll slip over to the hospital and tell your son personally I've just blown your brains out. You see I remember once when he considered you more valuable than the money he was going to get for me. Very insistent if I hurt you in any way I could expect a good beating and then I'd be left to burn up in the desert. But it would seem you consider yourself less valuable than the money you've collected for that son of yours. He'll be really grateful for your consideration when he's still got money to pay his bills and bury you."*

Karen raised the gun to her head. Saeed's mother panicked, the girl was so matter-of-fact and actually was going through with it. *"I'll get you the money,"* she suddenly said.

"Oh..." Karen sighed. *"You're not playing fair today, this is the second time you've stopped me from using the gun. I would rather like to see if any brains came out of that head of yours, if there are any, as I suspect, they're all in your bottom."*

Saeed's mother said nothing and stood before making her way out from the bedroom and into another opposite. Inside there was a huge double bed with two wardrobes and a large chest set against the far wall. She pulled out a key from under clothes inside a drawer of an old dresser and opened the chest. Removing a black leather doctor's bag she threw it down in front of Karen. *"The money is in there. Take it and get out of my house."*

"Open it," Karen demanded.

She opened the top and Karen looked down. Inside she could clearly see bundles of notes. Not neat and tidy but in wads of mixed old notes. She bent down and pulled a bundle out flipping through to see if it was all notes and not paper.

"Thank you, old woman. I hope you'll send Saeed my regards? Tell him I'm sorry I missed him this time; perhaps next time when I pass this way, he and I can get together? Not for the sex bit, more for me to finish the job and send him to his maker."

"You are a very bad person, Karen Marshall, Saeed will hunt you down."

Karen shrugged, changing back to English. "You have it wrong old woman. It is you and your son who are the bad people round here. It isn't me who has taken young boys and girls and sold them into a life of hell. I suppose your son grew up in a loving family, played out on the street in safety. Sat round a table on birthdays to blow the candles out, maybe even received presents. You took all that away from the children who came through these doors and you have the nerve to call yourself a mother? I'm ashamed of you as a woman and you're very lucky I was brought up a Christian otherwise you would be dead now. Perhaps when your son finds out all his money has gone, he will decide to hunt me down? However, remember the hunter can also be the hunted."

Then she left the room, slamming the door shut, before going down the stairs.

Saeed's mother sat for some time until she was sure the house was empty. She was very frightened of this girl. A girl who Saeed should have just dropped off at a brothel as arranged. She had only brought disaster into their lives for the sake of a few more dollars. However, she knew there was only one man who could bring this girl to her knees, and he would pay money for information as to her whereabouts.

Shuffling down the stairs she went into the kitchen, pulling a book from a pile stacked up alongside the telephone. She opened it and went down the listings till she found what she wanted. Quickly she dialled the number. It rang out for what seemed an age - eventually it was answered by a not-too-happy person.

"I want to speak to Sirec," she demanded.

"Do you know what time it is woman, he'll go mad if I disturb him, call tomorrow."

"No you don't understand it's very urgent. Tell him..." she hesitated for a moment. "Tell him Karen is in the country and I know where she's heading."

"Wait, I'll tell him." Then the phone fell silent.

After a short while she could hear voices, someone coming down the stairs, then the handset lifted. "Sirec here, what's this about Karen?"

"Sirec, I'm Saeed's mother. She came tonight. She was with others and was heavily armed. She took all our money, but I know where she's heading."

"Tell me?" he demanded.

"I will, but we have lost everything and my son needs money to pay his bills," she replied, keeping her fingers crossed.

"I will pay his bills old woman, but I want the location

otherwise your information is worthless."

Five minutes later she replaced the handset. A smile was spreading over her face. "Let her go up against Sirec and see how she fares," she muttered aloud, then began laughing.

30

Karen and the troops were back at the helicopters. Angela had already been placed in one waiting until decisions were made as to what happened next.

The Captain and Karen were looking at the map after receiving coordinates for the addresses they had radioed back to control. Out of the three locations, two were large estates, one in a border town and the last one located in a compound just outside a village less than fifty miles from where they stood.

"I suggest we go for the most local, Lieutenant? We'll use one helicopter and send the others back with Angela and the medic. They can then remain on standby if we need assistance. After that pickup we high-tail it back to the ship and wait until nightfall before going on to the final two locations."

She nodded. "I agree it is pointless sitting it out in the day around here, after all we're far better going in undercover of darkness anyway and there's at least three hundred miles to the others after this one."

They watched the first helicopter leave and with six troops they set off for the next girl. The flight was without incident and soon they landed less than a mile from the house. The Captain didn't see the need to take all the troops so two, along with the pilot, stood guard over the helicopter.

The house was as the map showed on the outskirts of a small village, at five in the morning all was quiet as they approached. Then a dog started barking but was quickly silenced with a drugged dart. Once inside the compound they walked round the outside of the house, a soldier was trying each door and window to assess which would be the easiest to enter from. After a decision, and using a glass cutter, they soon had a hole by which they could unfasten a catch. One climbed in and opened a door allowing the rest inside. The house was large with many rooms. They started to move between rooms, checking and searching before going on to the next floor. Five of the rooms had people sleeping in them. Soldiers were waking each person and moving them quickly to one room. Within minutes everyone in the house was standing in a row with two soldiers guarding them.

Karen walked up and down the line, stopping alongside a man who was obviously, by where he was taken from, and his night clothes, important.

"You speak English or French?" she asked.

"I speak English, what is it you want?"

"You purchased a girl off Saeed? Where is she?"

He shrugged. "I know nothing of a girl."

Karen nodded her head up and down slowly as if in understanding, and then pointed to a young girl. "She's your daughter?"

"Marcela is my niece, what is it to you?"

"And the rest of the people here, are they relatives."

"Of course."

Karen turned to the Captain. "We take the girl," she said, at the same time winking at him so no one else could see.

"She's joining us in the helicopter then, Lieutenant?" he asked.

"Of course. The way I see it, he buys a girl, deprives her of her own family, unlike his niece who still has hers, so it's a fair exchange."

The girl was dragged screaming out from the room, her mother and others beginning to panic, not knowing what was going to happen to her, but they didn't dare intervene with two soldiers pointing guns at them.

"Who do you think you are? Coming into my house accusing me of taking some girl and now threatening my family?" the man demanded.

Karen grinned. "I'm not threatening; this is the reality of what you did to another family. Now it's your family. Maybe you'd better explain to the mother what's going to happen to her daughter, because until you produce the girl you took, she's not coming home? Mind you thinking about it, you don't seem to care shit about females. We will take the little boy as well."

He sneered. "You don't have the nerve to do that, Nasser's my son and neither him nor myself are afraid of you."

"I suppose you're not afraid of a woman, after all you're the sort who probably beats your women into submission. Mind you I'm not like that, so I'd advise you to be afraid, very afraid of me. Because I'll have no compunction in putting a gun to your head, or that of your son. In my book it's just one less child abductor in the world. But there is something I've been wanting to do since coming."

"And what's that?"

"I want to punish you where, with you lot, it seems to hurt the most. In the pocket."

He sniggered. "So how do you intend to do that?"

"I could probably burn the house down, well not burn it down exactly, more blow it to smithereens with my grenades. That could cost you." she replied grinning.

"You're insane."

"Yes, a few people have told me that."

At that moment the Captain returned.

Karen turned and looked at him. "Sorry, Captain, this man seems to have so little regard for women we could be wasting our time with the little girl, so we take the son as well."

When the Captain began walking towards his son, the man moved quickly between his son and the Captain.

"Take my niece, she's worthless, but you keep away from my son," he demanded.

Karen knew then she had him. "How can he be so thick, Captain, telling us what he values above all else? I vote we teach him a lesson and put a bullet in the lad's head. It's odds on he'll end up like his father, so we'd be doing the world a favour."

"Lift a finger to hurt my son and you, girl, will be hunted down and killed."

"Yeah, Yeah, I have that shit all the time," she said, pulling the handgun from the holster at the same time. Then she aimed it and fired, intentionally missing the son by inches.

"Shit I missed; maybe I'd better aim at the body, perhaps round the heart, that would be easier as I'm bound to hit something pretty painful?" Karen said, at the same time raising the gun once again to point directly at his son.

"For god's sake stop her, she's mad. The bloody girl's in the cellar; just take her and go."

Karen had a look of annoyance on her face. "What's up with you lot, you could at least have held out a little longer, I'm a good shot normally."

"Lieutenant, please will you put the gun away and go down and find the girl?" the Captain asked.

"Yeah okay, is the room locked?" Karen asked the man.

"The key's on a hook outside the door," he replied.

She replaced her gun. "Watch them," she said, and left the room.

The cellar door led off the kitchen and she went down. The passage to the cellar was lit with one small light bulb hanging from a hook on the ceiling, the wire tied to pipes running the length of the passage. As the man had said a door at the end was closed, a key on a small nail knocked into the pillar of the door. When Karen opened the door, the smell of sewage hit her hard. Again, as in the passage, a small single lamp lit the room. There was no furniture or bed inside, only a bucket, a tray with a cup and an empty plate, to the far corner a mattress with a figure on it, huddled and leaning against the wall watching her. She was clearly frightened seeing a figure stood there holding a gun and pulled the blanket even further up.

"I don't feel well tonight, I was told I could have the night off. Please leave me alone."

"I'm not here to hurt you, but take you home. What's your name?" Karen asked.

The girl's eyes widened when she heard an English girl's voice. "Stephanie Coops. Are you English?" she stammered.

Karen recognised the name. "Of course, my name's Karen Harris. And like I said, I've come to take you home."

"I'm really going home, and you're not tricking me again?" Stephanie gasped.

"Of course; are you coming?"

"God yes, thank you," she replied scrambling up quickly. Wearing only knickers and a t-shirt.

She followed after Karen into the room all the people were in, then stopped dead staring at the man who'd abused her for days, before leaving her in the cellar.

"Was this the man who bought you?" Karen asked.

"Yes…" she replied softly.

"Do you know where you could find your clothes, or at least something to fit you?"

"I never got any more clothes than these, Karen, but I'll check the wardrobes in the other rooms, there must be something I can put on."

When the girl left Karen went up to the man. "You owe that girl a great deal. How are you going to pay for the abuse and way you've treated her?"

He smirked. "I've paid enough, she's wasn't worth anything anyway."

Karen turned to the soldiers still watching the group. "Take everyone but him down to the cellar room and lock them in."

He grabbed her arm. "You can't do that, my sister suffers from asthma."

She shook him off. "Take them."

Stephanie returned wearing a woolly jumper and old jeans two sizes too big and shoes.

"Go with the Captain, Stephanie, I need to talk to this man alone."

She took one last look at him and walked out with the Captain.

"So what are you going to do?" he demanded.

Karen shrugged and leaned against the wall looking at him. "I'm still thinking about it."

"What's your name, so I can hunt you down?" he asked with a grin on his face.

"My name's Karen, and Saeed knows that name very well, after all he's now permanently in a wheelchair I believe. As for you, I intend to burn this house down, with your family in the basement. Maybe they will get out alive, if the stinking room you put a young girl in doesn't collapse. Anyway who cares, I don't."

He stared at her in disbelief, however he had also heard her name mentioned before. This was Sirec's girl, the girl he'd offered a fortune for her return and by all accounts a pretty nasty piece of work. "You can't do that, it's cold blooded murder? Those people down there are innocent, they knew nothing of her."

She frowned. "Wasn't Stephanie innocent as well? But that never stopped Saeed's mother from selling her into a life of abuse and depravity. You didn't even have the decency to give her some clothes, didn't put her in a room that was warm rather than leave her in some stinking cellar with just a mattress and a single blanket. A girl not even eighteen alone in a foreign country, her only future abuse until you tired of her, then she'd probably be sold to a brothel to get some of your money back?"

He kept quiet.

Karen looked at her watch. "Right… it's time I was gone, get down the stairs and into the cellar. Keep your hands on your head, try to escape, or go for me and I'll put a bullet in you."

He did as she asked. But as he walked down the passage towards the door, he suddenly realised they could all be locked in the room for days. It had no windows, was virtually soundproof and no one ever came into the cellar.

"I'm not going in there," he said turning to face her.

"Oh but you are. You will experience just what you put the girl through, if you want to live that is?"

"We could be in there for days, there are children inside, and they could die. Where is all this compassion if you're going to risk killing children?" he asked trying to play on her emotions.

"You really think I care about that? Maybe, if I get time, I'll call the local police and tell them where you are, once we're aboard our helicopter and safely out of the country that is. If I forget, so what, you deserve to die anyway. Now open the door, go inside and shut it, the longer you delay the more frustrated I'll get, unless you want me to shoot you anyway and let the others go?"

The man did as she asked and after locking the door she

wandered upstairs, shutting and locking the cellar entrance as well. Throwing the keys in a bowl on the kitchen table Karen joined the soldiers outside and they moved off back towards the helicopter. After half an hour at a fast pace they arrived at the helicopter but they stopped short. Close on forty troops were surrounding it, the guards they left including the pilot were lying face down on the ground, their hands high above their heads.

"Can we take them?" Karen asked the Captain.

He shook his head. "Not without casualties. Any suggestions?"

"We negotiate," Karen suggested, "after all we're on a humanitarian mission, they must have some shred of decency?"

"And if they don't what then?"

"That's your choice, Captain, for your own men. On my part they won't take me alive. I'll take them on."

"All right, you stay back here and I'll do the talking, Lieutenant."

Some of his troops hung back and settled in the undergrowth with Karen, their guns at the ready. The Captain with one soldier walked up to the officer obviously in charge.

"I'm Captain Saunders. Why are my men on the ground?" he asked.

The officer looked at him. "Why are you in our country?"

"We came on a humanitarian mission. A number of girls, British girls, were abducted and sold to people who live in this country. We have just collected one of them. When we found her she'd already been sexually assaulted, forced to live in a stinking cellar with nothing to wear except her knickers and a damp mattress to lie on."

"I am aware that children have been taken, Captain. I would like to question this girl in order for me to be certain in my own mind; that this is why you are here."

Stephanie was brought forward. The officer looked at her in the oversize clothes, her face streaked with dirt, her hair dirty and matted.

"You child, what's your name and where do you come from?"

"My name's Stephanie Coops and I come from Sheffield, England, Sir."

"Why are you in this country?"

"I won a competition for a holiday, but on the holiday I was drugged and brought here in a boat. A man bought me and I've been raped by him and his friends every night since."

"I'm truly sorry to hear of your ordeal, Stephanie." Then he turned to the Captain. "Where are your other soldiers, are they with you?"

"Yes, they held back in a defensive position awaiting my orders."

The officer began to talk to another officer stood by his side, but in their own language. Then he turned back to the Captain.

"I'm a family man, Captain. What has happened to this girl makes me ashamed of some of my kinsmen. But of course in every country there are also these sorts of people. You and your troop will be allowed to complete your humanitarian mission shortly. There is a time for soldiering and a time for compassion. This is a time for the latter; the child must go home and try to pick her life up again with her family."

"Thank you and yes you're right, this scourge on society, when a human sells another human, is not confined to one country, one race. But the fight with them should come another day. As you say the urgency now is to get this child home."

"I understand that, Captain, but among your troop do you have a girl with you called Karen Marshall?"

The Captain frowned. "Marshall? No we don't have a Karen Marshall with us. We have a Lieutenant Karen Harris, why do you ask?"

He shrugged. "Perhaps I have the surname wrong? But I have someone waiting to speak to your Karen Harris."

"Who is this person, and if she doesn't want to speak to them, what is the alternative?"

"I will not hinder your leaving the country if your Lieutenant does not want to talk, but unless she does; the chances of finding and collecting the final missing girls would be impossible, I can assure you."

"I will need to speak to my Lieutenant first," he replied.

"Of course, take as long as necessary, but point out to her the importance of this meeting."

The Captain walked back and joined Karen, out of sight of the soldiers.

"We can leave the country, Lieutenant, but there's a problem."

"What's that?" she asked.

He told her of the officers' conversation.

She shrugged but didn't admit to the Captain her real name. "Well I'll have to meet this person; after all we came for all the girls not just two."

"Should I come with you?" he asked.

"No, I'll be okay, you look after Stephanie."

The officer watched as Karen approached. There was something different about her, the way she was dressed, the equipment she carried. This girl was also the only one who had a diagonal ammunition belt with grenades attached, the straps holding them in the pouches already released, the safety on her gun still off. He had no idea why the man wanted to talk to her, but it was he who'd given the location of the helicopter and who had told him in advance just why they were here. Although he'd decided not to mentioned that fact to the British.

Karen stopped in front of the officer.

"Are you Karen Harris?"

"I am, who is it who wants to see me?"

"He will introduce himself, but first we'd all feel safer if you put the safety back on your weapon and secured the grenades."

Karen clicked the safety on the gun, clipped one grenade back down but removed the other, slipping her thumb through the ring, holding the grenade in her hand.

"I think perhaps I will protect myself. After all I don't know you, don't trust any of you and have no intention of being in a position that you could take me."

"But I assure you, you're perfectly safe, in fact I told your Captain that as well, and my word is law around here."

She gave a weak smile. "Yes, well I've been here before and last time I trusted someone's word, I often found it wasn't worth shit. So I'll keep my insurance."

He knew there was no arguing with this girl, but her statement about being here before may mean he had her name correct first time, and this really was Karen Marshall who had taken on the army and still escaped? However, he didn't pursue this line, if it was her, then this girl was extremely dangerous. Besides being very well armed.

"Very well, Lieutenant, if that's your decision, would you come with me?"

She followed him to a trailer fifty metres away from the helicopter. It was large and Karen decided it must be some kind of mobile command centre. They went inside where four soldiers were sitting at computers and communication equipment.

"Can you wait here, Lieutenant?" the officer asked.

She nodded.

He went through into quite a spacious meeting room at the far end, shutting the door behind him. A man was sitting alone on one of the six chairs surrounding a large table.

"The girl's waiting outside. She's heavily armed and holding a grenade with the ring around her thumb. There is no way we could disarm her without the grenade exploding. Are you sure you still want this meeting? We cannot guarantee your safety around a soldier as well protected as this," the officer said to the man.

"Is it Karen?" he asked

"The girl or rather Lieutenant claims she is called Karen Harris and also the Captain told me that was her name. But she also mentioned she'd been here before which makes me suspect this is the girl you want to talk to."

"Then I will see her, because if it is Karen, she can be very unpredictable, but her caution is understandable. Just send her in and leave us alone?"

When Karen entered the room, the man had gone over to a side table and was pouring two coffees; he turned holding them in his hands when she shut the door behind her.

He stood looking at her for a moment, his heart was beating

fast. She was a girl he had known only weeks, had photos of and yet even in combat clothes she looked stunning.

"I've poured us coffee, would you like to take a seat? Perhaps put your weapons to one side, I can assure you I'm unarmed and have no intention of trying to overcome you. You may even lock the door if that makes you feel safer."

Karen studied this man as he placed her coffee on the table. Olive skinned, six feet two, deep brown eyes with black hair combed back tight over his head and tied. His clothes, although casual, were immaculate. The man all told was particularly handsome and very well spoken.

She turned and locked the door, then pulled the coffee he had set down over to the far end of the table, in this position her back was to the wall and she could see the door and of course the man. Then she took her handgun out, made a point of releasing the safety and placed it alongside the coffee, before re-fitting the grenade back into its pouch on her diagonal ammunition belt. Finally she leaned her AK47 against the wall behind her and sat down.

He also sat down, smiling to himself at her actions.

"You asked to see me, said it was something to do with the missing girls and also knew my name, why is that?"

"One at a time, Karen Marshall. That is your real name I presume. Why do I know that, because for a week you lived in my home? You then spent the next avoiding the army before I finally decided that the risk to your life was so high I let you go home."

This time Karen's heart skipped a beat.

"You... you're Sirec?" she asked, her voice low and hesitant.

"Of course, and you don't know just how much I've looked forward to finally meeting you."

Her features changed; there was a coldness in her eyes. "Then you are a very foolish man wanting to see me without protection. You and Saeed are at the top of my list to kill."

"Me...why kill me, Karen?"

She leaned forward, her hand on the gun. He could see the hatred in her eyes.

"You have the nerve to ask me that? When for days I was

subject to a manhunt, forced to kill just to protect myself. Have you any inkling what that does to someone? The fear and hatred of the people that were doing it to you builds up in your mind, until you can think of nothing else. Many times I just wanted to put the gun to my head and end it, but even that's difficult. So you plod on, every shadow, every noise frightens you. I was injured, losing blood and with no food I was becoming weaker. I was no soldier, nothing, just a schoolgirl terrified of what would happen to me if I was caught. Then after all I'd been though, with a splitting headache, all I could see was hundreds of troops bearing down on me. So I hid in some stinking hole praying they'd miss me. God knows how, but they did, so again I moved on. Finally at the cove waiting to be picked up, a lorry full of soldiers came down a path, with nowhere to hide, nowhere to run I had to fight yet again. And you wonder why I want to kill my abductors?"

He stood, took a sip of his coffee and leaned forward, his hands on the table looking directly at her.

"For a start I saved you from a life of hell in the brothels," he replied sternly.

"Ha... and for what? Two weeks, maybe a month, before you tired of me and I'd end up in a brothel anyway?"

"Who told you that?" he demanded.

"Your own staff told me, that's who."

Suddenly his manner changed. "Karen, Karen you shouldn't listen to gossip. For years Saeed has been supplying girls destined for the brothels, mostly from the Asian countries and families who need the girl's income just to live. I admit I took a few, but only temporarily, never paid over five hundred dollars for them. But at least they were fresh and clean and not riddled with disease as you find in the brothels. But were they the sort of girl I'd want to spend my life with, have children with, meet clients? I don't think so. I have never paid forty thousand dollars for a girl to have just for a month. I'd never have a girl taken to the local shops, select nice clothes and sleep in a guest bedroom, if all I'd wanted is a quick romp. The moment I first saw a picture of you and read your details Saeed had been sent I knew you were the girl for me. But you were mixed up with Saeed; he'd seen the value of you and wanted his pound of flesh. I did everything in my power to have you looked after, my only error was not being there when you arrived, otherwise you wouldn't have been with Saeed for more than a couple of days. You have to remember, Karen, you'd already been abducted and were on your way. If I hadn't shown any interest and made an offer, you would have been left with the other girl who came with you. There would have been no chance of you ever escaping. By now you would have either have accepted a life of rape four or five times a day, week after week or been so badly beaten you'd have been good for nothing. Then you blame me for the man hunt. My home had been destroyed, some of my warehouses razed to the ground. What did you expect me to do, let the SAS go home? I offered rewards for their capture, but they had also taken you, so I was insistent that you were not to be harmed in any way. I saw you as an innocent party mixed up in what was a military operation. But as you know things went wrong, you were on your own a number of times and still fighting back. I was proud of you, Karen; proud the girl who I'd decided I wanted was proving herself to be competent and brave. I was also becoming desperately concerned, by the reports that were coming back telling me you'd take your own life, rather than be captured. I didn't want my girl to die, so I let you go but I didn't realise how much hatred Khan, the officer in charge of the search, had for you. He was supposed to deliver the SAS officers to the same cove you were heading for, but he took his own soldiers with the intention to kill you instead. I went to the beach and saw what you'd done. Knew it was your doing by the weapons and belt you'd left behind. To tell you the truth only then did I realise just how good you really are. I know of no civilian who has taken on a truck full of soldiers and won. I stood for some time where you left your weapons, trying to imagine just how you'd survived. A motley set of weapons, even the ammunition you carried didn't fit either gun, and yet you'd escaped. You were my sort of girl, Karen. Strong, determined, and I might add very dangerous both to yourself and others. I knew then I had to see you and explain."

Karen was looking at him, she'd gone cold inside, wanted to hate this man but it wasn't what she'd always believed. She had never realised just how much she owed him until now.

"How was I to know? I was really sorry to see your house destroyed, Sirec. They did it for fun, for a laugh. I could do nothing about it. The house and the grounds were beautiful and like you say my room was luxury. I'd even decided to really work hard and try to get you to like me, want to be with me so that you wouldn't send me on to a brothel, but by then I'd already called home and they knew where I was. If you found out, you'd have killed me, or sent me away. So I didn't know what I should do. Besides which, Saeed and his friends had raped me and I was glad you weren't there to pick me up. I was in so much pain, so scared of my future and worried if you'd seen me that way, you'd not have even given me the chance to show how loyal and loving I could be. Saeed had told me you'd not have a girl who'd been used and I'd be given to your guards, before being sent to a brothel. I cried myself to sleep the night I was raped. Terrified of what was going to happen to me."

He could now understand why she'd returned to Saeed's. Why the reports were coming back that they believed she'd take her own life. The girl had been more than scared, like she said, she was terrified. Because of Saeed, she'd no idea that the soldiers weren't looking for her, and just kept running.

"So why did you return, Karen, you knew the risks, the real possibility of you being captured. When you saw the soldiers today, what was going through your mind?"

She shrugged. "I had to come, Saeed was still alive. I'd thought he was dead. I was being chased all over England, caught twice but escaped. It was only a matter of time before they would get me. Then there were the girls he took. I knew what they would be going through, so when I found out it was Saeed's work I took the opportunity to finish our feud once and for all, besides find the girls. Was I bothered about the troops today? I don't think so, after all I'd been there before and whatever, it was either them or me, I've no illusions about that."

"Then you joined the army, why was that?"

Karen grinned. "I'm not in the army; I was told that I wasn't a team player. I was a loner and although they needed me to identify the house and Saeed, they weren't prepared to take someone who had no discipline, didn't even know how to use a gun correctly and was a complete wreck, taking drugs to stop the nightmares and keep my sanity. So they dumped me in a training camp, gave me a rank and that was it. When I go back I suppose they will fire me and I'll have to sign on unemployed."

"Do you want that?"

"Of course I do. I'm not cut out for this; after all I'm really very feminine under all this gear. All I want is a man to love me, to grow up with, have a fun time and one day have children of my own. When I was training on the moor in driving rain and gales all I could think of was being by the side of a pool in the tiniest bikini you could imagine, letting the world go by, not running around playing soldiers. Now I'm hoping after all this I'll able to walk down the street in safety and not keep looking over my shoulder."

Sirec refilled their cups and took the seat opposite. He liked this girl even more now he'd met her. She was not only very attractive, which first alerted him to her, but now talking to her he found she was also very intelligent, honest, sensible and determined about her goals.

"You realise that this is the end of the line as far as the missing girls that are left go? The last two you are looking for including the driver's little girl, were sold to men who live in the north. It's a region full of marauding bandits and it would take an army just to pass through the area."

She said nothing for a minute and then shrugged. "I didn't realise that, but now I'm here I may as well go anyway."

"Why, Karen, why are you so determined to risk your life? After all you've just told me you're not cut out for this sort of life."

Karen took a sip of her coffee and looked directly at him. "You want the truth?"

"It would be pointless if it wasn't, Karen, but I also want to understand you."

"I shouldn't be alive now. By rights I should have died weeks ago. After all I've killed for revenge, for protection and in error. I was brought up a Christian, believed God had abandoned me. I suppose now I realise why he has let me live, perhaps forgiven my breaking of his commandments? It was to bring these girls out. They are innocent, like I was, but they are also weak, unable to look after themselves and deserve every bit of help I can give them. Even if it means I don't come back, after all, if I failed God would no longer have a use for me and I should pay for my crimes."

"You're a very brave girl, Karen."

"Not so much brave, Sirec, more stupid, believing I can save the world. When in reality I can't even sort my own life out."

He pulled a case out of his pocket and removed a cigarette. After first offering her one, which she declined, he lit his own, then began drawing on it slowly before replying. In some ways he didn't want her to go, but could see no way in which he could stop her besides force and that wouldn't work with this girl.

"Well if you're determined to move on I'll help you. But without the SAS, it will have to be with local fighters. They can move freely through the areas, the SAS presence alone would bring hundreds of troops down on you."

"Why do you want to help me, after all I've not done very much for you, apart from cost you a great deal of money?" she asked confused.

He stood and walked to the edge of the room, leaning on the wall looking at her.

"You are right, there is a reason, Karen. The truth is I still want you as my girl. I want to prove to you that the money was just a means to an end, to get you away from Saeed, it has no significance. I'd like you to come and stay with me, after the girls are returned, and see if we can pick your life up again."

"You mean as a prisoner?"

"No, not at all, you would never have been a prisoner. You'll be free to go home if you and I can't get on. I believe we can, and we're alike in lots of ways. You will be at my side, meet my clients, not be locked away as some sex object to pass the nights away. Although…" he grinned. "I'm a particularly demanding and very good lover, so you will look forward to the nights, that I can assure you."

She smiled to herself at his comment. "I'll have to think about coming to live with you, Sirec. I do have a mum and dad and I'll have to explain to them why I'd be staying."

"I'm not asking you to think about it, Karen, the condition of bringing the girls out is you do come and stay with me. You become my lover; throw all you have into our relationship, so I can prove that I am the right man for you."

"And if I say no, what then?"

"Say no and you go home with the SAS, the girls are lost forever. Say yes and you leave today to collect them, but you stay at least six months with me. After that time if the relationship is not working for us you may return home."

"But that's blackmail, expecting me to exchange myself."

"Yes I suppose it is, but that's the way things are around here. You have to fight for what you want, so if I have to give you a shove to decide, you can't blame me, after all if you left with the girls you'd have tremendous pressure from your own family to forget me or more importantly, you would not know where to come back to, or how to contact me."

"Will you be coming with me to collect the girls?"

"No, I have a business to run. But you'll be looked after by my right-hand man, Halif, as Sirec's girl. That means, Karen, you demand respect, help and above all you will be as safe as you can possibly be. Although be warned, there are a lot of people out there who don't like me, who'd be happy to put a bullet in my skull. Those won't respect you being my girl, as even the mention of my name could bring retaliation on you to get at me. So it won't be plain sailing."

She sat quietly for a time in troubled thought, he never said another word. After his fine words about liking her, wanting to be with her, the bottom line was she'd be expected to pretend to love him, enjoy his demands on her body for six months, even if every time it disgusted her, there'd be no escape. Karen had also noticed he was taking no chances of her escaping when they went for the girls, his main man would be constantly at her side to ensure she did return. Maybe even his promise she could go home, if things didn't work out, would be conveniently forgotten over the six months and she'd never be allowed to leave. Could the families of the girls really expect her to give her freedom up in exchange for their daughters? Then there was the little girl of fourteen, what of her if she said no? Would she be abused for years, never see her mother again? All and more of these arguments were going through her mind as she sat quietly, Sirec watching her. Finally she decided.

"All right Sirec, you have my word. When the girls are on their way home I'll stay. The only stipulation I'll make is you give me time to settle and accept you as my lover. I'm not a prostitute or someone who treats sex as just something you do with anyone regardless. I admit I've had a lover, but I loved him, he treated me with respect and gave me time to get to know him before we actually made love. And of course Grant was also first and foremost my boyfriend, even if I didn't know the real reason he was with me. But if you expect me to share your bed on the first night then you'd put yourself at the level of Saeed and his friends. It'd just be rape in my book and every night you wanted me after that it'd be rape. But give me time to accept my new life, our relationship, then for me you'd be my boyfriend and I'd be a very different girl. I'd be faithful and I hope a good lover willing to learn how to please you, I can promise that."

He smiled inwardly, how he wanted this girl for himself. And if it meant she needed this time to settle, why not, after all he had every intention of her bearing his children far sooner than she could imagine, and a mother would never leave her children. "You have my word, Karen, like I've said to you; I can get a girl any time, but in you I want more, so I will give you the time you ask."

He stood and walked round the table taking her hand. She stood as well and he kissed her gently on the lips. "I have to go now, Karen, take care love and I'll see you when you return with the girls."

Following him outside Karen waited until Sirec had talked to the officer in charge, before he climbed into his car and left. She then approached the officer. Pulling out a small pad from her breast pocket she wrote the address of the house they'd been to, handing him the sheet of paper.

"I've locked the residents of the house in the cellar. The owner is in there with them. He was the one who purchased the girl with us and abused her. Perhaps you will inform the local police to let them out in a day or so? At least he will have had time to experience just what the girl had to endure every day."

"We'll forget the police, I will go with my troop personally Lieutenant, this man's actions and of course the shame he has brought to our country, necessitating armed intrusion, will not go unpunished. After you have talked to your Captain there will be a car waiting to take you to a place to sleep for the night."

Karen told the Captain what had been arranged, however she didn't mention the fact she'd not be returning with the freed girls.

The Captain looked concerned. "I'm not sure about this, Lieutenant, I should call control."

Karen shook her head. "This was always an expectation of Sir Peter, that I'd have to go on alone," she lied. "That's why I had my own agenda, with your task to secure and extract. Besides, I know Sirec, so this is why he's helping me. All you have to do is wait for my call, then bring in the rescue helicopters to pull us out. I'll be a couple of days at the most, and then we can all go home."

"Well if you're sure. Are you certain you don't want anyone to stay with you?"

"No I'll be fine, just be ready to come for us. That's all I ask."

31

Sir Peter gasped. "You've done what?" he asked unable to believe his ears.

"The Lieutenant has stayed on," the Captain repeated. "She was insistent that it was the only way to bring the other girls out. I must remind you she wasn't under my command; the Lieutenant had an agenda of her own. She said you were aware that it might be the case that she'd have to stay on alone, and I presume you'd already discussed that possibility with which I wasn't party to?"

Sir Peter looked round at the three other senior army officials in the room, then back at the Captain. "For your information, and that of you all, Karen is not in the army as such. She's only just eighteen, was a civilian just over a week ago until she agreed to help get the girls out. Mainly because she knew Saeed, his mother and a number of other unsavoury characters."

"Then it's your own fault. You should have told us. You presented her as an officer and she was treated as such. She had a meeting with a man called Sirec and it was agreed between her and him to use local soldiers."

Sir Peter shook his head in despair. "Why in god's name didn't you contact us? Sirec is a gunrunner; he's also the man who chased the girl halfway across the Lebanon in an effort to take her back. He paid forty thousand dollars for her, believes he owns her, and you have just handed Karen back to him on a plate."

The Captain shook his head. "No that's not true, the Lieutenant had moved off with local militia before we left. Whatever you think, or know about this gunrunner, he is helping her at this moment. Besides, we were already in a compromised situation, they were waiting for us and without serious loss of life we couldn't have re-taken the helicopter. Whatever we did would have been a compromise. They could have taken the Lieutenant, or whoever she really is, and we could have done nothing about it."

Sir Peter said no more but left the de-briefing of the Captain to be continued with the other senior officers. Making his way to the communications area of the ship, he entered a small room off the central communication wing of the carrier. A lady was busily keying in coordinates.

"Well is she transmitting still?" Sir Peter asked.

"She is Sir Peter, and moving steadily north. Does she know you have a tracker on her?"

"No, of course not, in fact I have two. Not that any of the army personnel know. This is for our ears only; it doesn't under any circumstances get out of this room."

"I understand, Sir Peter. My brief before leaving GCHQ and that of the other Communication Officer with me was that this operation is classified at level five and you were our only contact on this ship. We will be monitoring 24 hours and feeding back to GCHQ where they will be mapping the route she's taking."

"Can the bug be scanned for?"

"Yes but they are very sophisticated and will detect a scan. They automatically turn off until the threat is gone before re-starting. Provided she keeps wearing clothing the tracker is attached to, we will know where she is at all times."

Sir Peter smiled. "The girl's not only wearing one on her clothing, she's also got one buried in her body. It is a very low power one good for around a thousand yards but it will allow us to find her if we can get close enough. It was fitted during what she thought was a health check and injected under her skin. I'm taking no chances with her, she's far too valuable and it would seem, with her joining up with Sirec, she might just lead us to where he's living."

The lady pulled out a communication from the UK. "I received this while you were in the meeting. Two more members of Special Forces are already en route from the UK. They expect to arrive later tomorrow. I thought we already had Special Forces involved?"

"We do, but these two are specialists in covert work. If

Karen's in trouble and I believe she is, they will bring her out."

She turned to look at Sir Peter. "You're going all out to look after this girl, is she that special?"

He stood for a moment before replying and then smiled. "Yes she is. Karen has everything to live for but is still prepared to lay her life down besides now apparently give up her freedom to help others. In my book she's very special indeed."

"I can't help but agree with you, Sir Peter; we will do our best not to lose her."

"Thank you, keep me informed of any developments from what's expected please, day or night."

Then he left the room.

32

After Karen had left Sirec, and explained to the Captain the problem of where the other girls actually were, she climbed into a Land Rover along with Halif, Sirec's right-hand man, and they set off, soon arriving at a small compound. The amenities were very basic, but she had a good meal and was given a bed in a two-bedded room to sleep in. The following morning they were on their way, but not before Halif had told Karen to remove the British insignias and Lieutenant's label. Karen had no trouble removing them as they were just peel off-on Velcro and she pushed them into her pocket.

The first leg of the journey was long, uneventful and particularly uncomfortable. The vehicles were old, with little suspension, and seating for the gunmen riding in the back was boards and for her, alongside the driver, a very worn leather upholstered seat. After close on ten hours of travelling Karen was glad of the odd stop just to stretch her legs and allow the numbness in her bottom to go away. But it was already dark before camp was set up for the night and after dinner she was left alone. The majority were not able to speak English or French and the ones that could kept away. But the night was warm and she sat on a collapsible chair outside her tent, listening to music on a small MP3 player she'd brought. It was about an hour later when Halif joined her, pulling up another chair and lighting a cigarette.

"We enter an area of the country tomorrow that is controlled mainly by marauding groups of fighters," he began. "I told Sirec you shouldn't be here as a girl is at high risk of being taken, for shall we say, entertainment."

"What do you want me to do?" she asked.

"I want you to keep your cap on, stay back and within the main group if we are stopped. Hopefully they won't really think a girl is with us but as a precaution I'm putting you in the back of the lorry with the men. If we're stopped don't look at any of them directly, look down or away. You're unfortunately quite distinctive, but hopefully they will not expect a girl among the gunmen in the back."

"I understand, will the other men know you're doing this?"

"Yes, and they will bunch around you. By late afternoon, if we have no delays then we should be at the first house. It's where one older girl and the little girl were taken. I know of this man and you should prepare yourself. His sexual perversions are not nice and the little girl in particular could well have suffered very badly. The older girl has cost him a great deal of money, compared with his normal purchases, so she might have been treated better, but with him you can never tell, he's awash with money in his business. Either or both girls will need you, depending what they have endured, they will almost certainly be very wary of us, but you should give them confidence that we are here to get them out and not to take them somewhere else. As for security this man deals in drugs, mainly shipping them through this country en route to the US. There will be guards at the gate and one or two around the compound. The security is not that tight, unless he has a shipment in, then it's very tight. You have to remember this man needs to keep in with what he'll believe we are, militia, and so would always offer refreshments. While this is going on you and I will enter the house to meet him. You say nothing; and again keep your hat on."

She looked concerned. "Is this very risky for you as well?"

"Life's a risk, Karen, particularly in the gun running business. But to make money in this country it's the only way. So to answer your question, just coming into this region will always be dangerous. The people who live here don't like intrusion; they keep to themselves, unless you are part of a faction that opposes one thing or another, that is. You see there is little opportunity for work, if you want a family or are even trying to raise a family they have to be fed. So gun running, moving drugs or even people is okay, so long as someone is paying."

She said nothing more. Halif finished his cigarette and stood. "I'll say goodnight, we leave at dawn."

33

The small convoy came to a halt; Halif looked into the back of the lorry. "Put your hat on, keep close to the others, we have company," he told Karen.

She sat there listening to Halif and two other voices arguing. Then a face looked into the back of the lorry, saw all the gunmen and backed away. It seemed an age before the lorry started up once more. Halif climbed aboard and slammed the door. Moments later they moved on.

"It was only a small group looking for something they could sell. They didn't realise the truck was full of armed men, changed their tack completely then," he shouted back to her.

"Have we far to go?" she called back.

"No, about an hour, but I've been informed there are no drugs there so he's only got basic security. That is good."

The hour was more like two before the lorry slowed then finally stopped and the engine cut. They had arrived in a compound and she could see through the back, as the flap was pulled away, many people milling around. All had guns.

She climbed out with the rest, glad to be able to stretch before joining a small queue for the toilet. Once inside she wished she hadn't, the room was infested with flies and smelt terrible. But Karen needed to go and held her breath, getting out as quick as she could.

Halif came up to her. "Okay the men are going to eat, I've been invited to go to the house, you'll come with me. Leave your pack and gun in the lorry along with your ammunition belt. You can keep your waist belt, with the handgun, that's acceptable. Remember, speak only when I speak to you, women have little value and know their place. His name's Salem. I'll introduce you as Sirec's girl, which you are now. I'll tell him you've been sent with me to, I believe, keep an eye on things for Sirec. He'll understand that as he knows Sirec likes to know what's going on all the time."

They went inside; the guard at the door just gave them both a cursory glance. Inside, the house was the height of luxury and a man, around his forties, small with a large belly, came to meet them and shake Halif's hand.

"It is good to meet you again, Halif, you are well?" Salem asked in his own language, which Karen couldn't understand.

"Very well, Salem. This girl with me is Karen, I asked her to join me to meet you, I hope you don't mind?"

He looked at Karen for a minute. *"Not at all, can she understand us?"*

"No, she speaks only French or English," Halif replied.

"She's a pretty girl," Salem replied looking Karen over once more.

On Karen's part she felt decidedly uncomfortable with the way this man kept looking at her. Why that was she didn't really know, but she certainly didn't like him.

They all went into the dining room.

"So why is she with you, is she your woman?" Salem asked as the soup was served.

"Karen is Sirec's girl, he is away for the moment and because we have some private business for Sirec in the area, he said she should come with us. I think she also reports back to him regularly. I had no problems in that, besides, at times his girls can be useful to entertain special guests," Halif lied.

Salem smiled to himself as he listened to Halif's lies. He was not stupid and knew exactly why this girl was here. However, he had no intention of saying anything to Halif.

"I was told by Saeed, you have purchased two girls recently?" Halif asked, when Salem didn't comment.

"Saeed shouldn't be telling you about any of my dealings with him. But it's true; I've two and purchased them at one of Saeed's auctions. One of them is just eighteen, the other fourteen. They are lovely girls, both work hard to please me after their, shall we say, initiation."

Halif noticed the change in Salem's tone of voice, displaying pleasure when he mentioned the word initiation. *"What do you call initiation?"* he asked.

Salem grinned, more than happy to explain his pleasure at

what he did to the two girls. *"It's something I always do with girls for my pleasure to show them who is the boss around here. She is always taken into the punishment room on day one. Stripped and strung up, where they experience my leather strap across their bottom, quickly learning what they can expect if they step out of line. I've never had a girl ever step out of line after that induction. Take Sammy the older of my new girls. She was very strong willed and needing sedatives to control her, before she met me. Now she is perfect works hard to please and can't do enough for me. I never normally offer her out, but as you're Sirec's main man you may have her for the night in exchange for this girl with you. My Sammy is still learning but, unlike the ones from the brothels, she's clean, looks after herself and is very affectionate."*

"I will take her, Salem, but I'll have to talk to Karen for you. All Sirec's girls are usually up for a night of sex, so I can't see there being a problem. So what of the other girl you have?"

He grinned. *"She was a very good buy, Halif. Fourteen, is beautiful, obedient and a very bright kid. I've spent time with her during the siesta showing her ways she can please me. I intend to use her when Sammy is not available. Already she is proving to be a very good learner. But last night was something else. I did my random check of their room. It is something I do often, checking the drawers, the wardrobe in fact everywhere. It is important I keep them on their toes and ensure they are keeping to my rules. I pulled back their bedcovers and seeing her lying there naked, I wanted her there and then. So I gave Sammy a night off and she took over from Sammy completely. I tell you Halif, it is to be recommended taking such a naive young girl to your bed. They are so tight, squeal a lot but she still wanted to please."*

Halif was well aware that children even younger than fourteen are often married in many countries. But in his own mind he considered them still to be children and felt sad to hear this man enthuse over what he'd done with her. In this way he was glad they'd come to get the girls out. However, for the moment it was essential to keep the facade up, in order to locate the girls. *"I can believe that, Salem, you're indeed a very lucky man to have acquired such a girl. Where do you usually keep the girls?"*

"They're kept together, that's all you need to know. Sammy will be brought to your room after you retire." He answered in a way that indicated Halif should not to be pursuing this line of enquiry.

After lunch Karen was left alone to wander round the

house. Halif and Salem had gone into his study, shut the door and were engrossed in conversation. She could never understand these people. Outside the house was often left in an unkept condition with rubbish around. While inside the houses were immaculate, opulent and expensive. She must have, over the afternoon, checked every room as discreetly as she could, but the girls were not here, of that she was sure, although one room she was certain was a girls' room, it had everything inside you'd expect for a room in constant use by a girl or girls. Eventually, fed up, she went outside and settled down in an area set aside for outside dining. Karen was disappointed; she'd thought they would be leaving with the girls by now, like the last girl, but it seemed it was going to be slow going. She also didn't like this man; he was too laid back, as if he knew something they didn't.

Halif joined her outside, taking a seat at her side. "He has the girls, I'm to have the older girl for the night, but he won't tell me where the other girl is. So Salem needs to be distracted tonight, Karen. It will give me time to sort out with the older one just where they are being kept. Once I find that I'll use my men to sort out the guards. Then we'll be on our way."

Karen frowned. "When you say distracted, how do you expect me to do that, unless you intend to retire early with this girl and I play cards with him or something?"

Halif grinned at the girl's naivety. "Salem fancies you. He's not interested in cards. I told him you're a Sirec girl and his girls are always up for a night of sex. Saeed told Sirec you've already plenty of experience in pleasing a man; he even enthused over your lap dancing techniques, so give him a night to remember while we find the girls."

Karen glared at him. "You have to be joking; I've no intention of spending a night with a complete stranger and even more so letting him fuck me."

He leaned closer to her and gripped her arm. "Listen, you do as you're told. I'm not pissing about the country looking for a couple of worthless girls while some skinny eighteen-year-old female Sirec's bought and paid for, tries to dictate to me what she will and won't do."

Karen shook his hand off her arm and turned to face him. "What's this bought and paid for bit? I've agreed with Sirec to be his girlfriend. In return he promised to treat me with dignity, on an equal footing. Give me time to settle and get to know him before we even think about sharing a bedroom. And I'll tell you this, nothing was ever mentioned about me being handed out to any Tom, Dick or Harry who wants something to fuck, otherwise I'd have been on that helicopter with the soldiers. As it is I've agreed to a six months' trial in exchange for the girls."

Halif began to laugh. "You have no idea what you've got yourself into have you?"

"Excuse me?"

"From the day Sirec paid for you, you were his property. You escaped yes, but you're so arrogant, so full of yourself, you had the audacity to walk back in, wielding weapons and believing you were invincible. Well, Karen Marshall, you're a bloody fool. You even saved us the cost of bringing you back. Walked directly into Sirec's clutches demanding he treats you like a girlfriend. He's no snotty eighteen-year-old lad trying to impress a girl to get inside her knickers. Oh he'll be courteous, kind and considerate, that's until you object - try to tell him, rather than he tell you, then you'll see another side of Sirec. It is a side, Karen, which will have you on your knees begging forgiveness, promising never to answer back again and doing whatever he demands."

"So it was all lies, he never really wanted me for who I am, my personality. I'm just something he owns and nothing more?"

"You have it in one, so you'd better get used to it. You're never going home. You will certainly bear his children, share his bed the very first night you're back and sometimes, like this time, you will entertain another man for him. Now as I said you're going with this man and I don't want to hear any more objections. You're not a shy girl, besides being well used to taking your clothes off around men, even dancing naked in front of them. So I'll expect you to be pleasant, let him fuck you, or give him a blow job. I'm not bothered. Do either, or both, so long as you give him a good time and he's not getting in our way. Do I make myself clear?"

"And the alternative?" she asked.

Halif laughed. "There is no alternative. You'll be handed to him whether you agree or not, for his pleasure. Struggle or object and I understand he has a punishment room which he uses on any girl who refuses his advances. He tells me he strings her up naked, like a carcass of beef, and lays in with a leather strap to her bottom. Perhaps I should ask if I can borrow the room to loosen you up for him. It's up to you, but personally I'd accept his bed, Karen, it's less painful and could be infinitely more enjoyable."

Karen knew there was no way out. She was now in a world where no matter what she wanted, they had no interest in her as a human being, she was just something to be used and bartered with.

"So how long do you expect me to let this man fuck me for?"

"As long as it takes. You stay in the bedroom with him. You give him the time of his life so he doesn't want to come out, because if you fail to do that and he does come looking for me, Karen, I'll be in there and tie you down on the fucking bed myself. Has that answered your naive question?"

She sighed. "I suppose. Like you say I don't have an option, I'll do as you ask."

"Good... dinner's in an hour, get upstairs to the bathroom, wash your hair and clean yourself up. Perhaps you can make yourself look more desirable, rather than some scruffy excuse for a soldier. A dress has been found for you the girl Sammy uses, she's your size so wear it. Be pleasant over dinner and when he asks you to join him later, which he will, agree."

Later, after finishing combing her hair in front of a mirror she slipped on a long dress that had been left on the bed. It didn't quite fit, but was preferable to the army clothes. Karen felt very down. She'd thought at least she was in control of her future. She'd even begun to look forward to building a possible relationship with Sirec. Happy he was going to give her time to accept him and her new life. But Halif's words had burst that bubble completely. His attitude that she was bought and paid for, and could be just handed over to someone for a night without even a consideration of her feelings was the reality. This was a taste of the life she'd have had to endure, if no one had come to her rescue and stupidly she'd fallen for Sirec's lies, like the naive schoolgirl that she really was, and agreed to stay with him. Looking at her watch she found it was coming up to seven, time to go down for dinner. After one last look at herself in the mirror she left the room.

"Ah, you are here. You are a very beautiful girl," Salem said in English as she entered.

She smiled thinly before taking her seat at the table.

After dinner the three of them went through to the lounge. Salem put his arm around her shoulders, slowing her and allowing Halif to go ahead. "I want to spend time alone with you tonight, Karen," he said in a low voice, while at the same time his hand had moved down her back and was rubbing her bottom. "When Halif retires, I will come to your room."

Karen wanted to slap his face, but just looked towards him and smiled. "I will look forward to your visit, Salem," she replied.

A large grin came to his face, but he said nothing more.

Salem and Halif were still in the lounge when she went to her room. After cleaning her teeth and washing she climbed into bed. Wearing knickers and t-shirt she lay there in the dark. All the time she'd sat in the lounge with them she'd tried to think of ways to get out of it, from it being the end of the month through to feeling unwell. Finally she realised they'd not be interested with whatever excuse she came up with, so she'd just resigned herself to letting him do whatever he wanted with her. The longer she waited the more the trepidation of what was going to happen made her feel strange. Now her body was shaking a little, her stomach was tight, the expectation of being with a man again seemed, in some ways, to be exciting her physically and yet she couldn't understand why. The man was gross, stunk of tobacco and was nothing like her Grant or even Sirec, who was tall, muscular and good-looking.

She heard the door open silently, then close, the lock being turned before the light was switched on. Salem was stood there. "I see you're already in bed, Karen? Perhaps if you can just get up for a moment and step away from the bed, I can satisfy myself you don't have any nasty surprises hidden away."

She climbed out and stood away. He pulled back the bedclothes and then the pillows, before running his hands under the side of the mattress.

Karen was thankful, while watching him check, she'd not placed the knife, as she'd intended for protection, under the mattress. This man seemed to be very careful in ensuring she had nothing to harm him with. Why, she wasn't sure, after all, as far as he was concerned, this was just a night with Sirec's girl, she thought? However, it worried her in as much that being in his house with no access to her main weapons, importantly her grenades. Karen was brought out of her thoughts when he stood away from the bed, obviously satisfied she'd hidden nothing.

"Now before we can relax the clothes as well please. I'm not into girls starting off having clothes on in bed. It wastes time removing them and has no value, so just get them off and then lie down on the bed," he told her, at the same time kicking his shoes from his feet and unfastening his trousers.

Karen removed her t-shirt and knickers, placing them on the chair with her other clothes, before returning to the bed. She wasn't bothered, she'd lose them anyway and the embarrassment of being naked around a man had been well and truly knocked out of her during her time with Assam and Saeed.

He turned the light off then joined her, putting his arm round her neck and kissing her long and hard. Karen reacted positively as Halif had demanded she should, and soon he was exploring her body. Kissing her breast and moving his hand down between her legs, exciting her until she was ready for him. She closed her eyes momentarily as he entered her, trying to imagine it was her Grant as they used to be when they first met, and not some man she'd only met hours before. He went at her gently at first then began to be more aggressive as her body responded to him. Karen lay there making the appropriate noises trying to make him believe she was enjoying the intrusion into her body, but the reality in her mind was very different, this was rape and she despised Halif for forcing this man on her. Even at the outset she'd decided to give Salem no real encouragement, hoping by being this way, he'd decide she was useless as a lover and he'd tire of her quickly. But he didn't seem to notice her reluctance and pulled out telling her he wanted a new position. Karen realised now this was not going to be quick like she'd hoped, so she began to make it even more difficult for him, by not moving as he kept telling her to do, or when she did, getting herself in the wrong position. With this Karen was determined more than ever to put him off, and he'd leave her alone. But Salem was very experienced in dealing with girls who didn't want sex. So he pulled back urging her to lie face down, kissing her on the back of the neck, running his hand down her back and rubbing her bottom gently, in her view trying to relax her.

Karen was smiling to herself, she believed it was working he was getting frustrated with her, soon he'd just become fed up and turn away.

"You believe, no I suspect, you think you're being very clever by doing your best to make life very difficult for me," he suddenly said.

Karen didn't reply, not sure how to answer.

"Ah...silence as well, so I must be right? But you see I've met girls like you before...none have won," he said, at the same time raising his hand high and bringing it down very hard on her bottom. It was a sharp stinging slap that made her gasp involuntary, immediately taking her thoughts back to the time she was held over the side of the dinghy and Assam had taken his strap to her bottom. This was something she didn't want repeating and she was annoyed. So much so she was considering some sort of retaliation.

He grinned hearing her gasp, before dropping his head to hers whispering into her ear. "Now little girl, like it or not you're going to be fucked hard tonight. With difficult girls I always give them a taste of the punishment to expect, it's far better than a threat. However, any punishment will be by three strokes of my leather strap, one to the bottom, the others to the top of the legs," he began, rubbing his hands gently over her still smarting bottom. "My Sammy and Natasha received this when they first came to my house. Both were strung up in my punishment room where I used the leather strap on their bottoms. Since their, shall we say inauguration, they have been a delight. So how do you want to play it, three slaps of my hand to this tight bottom of yours to show how serious I am in my threats, or would you rather I called for help and have you taken to my punishment room, if you really are still determined not to play ball, and have a desire to feel the leather strap across your legs and bottom? Of course you could avoid all of this now you're aware just how painful it can get for you, by relaxing and giving everything you've got, then we both enjoy the experience."

He fell silent a moment. "What's it to be then?" he demanded, at the same time beginning to rub her bottom and preparing to give her the three promised slaps.

Karen knew then she'd no option but to do as he demanded, that was unless she wanted constant punishments? Which with her bottom still smarting from his initial slap, she didn't relish. Besides, she was also nervous of Halif, who'd demanded she keep him occupied, and less than half an hour on a bed was not keeping someone occupied, so she risked little sympathy from him as well. Karen sighed inwardly, it would seem her sex life was still dominated by people forcing sex onto her rather than wanting her for what she could offer in a loving relationship. So she turned over and put her arms round his neck, pulled him closer to her and gave him a long kiss.

"I'm sorry, Salem, you're right I'm not playing fair, I was only testing you just to see if you wanted me for a quick shag and it's over, or as I really expected a night we will both remember," she lied. "Let's start again and I'll show you what I can really do for a man?"

He smiled to himself, the girl was lying of course, but he wanted this girl in his bed, not to punish her with the strap. Because if he did have to go that way she'd be in no fit state to use tonight, or even the rest of the week. However, he had no such worries, Karen did as she promised, throwing herself into it and beginning to enjoy the experience, like she always had with Grant. Although Salem would never be her choice, his attentiveness and the way he was now treating her wasn't in any way derogatory, like the rapes she'd had to endure. But he was firm and aggressive in his demands, which she liked in a man, constantly making her change position, kissing and caressing her body with each change. He had an ability to bring her to heights she'd never experienced and she was unable to believe how this overweight and small man could carry on like he was. But he'd been at her for over an hour, Karen had had enough, she wasn't used to such demands on her body so after he'd finally brought himself to climax, she sighed a sigh of relief when he fell back on the bed, settling down at her side. She lay there still shaking, even Grant couldn't have kept up with this man, but she'd had her fill of him, done her best to please, and hoped he'd leave her alone now. However, within twenty minutes, just as she had drifted off to sleep, he was leaning over kissing her again.

"God," she said to herself awakening with a start, *"he doesn't want more does he?"*

"No, I've had enough, Salem. I just want to sleep," she said pushing him away.

With his face inches from hers, he smiled. "It's obvious your other lovers have let you get away with too much, Karen. For a very fit eighteen-year-old I think you're only saying you want to sleep."

"I'm not just saying it, I really do want to sleep, Salem. I'm not used to this like you; besides, it's beginning to hurt me."

"Just words, Karen, just words, I'll soon have your juices running again. After all, you're very adventurous, besides being particularly well tutored in pleasing a man, as my good friend Saeed had said you'd be. That is of course after a smack by way of punishment, to remind you who was in charge. Which would you believe, he'd suggested I gave you first, saying you'd always need dominance by the man, you're that type of girl."

Karen glared at him. "What are you on about? I don't need violence in my sexual activities thank you. Besides, what's Saeed got to do with all this?" she asked, slightly confused and alarmed as to why Saeed's name was mentioned.

"Oh didn't I mention it? It must have slipped my mind with

all this fucking we've been doing."

"Mention what? I still don't know what you're on about," she said, now even more confused.

"Why, both you and Halif believing you could come to my house and just take my girls. I had a call, before you'd even set off, from Saeed. Plenty of time to prepare shall we say a little welcoming party. Although I delayed it, when Halif said I could have you for the night, I couldn't resist giving you a good fucking as a going away present. Anyway Saeed sends his best; after all you're soon to meet him again. But this time he has an even bigger reason to see you. Didn't you injure his mother and take his money a day or so ago? That, girl, was very foolish; his mother means the world to him, I'm sure he would have told you that when you last stayed at his house? You can believe you'll be working the debt off in ways you can't imagine, that's if he doesn't get fed up, and skin you alive, before leaving you to die in the desert."

"Why are you telling me this, after all I'm Sirec's girl, and I've no intention of going to Saeed?"

"Karen… Karen. Can't you understand simple English? This is the end of the line. Saeed's man is already on his way to collect you. In the meantime you'll be kept in the guardroom till he comes. It'll be hardly worth you putting your pants on though; my guards get very few girls round here. After I tell them how good a fuck you are, they'll be queuing out of the door."

Karen had gone cold, yet again she'd been deceived, but she needed to know if Halif and the men with him were involved. With that knowledge she could make plans as to how to get out of here, fast.

"If what you're saying's true, Halif has also conned me into thinking he was on my side, when all along he was part of your plan as well?"

"Ha, he knows nothing, still waiting for my girl to join him I would imagine. He'll wait forever; both girls are mine and mine alone. I don't lend either of them out, no matter what alternative is on offer. Soon he will have the choice of freedom or to die. He will choose freedom and go back to Sirec; you're not worth dying for. Besides the best part of is Sirec will never know Saeed has you. With Halif paid off the keep his mouth shut and claim you're dead, you'll rue the time you decided stupidly to take on Saeed."

Karen knew Salem was right, Halif would not think twice about leaving her to be taken by Saeed's man. She also knew Saeed would have given instructions that she was to be checked very carefully, maybe even taken naked; to make sure she carried no weapon. That's if she was in any state to object after being given to Salem's men?

Both these threats now decided her next action. Karen was close to the edge of the bed, one arm hanging over, the other trapped under this man who was leaning over her enjoying making her, in his view, squirm. Already he'd began to rub gently between her legs, trying she suspected, to arouse her again. She clenched her fist, as she'd been taught in close combat training. Dropped her arm back, and bent her elbow bringing her fist up to her shoulder. Every bone in her body was taut as she waited for him to pull away from her face.

To push him on she smiled. "Well if I'm to go back to Saeed, we may as well continue. After all, Salem, you're far more preferable to spend the rest of the night with, rather than the hired help."

He was ecstatic, believing this girl was really going to be submissive from now on, with the threat of being raped by his men; she'd give everything she'd got to stay with him. He kissed her gently, and then pulled away with the intention of getting back on top of her. That was all she was waiting for; he'd exposed his neck, and was clear of her body. Within a second, her clenched fist hit his Adam's apple with devastating force.

Salem was stunned into silence, his breath taken away from him as he began to choke and gurgle. Karen pushed him to one side, climbed off the bed and looked down, in the dim light, at the man holding his windpipe trying in vain to breathe, close to passing out. She'd been surprised how good the move actually was, before she'd always relied on her knife. Switching on the light she walked over to her clothes folded neatly on the chair, removing her knife from the sheaf. Then after slipping her knickers and t-shirt on, she walked back to him.

"On your face quickly, hands above your head," she shouted aggressively.

Salem was beginning to come round, still gasping, but could see the knife in her hand glistening in the light, so he turned over as she'd demanded.

"You're pathetic," she began, "but Saeed missed out one little point he should have told you about me. You see, everyone seems to believe I'm just a young girl, something to take to bed and worthless beyond that. Except I'm also close combat trained and already a killer, in fact quite a number of men have died by my hand. So why don't you tell me about the two girls, in particular where they are, otherwise I'll use my knife to extract the information?"

By now he'd just about got enough breath back to talk. "You'll get nothing from me. Besides, you're a dead girl for even touching me, you cannot escape from here."

"Yes, well I've had those threats made to me often enough, so don't expect me to fall to the floor begging your forgiveness. You should learn to keep your mouth shut and not boast about how clever you are. Especially how you've put off sending me directly to Saeed's because what's between your legs ruled your brains. Your stupidity also means we're unlikely to have any unwanted visitors until morning. I can't see your workers disturbing you somehow with a girl in your bed. So there's plenty of time to get you to talk."

He said nothing.

She pulled the bedclothes back, put her hand on his head, pushing his face into the pillow before forcing the knife between his legs directly through his penis into the mattress below. The pain must have been excruciating and he struggled to breathe, let alone be able to scream out as she held him down.

"Now Salem my next move with the knife means you'll lose that excuse of a dick you think so much of. Then you'd be useless for your women. They'd not be able to find even a stub left to give you a blow job. So I'll ask again, where are the girls?" she whispered into his ear.

Whether it was the very real threat of losing his manhood, or losing his life, Salem was not prepared to risk either for the sake of young girls, both of whom could be replaced with ease.

"Sammy's locked up in a room behind the guard house," he said.

"And the other one, she's there as well?"

"Yes, they're always kept together. Now get that fucking knife out of my cock."

She did that and he turned over, staring down at the blood oozing from the wound. He looked up at her. "Like I said you're dead, do you hear me, dead? I will hunt you down and you will pay for this."

She sighed. "You've done it again. Told me what your intentions are towards me. Saeed made the same error and he's now in a wheelchair, although I meant to kill him really. But you see I've no intention of being chased all over the world. I also don't like my bottom smacked or being offered out for sex with some short-arsed, fat pig before. And then, because I'd had enough, being threatened by you to spend the rest of the night with your men."

He grinned, even with the pain he still wanted to gloat. "Well this short-arsed pig, as you like to call me, certainly fucked you dry, so you've nothing to complain about."

"You think that do you? Actually I was just bored and fed up with your pathetic attempts to keep me interested and I much preferred to sleep. But I diversify, the point is, what do I do with you now? After all if you threaten to kill me, I should have the same right to return the threat to kill you."

Salem had decided that she'd delayed too long, by questioning if she should kill him. He'd no doubt she had the guts, but not the impetus any longer.

He looked at his watch. "A lot of talk, Karen, I know when a girl is enjoying the sex and you **girl** were doing just that. So for payment, rather than insult you and give you a few dollars for opening your legs, take the girls. You and Halif have five hours before I send my men after you to bring my girls back, oh and to kill you both."

Karen smiled, leaned forward and began to move the pillows behind him. "I'm really grateful for that, Salem. Tell you what, in order to make sure you do give me all that time I'll make you more comfortable before I leave shall I? After all I'll be locking the door and pulling the wire out of the telephone."

He sat there with a smug look on his face, managing to stem the blood oozing from his penis by stuffing the blankets round and pushing down hard with his hands. He couldn't believe her naivety thinking he'd give her a few hours' start.

"There you are, Salem, just lean back, it's going to be some time before they come and find you," she said quietly.

He leaned back on the pillows grinning at her as she turned away. "Look after my girls, till I collect them," he mocked.

Karen turned back and stared down at him. Then she shrugged. "What the hell, this is not like me I'm getting too soft, he'll never learn," she muttered, pushing his head back onto the pillow, before swiftly drawing the knife across his throat, then standing away watching.

"Sorry, Salem, I've changed my mind and decided it's best to kill you. After all you did threaten to kill me, or even worse planned to hand me over to Saeed. That was your biggest mistake, to tell me that, because Saeed is a man I have real reason to be very scared of, without any protection that is. I'll always remember you though; you've certainly helped me in my personal confidence. I was afraid I'd be frigid, unable to cope sexually with a man again, after being raped particularly badly by Saeed. I've also found out just how vulnerable men really are when they get the belief, with my acting submissive, I no longer pose a threat. How very wrong they would be by making that assumption. Why you might ask is that important to me? Because I have a date with just such a man, who believes he can deceive and treat me like shit the same as you. He will find to his cost I'm very capable of defending myself, even without weapons I was able to stun, possibly might have even killed you, as you've found tonight to your detriment."

He was staring at her, unable to believe he was dying and she was just stood there indifferent, rambling on about nothing. Slowly his mouth dropped open, his eyes still wide with shock as he lay slumped back on the bed, a pool of blood beginning to build up around his inert body.

Karen went into the bathroom and turned on the shower. She wanted to wash this man's sweat from her body and was under for some time, using plenty of soap. Finally, in her view clean again, she dressed in her army clothes and left the room. Closing it silently she locked the door. The house was quiet as she went down the passage into Halif's room. She sat on the side of the bed and shook him.

He stirred and opened his eyes. "What are you doing here?"

"Well for a start I'm not the replacement for the girl who was going to see you tonight. Secondly why are you not out looking for the girls, while I was entertaining that excuse for a man?"

"She never came; I think there was something in my drink as I just fell asleep."

"I know why she didn't come; he'd no intention of letting Sirec's hired help have either of his girls."

"How do you know that?"

Karen told him everything that Salem had said.

"What have you done with him now?" Halif asked.

She shrugged. "The stupid man threatened to kill me, said he'd follow me all over the world. So I cut his throat."

"You've killed him?" he gasped hardly believing this girl could actually have killed in cold blood.

"Of course, that's what you do with scum. Besides, if he'd lived I'd have another Saeed on my back, and just him alone pisses me off."

Halif stood and began to dress. "You realise what you've done?"

"Yes, killed Salem."

"Apart from that, Karen. Your stupid action will also bring the whole bloody region down on us. We'll be lucky to get out of the area alive."

"Well you'll have to be creative won't you, besides I saved your life. He was going to kill you in the morning anyway, so you owe me," she lied.

"Just how do you suggest we be creative?"

"Let's have a fire. Us two will run out and poor Salem will perish. When I was at Sirec's house the SAS did that and destroyed any evidence that two people inside were shot. Anyway while they're struggling to put it out, we'll tell them we have to move on and will take the girls back to Saeed, to be looked after."

Halif didn't want to correct her assumption the evidence of Salem being killed beforehand would be destroyed, except the girl was right in one way. There would be a delay in finding out Salem was already dead, which meant they would be well away from the area.

He fastened his trouser belt and looked at her. "It might work."

"It'd better; otherwise you'll be in the same boat as I was in, last time I was here."

"What are you rambling about now, Karen?"

"Chased by hundreds of soldiers, that's what."

He sighed. "Come on, let's start the bloody fire and get out of here."

Twenty minutes later the bedroom Salem had died in was not only on fire but the entire house was threatening to be engulfed. The soft furnishings inside were quickly turning it into an inferno. His guards were running everywhere trying to stop the fire spreading. Halif went to get Sirec's men together, while Karen replaced her ammunition belt, collected her gun and went to the guard's accommodation building. It was empty as everyone was fighting the fire. She soon found the locked door but no key. However in seconds she'd kicked the flimsy door open. Inside were two girls, huddled together on the bed, a single blanket covering them, not even looking up with the noise.

Karen went inside. "Don't argue or ask questions at this moment. My name is Karen Marshall, I'm English and I've come to take you home. Get dressed quickly, and then we go."

Both girls got up without saying a word and dressed in jeans, t-shirts and jumpers as she asked. Then they all left the building and ran over to the waiting lorry. Moments later it set off along with the other two vehicles of the convoy.

34

Saeed replaced the telephone in its handset. He was deep in thought. The man he'd sent to Salem, to collect Karen, had just telephoned and told him of Salem's death in a tragic accident. By describing Karen to the guards the man had confirmed she'd been there, but moved on during the fire. Saeed wouldn't have thought any more about it, except that Salem's two girls had also left with Karen. Now Saeed was convinced she'd had a hand in it, but he wasn't certain. However, there was nothing lost in planting a seed of doubt.

Dialling another number, he waited a time before it was answered. "Is Ishmael there?" Saeed asked the person who'd answered the phone.

A few minutes later Ishmael came to the phone. "I can't talk now Saeed, my brother has just died in a fire at his home. I need to go there."

"Yes, Ishmael, I've just heard. But if I were you I'd look into the death very carefully. It just seems a coincidence that Sirec's man Halif and Karen, Sirec's new girl, were also there and have collected Salem's girls."

There was silence on the other side of the phone for a minute or so. "Are you suggesting Sirec's man has got something to do with my brother death?"

"Not only suggesting it, but you can be certain if Sirec's girl is also around, it was no accident."

"Then Sirec will pay with his life. My brother was a kind, simple man who would hurt no one."

Saeed rolled his eyes back, Ishmael had no idea just what Salem had been up to all these years. But if he wanted to believe that, so be it, after all you can be certain if Ishmael found Sirec was involved, it would be war between two very powerful men.

"I suggest you intercept them and perhaps have a little chat,

Ishmael, they are on their way to see Lomax. But I'd like a small favour if you will?"

"What is that?"

"Karen, Sirec's girl, injured my mother. You know what a kind and loving mother she is. I was very upset by the way she was treated. I'd dearly like to have Karen apologise to my mother personally, before she's handed over for punishment, to the authorities."

"If we manage to catch up with them, you can be sure I will arrange it for you Saeed. You are right, your mother was so very kind to me and my wife on our visit to your house."

"Thank you, Ishmael, you are most generous."

Replacing the receiver, he lifted it again and dialled another number. "Lomax, Saeed here. How's the girl?"

"Saeed, good to hear from you. The girl is very well. You couldn't have found me a more loving and obedient companion. Besides she is very beautiful and admired by all my friends."

"That is good, Lomax, but we have a problem with Sirec."

Lomax was also a gunrunner, like Sirec. However he was nothing near the size of Sirec's operation, selling mainly into the African states. "What's Sirec got to do with me?" he asked.

"Sirec wants your girl. In fact he's sent Halif to collect her. But Halif is not alone he's travelling with a few of Sirec's gunmen, and would you believe Sirec's girl."

Lomax thought for a moment. "That's not the girl who escaped and he offered silly rewards for her return is it?"

"The very one."

"So why does he want my Annette, if he has her back?"

"You know Sirec, he doesn't keep his girls long and has heard good reports about your girl," Saeed lied.

"Well he's not getting her. Thanks for the information, Saeed; I will see you're rewarded for it."

"That's okay, Lomax. I will call you if I hear anything else."

Lomax rang off.

Saeed leaned back in his chair. Now the seeds were sown, either man could bring about Karen's downfall.

35

"Are we going straight home?" Sammy asked Karen, as they travelled in the back of the lorry. Natasha the young girl was asleep, huddled close to Sammy ever since they had left Salem's.

"No, we have Annette to collect first. Then you're going home."

"What about the others, have you found them?"

"Yes, there's already three on their way home. Anyway, how did Salem treat you?"

Sammy looked at Karen, her voice low. "He treated us well, if you can accept being raped regularly as being treated well? But that was preferable to our first day in which he showed us the alternative to refusing to do everything he wanted of us."

"How do you mean?" Karen asked, although she knew what Sammy was going to say, but felt it prudent not to mention her hours with Salem.

Sammy went on to tell her of the barn.

Karen shook her head. "You know the actions of these people don't bear thinking about."

"I agree, but Natasha didn't deserve any punishment, she'd done nothing, never spoke out like I did. God knows what they had against her, even at the auction, they'd virtually starved her, used an electric stick on her for amusement, then for Salem to string her up, I don't know how she's held herself together. When I was fourteen I'd have been a blubbering wreck, but she's never once complained and there couldn't be a more sensitive and loving girl you could ever meet."

"I know what you mean, the more you hear, the more you realise these people seem to relish depravity to others. So how did things go after the barn?"

"We were treated better, had a nice room to share and Salem promised Natasha one of her own, but it didn't materialise.

We worked in the kitchens and cleaned the house in the mornings, then lounged about in the afternoons. Salem would sometimes take Natasha in the afternoons. He was teaching her how to please him and she'd be back for tea. Often she'd return to the bedroom in tears, embarrassed with what he wanted her to do to him. The girl is young, not developed and he had this belief she accepted and understood what he wanted of her. But if I tried to tell him, he'd have taken me back into the barn to be strapped. I'd have taken the punishment if it would have made any difference, but it wouldn't. We'd often have to dance for him and his friends early evening wearing very short skirts and crop top." Sammy scrunched her nose. "They always wanted us to wriggle our bums a lot, which wasn't exactly dancing. Thankfully though we were never allowed to remove any clothes. Salem was very possessive of us, and loved to show us off, but never let any of his friends see us naked. My turn alone with him was from around eleven at night when he retired till the early hours, then I was sent back to our bedroom. I was really worried I'd get pregnant, after all he was at me very nearly every day, but the cook told me he was impotent, had to take pills to even have sex. It made us laugh, realising he wasn't the super stud he'd tried to make out he was, but a blue pill junkie unable to get it up without any. Natasha was missing her dad desperately, believing he'd come for her and take her home, but as the days went on she was becoming more depressed and cried herself to sleep by my side at night, before I'd have to leave her, and entertain Salem in his bed. The night before last I could have killed him. He always insisted we wore no nightclothes, didn't believe in them he said. But I think it was a way to make sure we carried no weapon into his bedroom when he came for us. I'd always have my hair down and he'd run his hands through, very carefully, before I was allowed to get into his bed. Anyway he'd often come into our bedroom, look around, check the drawers and cupboards. I suppose looking for something we might have hidden, but we never did, besides having nothing to hide really. Even the cutlery at meals was counted, washed and placed back in racks so they could see if any had gone missing, and that was before we could leave the table. He always pulled the bedclothes back and looked at us both lying there naked, then he'd take me to his room. But that night he took Natasha instead and used her like he used me. Up to that time she was a virgin and when she came back she could hardly walk, with dried blood between her legs. I had to wash her down then kept her cuddled close to me. She was so frightened and just wanted to die."

Karen felt relieved at hear that Salem was impotent. It had been at the back of her mind that such a long session, without any protection, could well have increased the risk of pregnancy, the last thing she wanted. She also realised now why he was so demanding, it was the pills, no wonder she was struggling to keep up. Putting it to the back of her mind she gripped Sammy's hand. "Well it's nearly over now; it's time to pick the pieces up, Sam, and get on with your life. Salem is dead, so he's paid dearly for his crimes against you and Natasha," Karen said quietly.

"How did he die?" Sammy asked.

Karen grinned. "I did what they do when they slaughter any pig. I slit his throat."

"I'm glad he's dead, Natasha will be too. But I don't know how you coped, Karen, when you were with these people. I remember reading a little in the paper about you. It sounded so far-fetched that there were people, in this world, who would do such things to another human being. When they took me, only then did I begin to understand just how strong willed and capable you really must have been to get out and fight back. I now know how helpless you are in their clutches and the guts it must take to go up against them. My will was broken after the punishment, too scared to even utter a word."

Then she looked down at Natasha, still sleeping. "He deserved to die like that; in fact all of them deserve to die, after what they have done to this little girl. She will take a very long time to get over it, if she ever does."

"And what of you, Sam, will you get over it?"

Sammy didn't answer directly; she just looked back at Karen. "Have you, Karen?"

Karen shrugged. "I live on borrowed time, Sam. I already walk in the shadow of death, there are people out there who want me dead, so for me it won't be a question of me getting over it. It's more the question as to just how long I'll survive before one finally succeeds in taking me out."

Sammy's mouth dropped open. "But you can't give up, Karen. You've come for us, for the others; surely you're going home with us to take up your life again?"

She shook her head. "It's not quite like that. To actually find you both I had to do a deal with the man who arranged this operation. Why do you think we're with gunmen and not British soldiers? Don't get me wrong, I was very happy with the arrangement, I like the man a lot, he's my type and we'd be good together. But I've found out over the last day or so it's not quite what I believed was going to happen. So I'm going to kill him and hopefully a man called Saeed. His mother was the one who prepared you before the auction. Believe me when that happens, I won't get out alive."

Tears were coming to Sammy's eyes. "You shouldn't have come for us, Karen. Neither, me or Natasha would ever expect, or want, someone to lay down their life for us. We would have survived, how long I don't know, but we were coping, just about."

Karen grasped her hand tighter.

"Soldiers came for me, Sam. They had families, their whole life in front of them, but they came for me and none returned. I felt the same, couldn't understand why people would do that for a stranger. Now I know. I believe God has kept me alive to help get you all home. In particular Natasha, who is still just a child and has never done anything to anyone to have been treated the way they have with her. Even if she'd been the only one missing, I couldn't have left her there, because I know what she and all of you were going through. If I don't go on to finally finish it with Saeed, the abductions will never stop. He and his mother couldn't care less what their greed has done to so many children. Believe me they deserve to die."

Sammy looked at her for a minute. "Then I'll come with you. We finish it together, Karen. I wasn't brought up with a silver spoon in my mouth. I was brought up in the East End of London where you fought your own fights and never turned the other cheek. You're not going to fight my fight while I run away like a scared rabbit. That man sold Natasha, his mother treated the little girl like shit. They will pay for that, believe me they will pay."

"I understand your anger, Sam, I really do. But what you have been through is nothing to what can happen. There would be a very high risk of you falling into their hands again, which for you, does not bear thinking about. You will need the guts to kill a man, maybe a woman. You will need the guts to be able to take your own life. That, Sam, is the most difficult. Your mind will fight against you, self-preservation will kick in, and you won't be able to pull the trigger. Then it'll be too late, you'll be caught, never have the opportunity again."

"And can you, take your own life I mean?"

Karen shook her head. "I don't know, I can only hope I can. But if I think back to when there was one moment I'd asked a soldier to take my life, I clutched at a very tiny straw to stop him. I hope the next time no straw will be offered."

They couldn't continue the conversation as at that moment the vehicles came to a halt. Halif looked into the back of the lorry. "Karen, can you come with me," he asked.

She turned to Sammy. "Stay here, we'll talk about what we've been discussing later." Then she climbed out of the back, dropping to the ground.

"Lomax's place is about a mile further along this road. He's a gunrunner and will, like Sirec, always have guards. I think we can assume he's already got knowledge that we're coming, it gets round these people like wildfire when there's a risk of trouble. Anyway this entrance we've stopped at leads down to a disused quarry. It's a good quarter of a mile and it's unlikely anyone would go down there. The girls will have to remain there with one guard until we return."

"Will they be safe?"

"As safe as anywhere, Karen. The guard I'm leaving is a family man, will look after them and get them to Sirec if we don't return. Sirec may be a lot of things but he has never condoned such a young girl like Natasha being forced into prostitution. He will get her home believe me."

"And Sam, will she go home?"

Halif smiled. "Yes, Karen, he will keep his word to you and send Sam as well."

Karen believed him. In lots of ways she had to, there was no other option. So after telling Sammy what was to happen, she left with the main troop for the last girl, Annette.

36

Lomax was handing guns out to his men. He'd already received telephone calls to tell him the convoy had been spotted and was heading this way.

"Who are these people, Lomax?" his top man asked.

"Sirec's men. He has some stupid notion that he wants my girl. I paid good money for her and she's mine. I've just had a call to say they'll be here within the hour. So get into position, I don't want them to get close to the main house."

The men spread out, however, Lomax's caller was too late in his warning, Halif and his men had already arrived. But rather than drive directly up to the main house, like they had at Salem's, they had stopped short and were approaching on foot.

Lomax went into the lounge with two men. He'd an idea Halif would use his gunmen to keep the guards occupied while he tried to enter from the rear. Lomax had deliberately left that area vulnerable to entice him in. Sirec's gunmen would give up and go home if he caught Halif; there'd be nothing to fight for.

Karen stayed with Halif, their intention as Lomax anticipated, was while the men distracted Lomax's guards they would make their way to the house by the back way. Already a gun battle had started and Sirec's men dug in for a long fight. Taking a wide berth of the house and compound, where the battle was taking place, both Karen and Halif found only two protecting the rear. It was Halif who took them out. Karen was surprised how good he really was in a battle. He helped her over a relatively high wall and they dropped down into the compound behind the house. Keeping close to the wall, they went through the unlocked back door into the kitchen area. It was a large house, with many rooms. Outside they could hear the sound of small arms fire, but the house seemed deserted.

"You take the bedrooms, I'll check downstairs and the

cellars," Halif told Karen.

She nodded and went up the stairs. With five bedrooms she'd no trouble searching them. The third one was locked, although the key was in the keyhole. She unlocked it and went inside. Annette was on the bed reading, dressed in jeans and t-shirt. She looked up as Karen entered the room.

"Hi, I'm Karen. Are you Annette?" Karen asked casually, so as not to alarm the girl.

"Yes, but what are you? Where are you from, dressed like you are?"

"I'm Special Operations, British Forces."

"So there's a load of you then?"

"No, only me and another man, the rest are outside, why do you ask?"

She sighed. "Well if there's only two of you in the house it's all a waste of time. Lomax has been expecting you, and set a trap."

Karen shrugged. "So what, besides it's a bit late to turn back. Shall we go and see what sort of trap he's set?"

She looked at Karen wide-eyed. "He'll kill you. Leave me and try to get out yourself. He's determined to keep me anyway; alone you two might just succeed in escaping."

Karen took out her British army insignias from her top pocket and attached them back onto her shoulders and cap, followed by her lieutenant's label. She'd an idea this rescue was not going well, but in her mind she was still a British soldier, maybe only temporary but if she was going to die, she wanted everyone to know that, and not die a nobody. Then Karen pulled a grenade from her belt, slipped the ring through her thumb and smiled to herself. *"Try taking me alive now,"* she thought, then she turned to Annette. "Come on, whatever happens, by the sound of it, he won't shoot you. He'll go for me. If we get through we're out. If we don't you're no worse off. What do you say?"

Annette frowned. "What's that you've got in your hand?"

"Insurance that's all. You see, Annette, I'm wanted by so many people, I can't risk being taken alive. Anyway come on; let's see if we can have some fun shall we?"

"Excuse me, I've just said he'll kill you and you call it fun. I call it madness."

"So; we don't live forever. Besides, do you really want to stay with this guy and not try to get home?"

"Of course I want to go home. I just don't relish dying in the process. But if you're hell-bent on doing this stupid thing, I'll come with you. But don't blame me if he kills you."

"And how can I do that if I'm dead?" Karen mocked.

"You know what I mean, Karen. I'll get my jacket," she replied grinning.

Annette took out a leather bomber jacket from the wardrobe and slipped her shoes on. At the same time Karen had gone to the door opening it gingerly. She was worried; Halif hadn't come up the stairs. There weren't any sounds, apart from what was going on outside. This could, as Annette had said, be a trap. She swung her AK47 round, set the output to maximum and with the strap over her shoulder she held it firmly in one hand, in the other of course was the grenade. They both went to the top of the stairs ready to go down, when Karen came to an abrupt halt. Four men, all carrying handguns, were stood in the hall below. Halif was on his knees, a man had a gun pointed at his head.

"It's about time you came out of Annette's room, we've been waiting ages," one of the men said. "Why don't you come down and join us?"

Karen looked around the hall, then the landing and the closed doors. She was expecting others to be hidden inside some of the rooms, but couldn't detect any movement from the doors.

"Stay well back to the wall and shout if you see someone coming up behind me. Can you do that?" Karen whispered.

Annette gave her a withering look. "Of course I can, but that's Lomax standing down there, which means you're dead anyway, so what's the use? I may as well go and wait in my room."

Karen knew the girl was right, this was the end, she'd failed but at least some of the girls would get home. However, she was not going to admit that to Annette. "Stop wishing me dead all the time?" Karen answered back. "I'm not dead till I'm dead. So will you do that little thing for me and just maybe I can be confident enough to know someone's watching my back."

Annette never replied but backed off leaning against the landing wall. She pulled out a packet of cigarettes from her pocket and lighting one, she took a long draw. It was as if the girl was waiting to see Karen killed, before returning to her room.

While Karen had been talking to Annette, Lomax had been studying her. He'd expected a girl, perhaps in jeans and maybe holding a handgun, but stood there was no civilian, no conscript, but a fully armed British soldier, protected with a bulletproof jacket and carrying a formidable arsenal of weapons. He would have to be very careful with her, with the bulletproof vest the chances of an instant kill was remote and barring a very accurate hit to the head, he could only hope to injure her before she brought her own weapon to bear on them.

"I presume you're Karen, Sirec's girl?"

"I am, what's it to you?"

"Nothing really, except Sirec seems to have the intention of taking my girl. So I thought I might just take Sirec's girl instead. After all, get rid of that military gear you're wearing and you'd probably not be a bad looking kid. Besides it would piss Sirec off to know his girl's with me now, and I still have my own."

"Think a lot of yourself don't you? Apart from which, you're hardly in any position to even have a hope in hell of getting close to me, before I blow your brains across the hall."

"Aggressive aren't we? Do you really believe you can escape from here? There's close on thirty men outside, all with guns. I only have to say one word and you'll die in a hail of bullets. Do you want that?"

Karen grinned. "So; we all have to die sometime, personally I couldn't care less, but you can be sure a few and maybe even you, will go with me."

Lomax nodded his head up and down slowly. "Yes whatever little girl. Anyway enough talking, it gets us nowhere. Just put the gun on the floor and come down, or your boyfriend's right-hand man is dead. Then try to explain to Sirec how you let him die," he replied softly.

She shrugged indifferently. "You think I'm disarming for him? Do what you want; I've no allegiance to the hired help. I'm leaving with Annette. Perhaps, if you've the guts, you'll come after me, and then we'll see what sort of man you really are. At the moment you're all looking pretty pathetic holding peashooters against my AK47."

A man at Lomax's side moved a little closer. "I can take her out, Lomax."

Lomax glared at him. "How the fuck do you expect to do that? She's got a bulletproof vest on and if that gun's set to max, which if she's any sense it is, we are all fucking dead," he hissed.

The man moved away, he'd not known her jacket was bulletproof, thinking before Lomax had told him about the jacket that he could have fallen to the floor, reduced her target on him and let go eight rounds at her very fast.

Outside the gunfire had suddenly fallen silent, and a man ran through into the hall stopping dead when he realised he was between a girl holding a gun at the top of the stairs and Lomax.

"What the fuck do you want?" Lomax demanded.

"Sirec's men have surrendered, Lomax, we're in control."

Lomax grinned, then turned and shot Halif in the head. He fell forward silently, blood beginning to spread across the floor.

"You hear that, Karen? We've won, Halif is dead and you're alone, so let's call it a day shall we, put the gun down carefully and I promise you won't be hurt?"

Karen was still trying to decide her next move, when Annette spoke. "What are you going to do, Karen, do you want me to go back to my room?"

Karen stood silently, it had shaken her to see Lomax just shoot Halif in the head. However, in her book a man who could do that so callously, after he'd won, wasn't to be trusted to keep his word to her.

"I seem to have a tiny problem here. In fact when the shooting starts I'll be lucky to get out alive. You'd better go back to your room, Annette, if you want to live?"

Annette didn't need telling twice, she was already scared, if they started shooting she was stood directly behind Karen and would more than likely get hit.

"Sorry, Karen, good luck. But I did warn you it was a trap," she said and ran back down the landing slamming her door.

Lomax watched his girl go; now he was more relaxed, at least she was safe. "Okay, Karen, put the gun into safety, remove your belt, and then throw them down the stairs."

Karen made to begin to take the gun off her shoulder, but at the same time was moving her thumb and slipping the pin out from the grenade hidden in her other hand, allowing the catch to release. Then she began counting. "Here; catch this, while I slip the safety on my gun," she said casually, before throwing the grenade underarm towards them.

One man, next to Lomax, went to catch what Karen had thrown. Lomax had relaxed a little when she said those words, convinced she'd realised the futility of holding out against so many. Then his mouth dropped open as he recognised what she'd thrown; flying towards them, spinning as it came. There was nowhere to run, the doors shut and locked to prevent her escape except the front door ten feet away which was too far to reach.

"She's thrown a fucking grenade, hit the floor," Lomax shouted.

The man who'd moved forward to catch what she'd thrown stopped dead staring at it coming towards him. The next moment it exploded, still feet from the ground. The noise, the percussion effect of the airborne explosion, besides the shattered pieces of the grenade itself, killed some instantly, mortally wounding others.

Karen had also hit the floor, her hands over her ears, but this was a very modern grenade, unlike the type used in earlier wars, designed to stun besides kill very efficiently, and Karen was not immune, being in the same confined area as the shrapnel flew everywhere, the noise unbelievable. Her ears were ringing, she felt disorientated, but tried to pull herself together, the threat still very real until she could be sure everyone below was either dead, or no longer able to retaliate. But the place was full of smoke and dust, she could see nothing.

Finally, still with the ringing in her ears the dust cleared to a point where she could see what had happened. Karen stared in disbelief, she felt sick inside. The four people who were downstairs were all obviously dead, body parts from some missing. The others badly disfigured.

Scrambling up she heard a sound behind, and spun round, her gun ready. It was Annette.

"What the hell happened?" she whispered.

Karen shrugged, trying to act indifferent. "I threw a grenade; it seems to have done quite a lot of damage though. Well more than I thought it would anyway."

Annette looked down, feeling decidedly sick at what she saw. "Seems, Karen? You've blown everyone into little bits."

"Yes, I can see that as well. Besides, I didn't know it'd do so much damage. Anyway are you ready to go. I've got a feeling we'd better get out of here fast."

The two girls ran down the stairs, trying to ignore the carnage. The kitchen door originally locked by Lomax had been blown open by the blast, so they ran through the kitchen and outside.

"Where now?" Annette gasped looking down at two men lying dead, shot earlier by Halif.

"Can you use a gun?"

"Excuse me, how would I have learnt to do that, it's not on the school curriculum you know?" she replied.

"No matter, you'll soon learn, like I had to. Take his gun," she said pointing to one of the guards, "and we'll make our escape over the back wall, come on I'll give you a leg up and then you pull me over."

They both scrambled over the wall, jumped down and ran for their lives. Taking a wide arc round and up a quite a steep hill, they followed the track away from the house. Karen had come this way with Halif originally and knew the direction to take. The two of them came to a halt looking down at what was going on.

They could see people stood some distance from the main house, already six of the gunmen who'd come with Karen lay face down on the ground with their hands on their heads.

"It's pointless hanging around here, Halif's men have lost. Mind you, now your boyfriend's dead, they might wonder where the wages are going to come from. So with luck, maybe they'll ransack the house for valuables and forget us," Karen said,

"He wasn't my bloody boyfriend. I don't go out with slimy gets. I bet when your arse was up against the wall, you'd let anyone shag you?"

Karen grinned; perhaps she'd used the wrong word calling Lomax her boyfriend? "Don't be so touchy, I was only kidding you know, trying to lighten the position we're in."

"Yes well, I'd prefer the kidding not to be directed at me having to put up with some scumbag, who raped me every night, referred to as a boyfriend, thank you. And while we're talking about the position we're in, perhaps next time you come and rescue me, the others should come inside the bloody house with you. That might have reduced the risk of having to blow the bloody place up with a hand-grenade, while I'm still in there. My ears are ringing even now."

Karen began laughing. "Tell you what Annette, why don't you just go back, then when they actually give me a small army to help, plus transport, I'll come for you again?"

Annette's face changed. "I was joking, Karen. Anyway where are they?" she asked quietly.

"Where are who?"

"The troops, the British SAS, whoever you came with."

Karen's face fell. "I don't have anyone with me, British that is, Annette. Even Halif is dead and his men are captured. Now we've a long way to go in hostile territory. That's before I can get you to a place where the British forces can collect you."

She stared at Karen, open-mouthed. "I don't believe this, it's another of your jokes; isn't it? You're dressed as a British soldier; they must be here with you?"

Karen shook her head. "It's no joke. I was with the SAS; I split up from them two days ago, after we'd collected two of the girls. I came on alone with Sirec's men. You're the last to be rescued. Three are on their way home and another two including a younger girl, who apparently was just along for the ride to the desert camp, I've already collected. They're waiting for us about a mile or so away."

"But you're just eighteen, like me, how in hell have you managed to do this?"

Karen shrugged, trying to look indifferent. "Luck I suppose, like with Lomax. He believed I'd crumble seeing Sirec's man with a gun at his head. Personally it meant nothing to me, it can't. You see for me to give my gun up means being forced into a life far worse than what you've had. So I live or die by the gun, there's no surrender, no alternative, for me that is."

Annette sighed. "You're no Rambo, Karen. Have you looked at yourself? You look like someone from one of those spaghetti movies; they used to have an ammunition belt strung across them as well. Anyway, just because you're dolled up with weapons and dressed in an army uniform, you can hardly take on the bloody world. This is as real as it gets. It's not a film, where we all go home after. Now your actions have probably put us in a position, if we're caught, of being sold again to god knows what sort of man this time, or even worse killed."

Inwardly Karen was already scared. She never imagined it was going to be like this. She'd expected to have just collected the girls with Halif and his men, finding little opposition, and gone back to Sirec. The last thing she wanted was what little confidence she had being pulled down by this girl.

"I know you don't think much of me, Annette, but I will get you home, I promise you that."

Annette didn't ask the obvious question as to how she intended to do that, she was interested in why Karen was really here. "I read in the paper, before I was abducted, you got yourself home, didn't you?"

"Yes, why do you ask?"

"So you admit you were actually home and away from all this?"

"Yes."

"Then why come back?"

"To get you and the other girls out."

Annette took a cigarette out and lit it slowly, and then she looked at Karen. "You're telling me out of all the resources of the British army, it came down to them giving a girl, just out of school, a few weapons for her protection and telling her to go alone into a country, already embroiled in a civil war, because she was the only person stupid enough to actually agree to do it? Come off it, even I'm not going to believe the government would let the military do that?"

"I suppose you could have been right, they may have stopped me if they suspected I was actually going to stay here. But the Captain in charge never checked, just accepted I had my own orders he wasn't party to, so that's why I'm here," Karen replied.

She frowned. "Then they really were the SAS you walked out on?"

"Yes, what's that got to do with it?"

"A great deal, Karen, when you're talking about people's lives, particularly mine and by what you're telling me two other girls'. Because, correct me if I'm wrong, we're in a foreign country on the run from god knows who, just because you had this idea you can run around a country shooting and killing, and no one would notice? Now you seem to be saying we're miles from a point the British army can pick us up. Isn't that a bit naive on your part?"

Karen put her hands to her face, she didn't need this. Then she looked at Annette watching her. "You're right, this is hostile country, but the British Army couldn't get near you, it would have started a war. So you would have been lost to your family, to your friends, forever. I'm no female Rambo, Annette, nothing special. Sirec, the man who purchased me wanted me back, so I agreed to exchange myself for the three of you. He supplied help and transport, that's why I'm here. When you get on the helicopter to go home, I can't, I have to stay. Now please, we have a long way to go and this really isn't the time to discuss the rights and wrongs."

Annette stared at her, unable to believe what she'd just heard.

"You're wrong. This is the time, Karen. You really are insane aren't you? Why would you think we'd accept that our only way of getting home is to swap ourselves for another girl? I for one won't and I'm bloody sure the others won't either. We got ourselves in this mess; you're nothing to do with it. Now you're expecting us to just go home and forget a girl has given her life, her freedom up for us? I'm sorry, it doesn't work that way. You stay, we all stay, otherwise you come with us."

Karen stood and looked down at her. "I'm not insane, maybe a little stupid for even bothering to come to collect a girl with your attitude. I've done my best, risked my life to get you out. The least you can do is humour me and believe I'll get you home."

Annette stood; she could see tears forming in Karen's eyes, so she put her arms round her, holding her tight. "I'm sorry, Karen. I accept you've done your best and risked your life. I witnessed it in that house. You've got more guts in your little finger than I've got in my whole body to actually take on these people. I really am grateful you came. But no matter what you say or think, I will not leave this country without you."

Karen sighed. "I'd think very carefully about those words, Annette. Because I'll tell you now, come with me to take Saeed and Sirec out and you will be signing your death warrant. Because if we fail and my back's up against the wall, I will kill you rather then let them take you again, have no doubt about that," she said softly. "Anyway we really must go; we need to get back to the two other girls. They'll be getting panicky if we delay too long."

They set off, keeping close to the side of the road, ready to scramble for cover if anything approached. Only two vehicles travelling the other way passed them. Each time they had plenty of notice to hide from view, in the scrub on either side of the road, until they passed.

"So how have you coped?" Karen asked as they had now left the main road and were heading down the track towards the quarry.

"All right I suppose. Lomax was really nice in lots of ways. My clothes were all new and he took me to choose them. I always ate with him and we'd talk, watch movies, then he'd take me to bed. I hated that part. I was just something to shag until he'd had enough of me, then he'd push me away and I'd have to go to my own room. There was no affection, no love. In his book I was bought and paid for, so I did what he wanted, not what I wanted. The hardest part was not being able to talk to my mates, see my mum and dad. I was facing the rest of my life alone. He told me

I'd soon have kids, but I didn't want kids at my age. I wanted to go out and party, but he never took me out, not in public anyway. I did go to another house last week and sat around a pool all day, while he was in some sort of meeting. There was a really cool lad there, my age. I think he was the owner's son and he kept looking at me. Mind you, it was understandable, I had this bikini on to die for, and with my long legs, I knew I looked good with it on."

"Sounds like you'd settled and started to enjoy it," Karen said.

Annette stopped and looked directly at her. "That's not true, Karen, again you're using the wrong words. I was doing my best to try to live, as a prisoner has to. They at least get to see their loved ones; I got to see no one. I may as well be dead. The first nights I cried myself to sleep. But no one came, no one listened or cared. What could I do? I threw myself into it, tried to act pleasant to a man I despised. I dreaded the day I'd be pregnant and then have to bring up a child in what was a prison. He'd even said he didn't want girls, only boys. I began to imagine he'd want to terminate my pregnancy if it was a girl. How do you think that made me feel? I may not want children yet, but if he'd made me pregnant, like any mother to be, I'd want to keep my baby not keep terminating till he got what he wanted. When you came in the room, I was really happy I'd been found and was to go home. But after the night before with Lomax boasting all the time how he'd send Sirec's man home, with his tail between his legs, and also take his girl, you can understand I didn't have much confidence in being rescued. I'll tell you this though. If you'd said in my bedroom there was only you who'd come, wild horses wouldn't have got me down those stairs."

Karen sighed. "I suppose I can't blame you for thinking that. But at least everyone believed you were still alive. When I was taken they thought I was dead, drowned in Wales so no one would have come to find where I was."

"Yes, I can understand that, it must have been devastating for you. What of the other girls, how did they get on?"

"They have both had a bad time, particularly the young girl Natasha, who's just fourteen and has already been raped, and beaten into submission. We're still a long way from being free, so we have to keep Natasha's confidence up that she's going home. The girl would fall apart if she got the idea she might be taken by these men again."

"So would I, but do you really think we'll get home?"

Karen shrugged. "There were lots of times I didn't think I'd get out last time, but I did, so yes we have a good chance, if we stick together."

They arrived at the vehicle to find the two girls sat on the banking and the soldier asleep by the side of the front wheel.

"Hi, Karen, we were wondering when you'd get back. Is this Annette?" Natasha asked.

"Yes, Annette, meet Natasha and of course you know Sam from the hotel. Now we should all sit together and I'll try to explain where we're at."

By now the man looking after them had woken and he too joined in the meeting. He could speak English, which saved a great deal of gesturing.

"First of all," Karen began, "I'm not sure just what is happening at the Lomax house. By the look of it, Sirec's men who came with us have been captured, that means we're alone and will need to travel at night. I've been on the roads then myself and it's practically deserted. With Halif dead I've decided to try to head for a lady I know. Hopefully from there I can call the UK by phone and speak to Sir Peter."

"Why would you want to speak to a Lord?" Sammy asked.

"He's head of MI5 or some other oddball department and with three English girls rescued, but on the run, they may just be able to convince the authorities here to help us. Alternatively they will send in Special Forces by helicopter and get you out."

"But what about Saeed? You said you were going after him?" Sammy asked.

"I am, but alone. I can travel faster that way. I'm also carrying enough firepower to take him out."

"Not without me you're not. I told you, Karen, Saeed and his mother owes us. Particularly Natasha who shouldn't even be here. You are not fighting our battles. You fought your own, this is ours," Sammy replied.

"I've told her that as well, Sam," Annette added. "She sold me to be raped every bloody night. I'll break her fucking neck for that."

Karen smiled. "I'm sorry but you all have to go home. Leave it to me. They both owe me as well. Besides this is a particularly risky operation to go back into their houses, so much could go wrong and I can't afford to be taken alive. What you have all gone through would be nothing to what they'd do to you the next time. So as a last resort, if I was up against the wall with nowhere to run, I'd take my own life. You would need to do the same, you couldn't risk being taken again, Saeed would make life absolute hell, believe me, he has the outlets to do just that."

"She's right girls. You're all valuable prizes in a country where young white girls command very high sale value. You've already had a taste of what could happen, you shouldn't risk losing your freedom for vengeance," the man added to Karen's words.

"Well that's where you're both wrong. Like I said, Karen, if you stay, I stay. I refuse to allow another girl to take my place. So you'd better get used to it or come up with a plan that gets us all home. What do you say, Sam?"

"I'm with Annette, Karen, I too will stay," Sammy said.

Both girls looked at Natasha.

"If I understand what you're all saying, is that Karen intends to exchange herself for me," she asked.

"Yes she does, Natasha," Sammy replied.

The young girl looked at Karen. "Thank you, Karen, for offering. But I won't let you. I'd rather return to another Salem, than expect you to go through what I have, just so I could go home. Besides, mum and dad would both understand and I think agree with me."

Karen now wished she'd not mentioned it, but she had, trying to defend herself as to why she came. She looked at Sirec's man.

"What's your name?" she asked.

"Abed."

"You heard them, Abed, you know Sirec. What happens

now?"

"As far as I am concerned, Karen, I did not know of the arrangement between you and Sirec, only Halif knew among all the men who came and he's dead. I will take you all where you want to go and drop you off. You girls should not be here, should never have been taken and must go home. It will be up to your government to do that, I cannot."

"Thank you Abed," Karen replied. "We will all go home then, me as well."

"Yes, thank you, Abed, from us all," Sammy added.

"Okay, now we have some sort of plan," Karen began, "I intend to sleep. I've been up for nearly two days and we've a good five hours till dark. You must all take turns to rest and keep watch. Wake me if you see anything; keep well down and out of sight. This is not a holiday camp. They could come to look for us, or just ignore us, I don't know, but we have to be prepared for either."

"You get some sleep, Karen, and don't worry," Annette said. "We all understand the dangers and what we need to do."

37

Sir Peter was studying a wall map in the operational room where they were following Karen's progress. According to the map she had travelled three hundred miles and seemed now to be returning.

"Is this data up-to-date?" he asked the lady monitoring the tracker signals.

"Yes, Karen has transmitted her position a number of times, Sir Peter, with her mobile GPS unit. That has confirmed our tracker. She's travelling by night and turning off the road onto small tracks in the day," the lady answered.

"Why is she so slow coming back?" he asked.

"GCHQ suggest the road she's travelling on is through areas where the civil war is very active. A number of times she's turned off and waited for an hour or more before moving on. We suspect she's either being stopped or staying out of sight if there's traffic on the road. Karen is currently stationary half a mile off the highway and looks like she has settled down for the day. It's been the same pattern for the last three days. When she sets off tonight, we expect her to reach the area close to Talia by four in the morning, where she was collected by submarine last time she was there."

"Well this time I intend to send in rescue helicopters, I want this girl out, whether she has succeeded, or not, in her attempt to find the other girls."

He left the room and made his way down the corridor. An hour before, Sir Peter had requested a full operational meeting. They were already waiting, but before he joined them he wanted to be sure Karen was still following the same route out of the area they had tracked her going in.

Standing in front of the assembled people he called order. "Gentlemen, thank you for coming. Lieutenant Harris has for the last few days been tracked by satellite as she has moved further into an area where civil war is at its most active. She is now returning. We don't know if she's found the girls? Has been captured and is now being brought back or she's alone trying to get home? Personally I don't think she's been captured, as GPS data is still arriving at regular intervals. The Lieutenant is also travelling at night, exactly the same as when she was last in the Lebanon. It would seem illogical, if she had been captured, to allow a prisoner to still carry the GPS and also travel at night. So we must assume she's coming back, still under her own control, to be brought out. With that assumption it's a go for 'Operation Clean Snatch'."

"What is her ETA, Sir Peter?" the Captain who was running the operation asked.

"We are estimating o-four hundred hours. The weather reports say it will be clear skies and satellite infrared surveillance of the area is now very possible." Sir Peter looked around the room. "No matter what Lieutenant Harris says, whatever excuse she tries to find to want to stay, you ignore it, the girl comes out. Our original intention was to see if she might lead us to Sirec. The government has decided this is far too high a risk for such a high profile girl and as such that part of the operation has been aborted. All I ask is you find her; protect her and get her out. Now before I pass you all to Operational Control for your own briefing, a word of warning. The Lieutenant is carrying a formidable arsenal of weapons including three grenades. Among them is a special grenade. It has a red band round it. She has only one, but it has no timer. The moment she pulls the pin and releases the lever it will explode. She requested it for her own personal protection, and that girl will take her own life if she feels threatened and has no way out. So I'm asking you to be very, very, careful and don't take risks. I do not want to lose anyone in this operation."

Leaving the military to complete their planning, Sir Peter went up on deck, leaned on the rail and lit a cigarette.

"Penny for them," a girl's voice came from behind.

He turned and smiled. "It's good to see you up, Angela,

how are you feeling?"

"I feel fine, the injection worked wonders, but it'll be nice to get home, or at least be able to call mum and dad. Are you allowed to tell me how everything's going? Are we close to making it public that I'm out?"

"Not long now, in fact if all goes well, tomorrow."

Her face lit up. "You mean the other girls are safe?"

"We don't know that yet. But Karen is close to where we can pick her up, and then we will know for certain if they are lost forever."

She leaned on the rail alongside him looking out across the still water. "You know when I was in Saeed's house, I'd given up. I knew I was dying. I was being sick every hour or so, the pains in my stomach often brought me to tears. I'd not eaten, only taking water, even that, like I said wouldn't stay down and they still tried to force medicine into me, insisting I'd food poisoning, pneumonia, in fact everything they could think of, but I knew it was none of those and soon they'd give up. I suppose, I was hoping they'd kill me and finally finish it? Unless of course I died naturally before they lost patience. I was so lonely, and scared. I begged the woman to send me home to die. I even asked her to just leave me at some embassy gates. But she wouldn't hear of it, said I'd get better, I was already sold and her Saeed doesn't like losing money. I lay there for hours alone, wishing I could see mum and dad just once more and say goodbye. When on that last night I woke to find Karen knelt by the side of me in that room, my heart skipped a beat. I was lost for words that she'd come to find me. I thanked her for coming but when I told her I didn't think I was well enough to go, she just brushed it aside in her usual casual way and produced a stretcher. I believe, if she's on her way back she'll have the girls with her. I don't think Karen would ever give up and just come home."

"You seem very confident about Karen, Angela?"

"I suppose I do, but you've met her, she seems to exude confidence. Mind you the way she was dressed, the weapons she carried, I'd not like to be on the receiving end. I would think she could be very dangerous if you crossed her?"

Sir Peter thought back to the time she was ready to board the helicopter. Angela was right; he also had confidence that Karen would see it through, no matter what. "You're right, she can be very ruthless in dealing with people who get in her way, as a few of her adversaries have found to their cost. But deep down she really is a very feminine girl, who just wants a boyfriend, someone to love her for who she really is."

Angela looked at him. "Aren't we all just as feminine? It's in our nature to love and want to be loved. But Karen's the sort of girl who will do anything to help you. She doesn't look down at you; she thought nothing of stopping and helping me in the airport. The majority of girls would have looked the other way, particularly with the press around, Karen didn't. But more importantly she saved my life. She came back for me to a place that would certainly have held so many bad memories for her. I'll always be grateful for that. But what do I say, when I meet her again, to someone who's prepared to risk her own life for you?"

"You'll think of something, anyway what are your plans when you get home?" he asked changing the subject.

Angela frowned. "I don't really know. Life seemed so simple when I was planning university, leaving home, and going to bunk up with other girls to live as a student for a few years. Now I'm not so sure mum and dad would want me away from home, what with my health problems and fear of me being taken again. So I might not go now. I was also thinking how my boyfriend will look at me."

"In what way? I'd think he'll be over the moon to find you're safe." he said, a little perplexed with her answer.

"I suppose, if I can convince him nothing happened, beyond the preparation and sale. We may be okay, but I'm not confident that he'll believe me. He's very possessive and was quite put out when I won the holiday, and I preferred to go on that rather than join him and his friends for a week in the nightclubs of Spain."

Sir Peter took her hand. "Come on, let's you and I grab some coffee. That's if you don't mind having a drink with an old man, or would you rather have a drink with one of these fit young sailors walking around?"

Angela grinned. "I couldn't wish for a better companion, Sir Peter, apart from which my street cred will go through the roof at home if they know I've been drinking coffee with a real knight."

38

Karen's plan of travelling at night was on the face of it good. The first night they met only one vehicle, however by five in the morning traffic began to appear so even travelling in the lorry they were only managing around twenty miles an hour, making it very slow going. They had little food and everything was rationed including water.

The days were hot and humid, but they did find good vantage points that allowed them to see the road and not be seen themselves. Karen checked her GPS, and then began to work out just where she was as they moved closer to Talia and where Martha lived.

Karen had just come off watch with Annette taking over. Sammy settled down at her side, Natasha lay out in the sun.

"How far have we to go now?" Sammy asked.

"Around a hundred miles."

"Then what happens?"

"We're going to stay at the house of someone I know. There's a good hiding place there, and more importantly a telephone. I'll call the UK and find out what they can do for us. If there is no instant way out by air I have a contingency plan, which activates if all else fails, so we will get out. But we'll have to lay low for a few days. I know it's not a good plan, but it's all I've got."

Sammy frowned. "I think it's a good plan. After all we can hardly get on a bus or train home."

They both fell silent.

"We could if things got too bad," Karen said after some thought.

"How do you mean?"

"Well in this country they use the veil a lot. If we could get the clothes we might just be able to travel to the border without attracting attention. Admittedly we don't have passports so we'd have to sort of go round border control, but it might be possible."

Sammy grinned. "You could be right, but how many are five nine like we all are? Apart from Natasha that is."

Karen laughed. "Well I didn't say it was perfect. Anyway it's a long way from that yet."

"I was going to ask you something, Karen."

"What?"

"Are you in the army now?"

"Sort of, well no not really. They signed me up for a month. Made me a Lieutenant, even gave me good pay. But it was only to go to a training camp to learn how to use my guns, without the risk of killing someone every time I used them."

"Then you're not going to stay on, because I think you're well suited for it?"

"I have thought about that, but to sign up means I'd have to start at the bottom. I wouldn't want that, it'd be demeaning after being an officer. Although the lads are something else. There must be a ten to one ratio and I had so many offers to take me out it got embarrassing."

"Come off it, Karen, you're really attractive, you'd get offers anywhere you went."

"I suppose, but you have to remember I was at school before all this and didn't go to nightclubs or many pubs for that matter. So the only offers I used to get, besides Grant who you can't count, was from school lads, not twenty years plus and decidedly fit."

They fell silent for a few minutes.

"Have you got a boyfriend?" Karen suddenly asked.

"Yes, well I hope I still have. I'm feeling a little nervous about meeting him again. Especially when it gets out what I had to do, just to survive. Lads are funny that way. It's okay for them going with another girl, but they whinge like hell when their girlfriend does."

"I know what you mean. But it was hardly like you were two-timing him and if you were I don't think Salem would have been your first choice."

"I'd agree with you there, Salem wasn't the sort you'd take down to the club to show off, it's no wonder he had to buy his girls. How did you feel, Karen, after you'd been raped?"

Karen sat for some time deep in thought. How did she feel? Was she really raped by Salem as well? After all she could have just killed him at the outset. Or even when he smacked her bottom, with the threat of more punishment, which would have been a more fitting time to have killed him. If she'd had Halif would have had all the time in the world to look for the other girl. However, for Karen, the time with Salem would always be her secret. The only people who knew were dead, besides which, to admit to Sammy she spent the night with him as well, would place her own credibility as someone strong and resilient, down to the same level of her or Natasha by submitting to this man.

"I was a little different. Mine was a gang rape. Five men queued up to take me. But I killed all my rapists, apart from Saeed, who survived. For me it had a sort of closure, like someone being sent to prison for rape. What law there is in this country seems not to include women's problems, particularly the rape of a foreigner. So killing them was their only real punishment. Perhaps with Salem dead you will feel he's been suitably punished, and have the same attitude as me? The only thing I was worried about, after my story in the paper, was people would think I was an easy target, at the screwing level I mean, and would take me out just for what they could get. They'd have a nasty shock, I'd never go to bed on a first date, in fact it'd have to be at least a month before I'd even think about it."

"I suppose you're right there. I mean I could never walk into him on the street now, and I'll never have to endure the thought that he'd be somewhere in the world, doing the same thing, probably gloating over what he'd forced me and Natasha to do with him. In fact I could even turn round and tell the world we were treated well and rescued before anything happened."

"You could, if it makes you feel okay over it, after all the man doesn't exist anymore. I don't think Natasha will feel that way, she will find it very hard, and you might have to admit it, when they counsel you, in order to help Natasha through the healing process?"

Karen moved her backpack and lay down, placing her head on it. "I'm going to try to sleep for a short time. Unless you want to talk more?" she asked Sammy.

"No, you go ahead. You've given me a lot to think about, Karen. Besides I'm tired and will probably fall asleep anyway."

By dark they were all ready to move on. Progress was decidedly slow. Twice that night they had to turn off the highway and wait while large convoys passed, heading for the trouble areas. Once they actually waited for close on two hours when a tank transporter had a tyre blow-out, which had to be replaced. However, by daybreak they had still managed fifty miles, which placed them less than fifty miles from Karen's target area.

Settled down for the day, all the girls were asleep apart from Karen, who had taken the first watch.

Abed came over to her. "Tomorrow night, Karen, I will drop you around twenty-five miles from the location you're heading to. I'll be taking the road to Jina. I will be going home and see Sirec the next day, if he's in the area that is. You have a choice. I can tell him I brought you and dropped you off. Otherwise I'll say you never came back and the two girls with me refused to leave, convinced you'd come for them."

"Would he believe you?"

"On which option?"

"Either I suppose."

"Why not? None of us were told you were to be brought back for him, only Halif knew that and he doesn't tell you anything. As for leaving the girls, what did they mean to me? Besides I could say that I didn't think he'd want two abducted girls, one of fourteen and another just out of school, around his house."

Karen thought for a few minutes.

"I'd go on the premise that I didn't come back and you left the other girls. After all no one has seen us, we've kept well out of sight and not even collected food from any village. He's bound to have found out about Halif's death and the fate of his gunmen by now. He'll never think I'd come back this way, it's too far and it would have been easier for me to make my way to the border."

"If that's what you want, Karen, then I'll keep to that story. It will be logical that I was just making my way home through bandit country and couldn't call him. Sirec never gives his contact number out to people like me, we are nothing."

With this agreed, he wandered off to settle down for the day. Karen again checked her GPS location, marking it on the map. Then to pass the time she stripped her gun down and began to clean it carefully. Tonight it was possible that she might just need it, and it was essential that it was in good working order.

By ten that night they were on the road once more. Three quarters of an hour later they were stood at the side of the lorry.

Abed hugged each girl, finally he hugged Karen. "Look after them, Karen, and yourself also. But please don't ever consider coming back. It is a hostile and unforgiving country."

"I'll not be coming back, Abed, that's for sure. Twice is enough, to tempt providence three times would be one step too far."

They stood back and after one last wave he turned off toward Jina, his home.

Karen and the three girls set off, not following the road, but directly across scrubland towards Talia. She had estimated three miles an hour would be achievable, and although cutting it fine, towards daybreak they should make it.

Annette was a short distance behind them acting as rear guard and lookout. She still carried the gun she'd picked up from the dead man at Lomax's house. Karen had cleaned the gun, and checked it over. She'd fired just one shot to test everything worked and spent time explaining to and teaching Annette how to hold and more importantly fire it. They looked a strange bunch. Karen in her army combat gear with bulletproof vest and peak cap leading. Sammy and Natasha both dressed in jeans, t-shirt and jumpers a short distance behind, with Annette also in jeans, except she wore the leather bomber jacket Lomax had bought her.

After two hours they rested for ten minutes. The sky was clear, the moon giving just sufficient light to keep to well-used animal tracks. Karen checked the GPS.

"We've done well; we have already covered nine miles," Karen said after marking their position on the map. "At this rate we should reach the farmhouse by five. Plenty of time to hide out before daybreak, besides gets a call off to Sir Peter."

"I just want a bath," Sammy commented. "I have never felt so dirty, I must stink?"

Annette laughed. "I think we all stink, Sam. You just don't appreciate modern living until you don't have any of the perks."

Natasha frowned. "I don't think I smell?" she said trying to sniff herself.

"Oh you do, believe me. It's a good job we're not sharing a bed anymore," Sammy ribbed her.

Karen stood. "Okay, let's move on shall we?"

The going was still easy. Karen felt a little put out; the last time she'd been here, this journey had been a nightmare. Now it seemed like a stroll in the park. Soon they stopped close to Martha's house.

Karen called them together. "Right, gather round and listen. What I'm about to tell you is your way out, if things don't go to plan."

She removed the GPS tracker unit and switched it on. "You can all see the map and the small flashing light. This flashing light shows you where you are on the ground. As you can see I've programmed a route to follow on the map which will guide you to a pickup point if I don't come back. Basically you just follow the route and check the little flashing light which shows where you actually are. If I do return then we all go on from here, if I don't you have until Friday night to travel about twenty miles using the tracker. You should travel during the hours of darkness, lie low in the day, the same as we have done up to now. You have to be at the pickup point by twenty hundred hours, that's eight o'clock at night. They will wait half an hour then go."

She then pulled out her torch and placed it alongside the GPS unit. "Once you arrive at the pickup point you'll find it's a cove. Send three flashes out to sea every five minutes. When you get a return three flashes, if it's safe to pick you up directly, you return with two flashes. If it is not safe then send three flashes.

Your rescuers will know what to do, and they will try to help you. Now Sam, Natasha, over to those bushes and settle down behind and keep your heads down. Your white faces can be seen very easily, so no looking up unless you hear me call you. Annette, you take the bush over there," she directed pointing at another clump. "Again keep your head down, the gun at your side with the safety on; we don't want any accidents at this stage. I'll go and survey the house, make sure she's alone. I could be gone some time, after all she'll be in bed asleep, but don't get worried and decide to come and find me, I'll find you. Lastly if you hear shooting, don't hang around and wait for me, get out fast to about a quarter of a mile back in the direction we came. Keep your fingers crossed it wasn't me caught in the gunfire. If it was, and I don't come to find you, you have your instructions on how to get home. I can do no more."

"Good luck, Karen," Sammy said.

"Yes good luck and don't take risks," Annette added.

Natasha came over to Karen and hugged her. "Don't be too long and come back for us," she whispered.

"I won't, now into your places, so I can check you're all well hidden."

With the girls settled Karen moved on towards the house. Unlike the last time she was here, and fell over garden implements, this time she was very careful and was soon at the window. As expected the inside was in darkness, even the fire was out. But it was very early in the morning, in fact just after half-past four, so she could hardly have expected anyone to be up and about. Moving round to the door, she gazed at it for a moment, the door was partly open.

Alarmed that the door was like this, Karen unclipped the hand grenade with the red band from its pouch. Then holding the grenade in her left hand, with the ring through her thumb as in Lomax's house, she felt safe. This was a time to be cautious, going into an already open and inviting building and Karen did not want to be in a position where she could be taken alive. Now with her gun strap over her right shoulder, the gun in her right hand and the safety off, output at maximum, she pushed the door open very gingerly with her foot.

Suddenly all the lights came on, Karen blinked for a second or two in the strong light, but stood motionless. Two men stood looking at her from the other end of the room; both had guns similar to hers. Sirec was sitting in the armchair Martha had been in last time she was here. How she'd not seen him through the window she didn't know, but she hadn't. But what annoyed her more was she'd fallen for the same sort of trap as she had with Lomax.

"Dead on time, Karen. You're so predictable. Why don't you take a seat, I'm sure you would like a drink? Maybe we should call the other girls in as well? Your good friend, Saeed, is in the kitchen waiting to take them away and of course you. But he assures me you'll not be going up for sale to a private bidder, as are the others. He says you're more of a party animal, well able to satisfy a number of admirers all at once, saying you like it that way, spread over a table."

Karen didn't move from the door. "Where's Martha? Why are you here? Who told you I was coming?" she asked ignoring his derogatory words.

He smiled. "Such a lot of questions but I will answer them for you. First of all Martha is dead. We found her on the floor in the kitchen. She'd died of a heart attack. We've had no time to bury her, so she's in the barn. We've been following you for the last few days and knew you were coming here, after all this is where you hid out last time, isn't it? And of course Abed called me only three hours ago, telling me of your new plan; that no longer included you and me. I thought we had a deal, Karen? You're so fickle girl, and then to kill Halif was not the right thing to do."

Hearing that Abed had lied to them and contacted Sirec, in some ways didn't surprise her, after all she'd found many in this country lied as a matter of course. However, she realised it was her fault for trusting him, he was a Sirec man after all. But she decided it was a waste of time showing her annoyance to Sirec, he'd probably laugh at her for being so trusting. However, she was glad she'd not told Abed about the final way out if all else failed.

"Yes well your plan for me, according to Halif, wasn't quite what we agreed either, was it? And while we are talking about Halif, I never killed him; Lomax shot him in the head. I just took out Lomax afterwards," she replied.

He shrugged. "An easy mistake if that's true, Karen, after all you blew them to pieces, and so it's a little difficult to prove one way or the other now. But I must thank you for killing Lomax. I've been able to take over his patch, which will make up for the money you've cost me. What with paying Saeed, supplying men and all manner of things, including having to replace my home, which you and your SAS friends kindly destroyed for me, it adds up to quite a figure."

She sighed, but still didn't move. "Why the girls, Sirec? I can understand you want me, but the girls. They've been through so much; it's inhuman to let Saeed sell them again?"

At that moment Saeed was pushed into the room, from the kitchen, by his mother.

"Why inhuman, Karen, that's their function in life, to please a man. Besides, you took their payment off my mother, so you have only yourself to blame if I have to now re-sell them to get it back," Saeed said.

Karen looked at him sat in the wheelchair grinning at her.

"I thought I'd killed you, Saeed? But by turning up here you've saved me the trouble of coming to find you and this time you won't be so lucky, you should have remained in the sewer, like the stinking rats you and your mother are."

"Just as arrogant and stupid I see?" Saeed began, "I warned you what would happen if you touched my mother. Now Sirec has released you to me, you can expect no favours. But I'd think twice about trying to make a run for it, there's two guns trained on you from behind, you have nowhere to run this time."

For Karen to hear those words, confirmed to her she'd lost. This was the end of the line. Secretly she'd always hoped she would get out with the girls. But Karen had had enough of this country, the people and the value they put on life. In her view her life was valuable, very valuable so they would pay dearly, because if she was to die, so would all of them.

"I don't intend to run," she replied quietly, at the same time moving her thumb and slipping the pin out of the grenade, and releasing the catch. Now all that remained was for her to open her hand, to allow the trigger to release.

"If that's the case drop your gun, like Sirec told you to. It's time we were gone, after I collect my girls of course."

Karen stood there, the nightmare that began weeks before was finally coming to an end. In minutes she'd be dead and all she could do now was pray her death would be quick.

"Sorry to disappoint you, Saeed, but you don't seem to understand. I'm not going to run or put my gun down, because I intend to kill you, Sirec and your mother. You see, you can have a hundred gunmen outside, it means nothing, because I am going to make sure that the misery and despair you've brought to so many children, which both you and your mother have wallowed in for so long, will finally finish now. I realise I'll have to die to achieve this; it's inevitable, but what's one if it saves hundreds?" Then she just shrugged indifferently. "Anyway I've lived on borrowed time for so long, I'm no longer scared, and for me it will be a release."

"She's insane, kill her, Sirec," Saeed urged.

However, Sirec was beginning to become worried. This girl standing in front of them seemed very confident that she could kill them all. But even if she could get her gun to fire before his men took her out, she'd struggle to kill everyone. Unless, that is, she had an alternative to using the gun? Suddenly he went very cold. Of course, Lomax's house, didn't she blow them all up?

"Shut up, Saeed," he demanded, then lowered his voice. "Tell me, Karen; is that a grenade in your left hand?"

Karen just shrugged. "You know, Sirec, you were very stupid to leave the front door open for me. You see it rang alarm bells deep inside. I'm a very untrusting girl at times, especially when a door that should be shut and bolted, is not. So it seemed prudent to set my gun at max, the safety is off and already, like you suspect, I hold a grenade with the pin out. But this is a very special grenade. You being in the arms trade may have heard of them? It's a zero delay grenade, so when I open my hand that is it. I can assure you no one will have time to leave this room. No one will survive in this room. I suspect you've seen, or heard about the devastation in Lomax's house, of a hall twice the size of this room? So as I've just said about the gunmen outside, I'd forget them, they can't help, because no matter what they could do, I will have time to release my hand."

The men behind Sirec, Saeed and his mother stared at her open-mouthed. She really did intend to kill everyone in the room and as she said, they could not escape.

Sirec, on the other hand, took a cigarette out of a packet and lit it carefully. "Let's not be hasty, Karen. It's clear you're not such a stupid girl to want to die yourself. So as you have the upper hand, what is it you want?"

She gave a weak smile and sighed, looking down at her gun. "You're right, I don't want to die, I'm only just eighteen. All I ever wanted was my life back. That wasn't too much to ask, after all I'd won and you'd lost. But of course I've found to my detriment, while you live and Saeed for that matter, you'll never let go, still believing you own me. When I told Saeed once no one owns anybody, he just laughed and ridiculed my beliefs. Even now he prefers to say nothing, still believing he will leave this room alive. Well, Saeed, you should listen to your mother, she will believe, because she has read my future. I've always walked on this land with the Angel of Death at my side; the only difference now is, he's not only come for you, your mother and of course Sirec, but me as well."

Saeed's mother hated this girl, and like she'd said she'd read Karen's hand. For her the story any hand told was absolute. Everything she'd predicted had come to pass, except one tiny point. At no time did she see Karen's death, and to her, a hand reading had never lied. She leaned close to Saeed, her voice very low and in their own language. *"The girl's bluffing, Saeed, I read her hand. Karen's death is not there. Take this knowledge - I am not wrong."*

Sirec drew carefully on his cigarette. While she talked he was weighing up the possibility of taking her on. But she was too well armed, too well protected, with her bulletproof jacket reducing the kill area considerably. It was a grave error on their part to underestimate, Karen. She was a girl of principle, absolutely focused in what she must do. But for them no matter what, no one can protect themselves from a suicide bomber, and that's effectively what she was intending to become.

"You may have your life, and that of the girls, Karen. It's not necessary for you to die or me for that matter."

"What are you offering, Sirec? Karen's mine and the others not yours to give away," Saeed shouted.

Sirec swung round and glared at him. "Are you out of your mind, she's holding a bloody grenade if you haven't noticed? If she drops that, like she said, we're all dead," he retorted.

"Yes… yes… I know that, but she's bluffing," Saeed replied. "I know Karen; she's all talk, that's all. Give her an hour's start to escape, and she'll take it. But no longer mind, she's worth not a minute more, and then we go after her."

"We have a say as well," one of the gunmen cut in. "I only get paid to protect, not die for you fuckers."

"Excuse me, I'm still here you know?" Karen cut in. "But I do have an offer, for Sirec's gunmen, if you want to live that is?"

"What's that?" the gunman asked.

"It's simple really. You call the other two from outside, all of you leave your weapons, the guns with magazines out of course, and you may go."

"Ignore her, it's a trick, she'll shoot us, we'd have no protection. Besides you work for me, I pay you, so I say if you go," Sirec demanded.

The two looked at each other, nodded, then one turned his gun on Sirec. "Sorry, Boss, with someone stood holding a grenade and you demanding we stay, there's no contest. No hard feelings, but you and Saeed got yourselves in this mess, you sort it out, I quit. So remove your gun from inside your jacket and throw it on the floor. You do the same as well, Saeed. If either of you try anything, this girl won't need to kill you, I will."

Karen stood motionless, her hand still around the grenade. She never expected this turnaround, but could well understand it. After all, who'd want to die for a few dollars pay, unless they are completely stupid? However, both Sirec and Saeed did as the man asked.

The man turned to Karen. "Come further into the room

and stand to one side of the door. My mate will call the two outside?"

She remained still for a moment. "You're sure if I move they won't shoot? This grenade in my hand has no pin in, and will explode within a second if I let go."

"They won't fire, they are under instructions only to fire at you if you try to make a run for it, not come further inside."

Karen moved in and stepped to one side of the door, now out of the line of fire from anyone watching from outside. The other man placed his gun on the floor and walked towards the open door and shouted in the local language.

After a short time two men appeared at the entrance, they looked inside and pointed their guns directly at Karen. She never moved, resigned now that it will be only minutes before she would be dead. In some ways Karen had become detached to what was happening. All her life had been around the church, even her schooling was directed towards the Catholic faith. Now her only thoughts were what she was going to say in her defence, when stood in front of the Almighty.

She was abruptly brought out of her thoughts when the man, who seemed to be taking charge, shouted at the two who'd come to the door in his own language. They hesitated, and then one saw the grenade in Karen's hand. Immediately he pulled the clip from his gun and threw both the gun and clip to the floor. The other followed suit, before both of them turned and ran back outside. Once they had gone the two gunmen who were inside the room followed suit. Now there was only Sirec, Saeed and his mother. However, the circumstances were very different. All of them unarmed, Karen holding both her grenade and the AK47, fully primed and ready to fire.

"So where do you go from here, Karen?" Sirec asked.

Where did she go? Karen wasn't sure except in her eyes there were two alternatives. Kill them or let them go.

"I suppose I may as well just shoot you all and get my way. After all there is no one to stop me now. I live, you lot die. It's the way of the world," she replied with some indifference.

When Sirec answered her, he sounded hurt. "I can see that

with Saeed, Karen. But I've done nothing to you that you should take my life. In fact I've kept to my side of the bargain. You can't blame me for being a little put out - after getting the girls with my help, you decide to renege on our arrangement and go home."

"But your arrangement with me was not what we talked about, according to Halif. I was just some shit under your foot, to play around with, be handed out as a common whore at your whim."

He shook his head. "There you go again, Karen, listening to the hired help. Won't you ever learn to trust someone's word?"

"I wanted to Sirec, I really did. In fact I was looking forward to a life with you."

"So what's changed, Karen?"

She sighed. "I've had enough of the whole sordid mess. I just want to go home, that's all. Forget this life, the broken promises. I really don't understand what I've done to deserve all this. I was brought up to respect my elders, to trust people's word. It all makes me look a fool, a gullible and naive young girl trying to grow up and just, I suppose, survive?"

"Then you should go home, Karen. Give me the gun and I'll get rid of Saeed and his mother. All they have done for this country is bring shame on us. You have the girls back, your work is done and this really isn't your fight any more."

It was at that moment British soldiers burst through both the front door and from the kitchen. To say Karen was shocked would be an underestimation. In fact so much so she nearly panicked and dropped the grenade. But how did they find her? And more to the point why hadn't she seen them?

"Captain Masters, Lieutenant. We will take over from here."

"Captain," Karen replied. "Please move your men to a safe distance and take the girls home. I won't be coming. Saeed cannot be allowed to live. I'm not prepared to go through my life with the constant threat that he'd try to take me again."

Both Sirec and Saeed remained absolutely still; they knew just how dangerous a situation they were all in. This girl was so unpredictable neither of them had a doubt that she would release her hand if she was threatened. It was only the Captain now who might be able to dissuade her.

The Captain moved closer to Karen, his words very low so that only she could hear. "They will not go their own way, Karen," he whispered. "We're taking them with us. Saeed and his mother will be tried for people trafficking, rape and abduction besides being implicated in murder, at a closed international court. Sirec will be handed over to another power desperate to get their hands on him. He has very important information about the gunrunning operations from this area, which they need to know about. This knowledge will save many lives believe me. I promise you, none will ever be released. Now please leave it to us. You've done your part?"

Sirec was wondering just what this man had said to her because Karen hadn't moved or even reacted to his words. Everyone held their breath as the seconds ticked by.

"Will you take my gun, Captain? Be careful it's set to maximum and the safety is off. Then you and your men leave the room and stand well away from the house. I'm holding a very special grenade with the pin out - it has no time delay. I'll try to make it safe," she said the tone of her voice showing how nervous she was.

He leaned forward and clicked the safety on before sliding the strap from her shoulder, then looked round at Sirec and Saeed. "Do not move; don't attempt to go near the Lieutenant. My men will be stood outside while she makes the grenade safe."

With this advice he left the room.

"So, Karen, was that an excuse to get them to leave, because you really are going to kill us all?" Sirec asked.

"She's not going to kill herself, believe me it's not in her destiny to die just yet," Saeed's mother cut in.

Karen shook her head. "You're wrong old woman. I make my own destiny, but again your actions have forced me to kill as you read in my hand. However, there has been enough killing, so this time I'm going to allow you all to live. Death is too final for people like you. You need time to contemplate your actions against your fellow human beings, before you meet your maker. But believe me one day you will, as we all have to. I hope then He damns you for eternity." Karen carefully moved the grenade across to her other hand. Everyone left in the room had their eyes fixed on her hands. They could now see the pin was out as she'd claimed. Sirec especially recognised the red band around it, very aware that the grenade had no timer. In this condition it was extremely dangerous, a wrong move and the grenade would activate immediately. They watched as she very carefully slipped the pin into its hole, before placing the grenade back into the pouch on her ammunition strap.

"The grenade is now safe, Captain," Karen called.

He returned to the room.

"That's good, Lieutenant, now please go outside," the Captain replied, with obvious relief in his voice. She turned and gave him a weak smile, even she'd felt the tension, the seconds that seemed to her hours as she made the grenade safe once again. Karen took back her gun, as soldiers pushed past her into the house.

"I'll get the girls shall I?" she asked when he came out of the house to join her.

"We already have them, Lieutenant."

"So you saw me arrive and come to the door then?"

"Not exactly; we arrived just to see the other gunmen running from the house. We stopped them and one said you'd a live grenade with the pin out, and intended to kill Sirec and Saeed. We had to make sure the area was clear even though I realised just how dangerous a position everyone was in, besides not being certain which grenade you were actually holding. As for the girls, with them not being with you, it was a simple matter to backtrack and find them hiding. Mind you, you gave us a few tense moments when we heard you were holding the zero timer grenade."

She grinned. "I was shaking, even more so when I had to put the pin back. I'd never been so scared looking down at it."

"I can understand that, a grenade is very unpredictable once the pin is out."

"But how did you find me, I've not called Sir Peter to give my position yet?"

"You have a tracker on your person, besides the GPS unit

giving your position. Once we were on the ground our detection equipment told us to a metre as to where you were."

"Well that's bloody charming, I'm even bugged," she replied indignantly. Then she changed her tone. "Have you seen Martha, this is her house and Sirec told me she had died. But he can't be believed about her death, and that he wasn't implicated in some way?" Karen asked, changing the subject.

"There's a lady in the barn. I'm afraid she is dead. She had been moved there, perhaps from the house. But our medic believes she died from a heart attack. There are no marks on her body and she's been dead for some time."

Karen lowered her head; tears were beginning to trickle down her face. Would there be no end to death around her?

"Can we bury her, Captain?"

"Of course, it was our intention anyway, Lieutenant."

Twenty minutes later, after the Captain had said a few words over Martha's grave, they left Karen alone. She knelt down holding a cross from a wall inside the house. A cross that she first saw last time she was here, only weeks before. After a small prayer of her own, she laid it on the still soft earth.

"Thank you for my life, Martha," she whispered. "I can finally go home now and try to pick up the pieces."

39

Sir Peter was stood at the entrance to the flight-deck of the carrier, watching the last helicopter approaching. Already three had arrived back some time earlier. The girls were in the first one that landed, and whisked away quickly before the next two containing the prisoners arrived. Karen, he'd been assured was safe and aboard this final helicopter.

As it came to land and the rotors stopped, Karen was helped down. She stood for a moment; saw Sir Peter, smiled and then began walking towards him, at the same time pulling her peak cap off allowing her hair to blow freely in the wind. Her AK47 slung nonchalantly over her right shoulder, as if she'd not a care in the world. The Captain was at her side.

Sir Peter smiled to himself. This was a very special girl and he was glad she'd survived. Karen stopped in front of him, unclipped the cross belt holding the grenades and spare clips of ammunition, handing it and her gun to the Captain, before putting her arms around him, hugging him tightly.

"It's good to have you back, Karen," he whispered in her ear.

She pulled away. "It's good to be back, Peter. There were a few times I didn't think I'd make it this time."

"Yes, I can understand that. But next time Karen, please don't go off on your own. You were lucky we had the foresight to place a tracker on you. Otherwise things could have turned out very differently at the farm."

"Yes, the Captain said I was bugged. You never told me. So where did you hide it, in my clothes?"

He smiled. "Of course, I wanted to know where you were, after all you're a very valuable asset, so I had no intention of losing you. Besides every time you used your GPS, it confirmed your position. But forget those minor points, Karen, you must be starving, get yourself off for breakfast, then some rest and join me for dinner tonight."

"I think I will, Peter, I'm absolutely shattered, if they can find me a bed that is? And thank you for inviting me for dinner later, I'd love to join you."

"If you go direct to the ship's dining room, Lieutenant, I'll have someone collect you in about half an hour to take you to your room. I'll also hang onto your weapons, particularly the grenades," the Captain said.

"Thank you, Captain, but shouldn't I sign them back in? Oh and I've used a grenade," she replied, at the same time removing the hand gun from its holster and passing it to him.

"Usually yes, though in this case, because of the special grenade and the risks associated with carrying such an unpredictable weapon onboard a ship, and with you being so tired, I'll do it for you. But we will need a complete operational report later, and most importantly where and why you used one of the grenades."

She said she would do that, then left them and headed for the canteen. Sir Peter was right, when she entered the dining room and smelt the food it reminded her how hungry she really was. But she didn't like the fact that they'd bugged her and it was considered a minor point, so she'd decided to look for the bug herself later.

"Karen... Karen," a voice shouted across the large dining room."

Karen was standing by the counter waiting for her breakfast when her name was called, and she turned to see Angela at the entrance. Angela ran over and flung her arms round Karen hugging her tightly.

"I couldn't believe it when they told me you'd finally arrived, I'm so relived you're safe" she said still hugging her.

"Yes I came in a few minutes ago. You look well, why don't you join me for breakfast and we can talk?" Karen asked.

Angela collected a Coke with a slice of toast and they found an empty table in a corner.

"So how are you feeling?" Karen asked as she poured a little sauce on the side of her plate.

"I feel great since the injection and decent food," Angela began. "I've just got off the phone telling mum and dad I'm safe. She was stunned, couldn't believe you'd found me and told me to send you her thanks, besides to tell you that you were wrong. God was with us both and he brought us home. Anyway I met Sam on the way to the showers, but she couldn't tell me what had happened to you. She was shattered, after being up all night."

"Yes I'm a bit knackered as well."

"I've been told all the girls are leaving at six forty-five tonight. We're being taken to Cyprus and then home. Are you coming with us?"

Karen shrugged. "I don't think so. I'm still in the army and they have to debrief me yet. But I'm looking forward to going home. It's been pretty hard, these last weeks."

"You'll keep in touch won't you? And you promised to come and stay for the weekend?"

"Of course I will."

At that moment Stephanie came into the dining room, she looked round and headed for them. Karen stood and gave the girl a hug while Angela went over to the counter and collected a Coke for her.

"So how are you?" Karen asked as they both sat down at the table.

"Not so good Karen. I'm on medication and can't sleep. I keep waking up all the time with nightmares, still thinking I'm in that man's house. But I'm really grateful you came for me, and they let me finally talk to mum and dad this morning which made me feel tons better."

Karen leaned forward and took her hand. "It goes Stephanie, believe me it goes. You just have to pick up your life and throw yourself into it."

She looked at Karen. "I'll try, but it'll be hard."

Angela came back with the Coke. "Sam and Annette are here as well, Stephanie," Angela told her. "Karen got us all out. I was talking to them earlier and we're all going to get together and have a big party after Christmas. You're the main guest, Karen."

"Sounds fun, are we clubbing it after?"

"Of course. It'll be in London. Sam lives there and knows all the places to go."

"What happened to Natasha?" Stephanie asked Karen.

"She's out as well; she was sold to a man who also took Sam. The girl was treated very badly and still doesn't know her father was killed by these people. I think out of all of you, she'll take the most time to come to terms with what happened to her," Karen answered.

A sailor came into the dining room looked around, saw the girls and walked over. Karen looked up at him.

"Your room is ready, Lieutenant, when you've finished your breakfast."

Karen had finished her food. She stood and looked down at them both. "I'm off for a shower, then sleep, I can hardly keep awake. I'll see you before you all leave."

They nodded and she left with the sailor.

Angela sighed. "I didn't really know what to say to Karen. I owe her so much and yet she seems so laid back, as if she's been on some holiday. But Sam said Annette had told her how Karen had taken on the man she was staying with, and never batted an eyelid with four guns pointed at her. She said it was as if she wasn't afraid to die."

"I know what you mean. I didn't know what to say either. All I could talk about was how badly I was coping. She went through ten times worse than I ever did, and yet I didn't even ask her how she was. I feel really embarrassed not doing that."

Later that day, Karen hugged each girl before they climbed onto the helicopter. Natasha was last and Karen held the little girl even tighter.

"Thank you for bringing me home, Karen. You will come and stay with me? Mum and dad would love to meet you," Natasha said.

"Of course I will, besides you should also come and stay with me sometime. We'll have a great time going round the shops."

The girl's eyes lit up. "Can I, can I really?"

"Why not, we're mates now aren't we?"

"Of course we are."

"Then we should keep in touch."

"I will, I promise."

Natasha gave her one final hug before she went over to the waiting helicopter. Then, with a little help, she climbed inside and in seconds it rose from the deck. Karen gave them all a last wave and it soon disappeared, heading towards Cyprus and their final leg home.

Walking back inside she made her way to the officer's dining room. Already a number of the ship's officers were there and one handed her a drink. Sir Peter, along with the ship's Captain joined them. It was a good dinner, with plenty of conversation. However, by ten Karen and Sir Peter were sat alone. He poured them coffee and lit a cigar then pulled out two envelopes, placing them on the table.

"Here's the letter to your parents back, Karen, do you know what this other envelope is?" he asked.

She nodded. It was her will.

"But before I give it back to you, what are your plans now, Karen?"

"In what way?"

"Well, where do you go from here?"

She smiled. "I'm going home of course. It's been very hard for me, Peter, but now I know I can relax and not be on constant guard. Although for a time I will carry a knife. I know it's illegal, I know I can get in trouble, but for my own piece of mind it will give me confidence."

"Why don't you stay in the army, in Special Services? There are still plenty of others out there, desperate for your help."

She shook her head. "Oh no…this is it for me. I've been too close this time in losing first my liberty, then my life. I'm going home to work as a shop assistant, a secretary, in fact anything that does not include a gun."

"I suppose you could, but you're still in the army and you should do as you're told," he came back at her.

"Then I'll resign, after all my contract runs out in a few

days."

"We've extended it, Karen. Indefinitely, besides you're an officer and we'll refuse to accept your resignation."

Karen stared at him. "You can't do that to me; mum and dad would go berserk if they knew I was even here now. They think I'm still in a training camp."

"We can, you're a British subject and this girl is your military service," he replied with a wink. "But seriously, Karen, it is the life for you. It's a world you now understand. A cruel and desperate world for those caught up in it. Already governments are waking up to just what's happening. They, like the Lebanese, are prepared to help and more importantly work with us to clean up their own backyards. I want you to be part of it. To finish your training and finally get this maverick side of you, that believes she can take on the world alone, sorted out once and for all. Then you will become part of an international elite group, have the power to go in and sort these people, who still believe we live in the Middle Ages, and can sell others into slavery. They will learn to their cost, they can't, because people like you will stop them."

Karen said nothing for a short time. He was right, this was only the beginning. There were people like Debby who Saeed had sold into a brothel still out there. Children like Natasha, Sammy and Angela who had no one coming for them. They too wanted to go home, to pick up their lives.

She gave a weak smile. "You're right, Peter, I'm not going to resign just yet. I'll see how the training goes, and more importantly how I feel in myself. I've been minutes from death a few times now, and it doesn't get any easier. But one thing that may convince me to stay, after this last trip, is that life would soon become very boring, and I do get to be among lots of hunky and very fit soldiers. What more could a girl ask for?"

He picked the will up and slipped it back into his pocket, but left her other envelope on the table. "I'll hold onto this shall I, then? But you won't regret a yes decision Karen, and there will be lots of children who will be glad you did decide to stay. Now I must leave you, I have a number of telephone calls to make. Call home yourself; let them know you're safe. I'm told you've got some leave coming your way, after you finish your training, still as a Lieutenant of course. So why not take a holiday, sort out that skimpiest bikini you dreamed about wearing on that beach of yours, when you were freezing your butt off on the moor, and recharge your batteries?"

Karen knew he was right; she needed that holiday, particularly the beach. But how did he know about what she'd said to the lads on the moor, was there nothing secret in her life?

40

It was Christmas Day; Karen was helping her mother with the dinner. The house, as usual, was full of relatives. She had returned not to the original training camp, but was sent to Sandhurst, to begin her training as an officer. All the usual acceptance procedures had been put to one side for her, after all she had already proved herself as a potential leader, and as Sir Peter promised, she was to keep her rank. During her time at Sandhurst, she'd been flown to a new camp, located in Europe, to look around and meet the Colonel in charge. This was the camp Sir Peter had told her about. Already a multinational force was assembling. Specialists of all kinds were arriving daily, particularly in communication, surveillance and covert operations. Karen was to be attached to a special incursion group. A fast and efficient force, with one term of engagement, which was to take out any opposition, no matter who they were, and bring out people caught up in the trafficking trade. When Karen left for her Christmas break, already she was looking forward to returning in January, completing her training, then taking on the traffickers once again. But this time not alone.

They had just finished dinner and were all still sat around the table, drinking coffee, when there was a knock at the door. Karen's grandmother, nearest the dining room door, went out to answer it, soon she was back.

"There are three military looking men at the door, Karen; they want to speak to you. I've asked them in, I hope you don't mind?"

The room fell silent as she went through to the hall. They were stood inside. All were Commandos, one a junior officer and very smart.

"Lieutenant Harris?" the Officer asked.

Most of the relatives looked at each other. "Karen, a

Lieutenant, since when? And why is she using our surname?" her grandfather commented.

His daughter, Karen's mother, touched his arm. "It's a long story Dad, I'll tell you later," she whispered.

"Yes I'm Lieutenant Harris, what can I do for you?" they heard her reply to the officer's question.

"I have been ordered to deliver this communication. Can you sign for it, Lieutenant?"

She took the very official looking envelope from his hand and signed their document. They made to leave.

"Wait a minute, can I offer you all a drink? It is after all Christmas Day," she said.

The officer stopped and turned. "That is up to you, Lieutenant, you are the ranking officer here," he replied.

"Well if that's the case, come and join us," she said grinning. "And my name's Karen, in my own home."

Coffee was poured, with a tot of whisky in each. But everyone was urging her to open the envelope, which she did with trepidation believing they were new orders and her holiday was to be cut short. However, besides a letter, the envelope also contained a beautifully ornate invitation. Karen read the letter, then looked at the invitation, her mouth dropping slightly.

"Well love, what does it say?" her father asked.

She shrugged, trying to pass it over as if of no importance. "It's nothing, Dad, just an invitation. I'll sort it later," she replied pushing the letter and invitation back into the envelope.

He looked at her sternly; he knew his daughter and the word 'nothing' meant it was something. "Karen, let me see it please?"

She hesitated, nervous of him reading it.

"Now, Karen," he repeated holding his hand out.

Karen handed the envelope to her father.

He read the letter and gasped after looking at the accompanying invitation. "It's an invitation to the Palace," he began his voice breaking. "Karen has been recognised in the New Year Honours and awarded the Conspicuous Gallantry Cross for the exceptional personal bravery she portrayed, in going into a hostile area alone."

Everyone had fallen silent, even the soldiers were looking at her.

Her mother took the letter and invitation from her husband and read the citation carefully and then the invitation before looking up at her daughter. "When was this, Karen?" she asked quietly.

Karen just shrugged. "A few weeks ago, Mum, I just helped out that's all, nothing special."

She sighed, "I'm sorry, Karen, but that isn't good enough. Somebody just helping out does not receive one of the highest awards in the land. The truth is both Sir Peter, and that General who came to the house lied. They put you in a position where your life was at risk, without us even knowing you were in such a situation. It's not fair for you to have done this to us. Last time was hard enough, not knowing where you were, thinking you were dead. It would seem this time you have done the same thing again, but voluntarily, with no thought for us? But I'm telling you this, so you and the rest of the family understand. While you live under our roof, we want the truth about just what you're up to. If this is something you feel you can't do, then you must move out."

Karen looked around at them all still watching her silently. "I couldn't tell you, Mum, they wouldn't let me, for my own safety no one was to know I was back in the Lebanon. We went in for the five girls who were abducted - by the same man who took me. Two of the girls and another younger girl of fourteen were three hundred miles away from where I was kept. They were in an area where the civil unrest was the worst. A large British military presence travelling to collect them might have caused a war." Karen sighed. "The little girl was so brave, she'd been beaten and raped but was still keeping herself together, looking forward to being with her mum and dad again. She didn't know the abductors had shot her daddy. I had to get her out, so I joined up with local gunmen and went on alone, what alternative was there? I don't deserve an award, let alone some sort of medal. I was glad I could do for her, the same as others had done for me; the only difference is, I returned, they didn't."

Her father was staring at his daughter stunned. "Are you

telling us, Karen, it wasn't the SAS as the papers reported, but you who brought out the last three girls? That you travelled six hundred miles inside the Lebanon alone and at risk of being taken again yourself, even after the promise of that General - who came to this house - and told us categorically that you'd be looked after?"

"Yes," she replied meekly. "But I was in the SAS, well Special Operations, so the papers weren't really wrong. The girls I brought out were told never to speak of how they were actually rescued, except just to say the SAS came for them."

There was a pregnant pause, no one knew what to say or do. Every person in the room now realised just why Karen had been awarded the medal.

"If I may speak?" the officer asked.

"Of course," Karen's father replied, in lots of ways relieved that the silence had been broken.

"We join the armed services in this country voluntarily. I, like all my colleagues hope that the things we do, the help we give, no matter where in the world, has an impact for good. Some of us will die, many will be injured, but we still do it. Karen has done what every soldier would do, tried to help those less fortunate. You shouldn't shun her, pull her efforts down. I know I speak for every soldier in this country, no matter what the rank. For your daughter to be awarded the Conspicuous Gallantry Cross, you should be the same as we are - proud of her. Proud so much courage was displayed that it has been recognised, and the honour is to be awarded by the head of all the services, our Queen."

He then came to attention, the other soldiers at his side also. "I'd like to be the first to congratulate you, Lieutenant. To shake your hand and salute you on behalf of my regiment, the armed services and my country. I hope, if ever a time comes, and I'm called upon to display the courage you must have shown, I pray to God I can."